ALAN DEAN FOSTER

Intelligent.
Inquisitive.
Insidious.
Inhuman.

Life Form

PRAISE FOR ALAN DEAN FOSTER AND HIS BESTSELLING NOVELS...

"Refreshing."—**Piers Anthony**

"The kind of book that makes you miss sleep and be late for appointments."—**Roger Zelazny**

"Foster's imaginative creations...keep this light, brisk story clicking!"—***Publishers Weekly***

"Great fun!"—***Science Fiction Chronicle***

"Excellent fantasy!"—***Rave Reviews***

"A page-turner!"—***San Francisco Examiner***

Life Form

ALAN DEAN FOSTER

ACE BOOKS, NEW YORK

This book is an Ace original edition,
and has never been previously published.

LIFE FORM

An Ace Book / published by arrangement with
the author

PRINTING HISTORY
Ace edition / July 1995

ISBN: 0-441-00218-8

ACE®
Ace Books are published by The Berkley Publishing Group,
200 Madison Avenue, New York, NY 10016.
ACE and the "A" design are trademarks
belonging to Charter Communications, Inc.

PRINTED IN THE UNITED STATES OF AMERICA

10   9   8   7   6   5   4   3

For Rodney Fox . . .
Under whose friendly guidance I have
Snatched from its lips a tooth of the White Death
Ridden the back of the Great Fish
Seen the green flash
Marveled at the hidden portraits of the Dreamtime
Been bitten in the eye by an angry green ant
Played tennis atop a mountain of iron
Toyed with a living emerald
Communed with the shadow of a thermonuclear explosion
Walked the finest beach in the world
Dived the reefs still primeval
And more importantly, shared silent wonders, quiet
    moments, and good humor.
He also ain't a bad field cook.
With many thanks and best wishes to him
And blessings upon his good wife and progeny

I

Twenty-four hours to wake up, and in all that time you didn't even get to yawn once.

Stevens studied the monitors, his practiced gaze flicking successively from one readout and screen to the next. Eventually his eyes came to rest on the vids that monitored their somnolent cargo. There was a separate pickup for each capsule, separate readouts for each individual life-support system.

Revivication/awakening procedures had just reached the ten-hour mark, with fourteen still to go. No yawning, no rubbing your eyes. It was a delicate, instrument-intensive process. When someone's been in deep sleep for over a year you don't just set off an alarm clock next to their ear and expect them to pop up inquiring if they're late for the morning commute to work.

Actually, their work was doing the commuting for them.

There were four worlds circling the central G-type star, which its optimistic Brazilian discoverers had enthusiastically named Xica da Silva, or Xica, for convenience' sake. The outermost was a gas giant, a lonely but colorful banded sentinel the size of Neptune. It had collected five moons, all interesting but dead, and was flanked inside and out by a pair of asteroid belts. The two innermost worlds were scorched and torn by clashing tectonic

1

forces, broken paving stones on the path outward from the sun.

Xica III . . . Xica da Silva . . . was a possible miracle.

One of many similar long-lived mechanical servants of humankind entrusted with the Long Ride Out, the Xica probe had reported back the presence of a breathable atmosphere, reasonable gravity, and oceans of hydrogen dioxide. Despite the dispatching of dozens of identical devices, these conditions had been encountered only twice before outside the solar system. The probe subsequently strongly suggested but could not confirm the presence on the two main land masses of a biota of consequence.

As nothing more advanced than primitive fungi, lichens, and segmented worms had been found on Tycho V or Burke, when the prospects for Xica were reported, competition among qualified scientists for places on the *James Cook* grew more than spirited, with several notably sedate individuals coming to blows once the final selections had been announced. Stevens hadn't been involved. Though he had a deep interest in exploration, he was no scientist. Somebody had to drive the truck while the brains rode in back, arguing over prospective Nobels and Sakharovs. That task fell to him. Him and Lastwell.

He swiveled slightly in his seat to regard the captain. The two men had worked together for some time. Each knew and respected the other's limits and abilities. Stevens had youth and energy, Lastwell great practical experience and determination. Together they comprised the entire crew of the *James Cook*. It was all the vast ship required.

Most of the time it needed no crew at all, the redundant automatics handling routine functions silently and efficiently. Only when it had begun to slow from its long journey a month ago had it awakened its crew. Both of them. Now that all systems had been checked out and the ship was in Xican orbit, it was time to rouse the vessel's somnolent scientific compliment.

Stevens looked forward to meeting them with a mixture of expectation and apprehension. The committee that had chosen the fortunate few had gone to great lengths, just as they had prior to the journeys of exploration to Tycho V and Burke, to ensure that all members of a team would be compatible. Scientists and researchers were chosen to crew such voyages as much for their ability to get along with others as for their mental skills, but no selection process was perfect, Stevens knew. He'd worked with some who'd worn an air of superiority like dirty underwear.

He had never met nor did he know any of them. Unlike the crew, they'd been put on board already in deepsleep, like so many cocooned worker bees, their individual capsules shoehorned into the waiting empty sockets like jewels into findings. The transparent cylinders showed him what they looked like, but not what they were.

That would be learned soon enough, he knew.

He remembered the rush of final preparations, the pulling back of the support vessels. Then he and Lastwell had cut on the fusion engines and, ever so slowly, the *James Cook* had begun to move. Away from Earth. Away from Home. Checks and rechecks and final checks, and then it was time for the Long Beddy-bye for the pair of them as well.

Now he'd been awake for a month, and looked forward avidly to having someone to talk to besides Lastwell. No doubt the captain felt the same way about his mate.

He glanced again at the nine sets of life-support monitors. Every readout was equable and within designated parameters. No one was sent into deep space, no matter how brilliant, if they weren't healthy. The *James Cook* had facilities, but it was no hospital. Its cargo had to be able to breathe efficiently on its own.

Lastwell muttered at him, preceding and concluding the request with a ripe invective. The captain could be inventive as well, but preferred to reserve his best efforts for special occasions. The obscenity did not trouble Stevens. It was merely Lastwell's manner of speech, a form of specific punctuation not unlike the singsong of Mandarin or the click-stops of the Xhosa. He complied without thinking as he turned his attention to the vid screens.

The six men and three women represented an extraordinary range of talent and abilities. Intellectually, Stevens knew the least of them could spin him dizzy. But he doubted there was one among them who, no matter how much time they were given, could fix a broken food service unit. In his own skills, however plebeian others might consider them, he was supremely confident. With eleven lives hanging in the balance on the work he was expected to perform, this was a good thing.

Several of them had been on pioneering expeditions to Tycho V or Burke. Two had been to both and were therefore, to a certain extent, possessors of that peculiar attribute known as fame. Stevens and Lastwell had taken the *James Cook* twice to Burke, but not in company with any of those currently in their care. Like Stevens, the youngest among them was near thirty. At fifty-two, Cedric Carnavon was the eldest.

Stevens had had plenty of time to study their records. His passengers represented a wide range of specialties and interests. He hoped they could be relied upon not to do the stupid thing the first time. From experience he knew that most scientists had a worrisome habit of becoming dangerously preoccupied with their work, even to the extent of ignoring personal safety. All the honors and degrees in the world couldn't help someone trapped in a crevice, or stranded on low power in an arctic environment.

"Stop staring at number Seven, ya mucky pervert!"

"I wasn't staring at Seven any more than any of the others," Stevens shot back. He swiveled fully to face Lastwell, who grinned back at him. Seated in the command chair, the older man affected the aura of a minor potentate. His skin was pale, the face chiseled underneath but slightly puffy on top, his blond hair graying and thinning. A man of action rather than contemplation, he abhorred delays or hesitation of any kind. Even as he was accusing his assistant he was carefully monitoring a battery of readouts, wondering just how accurate the old probe's report had been. Too many light-years to travel only to verify inconstant data.

"I said I wasn't staring." Stevens was insistent.

Still smiling, Lastwell replied without looking up. "Don't try to fob me, Mate. This is Frank you're talkin' to. I've seen you take a stroll through the sleep room to have a private peek or two."

"Of course I've looked in on them," Stevens protested. "So have you. It's part of the job."

"Fob job." Lastwell chuckled, maintaining his ever so slight but inescapable air of superiority. Stevens was used to it, and ignored it.

"I've run the standard in-chamber checks every day for the past twenty-eight, as per regs. Just like on the two cycles to Burke."

"And lingered longest at the ladies' capsules, *unlike* on the two cycles to Burke."

"You haven't done anything of the sort, I suppose."

The captain frowned momentarily as he leaned forward to squint at a readout. He nudged a small switch, grunted at the result, and settled back in his seat with an air of contentment.

"Oh, I've taken a glance or two. Not near as long as you, though. I'm a married man."

"The homefires burn dimly from here, Frank."

Lastwell turned to his friend and assistant. "Maybe so,

but married I still am. About all I can do is look. Legitimately."

"You've seen the two in Seven and Eight. Would you do otherwise if you had the chance?"

The older man blinked at his own set of capsule monitors. When he replied, there was a wistfulness in his voice that belied his usual explosive good humor. "According to their individual stats, there isn't a one of them that doesn't muster twice my pan power. That would make any kind of relationship awkward, though neither of them could handle a ship. And I think that's about enough of this business, Mate. Let's let it go, right?"

Stevens turned back to his instruments, but Lastwell wasn't through.

"And you remember that we're out here to do a job. The Council pays us more than we're worth to spend most of our time sleepin'. Not a bad life, no. So don't you go screwin' things up, in every sense of the word."

It was Stevens's turn to smile. "Have I ever given you any problems, Frank?"

"No, you crazy wanker. Never. But we've never before convoyed a pair of heavy thinkers that looked like Seven and Eight, either."

The mate considered the pallid closeups supplied by the monitors. "They all look pretty washed out."

"Who wouldn't," Lastwell muttered, "after not takin' a breath or sucking on a glass of water for more than ten months? Deepsleep's amazin', but nobody ever said it was fun." He stretched emphatically. "Damn glad to be out of it myself. They'll be wanting water first. That's what they always want."

"At least they're not all novices," Stevens murmured. "We won't have to wet-nurse each of them. Carnavon and Simna have outspaced you and me."

"Too bloody right. It's the other seven we'll have to keep

an eye on." His smile returned. "*All* seven of 'em, and not just the two."

"They're all pros, or they wouldn't have been selected to make this trip. You and I didn't have to compete to be chosen. Our names just came up."

"Not by accident, though," Lastwell insisted. "Not by no bloody accident. I suppose we ought to be flattered, Kauri, old boy."

"I don't feel flattered. Just tired."

"Better suck it in. It's only going to get busier when that lot wakes up." The captain absently thumbed another control. "Be a helluva lot simpler if all this exploring could be done by automatics. They do what you tell them to, and they don't argue or talk back. Can even give you some decent conversation if they're properly programmed." He aimed his voice at a pickup. "Ain't that right, ship?"

"Too bloody right, Captain Lastwell," the synthesized voice replied tersely.

"But you can't talk to automatics at length," Stevens pointed out. "You can't have an extended conversation."

"How many people can you do that with, and be comfortable the whole time?" Lastwell loved a good argument almost as much as he did the *James Cook*. "Give me automatics any day. Sound mechanicals, open space, a fixed destination." He stared out the foreport at the untouched, unexplored world drifting beneath them, an entirely different kind of expression on his face.

Then he blinked and glared at Stevens. "Don't play mind games with me, Kauri. Just tend to your work. If you haven't got anything better to occupy yourself with, I'm sure we can scrounge something up for you."

Stevens said nothing. His attention returned to the monitors that showed capsules Seven and Eight. Inside, he was churning. Seven and Eight presented a situation he'd never had to deal with on either of his two previous outspace journeys. Not only were the botanist and biologist asleep in the two capsules unmarried, they were his age and unfairly attractive.

The corner of his mouth twitched. He'd dealt with more serious problems. He would manage to deal with this one.

But it would have been a lie to say he was focused entirely on the business at hand.

* * *

Jack Simna blinked as the glassy, transparent upper half of his capsule slid back on silent runners. Actually, it wasn't quite a blink. More like slowly wrenching apart two pieces of paper that had been glued together, stretching them until it seemed they would rip. His mouth had the familiar taste and feel of a salt pan in the middle of the Kalahari. It was a sensation he had experienced several times before, and one he had not been looking forward to enjoying again.

He tried to move his arm. In response to the command from the brain, individual cells seemed to bank together to protest.

Instrumentation and unseen equipment hummed softly all around him. The gentle pastel luminescence cast everything in waxen shades of peach.

Experience and foreknowledge of this moment did nothing to alleviate the actual physical discomfort. Knowing better than to try to lick his lips in the virtual absence of saliva, he carefully engaged his vocal equipment.

"I'd like to sit up now, please. Sixty degrees, no more."

With a slight whirr, the upper half of his bed rotated up and forward, raising him to a sitting position. At least that much of the *James Cook* was functional. He'd seen the vessel that had been his home for the past half year of his life only in pre-departure vids, having been put aboard already encapsulated.

He remained motionless and let his eyes rove. They'd been kept moist by the capsule's equipment. His fingers and then hands slowly responded to direction. As he advanced through the wake-up exercises, he employed his voice a second time.

"Water, please. Lightly chilled, not too cold."

A compliant blue tube an eighth of a centimeter in diameter extended toward his face, sensors halting it short of his mouth. Turning slightly and ignoring his twitching facial muscles, he took the end of the tube between his lips and sucked as best he could. The shock of the first drops entering his mouth and sliding down his long-disused throat always reminded him of the time he'd gone over the falls while body surfing a four-meter wave off Noumea. On that occasion he'd swallowed enough salt water to make him throw up. That was the wake-up tube he now held loosely in his mouth: the Banzai Pipeline of soda straws.

As he sipped, the discomfort faded. Each successive swallow smoothed the way, psychologically as well as physically, for the one to follow. He forced himself to stop before he was sated. Better to feel fifty percent better and stable than a hundred percent better and likely to heave. *The weather's all inside me,* he mused. Drought, turning wetter, with a high pressure system due in soon. His stomach began to growl. *Time to take the equipment out of storage.* Time to pull the sheets off the furniture and make ready for company.

By now he could turn his head enough to see other capsules opening. Among his estivating colleagues only Cedric Carnavon was also sitting up. From out of his kindly face he flashed Simna a congratulatory smile. They'd made it this far, however far that actually was. Simna struggled and managed a wave. Carnavon gave him a thumbs-up by way of return. He was slightly older than Simna and in excellent physical shape.

As was his wife Millie, who sat up and ran her fingers

through her lightly grayed hair as Simna watched. He smiled at her and she grinned back. She was nearly as tall as her husband, and Simna knew that her petite expression was the only fragile thing about her. All three of them had participated in one of the early expeditions to Burke. They could and would rely on one another. Though psi-powers remained in the realm of imagination, as men of similar mind and experience he and Cedric Carnavon could and often did communicate without words.

Carnavon was more of a field man than Simna. While Simna envied his older colleague his exploration experiences, Carnavon admired Simna's interpretational abilities. They complemented one another and would no doubt do so on this journey as they had before. No envy festered between them. Like all truly competent individuals, each respected what the other could do.

Levering up the heavy log that was his arm, Simna rubbed at his forehead where the hair was thinning ungracefully. It itched, but then there weren't many places on him that didn't. Despite the capsule's built-in computer-controlled moistening gear, dry skin was an inevitable consequence of more than a month in deepsleep. Perhaps not a scientific priority, but certainly a personal one. The prospect of standing beneath a pounding, warm shower of recyclable water brought travelers out of their capsules far faster than any threat or promise.

Salvor Prentice let out a moan of irritation as he raised his bed. Respected head of his department at a major university, he was the nominal leader of the expedition, with Carnavon second in command. That was fine with Simna. Having been in charge on a previous expedition, he knew that the responsibilities of leadership would take time away from his own work. He was perfectly content to let others make any necessary decisions. If the situation demanded, he was already to raise his voice, while preferring not to.

Prentice had been on Tycho V. Let him and Carnavon handle the requisite mundanities.

By now the sleep chamber was filled with voices. Halstead and Ramirez were chatting to one another while Noosa, typically, was already voicing concerns about the condition of his equipment, wondering how well it had survived the long journey out from Earth. Mixed in with the masculine babble was the higher-pitched chatter of O'Sandringham and Lejardin. Other than the normal, expected complaints about the discomfort of awakening from deepsleep, everyone seemed to be in good shape.

While each had been carefully chosen by committee, it fell to Simna, the Carnavons, and Prentice as the most experienced and senior members of the expedition to ensure that things ran smoothly. There had only been time for a couple of brief get-acquainted meetings prior to departure, and he was looking forward to talking at length with each of his colleagues. There would be ample opportunity. They were going to be working together for anywhere from a year to a year and a half, depending on what they found.

Disconnecting himself from monitors, sensors, and tubes, Simna climbed carefully out of the capsule, leaning against the plastic for support until his disused legs steadied. Like a butterfly exercising its wings upon emerging from its cocoon, he told himself. He sniffed. No doubt newborn butterflies smelled better.

As he ran through the designated series of awakening calisthenics he caught sight of Lejardin doing likewise nearby. There should be laws passed against such individuals, he knew. No one had the right to be that intelligent and that beautiful. Definitely a prosecutable offense. He looked away. It was much too soon for such nonsense, and there was work to be done.

Besides, having matriculated as the proverbial intellectual geek, he was quite used to such women looking over or through him as though he didn't exist. His having become in maturity a somewhat famous scientist and outspace explorer had altered women's attitudes toward him, but emotionally and mentally a great deal of the uncertain adolescent still clung to his personality, as it did to a number of his equally respected colleagues. It could surface at the most inopportune moments. He knew from experience it would be easier as well as more sensible to keep things on a purely professional level.

But it wasn't going to be easy.

Lejardin, O'Sandringham, Halstead, and Prentice had served at the same academic complex and knew each other well. They did not form a clique so much as a body of knowledge, one they were eager and willing to share with others. To a certain extent their close relationship made Simna feel like an outsider, but that was no problem. No matter who he was with he always felt like an outsider. Not that he was antisocial. He simply felt more comfortable with Nature for companionship than with the humans who inhabited it.

As they had been awakened to the sound of softly humming machinery and not alarms, he presumed that everything was proceeding according to schedule. The absence of any evident emergency meant that they should be close to their target by now. Xica. Xica III. Very soon they should be able to determine whether a small group of Brazilian astronomers and analysts were going to become merely famous, or canonized.

With its kilometer-wide nets of advanced fungi and its herbivorous worms, Burke had been a revelation. Xica tempted with the promise of more, much more. Promises to keep, he murmured to himself, and parsecs to go before I sleep. At the moment he could only hope. It was tough to contemplate the very real possibility that he might be giving a couple of years of precious existence to study rocks that might be green with copper instead of life. Only much closer examination than the probe had been able to manage would reveal the truth.

As he finished his knee-bends he found himself wondering about the ship's crew. Other than the fact that they had piloted two trips out to Burke, he knew very little about them. He'd heard that they could be brusque, especially the captain. That didn't trouble Simna. Give him a loud-mouthed, socially inept, half-soused expert over a cheerful incompetent any day. Especially when lives might be at stake.

Besides, he was usually able to get along with anyone he met. It was one of the reasons he'd been chosen for the mission. In the often charged atmosphere created by many intelligences forced to function in close proximity many light-years from home, serious arguments and even violence were very real possibilities. Simna had the ability to act like a carbon rod in an old-fashioned fission reactor, soaking up heat and fury in exchange for calm and reason. Since he rarely took sides in personal arguments among colleagues, his judgment was often accepted by both contenders. Having no axe of his own to grind, he was frequently able to blunt others', often without them even realizing it. Carnavon in particular recognized this ability of Simna's, and had made use of it on both journeys to Burke.

"Anti-fractious," Carnavon called him. Simna took no especial pride in the talent. He honestly hated to see people fight. Not only was it a waste of time, it burned protein.

Should have been a psychiatrist, he mused. Except that psychiatrists spent their lives sitting in small offices, listening to the small woes of others. Such isolation from the natural world would have driven Simna crazy. He was too much the explorer, too much curious about what lay just over the next rise or under the next wave. Like Carnavon.

His curiosity about their crew was at least partially satisfied by the announcement that reverberated over the chamber speakers. The voice was rich, loud, and mildly impatient.

"Come on, you lazy lot! Get up and out of there so we can disinfect it. Don't any of you want a shower? Isn't anyone hungry? There's a bleedin' whole new world out here just waiting to be looked at, and you the lucky ones picked to do the first looking. Ain't this side of two hundred days of sleep enough for you? Now, who wants to go for a jog?"

Good-natured complaints and moans filled the chamber, which Captain . . . Lastwell? Yes, Lastwell, Simna remembered. Which that worthy would no doubt ignore. It was clear they were not to be coddled. Good. Simna much preferred it that way.

The unseen captain was quick to respond. "That's it; get to bitching already. I know your kind. You're already arguing about who's going to be first out, whose degrees are the most prestigious, who's published the most papers. I've nannied plenty of you.

"Speaking of which, I know how hungry you're going to be in a little bit. The kitchen's been up and humming for a month now, and I'm getting damn sick of Stevens's conversational limitations. I'm sure he's equally disgusted with my face. Get clean, get dressed, and get out here, and we'll feed you all up. Then we can start talking about doing some *real* work. The ones who can't handle solid food can go puke in private while the rest of us get down to business. Lunch in one hour."

"Charming fellow, our captain," Cedric Carnavon commented affectionately.

Behind him Ramirez, their self-designated point man for field work, snickered ebulliently. Dark-skinned and long-haired, he was now wide awake and full of life and himself. From his occasional grab at a support it was clear he'd rushed his wake-up. Simna said nothing. Minor errors in judgment made on board were harmless and even educational. On the surface it would be a different matter.

He peered appraisingly at Halstead. It had to be Halstead, Simna knew, because he was the biggest member of their party. A hulking, gentle giant, his forte was reconnaissance and recording, procedures in which he was supposed to provide assistance to others. Technically he was a general biologist with a particular interest in invertebrates. Perhaps Xica might provide one or two for him to study. Hope sprang eternal.

"How you doing?" Simna asked.

The big man stretched, and air bubbles popped in his joints. "Waking from mummy-land. You?"

Simna smiled. "Not too bad. You don't get used to it, but having been through it before at least you know what to expect."

Halstead nodded and relaxed. His manner was gentle and easy but not in any way dull. "Can't say as I envy you the experience. Only the trips." He stared past the older man.

"Anxious to check out your gear?" Simna asked him.

The biologist nodded. "I hope it's in better shape than I am."

Simna grinned. "You aren't bad off. You just look that way."

"Thanks."

Short, fit, and eager to trim the pale blond beard that decorated the line of his jaw, Cody Noosa was even more anxious than Halstead to have a look at the precious equipment lockers. Both men would have to restrain themselves until later, Simna knew. Since social proprieties aboard a deep-space vessel were few, it was incumbent on everyone to observe them. The fulfillment of individual priorities had languished for months. They could wait an hour or two longer.

Noosa made a last check of his capsule, his movements terse, jerky, and efficient. As the others made their way in their sleep shorts toward the shower room, he and Halstead compared mental notes. Simna shook his head. He could understand and sympathize with their eagerness, but it was impossible to rush matters. The surface of Xica was a lot closer than it had been ten months ago, but it was still not within walking distance.

A glance showed the three women moving toward the other shower area, with the experienced Millie Carnavon already taking charge. He let his gaze linger longer than was necessary or even polite, but no one noticed him. Not that anyone should object. Gazing at any face after months in deepsleep, reacquainting oneself with the human physiognomy, was an understandable and accepted condition.

The vision he saw was akin to one brought on by a momentary fever, and he forcibly shook it off. Let the others gape, he told himself. You can and should be more professional. Be an example to those who haven't done deepsleep before. He tried to recall the number of times he'd served as an example to others, lost count, and realized he'd hated just about every incidence.

Think about food, he told himself. The notion, if not the physical anticipation, was attractive.

He'd never been on the *James Cook* before but the deepsleep chamber was identical to those on other far-traversing ships. Personal effects lockers would be off to the right. To the left would be a corridor leading to the men's hygienic facilities. For ten minutes or so he could relax in the luxury of an upright, damp stall instead of a dry horizontal one. He ambled off in that direction, noting that Carnavon was already ahead of him.

Noosa, Halstead, and Ramirez chose to first check their own lockers. Simna grunted to himself. He didn't understand the urgency. If his gear was there, all well and good. If not, there was nothing he could do about it and certainly no one he could file a complaint with. Better to spend the extra time in the shower.

Fighting the lingering dizziness that was an inevitable

consequence of emergence from deepsleep, he chose a stall, told it a temperature, and activated the spray. The first gush of warm water was indescribably pleasurable. There was soap and shampoo, both of which he employed lavishly. A few minutes later the others filed in and six of the eight stalls were in use simultaneously. Conversation and jokes rose above the flutter of cascading water. He felt no guilt. The *James Cook* was an enormous vessel, and everything it carried that could be recycled, was.

The water had a slight chemical odor that didn't trouble him. He savored every sensation, glad to be conscious and mobile again.

As he dried off he noticed Carnavon slipping into a clean white on-board jumpsuit. "Feel better?"

The other man favored Simna with the familiar gentle smile that belied his far more adventurous personality. Cedric Carnavon was nobody's kindly uncle, ready for rocking chair, slippers, and book. He brushed a hand through his thinning gray hair, his eyes crinkling.

"Ready for a bit of a walk?"

"More than ready."

"We'll be off soon enough."

"Waiting's tough." Simna toweled droplets from his shoulders. "I'm trying hard not to think about what we might find here."

Carnavon's eyes twinkled. "Something beyond the nematoda? Or maybe even something with legs? Wouldn't that be exciting."

"I'm not going to hold my breath," Simna commented dryly. "Not after Burke." Steam carouseled ceilingward, sucked out through recycling vents to be recondensed and reused.

"Ah, but this isn't Burke," Carnavon reminded him unnecessarily.

II

Dressed, dried, and clad in white ship duty jumpers, they assembled in the Mess. Noosa was preoccupied and Ramirez looked a little worn, but that was normal after emergence from deepsleep. O'Sandringham and Lejardin were spontaneously radiant.

Simna forced himself to focus on their two-man technical support team. Stevens and Lastwell differed in age, appearance, and probably personality. So long as it didn't interfere with their work, he didn't care if they hated each other's guts.

"Here she is." Lastwell was as forthright in person as he'd been over the intercom. As everyone dug voraciously at their first meal in ten months, a large screen at one end of the room brightened to divulge their first close-up view of Xica III.

"Beautiful. Much prettier than the probe suggested." O'Sandringham neatly sliced the steak in front of her. Her eyes were blue, Simna noted. Brilliant blue-eyed blonde. Nice alliteration. Apparently Stevens thought so too. The mate hardly took his eyes off the botanist.

As Lastwell manipulated the screen's controls, the slowly rotating image drifted off the screen to hover above the center of the table, not far from the dinner rolls. In situ visualization conformed closely to the mapping carried out years ago by the drone probe: two large continental masses each about the size of Africa separated by a great deal of ocean. There were several sizable islands and a lot of small ones, all of which the probe had missed.

As they ate and watched, the full-color holo expanded and contracted. High-power scopes aboard the *James Cook* zoomed in on areas of potentially greater interest.

What struck Simna initially was the predominant color of the continents: browns and reds, not unlike Mars. Unencouraging, especially in the utter absence of ice caps. Nor were there any signs of large inland lakes. But analysis confirmed that the vast seas were water, albeit somewhat saltier than Earth's. Surely in the presence of so much water there had to be some kind of life. It was unconscionable (not to mention depressing) to think otherwise.

Lastwell took note of their expressions. "Not real promising at first sight, is it? But have a look at this strip along the west coast of the smaller continent." In response to his command the holo rotated smartly and a section of sea and land seemed to leap out at them. Food paused halfway to mouths. There were a few sharp intakes of breath.

Carnavon's eyes were shining. "That's an awful lot of green."

"Too much to be caused by lichens," O'Sandringham added.

Prentice was his typical cautious self. "Could be the result of algal blooms, or even copper minerals." Lejardin threw some ice cubes in his direction.

"That's more than a stain on the ground," she contended. "It *has* to be."

Lastwell was nodding. "My feelings likewise. It's hard to tell underneath all that cloud cover, but we'll find out soon enough. I propose setting down somewhere along that coast. There are some good landing sites tangent to the green areas." He glanced expectantly at Prentice.

"No objection, Captain."

The older man nodded, then offered a sop to protocol. "When would you like to drop? We can execute additional ranging from orbit or . . ."

Prentice preempted unnecessary discussion by responding quickly. "As soon as we've completed the requisite health checks and preparations I see no reason why we shouldn't make landfall as soon as is feasible."

"All right!" The ever-exuberant Ramirez punctuated his approval by smacking the table. His food jumped while remaining largely in place. Lejardin frowned at him but said nothing.

"As far as preparations," Lastwell informed them, "Kau and I have been seeing to little else all this past month while you lot have been sleeping like babes. One of our two landers is all checked out, stocked, and ready to go. Everything we should need is on board, barring your personal gear and equipment. Shouldn't take long to load that." He nodded deferentially to Prentice, then Carnavon.

"We can caucus on this whenever you want to pick a precise site. With a number of possibles, the more input on the final decision, the better." His gaze roved the table. "I'm sure you're all as anxious as I am to set foot on solid ground again. Especially ground no one's seen before."

Simna decided the captain enjoyed the build and look of the squat ex-footballer who'd savored a little too much of the good life. Nevertheless, he wouldn't have bet against him in a tight spot. Hopefully they would encounter few such on the surface. He knew many men like Lastwell, deceptive in appearance, who when pressed could muster surprising talents. His eagerness to explore set him immediately apart from most of his kind, who wanted only to sustain their ratings and fulfill their narrow job assignments. A technician with real curiosity was someone to be valued. Most of them could care less whether they were assisting scientists or politicians, so long as they were paid on time.

The mate was a little harder to read. Convivial, sharp, wholly competent, he was clearly more approachable than Lastwell. Nor did he seem overly intimidated by his more educated charges. Simna wasn't sure of him yet . . . it was far too early to render judgments on personalities . . . but the signs were encouraging. On his last journey to Burke the scientific complement and the tech staff had hardly conversed at all, much less established any friendships.

Though the kitchen was fully automated, Millie Carnavon took it upon herself to supervise its output. If Lastwell and Stevens were offended by her imposition, they didn't show it. More likely they were glad to concede its functions. Simna marveled at her quiet efficiency.

"A hobby," she told him when he queried her about it. "I'm sort of an incurable domestic. Since I can't bring my home life with me, I try to improvise one no matter where I am."

"Personally, I'm grateful for the interference," he told her honestly.

"Even automated food service can be improved upon."

"I agree. We should get along just fine, Millie. You like to prepare food, and I like to eat." They exchanged smiles. Millie Carnavon was the sort of person who would always take pleasure in seeing to the comfort of others before thinking of herself. He doubted he would have to do any work with her.

Not for the first time he found himself thinking that the authorities should put a professional on these trips. Time spent providing therapy often cut into his own work. At such times he wished he could escape his reputation. Unfortunately it always caught up to him, when it did not precede him. And the Authority's point of view was hard to argue with. Why try to make room for another specialist when a generalist like Simna could do multiple duty? They always managed to convince him to take on the assignment. When offers of monetary compensation failed, they could invariably succeed by appealing to his ego, which was certainly no smaller than that of anyone else on board.

He knew he was being manipulated at such times, but it didn't matter. He was flattered by the manipulation.

"Time to fly." Ramirez's black hair brushed the back of his neck. He was clad in a fresh white jumper, only slightly stained from working with his gear. His excitement was so palpable it was clearly difficult for him to stay in his seat.

Wonder if I ever had that much enthusiasm, Simna mused. He was so organized, so logical, so prepared that he sometimes missed things that someone like Ramirez would go straight to. Which was just as well. They would blaze different routes to the same destination. Simna would reach a conclusion through careful thought and hard work, whereas Ramirez or Noosa might stumble right into it. Each approach had its supporters.

One day Ramirez would probably fall into a deep, dark hole. Until then, he rode his unbridled enthusiasm for all it was worth. Simna simultaneously envied and was appalled by him.

They were finalizing last-minute preparations in the vast drop hangar, bustling about under the floodlights next to the huge delta-shape of the lander. His eyes searching the extensive open space, Prentice wore an anxious expression as he joined his colleagues.

"Where's Cody? I see everyone but him."

"Where d'you think?" Ramirez chuckled and nodded toward the piles of gear waiting to be stowed aboard. "Checking his instruments."

"Again?" Prentice was clearly miffed. "He missed breakfast. He ought to eat something before we make the drop."

"Lighten up." Ramirez checked the label on a small plastic bag he was holding and placed it carefully inside a shipping crate. "Cody's a pro. He knows what he's doing. We're all pros here." He turned and raised his voice. "Isn't that right, girls?"

Ramirez's humor was of the shotgun variety. Pepper as wide an area as possible in hopes of hitting something. Often he was on the mark. This time his sally went wide.

Only a couple of days out of deepsleep and already we have a team member exhibiting symptoms of foot-in-mouth, Simna mused. As he personally was immune to the side effects of that particular affliction (though occasionally vulnerable to it himself), he decided to make an effort to engage Ramirez in conversation on a regular basis. That would keep him from inflicting his individual brand of humor on others to a degree that was tolerable. For this Simna expected neither recognition nor thanks. It was part of his job.

Lejardin simply ignored the feeble gag. O'Sandringham was considerably less indifferent. She looked over from her workstation.

"Next time you call me a girl, Stew, you'll find yourself in one."

"Old joke. Ancient," he responded. But as he returned to his work, his smile was somewhat frayed.

Prentice wandered down the line, beneath the leading edge of the lander's expensive, gleaming delta wing. "Everything functional and on-line?"

Stevens glanced up at the senior scientist. "What do you think I've been doing for the past month?" He indicated the internally cushioned crates stacked on the loading skiff. "I've gone over this gear time and again. Anything I didn't understand I haven't touched. Shipping integrity seems inviolate. Not a lot of turbulence in deepsleep. And I've had a ship to look after, too. Or did you think our good captain did any more of the dirty work than was absolutely necessary?"

"Just checking." Prentice was a bit taken aback.

"I hope you don't expect us to carry it all once we're down." Both men turned toward Lastwell. "As well as look after your housing, life support, and daily needs."

"We're trained to take care of ourselves." Prentice took no offense at the captain's naturally brusque manner.

"I'm sure you can. No offense, but the last lot I piloted out to Burke was a disaster. Couldn't wipe their bums without Kau or I first plotting a course for 'em."

Stevens's expression showed how he felt about the most recent group to make use of the *James Cook*. "Somebody must've made a mistake in their briefing. Told them they were going to have the services of a couple of robots. Bring this, fetch that. You can imagine who ended up doing most of the bringing and fetching."

Prentice smiled reassuringly. "We're not like that." He indicated the rest of the group, busy with final preparations. "Simna and Carnavon have more offworld experience than either of you, and I'm no novice. Everyone else is experienced or qualified to a lesser degree. We'll take charge of our gear. You two won't have to extend yourselves beyond your classification assignments."

"Promises," Stevens declared.

"I'm glad to hear that." Lastwell clapped a friendly arm around Prentice's shoulders. "How much longer you estimate before your highly qualified folks have everything assembled?"

Prentice considered the activity around him. "Another hour. Maybe less."

"Great!" Lastwell performed some quick mental calculations. For all of his social awkwardness and blunt manner, he was supremely efficient at his job. "Any last-minute details you'd like me to run through for the group?"

"I don't think so. Everyone was thoroughly briefed before departure."

"Then we'll get on with it." Removing his arm from the other man's shoulders, the captain strode off to see the final loading, his voice trailing behind him as he preached to no one in particular. "Be good to finally get free of this bloated blimp, see something new. One goddamn delay after another. . . ."

When there was nothing more to be done, they assembled for a last time in the mess. Cedric Carnavon used a small controller to recall the Xican holo. As he spoke, the unit executed a series of zooms and retreats.

"We've settled on three potential primary landing sites," he explained. "All on the west coast of the smaller continent. The other landmass will have to wait."

"Detailed analysis carried out by the ship's instruments subsequent to our arrival indicate that the large red-yellow regions are most likely desert, as was initially suspected. As if by way of compensation, the green strips along the coasts look even more promising than we'd first hoped." Murmurs of appreciation came from those assembled around the table.

A topographic blowup replaced the rotating globe. "We've chosen this site here, about midway up the west coast. The actual touchdown site seems both sandy and flat, ideal for the lander. At the same time, it's a finger of desert that penetrates the green area almost to the ocean. There's also an extensive river-tributary system draining the plateau just to the north, occupying an unusual fracture zone in the crust." He smiled. "Plenty to keep us busy. I'll let Cody speak to the geology."

Noosa's short, muscular form rose from the seat alongside the older man. He took the controller and aimed it at the image.

"This portion of the continental plate has been sundered

by unknown forces. It appears tectonically stable, suggesting that the fracturing occurred over a long period of time." A pointer moved within the image. "As you can see, the main river runs straight as an arrow into the sea and all the tributaries enter it at right angles. An unusual but not unprecedented situation. The main channel appears navigable for most of its length."

"Everybody into the boat!" Ramirez chirped.

This time he generated a few smiles. "We'll certainly want to send a boat up there after we're established on the ground," Carnavon agreed. "To check on the estuarine life and . . ."

"Whoa," said Ramirez. "Aren't we getting just a little ahead of ourselves? Maybe we should pray we find something more advanced than lazy protozoans first."

Noosa grinned. When he did so, he looked like a contented but uncertain child. "Might as well be optimistic as not, Stew. The potential's there."

"Yeah. For green slime. Hey, don't get me wrong. I'm as hopeful as everyone else. I don't look forward to spending a year hunting for mites under rocks. I'm just being realistic."

"We're all trying to do the same," said Carnavon. "But it looks good, people. Real good. Much better than Burke, and infinitely better than Tycho." His eyes were shining with expectation.

"That's why we all fought so long for this assignment," Prentice put in. "That's why I worked so hard to assemble this particular team."

"What a waste of time," declared Halstead unexpectedly. There was silence for a long moment, then unrestrained laughter. Halstead's humor was low-key, but highly effective when he chose to employ it.

Even among this group of experienced, presumably jaded professionals there was a growing excitement, a charge in the air that could be sensed. They were about to set foot on an unvisited alien world, one that offered brighter prospects to the hopeful biologist than any heretofore visited by mankind. Simna felt like bursting into song, but had too much empathy for his fellow travelers to subject them to that particular brand of aural distress.

He kept a close eye on his colleagues, noting for possible future use character traits and personality quirks. Another might have felt that Lastwell and Stevens's constant verbal combativeness was a bad omen for the future, but Simna saw clearly that it was all bluff and sham, and that in difficult moments the two worked seamlessly together, becoming a single tool. The cursing and complaining was all so much letting off of steam. Both men were under a great deal of pressure. Until the team was safely down on the surface, everyone but the two techs was pretty much along for the ride.

Lastwell didn't let anyone forget it, either. His working vocabulary was inventive if not elegant, colorful and highly descriptive if not biologically sound. Occasionally it ran away with him, but most of the time he managed to keep it under control. In contrast, Stevens was not nearly as boisterous, preferring to vent his invective sotto voce.

Everyone pitched in with the loading. Simna moved to help Millie Carnavon, who thanked him politely even as she shooed him away with that piquant half-little girl, half-maternal smile of hers. Only later did an abashed Simna discover that she'd been a champion athlete in her youth and was in better condition than many of her younger associates. He was upset with himself not for making the chivalrous offer but for jumping to a conclusion, something he usually worked hard to avoid.

The constant evaluating and observing of one's companions was normal at the beginning of an expedition, he knew. You might have to trust your life to the person next to you. At such times printed résumés, no matter how impressive, were of little reassurance. Words on paper were an inadequate measure with which to size someone up. As time passed and they grew comfortable with one another, such constant scrutiny would fade.

Except for Simna. He never stopped watching, never stopped appraising. Occasionally it got him in trouble. There were those who didn't understand such attention, or misinterpreted it.

So far he'd seen no overt indications of weakness. This was a strong and competent group. With luck he might be able to largely ignore them in favor of exploration and study.

Ramirez was bouncing all over the hangar, chivvying everyone else on, frantic to be on his way.

"Take it easy, Stew." Halstead tried to restrain his colleague. "We'll get there soon enough. The sun isn't going nova and the planet's not going anywhere."

"Can't be soon enough." Given the appropriate command, Ramirez looked ready and willing to jump out of his skin.

Halstead put pressure on the top side of a heatseal, melting it shut. "You've waited ten months in deepsleep. What's the rush?"

Ramirez beamed up at the big man. "There's a whole new world down there. Maybe the first one we've discovered with something really worth looking at. Ground that's never felt the tread of human foot, atmosphere that's never vibrated to the sound of a human voice."

"It'll be there tomorrow," replied the placid Halstead. "Untouched and ready for you to violate."

Ramirez looked away, fingers working against one another. "I'm just anxious to get on with it."

"We're all anxious to get on with it, Stewart."

He looked over at Lejardin, who was running a final

check on her personal gear. "Hey, you can stay on the lander and do atmospheric analysis. Me, I'm out as soon as we make landfall." •

"Nobody's out as soon as we make landfall." Carnavon had eased up silently behind them.

"Why not?" Ramirez challenged the senior researcher. "We already know the air's breathable. Surely you don't expect to run into a host of airborne pathogens?"

"No, I don't. But we advance according to standard procedure. Regulations apply to the scientific complement as much as to the crew. No one takes any chances. That means no giddy, precipitous dives from the airlock." He looked to his left, to the top of a huge crate marked PREFAB #6B. "Isn't that right, Salvor?"

From his lofty location Prentice nodded concurrence.

Ramirez looked disgusted. "Why the anxiety? Burke and Tycho V are void of potentially invasive microorganisms."

"Always a first time," Carnavon said cheerfully. "We proceed with patience and by the book."

Ramirez rolled his eyes and groaned melodramatically. Nearby, Noosa shrugged, as though he'd be content to proceed either way. Simna said nothing. As usual, he just listened and watched.

One item of recurring interest was the attention Stevens was paying to O'Sandringham. He hovered about her with surprising confidence. Busy with her own work, she'd brush him off, only to see him return, placidly persistent, after a decent interval. Simna smiled to himself. He'd always been fond of the ballet.

She frequently had a small drink close at hand, but it didn't affect her work. Simna slipped the observation into his "O'Sandringham, Bella-Lynn" file without comment. Everyone handled a new landfall in their own fashion, everyone coped with the isolation in their own way. One thing you tried hard not to think about for very long was how impossibly far you were from the rest of humankind . . . and any kind of help.

It served to focus one's attention wonderfully well on one's work, though it had never bothered Simna. He was equally at home in a crowded room or atop an isolated mountain peak—though if pressed, he would have had to confess that he preferred the latter. As he watched his colleagues, he wondered who would be the first to start fantasizing about the absence of certain civilized comforts.

How long they actually remained on Xica would depend on what they found. They could stay and work comfortably for a maximum of two years.

Then there were no more preparations to make. Everything that could be put aboard the lander was in place. All necessary and appropriate standbys and shutdowns had been initiated. Final checks had been rechecked. Even Lastwell was satisfied. Eager and expectant, they filed aboard the craft and took their seats.

Though dwarfed by the fusion-powered hulk of the *James Cook*, the lander was still a vessel of considerable size. In the forward passenger compartment Simna sat quietly, motionless in his pads and straps as he listened to the euphoric chatter of his companions. Eventually he noticed Carnavon looking at him, and the two men silently exchanged a soothsayer's smile

III

Despite the formidable size of the lander, the drop was neither pretty nor comfortable. Going atmospheric never was. Strong jet streams buffeted Xica's stratosphere. Lastwell cursed all the way down while everyone else held on and was contrastingly quiet. Even the usually voluble Ramirez was subdued.

Though they were less disturbed by the inconvenience, the Carnavons and Simna kept silent, preferring to give at least the appearance of suffering in unity. Nothing worse to encounter than a happy, smiling face when you're being sick. Eventually they reached deeper, heavier air and the lander's delta wing began to bite more firmly. The wild swings slowed. Except for an occasional bump the bouncing and jolting was replaced by a steady vibration.

Not that the winds were unexpected. It would have been unnatural had the thermal circulation in the vast oceans not given rise to real weather. As Lastwell banked continentward the lander sliced clouds high above a pair of well-developed anticyclones. Just like riding the ram shuttle from Bombay to San Francisco, Simna mused. Except there were no ships below them, no inhabited islands. No one at all.

Burke's seas had been smaller and shallower, and those of Tycho virtually nonexistent. Momentarily abjuring reason, he strained his eyes in search of a sail.

As they dipped lower, Lastwell's vivid commentary was subsumed by the roaring of the lander's engines and the thunder of their passage. The vessel was no suborbital passenger shuttle. It provided no first class and everyone traveled steerage, same as the cargo. The Exploration Authority had no money for frills and could not pamper those they honored.

That didn't keep the captain from trying. He took every rough spot, every unexpected jolt, as a personal affront and, were such a thing possible, would have found a means of casting doubt on the legitimacy of the planet's lineage. Their rough descent occurred in spite of his efforts, not because of them. Simna found himself wondering how much of Lastwell's steady stream of invective arose naturally and how much was a conscious attempt on his part to fit some invented, idealized image of the robust and rugged commander that he'd constructed for himself.

As the ramjets reversed and slowed their descent, it grew quieter in the cabin. Stevens handled his duties in comparative silence, only occasionally responding verbally to Lastwell's irate orders. Apparently he had no trouble sorting the important kernels from his superior's verbal chaff.

Cocooned in his seat, Prentice struggled to see his companions. Simna was chatting easily with the Carnavons, which was to be expected. The three of them looked relaxed and at ease. Though he'd been on Burke with them and they'd worked smoothly together, he still had the feeling that Cedric Carnavon and Simna sometimes spoke in certain dialects he would never quite be able to master. Watching them, he was sure he was missing out on something. It did not cause him to feel inferior: only left out. Despite his steadfast good nature and ready smile, Jack Simna in particular would always be something of an enigma to him. There was an interior wall within the man a heavy particle beam could not penetrate. In contrast, Carnavon was much more open.

The lander rose and dipped, Lastwell called down imprecations on all designers of large delta wings, while behind Prentice someone moaned. He twisted in his seat as much as possible to look behind him.

Grim-faced and silent, stoic as one of the heroic statues of Ramses II, Halstead sat motionless, white-knuckled fingers gripping his armrests immovably. Lips tight, he sat looking neither to the right nor left. On his immediate left Noosa looked preoccupied. No doubt worrying down his equipment, Prentice supposed. His natural bluster having no effect whatsoever on his insides, Ramirez looked decidedly queasy. How much of his bravado was natural and how much was cover for the kinds of insecurities they all felt was a matter for speculation.

The athletic O'Sandringham looked like she was going to make it all right, but the more delicate Lejardin didn't look well at all. She was fighting the airsickness for all she was worth, but the Xican winds were winning. As Prentice watched she bent forward and retched softly into the suction device attached to the seat. He grimaced, knowing there was nothing he could do. If he unstrapped too soon to go to her aid, a sudden jolt could turn him into ceiling decor.

Simna contemplated an elegant joke, designed to appeal as much to the intellect as to the funny bone. Seeing that his companions were not in the mood either to think or laugh, he filed it for future use. His gaze rose to the front port, past Stevens and Lastwell. They were over land now, coming down fast, rusted hills and eroded gullies slipping past beneath them. Lastwell's voice grumbled in his headset.

"Almost there, ladies and gentlemen! This goddamn, piss-groomed bitch may not have much in the way of atmospheric dampers, but she'll get us down. Kau, ya lazy mucker, run a manual correct on that outside engine! We want full thrust or we'll come in too low. Goddamn computer redundancies; can't fly worth a dag!"

"I'm already working on the correction, Frank," Stevens replied softly. Simna had already noticed that the mate preferred to husband his obscenities for more private moments.

Vibration faded around him. They were cruising almost noiselessly now, the huge landing engines reduced to a faint whistling that barely tickled his cochlea. Desert continued to rush past beneath them.

Then he saw the first patches of green, as isolated as they were full of extraordinary promise. They formed odd-shaped blobs in visible depressions or tracked the courses of occasional streams. He wanted to yell, to shout for the lander to stop cold so he could step out and observe. As always, patience was a tough meal to digest.

Real vegetation, he thought excitedly. Advanced plant life. It had to be. But nothing was certain until it could be confirmed. First observations could be deceptive. He wondered what the air would smell like.

There was a loud *bang* and the lander dropped sharply, its fall punctuated by a couple of startled exclamations from those near Simna and some exceptional commentary on Lastwell's part concerning the sexual habits of aeronautical engineers who never had to fly the vehicles they designed. By now Noosa had joined Ramirez in looking decidedly queasy. Simna's stomach jumped, and he ran through the personal mental exercises he'd designed for himself. His insides stabilized along with the ship.

They were almost down. The surface was racing past too quickly to make out details

"Hang on!" Lastwell shouted. "This is it!"

Prentice tried to relax his fingers. Three years of preparation had gone into the Xican expedition. Three years carefully assembling material and crew. Then a month in orbit and ten more in deepsleep. Four years leading to the moment of touchdown. It wasn't easy to relax.

A different kind of jolt jarred the lander. Less slippery, more convincing. The great fist of the planet's gravity reached up and took incontrovertible hold of the vessel. Sand and gravel screamed beneath the nanocarbon landing skids as a towering rooster tail of fine sand plumed behind the ship, darkening the midmorning sunshine. The rasping howl penetrated the shielding and shook the passenger compartment.

Prentice kept his eyes closed. If anything went wrong, he would know it without having to witness it. He smiled to himself. As long as he could hear Lastwell's steady stream of invective he knew everything was all right.

Automatic stabilizers sensed variations in surface conditions and compensated accordingly. The crew was shaken but not stirred as the huge craft slowed perceptibly. The steady roaring both from Lastwell and outside diminished proportionately. They continued to slow.

And stopped.

Everyone was too relieved and exhausted to let out any whoops of triumph. Prentice helped Ramirez and Lejardin out of their seats and with their antinausea shots. Not quite as sick, Noosa vanished into the bowels of the lander to check on his precious equipment. After a long, lingering glance out the port, Halstead followed in his wake.

While Stevens and Lastwell methodically checked on conditions both in and outside the craft, Simna and the Carnavons unbuckled themselves and ambled over to the port to peer outside. After several minutes Cedric Carnavon called back to Prentice.

"Come and have a look at this, Salvor." There was an edge to his usually even tone. "I think we can now report with confidence that it was worth all the inconvenience."

As Lejardin tried to sit up, Prentice gently restrained her. "Relax. Nothing's going anywhere."

"I'd like to look." She was gazing toward Simna and the Carnavons.

He smiled down at her. "The surface'll still be there when you're feeling better. Give your stomach a rest."

"I don't want to be kind to my stomach. I want to look." But she remained where she was, albeit reluctantly, as Prentice left her to join the others.

As soon as he reached the port he knew that the heretofore grand discoveries of lichen and fungi on Tycho V and Burke had been instantly relegated to the realm of footnotes in the young world of xenobiology. Lastwell and Stevens had brought the lander to a halt at the very end of the finger of desert. The ship was surrounded on three sides not by algal blooms or lichenous mats but by actual low scrub. Just beyond the scrub were trees, a veritable forest. The trunks were gray rather than brown and their crowning verdure unnaturally sallow, but they were incontrovertibly trees.

"Look at that, just look." Millie Carnavon's eyes were shining as she whispered. "I'll bet some of the emergents are a hundred meters high."

"Easily," agreed Simna. "But see how they keep their distance from one another, and how open the understory is."

"This is just one patch," her husband pointed out. "Further in it may get denser." Simna nodded agreement.

"There's a lot of high grass or some kind of succulent fringing the sand," Millie noted. "The forest's first line of defense against encroaching desert. O'Sandringham's not going to know what to sample first. *I* won't know what to do first." She was holding her hands clasped together just beneath her chin, looking for all the world like a little girl surveying the Christmas display at a large department store.

Prentice spotted a clump of large beige-hued spheres nestled within a pair of bushes. Seed pods, or something else? He was desperate to go outside and get to work, but knew they had to proceed with caution. He couldn't very well counsel restraint to the others if he broke procedure himself. It wasn't easy. The lustrous-skinned pods beckoned to him.

"No flowers." There was disappointment in Simna's voice that had nothing to do with science.

Millie Carnavon was more hopeful. "Perhaps deeper in the forest, out of the direct sunlight. Or in another location."

Stevens turned from his position. "UV's pretty intense here. Ramirez, Lejardin, and Simna might be okay, but everyone else is going to have to be sure to slap on some shield before going outside or we're going to be dealing with severe burn cases before we even get set up."

Carnavon's gaze hadn't shifted from the forest. "We all know our own skin," he murmured softly. "God, I can't wait to get out there."

"We are blessed, my dear Challenger, beyond all scientists since the beginning of time," Simna murmured.

"What's that?" Millie Carnavon frowned uncertainly.

He smiled gently. "Favorite quote from a very old book. I'll run the sphere for you sometime."

Her husband looked over at him. "Twenty-four hours here would guarantee a lifetime stipend, a prestigious professorship, make a career. And we've got two years, should we need it. Xenobiology's about to become a serious science, and we're going to define it."

"You're pretty sure of yourself," Stevens remarked.

Carnavon glanced back at him. "Just look at this place. Even if there's no animal life at all above the microscopic, the maturity of the plants alone exceeds our wildest expectations. This is what mankind's dreamed of finding since he put the first artificial satellite into orbit around Earth."

"There'll be more." There was a look that came into Simna's eyes at rare moments, as though he were gazing out upon vistas others could barely imagine. He wore it now. "I know it."

"Is that an objective analysis based on observable fact?" Millie Carnavon enjoyed gently teasing him.

The slightly aquiline profile, with its sharp chin and prominent nose, didn't swerve. "Right now there's a fire in my mind, Millie, and I'm just listening to it crackle and hiss."

An enfeebled but strengthening voice sounded behind him. "Can't you just talk like normal people, Jack? Does everything have to be couched in melodrama?"

He smiled back at her. "What do you expect, Favrile? I'm a melodramatic, abnormal sort of person."

She was about to comment again but O'Sandringham was pushing past her. "It does look promising as hell, doesn't it? What's it like out there, Kauri?"

The mate flashed her a thumbs-up sign as he turned back to his instruments. "Hot and surprisingly sticky, despite the desert's proximity. We'll need shades and shielding to block out the UV, but the rest of the mix looks tolerable, unless anybody hails from north of the twentieth parallel back home. Air looks good, gravity's a bit under one point zero. Maybe the extra bounce in your step will help compensate for the heat and humidity. Frank?"

Lastwell grunted. "The bitch smells accommodating. Atmosphere's a bit heavy on the argon, but that shouldn't vex anybody. Everything outside's going to stink of the new anyway. Too early to tell about airborne bugs."

"We should be so lucky." Ramirez had recovered enough to rejoin them, though he was still a bit green.

"Nobody sticks so much as a foot outside until we've run

standard cultures for potentially inimical microorganisms," Prentice announced loudly. "I know nothing of the sort was encountered on Tycho or Burke, but we play it safe and according to procedure." Someone groaned unhappily but no other voices were raised in protest.

"If I know Cody and Ted," he added, "they're already processing samples. We should know in a day or two if we can breathe outside without filters or supplements. Meanwhile everyone should have plenty to keep them busy."

No one slept much that night as they worked on preliminary observations, atmospheric analysis, and unpacking gear. Initial results indicated the presence of plenty of airborne organics, but nothing that was flagrantly human-invasive. By midday following they had accumulated sufficient data for a conference.

"Computer models and standard test scenarios on the stuff we won't be able to avoid inhaling if we go outside without filters indicate minimal likelihood of respiratory complication." Noosa detailed their findings as he ran charts across the screen. "Simulated cultures of a microbial atmospheric cross-section were uniformly negative. Potentially active human pathogens appear to be absent."

"Preliminary conclusions?" Prentice inquired.

Noosa pursed his lips. "You'd run more risk of catching something on a deserted beach in Madagascar."

"That bad?" Ramirez scanned the room. "Anybody else up for a hike in the woods?"

"Take it easy, Stew." Prentice was firm. "I admit it looks good, but nobody goes outside for the first week without suits. Procedure." No one raised a voice in protest. They were all familiar with the prescribed routine.

"I'm as anxious as anyone else to experience Xica in the raw, but we take no chances."

"Let me," said Ramirez. "I don't mind taking a chance or two."

"Want to be able to say you were the first one out?" Halstead commented dryly. He glanced around the room. "How do we determine that? Draw numbers?"

"It will be decided on the basis of scientific priority," Prentice assured him.

Millie Carnavon was her usual prosaic self. "You're the nominal leader of the expedition, Salvor. If you want to be first out, I don't see how anyone could object."

"Or you could let me go first." Stevens ventured the suggestion from his place near the doorway. "That way if anything unexpected happens, the scientific integrity of the expedition isn't compromised."

"Doesn't matter what you decide." Carnavon turned to Lastwell, who was leaning up against the port.

"Why not, Frank?"

"Because while you've been talking the silent son-of has already beat you to it." Grinning, he jerked his head toward the transparency.

There was a rush for the port. Outside, a singular figure was strolling casually toward the edge of the forest, its manner as casual as if it were taking a Sunday walk in the park. It was clad in one of the thin, slightly reflective eco-suits. With the polarizing mask down over its face, they couldn't see who it was.

Cedric Carnavon didn't need to. "I wondered where Jack was. I should've expected this."

"He ought to have waited," Prentice muttered.

Carnavon looked over at the younger scientist. "People like Jack don't wait. They appraise the situation and then they act."

"Can't fault the bastard for boldness." Lastwell was masticating something pungent as he stared out the port. "Looks like he's doing okay. Unless something jumps out of the bush and starts noshing on his intestines, I think I'm going to join him. I'm fucking sick of recycled air."

"I'm going out too," announced Lejardin.

"Shouldn't somebody stay with the lander?" O'Sandringham wondered.

"What for?" Lastwell paused in the exitway. "Everything's operating optimum. Don't need anybody to stand by to fire the guns in case of native attack. No natives and no guns. Me, I'm going out." He vanished through the opening.

Prentice looked resigned. "So much for procedure. I suppose we might as well all go." He glanced out the port. "At least he had the sense to suit up."

"Frank's right." Stevens was heading for the doorway. "Everything's okay. The lander's not going anywhere. One of the backup water recycler's only intermittent, but I can fix that later." He winked at O'Sandringham. "Want to join me in taking the time to smell the weeds?"

"Don't be boorish," she snapped. But she didn't say no, either.

It was overwhelming in the forest.

So engrossed were they in the wealth of discovery surrounding them that Prentice and his dazzled companions found themselves stumbling on a regular basis. Sometimes it was over a projecting root, sometimes a rock, occasionally their own feet. No one took notice and no one cared. They were all drunk with enlightenment.

Simna had encountered and crossed a small creek. It looked as natural and free-flowing as any forest brook back home, though the slightly lighter gravity gave an extra bounce and tumble to the gurgling waters. The air was warm and stale-smelling, but Prentice suspected that might well be a consequence of breathing through their long-stored suit filters. It did little to mute their exhilaration.

Furthermore, Simna's impulsive supposition on board ship had already been borne out. Xica's astonishing plant life did indeed support a habitat for the first higher animals to be found outside Earth.

Already they'd observed two different kinds of fliers flitting through the trees, though neither had been scrutinized closely enough to assign to a class or even a phylum. Beneath their feet the rich red earth was alive with all manner of burrowing, crawling arthropods. Some looked much like terran insects while others resembled nothing this side of a fever dream. It proved nearly impossible to hold anything like a normal conversation because their suit receivers were swamped by a constant stream of astonished exclamations as discovery after discovery was announced.

A third type of flier soared gracefully over Prentice's head on a meter-wide wingspan, the bright light filtering through its membranous wings. It had a narrow, blue-scaled body, multiple eyes, and neither neck nor tail. Almost too thrilled to breathe, Prentice stared raptly as it disappeared behind him.

"Did you see that, did you see that?" Noosa was clutching his recorder in one hand and shaking Prentice by the shoulder with the other.

"I saw it," Prentice mumbled. "I'm not sure I believe it, but I saw it."

"Got it clean." Noosa shook his recorder proudly. "Looked like a giant carnivorous slug with wings." Had someone just handed him a bowl of opals, he could not have been happier.

There was far too much to see. Any kind of serious study was out of the question. It would be days before anyone calmed down enough to commence any real work. Prentice had to turn repeatedly to assure himself that the bulky lander was where it belonged, mounted on its footing of red sand, and that he wasn't back home in his own bed, or still lying in deepsleep, dreaming.

Though it boasted a plethora of fascinating undergrowth,

the Xican understory was too open for the landscape to be called a jungle. Dense clumps of greenery and grayery would unexpectedly give way to rocky features through which burst only occasional bushes and towering gray-flanked trees. Except for an occasional raucous screech, the alien woods were oddly quiet.

Eventually Prentice knew he would have to rein in his stunned party and regroup back at the lander. But for now he would let them roam free, like children in a candy shop. He was hard-pressed to control his own giddiness.

We will not be famous, he told himself. We will be immortal.

The next step was to set up a base camp, probably in the woods but still within sight of the lander. No one would want to sleep and live on board when they could be close to the subject of their studies, inhale organic instead of machine smells, breathe fresh instead of recycled air. The lander offered a hospitable but sterile haven. Once set up, the prefab camp would be equally safe and much more inviting. Erection would take about a week, furnishing with domestic and scientific gear another. There was no rush. It was likely to be their home for at least half a year.

Something dynamic went slithering past his left boot. It was yellow and blue, with a narrow, triangular head and broad spatulate tail. He couldn't see if it was moving on legs, cilia, or belly scales. When he nudged the tail with his foot, the arrowhead-shaped head jerked around to contemplate the interruption out of bright red eyes. For a tense moment, visitor and native regarded each other solemnly.

Then the fore part of the tiny body arched and with a twisting, screwing motion, the brightly hued creature proceeded to drill itself into the earth. Prentice gazed in wonder at the hole it left behind.

What had it been? A worm, some kind of reptile? Or the prologue to a completely new order? *Annelida Xicaria drillicus.* Divergent rather than parallel evolution. The stuff of any would-be xenobiologist's dreams. Returned alive to Earth, that single specimen would cause sensation. All celebrities Great and Small, he mused. Human as well as Xican. He wondered if he would have time enough to fulfill all the speaking engagements.

Xica would not only silence the skeptics, it would give a tremendous boost to the flagging interstellar exploration program. No longer would drones would be sent out one at a time but in bunches, like grapes.

He lifted his gaze from the hole to scan the forest. Where there were trees, there were membranous-winged fliers. Below the fliers were yellow and blue burrowers. And where there were burrowers, there could be . . . what else? He listened intently as he scanned the shiny, gray-sided boles through his suit's faceplate. They looked as if they'd been covered in foil instead of bark. O'Sandringham could make an entire career out of any one tree within his present range of vision.

Yelps of joy and delight continued to fill his headset as his companions made their own revelations. Ramirez dominated the shouting, unable and unwilling to restrain his enthusiasm. His dossier confirmed what Prentice already knew: that the researcher was erratic and undisciplined. He tended to stumble across discoveries rather than build to them. Such an approach was sometimes necessary as well as useful. You just had to keep an eye on him.

To his left and just ahead Prentice saw O'Sandringham displaying to Stevens something tuberous she'd just plucked from the ground. The mate had his arm cast around her shoulder in a manner that was only part brotherly. As Prentice looked on, she shook it off. Shaking his head and smiling to himself, he advanced further into the forest. First day out, and already closer relationships were beginning to form, emotions shifting like clouds. Not that twosomes would constitute a problem. It was the formation of cliques you had to guard against. He fervently hoped that wouldn't be a problem with this group.

He chided himself for worrying. Here he was, in the first moments of the first hour of the first day, worrying about others instead of glorying in his surroundings. It was the way he was, sometimes to the detriment of his science.

There was movement in the brush ahead of him. He froze, staring as something like a cat-sized cow lurched through the vegetation. It had four legs and a splotchy green-brown skin. He couldn't tell if the faintly moist epidermis was composed of short, shiny fur or chitin. Four tiny horns protruded from the long-snouted skull. It was followed in solemn single file by eleven duplicates of itself. Varying only in size and length of horn, they ignored him completely, their olive-green pupilless eyes staring at the smooth backsides immediately in front of them. Each eye was divided into four distinct quadrants. Primitive compounding, he wondered, or something more complex? He held his breath, hardly daring to breathe.

The Xican ecosystem was proving to be not only prolific but downright riotous. So much diverse life suggested the existence of predators, though they hadn't encountered anything like that as yet. They might, he thought, have to improvise some kind of protection, some kind of weapon. Expecting to find nothing more advanced than the higher fungi, the team had not been trained or equipped to deal with anything larger or more mobile.

With comical dignity the twelve pudgy aliens trundled off through the brush, their passage progressing noiselessly. He stared after them until the last disappeared, wondering if they always traveled in single file or in troops of an even dozen.

Something went *phut* and he jumped reflexively. A nook near his feet had been closed off by what looked like a silicon disk. Overwhelmed by so many biological riches, he marveled at the unknown burrowing creature that had fashioned such a remarkable door to its dominion. You didn't even have to go looking for wonders to study. Here they willingly offered themselves up for your inspection.

Two years on this world wasn't going to be long enough, he knew. A lifetime wouldn't be enough. No matter how intensively they applied themselves, there was little more they could do than make a beginning.

After making sure the rock she selected was devoid of organic life, Lejardin took a seat and silently considered the bush. The focus of her attention was a shrub radically different from any growing around it. Its verdure was a bright purple instead of the by now familiar gray or green, its amethystine bark electric against the background of its duller companions. Pointy-leaved gray giants towered all around, shading the cluster of rusting, iron oxide-rich rocks on which she sat.

The bush was thick not with leaves but with tightly curled tendrils, like the shoots of an antisocial fern. They expanded and contracted as she watched, giving the growth the appearance of an anemone feeding in a lazy current. A swarm of tiny gnatlike things helicoptered silently above the deep purple core, perhaps drawn by the thick, acrid perfume it emitted. Occasionally a tendril would flick lazily through the cloud, parting the gnat-things as it trolled the torpid air for its supper. Whether the bush was plant or animal it was too soon to say. For the moment she was satisfied simply to admire rather than classify its rhythmic elegance. Off in the distance a second bush was similarly engaged. In her current range of vision, they were all that moved.

Her thin suit's air-conditioning system was hard-pressed to keep the heavy, humid air at bay. It didn't trouble her overmuch. Heat had never troubled her.

She'd quickly and intentionally separated herself from the others. It was better this way. No irrelevant questions, no one professing awkward offers of assistance. They had no idea what was going on inside her, no notion of the personal crises she'd left behind on Earth. Her decision to partake of the expedition hadn't been wholly motivated by scientific curiosity. She'd had troubles to leave behind, and this was as far as it was humanly possible to get from them.

Remembering them, however, was not leaving them behind. She concentrated on the beautiful deep purple growth but was careful to keep her distance from it. Even if it fed on minute bugs, it was still carnivorous and possibly capable of mounting unsuspected defenses. If she got too close, it might react unexpectedly. Not unlike certain individuals.

Though fully qualified for the expedition, she was acutely conscious of the gap that lay between her and its senior members like the Carnavons, Prentice, and Simna. This perception of personal inadequacy troubled her more than it would someone more easygoing, like Ramirez or O'Sandringham. All it really meant was that she was going to have to work that much harder. Not to prove anything to them, but to prove something to herself.

IV

They spent the first week concentrating on straightforward audiovisual recordings; touching nothing, collecting nothing, removing not so much as a colorful pebble back to the ship for detailed examination. When not out amassing images to present to a disbelieving posterity, they worked on assembling the base camp on a level site well within the forest but still in view of the lander. Prentice discovered that the easiest way to avoid having to debate priorities with Ramirez and to a lesser extent with Noosa was to give them plenty to do and praise the results, which were certainly competent enough.

The self-sealing walls, floor, and ceilings went up quickly in the calm if humid air. By the third day, analysis having revealed nothing dangerous in the atmosphere, they were working in field shorts, shirts, and visored caps, free of the encumbering ecosuits.

Once structural integrity had been achieved, connecting corridors linking the various individual buildings were levered into place and attached. The big climate-control unit was dollied into position and secured to the vents and ducts built into the prefab walls and ceiling. A cheer went up when Stevens switched it on. As soon as the temperature and humidity within the buildings dropped into the comfort range, they started moving in beds, kitchen gear, lab equipment, and personal effects.

Camp consisted of one large dome for living quarters, subdivided into eleven individual cubicles (privacy being a vital and precious commodity on any such expedition) with shared hygienic facilities; a mess-assembly building with attached autokitchen and dispensary, and three smaller domes for laboratories and storage. There was also a separate large, non-climate-controlled shed for uncritical storage.

Thanks to the extreme humidity, the integral condenser was able to provide more than enough water for all their requirements, extended showers included. This freed them from the need to lay a pipeline to the nearest stream, while incidentally supplying water free of any possible contaminants. In the bright sunlight where they emplaced the solar collectors, the photovoltaic cells were soon converting at a more than adequate ninety percent rate. Storage batteries raced toward full charge.

The lack of any wind speeded assembly. Indeed, an occasional gust to stir the languid air would have been welcomed. None manifested itself.

Lejardin tested everyone daily, as well as sampling what the air filters collected. They all remained in disgustingly good health, probably better than they would have enjoyed on crowded Earth. Ramirez had to be restrained from tasting any of the native fruits or nuts they had found.

"Why the hesitation?" he chided Prentice. "This world isn't only harmless, it *likes* us."

"No ingestion of native vegetation until it's been thoroughly checked," Prentice reminded him. "If you're so anxious to sample the local cuisine, you can run the tests yourself."

"I'll do that," Ramirez responded, "as soon as we're allowed to get on with what we came here for."

"Tomorrow," Prentice counseled him. "When the last of the gear's been brought over from the ship."

"Always tomorrow," Ramirez grumbled, but complied with Prentice's directive, which was all that mattered to the expedition leader.

It was almost an anticlimax when they were allowed to start collecting. Since no one wanted to stumble about clad in one of the encumbering ecosuits and since it was too hot and sticky to search in the middle of the day, they limited their field work to the morning and evening hours. According to regulations, at least two team members remained in camp at all times. This couple was allowed to carry out all the lab work they wished so long as they periodically checked the central communicator.

On the ninth evening after touchdown Ramirez was absently tousling his black mane as he looked up from his workbench. "Wouldn't it be great if we found something that lived up to some of the old tales about other worlds?"

Halstead was hunched over a scope and spoke without looking up. "Bored already?"

"Bored? Hell, no! If we never found another thing here and had to work for the rest of the year just with what we've picked up in the past couple of days, I wouldn't be bored. I was just fantasizing."

The Carnavons were studying a meter-long segmented worm that might not be a worm. They'd dug it out of the ground a couple of meters from the main entrance to the camp. A line of mouth parts running along both flanks appeared to absorb nutrients directly from the soil. The fantastic creature had no eyes and no nostrils, though there was evidence of a rudimentary kind of internal sonar.

"No harm in that." Cedric Carnavon smiled understandingly. "Give me ten-ex on the magnifier up here, Millie."

"I know Stew," Halstead remarked. "He's not going to be satisfied with burrowers and crawlers. He wants to find something big and imposing, preferably with long, sharp teeth."

"If you want a little excitement," Prentice suggested to the other man, "unpack one of the power rappelers and go climb a tree."

Ramirez didn't hesitate. "That's not a half bad idea. Bet there are whole ecosystems up in the crowns. Maybe I'll try that one we found yesterday, the one with the bluish trunk that goes straight up for thirty meters and then just kind of explodes into ten thousand tiny branchlets."

"Doesn't look very inviting," O'Sandringham commented.

"I picked up a few of the ends that had fallen off," Ramirez continued. "They're mimetic. Try to straighten them or twist them, and they curl right back into their original shape. I'm going to try to measure how long the effect lasts once they've been separated from the parent tree."

"Maybe they're not branches." O'Sandringham looked thoughtful. "Maybe the tips serve as seeds, or shoots. Plant a couple and we'll find out."

Ramirez shook his head. "Not me. I'm no gardener. I'll give 'em to you, Bella-Lynn, and you can see if they sprout."

"I'll take them," the botanist agreed readily. Ramirez could be a real pain, but there was no denying the quality of his work. Having a point man not only willing but eager to do any of the dangerous jobs spared the rest of them the need to volunteer.

A contented Prentice observed the byplay in silence. Everything was functioning optimally. Although it was still early, all systems were up and running without any awkward personality conflicts having manifested themselves. Any arguments or differences of opinion had been relegated to work. Hopefully it would stay like that for at least a year. It would make his job so very much easier.

For his part Carnavon had been on too many such expeditions to be as sanguine, but he was hopeful. And if relationships grew testy, there was always Simna to smooth things over. He chuckled at how rapidly O'Sandringham and Stevens had paired off. On the surface they seemed to have little in common. O'Sandringham was not only far more educated, but the mate teased her unmercifully. To this she responded with insults that were carefully designed to do little real damage.

At first there was a certain amount of competition to see who could describe and name the most new creatures. Only Cedric Carnavon and Simna didn't participate. They didn't seem to need that kind of immortality. As long as accepted taxonomical procedure was followed there was nothing to stop Ramirez or Noosa or anyone else from naming various discoveries after themselves. Given the seemingly infinite variety of the Xican forest, the game soon grew old and was abandoned, personal nomenclature giving way to that which was properly descriptive.

Prentice had carefully live-trapped several small black creatures as they'd tried to return to the silicon-barred hole he'd encountered on that first day. As he conveyed them back to the camp he hoped he wasn't breaking up a family. The little creatures had green stripes on their underbellies that he suspected might be a form of sex-determinant and three bright green eyes apiece. Instead of teeth, their little round O-shaped mouths were lined with inward-facing grinding surfaces. They might eat anything from arthropods to rock, he mused. They made no effort to escape from the lightless collection box, the interior of which he hoped would approximate the conditions to be found naturally within their hole or tunnel.

He added them to the growing collection of boxes and holding cages in Dome Three, which was rapidly turning from a laboratory into a zoo. There were a couple of the cow-pig things, several fliers that had been trapped in nets and quickly tranquilized, a whole phylum of burrowers and crawlers, another of worm-relatives, and something utterly alien that looked like a loaf of wheat bread on wheels. Its method of locomotion consisted of gadding about on rotating, ballooning spheres. Noosa had found it and spent half a day trying to get it into a cage without traumatizing the creature.

There was also an immobile predator. The size and shape of an overstuffed footstool, it was squamous and lumpy, devoid of external organs or prominent epidermal features. In place of limbs were a cluster of long, whiplike tentacles near the top that Simna theorized served as sensory organs as well as grasping devices.

They'd observed pairs and trios of the Bellies, as Ramirez had ignominiously dubbed them, traveling at an agonizingly slow pace over the ground, feeding on whatever they encountered that was too slow or stupid to get out of their way. Indiscriminate as to diet, they readily plucked crawlers out of branches, burrowers from the earth, or tiny fliers from the air. Although too thin to threaten a human, the tentacle-whips were lightning-fast. It was as if all a man's energy and reflexes had been concentrated in his hands and fingers.

They'd collected their Belly by slipping a broad shovel beneath its slow-moving form and placing it gently in a large wheeled collection box. As much as out of customary concern, they took care because agitating a potential specimen could result in its doing involuntary damage to itself. It made no effort to escape, though as Halstead pointed out it could easily double its speed without drawing attention.

It occurred simultaneously to Simna and Carnavon that except for the fliers, they'd thus far seen nothing that traveled in what could be called rapid fashion. Noosa had found several sets of parallel grooves in the ground that hinted at a fast-moving animal, but it remained unobserved.

"There it goes!" Halstead shouted one morning.

"Where?" exclaimed Prentice.

Halstead shook his head dolefully. "Missed it."

Prentice blinked, then grinned. And so it went.

Ramirez wanted to track the groove-makers, but Prentice squashed the idea. They had far more than enough to keep them busy within an hour's walk of Base Camp. Bashing through the forest for days on end in search of Xica's more elusive inhabitants could wait a month or two. Ramirez protested, as usual, and acquiesced, as usual, before returning to the study of specimens already gathered.

Xica's bounty soon forced Prentice to send Stevens back to the lander for another load of assorted cages and holding containers. To everyone's joyful consternation, their biological larder was filling up fast. But it wasn't enough to gather specimens: you had to make some sense of them as well. Exploration without explication was not science. Gradually the first outlines of a crude schematic of Xican taxonomy began to emerge from their collective studies. Within that diagram animals and plants found their respective positions shifted repeatedly. Each dawn brought forth new discoveries and new precedents, all of them clamoring for accommodation.

It was at lunch on the first day of their third week on Xica that Halstead entered the mess with a peculiar expression on his face. Unusually, it did not reflect its owner's standard preoccupation.

He halted behind an empty chair. Most of his colleagues were halfway or more through their meals. Off to one side, Simna was trying to help Stevens adjust the beverage dispenser.

"You're late, Ted," said O'Sandringham. "Better hurry, or there'll only be four or five portions left." Halstead's appetite reflected his outsized frame and served as the foundation for a running series of good-natured jokes among his companions.

"I'm not hungry," he told her evenly.

Her blue eyes widened and her reply reflected mock disquietude. "Whoa! Call out the medics."

"Everyone have a good morning?" The big man's gaze wandered around the table.

Lejardin and Prentice exchanged a glance. "What's up, Ted?" the senior scientist inquired.

"Anyone paid a visit to the collection dome lately?"

"Lately as in when, Ted?" O'Sandringham asked him.

He peered down at her. "As in a few minutes ago. I think you'd better come have a look." He raised his eyes. "I think everyone had better come."

"Something wrong?" An alarmed Carnavon started to rise from his chair.

"Maybe. The natives appear to be restless."

"Say again?" Prentice made a face.

Halstead turned and headed for the door. "Anyone with more than a casual interest in their individual specimens ought to come along." He disappeared through the locktight that led to one of the cylindrical connecting tunnels.

"This better not be a gag." Lastwell muttered to himself as he pushed his meal aside and belched importantly.

Halstead peered back through the portal. "You can stay, Frank. You don't have any specimens to study."

"The hell I don't. They're *all* mine." He moved to join the rest of them. Only Stevens remained behind, wrestling unhappily with the recalcitrant appliance.

Unrestrained cries of dismay and astonishment filled the dome as the team members entered and rushed to their respective stations. O'Sandringham gawked in disbelief at her precious, now empty containers and collection boxes.

"What happened in here? What the hell happened?" Her

disbelief grew as she moved purposefully from one case to the next. "I had a whole collection of those little iridescent leaf-eating arthropods in here. Now there's only some oily muck in the bottom." She stared into a screened enclosure. "And those four-winged fliers we caught last week; they're gone too." Her eyes flicked ceilingward, but the presumed escapees were nowhere to be found hanging from the smooth interior ceiling of the dome.

It was the same with about half the cages and collecting boxes. Fifty percent of their specimens had somehow managed to flee. A concerted hunt for the escapees commenced.

Gradually most were located and returned to their original containers. Some were found scratching at the impenetrable floor, trying to burrow their way out. Others had concealed themselves behind shelving or benches, retreating to the dark. How they had slipped free of high-walled xicariums or latched boxes or screened cages remained a matter for everyone to speculate upon.

Carefully gathered back up, they offered no resistance as they were returned to their still-locked containers. Perhaps a tenth of the specimens they'd collected remained at large, including O'Sandringham's delicately tinted leaf-eaters.

"How could any of them get out?" Simna was inspecting the screen that covered a large plastic xicarium in which Prentice had placed his black hole-dwellers. There was no way they could climb the slick walls, and even if they could have, their sausagelike bodies were too thick to pass through the fine wire mesh that was securely fastened to the sides of the box.

"They didn't walk through the walls. Dome integrity's intact and none of the alarms went off." Noosa was bemoaning the loss of his own favorite representatives of Xican wildlife. "All four of those green Floater Pads I netted in the north pond are gone."

"None of them should have been able to get out of their

cages, much less out of this dome," Simna declared. "If half managed the trick partially and ten percent completely, what restrained the other half?"

"Maybe they like the food," Halstead murmured unhelpfully.

"We've got a lot of work to do." Carnavon was helping his wife check their own specimens. "We've missed something important. If Cody's right and the dome hasn't been violated, then the missing specimens are still hiding in here somewhere." He turned to regard his colleagues. "As to how they got out, I don't think we can discount the possibility that some disgruntled member of our party with his or her own private agenda let them go."

Protests from the assembled were immediate and vociferous. "Ced, we're all here to study Xica," Prentice avowed softly. "You can't have an agenda to liberate creatures you didn't know existed."

"Good point," Carnavon conceded after a moment's thought. "*If* our hypothetical specimen liberator is thinking rationally. Unbalanced people do unbalanced things."

"None of us is any crazier than average," Halstead insisted. There were a few nervous chuckles.

"Then the missing critters are still in here somewhere, as Cody says." Carnavon moved to another cage. "I'll dump at least half my suspicions when we find them."

Lastwell and Stevens went over the dome and the two prefab tunnels that connected it to other parts of the base complex with scanners, monitors, and their own five senses. They could not find a crack, a hole, or any evidence whatsoever of a breach in the structure. The alarm system checked out sound. It had not announced any unexpected exits from the room.

More than any other single factor, it was the lack of consistency in the disappearances that troubled Prentice. Why a cluster of arthropods should escape while a much smaller container of half-centimeter-long wigglers remained behind he could not fathom. A strong-limbed ground dweller they'd named Sneek remained contentedly in his open-topped xicarium while a limbless, wingless burrowing worm had managed to defect. There seemed no rhyme or reason to it.

As for the twelve specimen types the team had yet to re-claim, they shared absolutely nothing in common except that all were still missing. They remained missing for the next three days. On that morning Simna and Cedric Car-navon, who had journeyed further afield than anyone else to date in search of new and exciting discoveries, returned with a revelation that put all thoughts of the missing speci-mens out of mind. It was left to Prentice to wonder if there might be a connection between their new discovery and the festering mystery.

He was working alongside O'Sandringham and Lejardin at the sorting tables in front of the main entrance to the camp when the two older men emerged from the woody depths. Brushing sweat from her fine-featured face, Le-jardin looked up from her work to greet them with a smile, envying them their ability to appear at home in the most uncomfortable of surroundings.

"Find anything explosive, guys?"

Simna was noncommittal. "One or two items of interest. The usual assortment of minor biological miracles."

"We didn't find the most impressive one." Carnavon couldn't contain himself. His ruddy face fairly beamed.

"What are you talking about?" Now Prentice looked up from his own work and O'Sandringham turned curiously from the pile of plants she'd been sorting.

The two men exchanged a knowing glance. "Well," Car-navon went on, "it's like this, you see. This time the dis-covery sort of found us." So saying, he turned and gestured toward the trees. "It's all right. You can come out now."

They were words, Prentice later decided, that would go down in the history of science alongside the greatest pronouncements of Einstein and Darwin.

Lastwell had been finishing up a minor repair to the base's external wiring. When he saw what was happening he hurried over, took a long look, and sat down heavily on the bare earth.

"Bugger me for a Hindu whore." He shoved back the brim of the customized cap he was wearing and continued to gawk. Less colorful but no less astonished exclamations arose from those around him.

Prentice was on the communicator instantly, informing the others. They gathered outside the entrance, in the comfort of alien shade.

"We're not equipped to handle this." Noosa kept muttering it over and over to himself, like some sort of bureaucratic mantra.

"What are we going to do?" Millie Carnavon had her recorder out and running, as did about half of her companions. "No one foresaw anything like this."

"Well, for starters," her husband explained, "there isn't a qualified linguist among us. In their wildest dreams no one in the Authority envisioned a possible need for one."

"We don't know if they even have a language." O'Sandringham stepped forward for a better look at the . . . natives.

Though not particularly short, none were as tall as Carnavon or Halstead. Sexing was a simple matter of separating the obviously mammalian females from the stockier males. Indeed, they were sufficiently humanlike for the similarity to be frightening, in spite of some conspicuous differences. Flatter, barely protuberant nostrils, smooth shell-like ears that cupped rather than stood out from the aural cavity, decidedly elliptical eyes in shades of green, blue, yellow, and lavender (no browns or blacks), faint streaks that were mere shadows of eyebrows, long lashes on both males and females, all set in faces that were more heart-shaped than oblong, readily distinguished them from any branch of humankind.

Both sexes boasted long, straight hair that began at the apex of their skulls and fell halfway down their backs. In every instance the color matched that of the individual's eyes. Blue and lavender eyes were not shocking, but blue and lavender hair was. Tiaras of small flowers, the first the explorers had seen, adorned smooth, unblemished foreheads.

Slim, satiny arms and legs protruded from sleeveless woven tunics decorated with abstract patterns painted in broad strokes of dull red, brown, and a brighter black. Each hand ended in two long, limber fingers flanked by a pair of opposable thumbs, an arrangement evolved to provide exceptional digital dexterity. Small feet shod in handmade sandals displayed a similar arrangement, except that the two large toes did not appear to be prehensile.

Altogether there were four of them, evenly divided among the sexes, to gape back at the humans. Despite the disparity in size (Halstead must have seemed a veritable giant to them) they showed neither fear nor panic; only an understandable hesitancy to relax. The males carried long, thin spears fashioned from some dark wood, short clubs slung at their waists, and crude bows with attendant quivered arrows. Baskets strapped to the backs of the females were half filled with forest fruits and tubers.

Hunters and gatherers, Prentice mused, but by the looks of their attire and gear, fairly sophisticated ones. The small clubs the males carried were solid wood and the tips of their spears and arrows were fashioned from bone, suggesting that they might not know how to work stone, much less metal. He tried not to jump to conclusions. This was an event, a moment in time, not particularly conducive to deliberate, meticulous thought.

They were very attractive people, he decided. It seemed natural to think of them as people. Their intelligence was beyond question. Just as there was no question of their astonishing humanness, despite the indisputable external differences. Whether further similarities were to be found beneath the skin remained to be seen. It would take time to find out. Intelligent aliens were not candidates for vivisection.

Everything they had thus far discovered on Xica, the sum total of their achievements to date, paled before the arrival of the four petite natives. Hoping to find fish and bugs, they had found intelligence. That one simple fact would set them alongside Magellan and Columbus, Cook and Armstrong.

Simna spoke apologetically into the silence. "I've had some linguistic training." Somehow no one was surprised. "Nothing designed to deal with a situation like this, but then there *is* nothing designed to deal with a situation like this. They do have a language, by the way. They jabbered at us nearly all the way back." He smiled gently at the visitors and two of them smiled back.

"As you can see, the smile is just one expression we have in common. We're trying to proceed carefully so as not to make any mistakes. Their voices are high and musical. You could almost say 'sweet.' Their language sounds are not complicated except for a couple of thick glottal stops and one long nasal trill. I can't tell anything about their grammar yet, or the extent of their developed vocabulary, but they don't have any trouble communicating with one another. They're not shy about talking, either, and there seems to be no hesitation on the part of the females to join in."

"Why would there be?" asked Lastwell.

"Depends on the society." When Simna was concentrating really hard one could practically hear him thinking. "We've no idea if it's male- or female-dominated, or ruled by elders, or sexually unbiased. We don't know if they have an Athenian democracy, a more advanced variant thereof, or a hereditary chief. Culture influences language, and vice versa."

Lejardin put a hand on his shoulder, startling him. "Considering that you've just met, Jack, I think you're doing a damn good job."

He shrugged and looked a little embarrassed. "I'm just trying not to make any breaches in an etiquette we don't understand."

"Well, don't stop now," Carnavon urged him. "We don't want our new friends to think we're bored with them."

Simna nodded and stepped out in front of his companions, very close to the lead alien couple. With his right hand he tapped his chest several times, declaring as he did so, "Human . . . human."

The four Xicans considered this display and then conversed softly among themselves. Their language had the flavor of Mandarin mixed with French, punctuated occasionally by the trills and stops Simna had mentioned.

Prentice observed the discussion in a daze. The ordinariness of the visitation was overwhelming. No grand preparations had been made, no careful, methodical buildup to the great moment executed. There had not even been time for congratulations. Everyone was too busy getting acquainted.

Simna had turned and was pointing to his friends. "Human . . . human . . . human . . ." he announced formally as he went around the gathering. Concluding with Noosa, he startled O'Sandringham by grabbing her arm and pointing to her. "Female." He followed his announcement by repeating his delineation of his companions, this time singling them out and identifying them by sex. The Xicans observed all this with great solemnity.

Simna turned back to them and again touched his chest. "Human . . . male." Deliberately altering his tone from formal to familiar he added, "Jack Simna." Once more he went through the group, beginning with, "Human, female . . . Bella-Lynn O'Sandringham." Adding individual names took a little longer, but the Xicans evinced an admirable degree of patience.

It was too much to expect, but the slightly larger of the two males promptly took a step forward and pointed to himself with one of his two fingers. His flutelike syllables tinkled in their ears.

"Pendju," he proclaimed formally.

Simna nodded, pointed to the native, and echoed as best he could, "Pendju." Then he pointed to himself yet again and reiterated, "Human." Following this he gestured first to the speaker and then to his companion, saying, "Pendju, male. Pendju, female."

This yielded a quartet of grins so broad and elfin that it inspired a similar response among all the humans. Though not exactly childlike, it was suggestive of innocence and wonder, not to mention honest delight. It also hinted at the true extent of the natives' intelligence.

The speaker wasn't finished. Pointing to himself again he said softly, "Pendju . . . m'ale. *Boutu.*" Before Simna could respond, the Xican gestured at his companion. "Pendju . . . f'male. Mahd'ji." He went on to identify his two other friends as Silpa and Jesh'ku. It was an astonishing performance. Prentice could not have been more overwhelmed had Boutu produced a vid of his own and commenced to record the explorers.

Ramirez whispered to Halstead, "Rich, Ted. When we get back we're going to be rich as well as famous." He nodded to the mate, who was observing the encounter with as much interest as any of them. "Even you, Kauri."

"Suits me," said Stevens, hands on hips. "I can live with that."

"No more long journeys for me." Lastwell was smoothing the dirt with a sandaled foot. "Early retirement in the company of several women obscenely younger than myself." He raised his voice to Simna. "What else do they say, Jack? What else *can* they say?"

Simna turned and made quieting motions. "We don't want to rush things, Frank. We've just made the greatest discovery since fire, and as long as the discovery's willing to cooperate we don't want to do anything to unbalance the situation. For example, I've noticed that they hardly ever raise their voices."

Lastwell looked uncertain for a moment, then grinned hugely. "Right. I'll shut up, then."

Pointing to herself, Lejardin carefully approached the female named Mahd'ji. "Human, female. Favrile Lejardin."

"That might be a little tougher for them to deal with than Jack Simna," the senior scientist warned her.

After first looking to her male companion for what might have been reassurance or might equally well have been something utterly different, the Xican turned back to the biologist and slowly pressed all four digits to her chest.

"Pendju, *s'si* . . . *Mahd'ji*."

That was what the male had called her, Prentice remembered. He was delighted. Consistency was the foundation of understanding. If it held true, the *s'si* was hopefully the native word for female. Or, he cautioned himself, it might mean "me." Or pretty, sick, happy, wife-mate, or any one of several dozen other possibles. He was perfectly content to let Simna try to sort it all out. Basic intuitive language programs would help. Doubtless Simna thought so as well. He'd been utilizing his recorder from the beginning.

While Lejardin and Simna continued with the exchange, Prentice moved up alongside Carnavon. "Think we can puzzle it out?"

"Puzzle what out, Salvor?"

"Their language."

Carnavon shrugged. "Not my field. But I wouldn't bet against Jack. He's certainly the best qualified to try. Sometimes it's useful to have a generalist around."

"A Renaissance man," Prentice commented.

"Yeah, but which Renaissance?" the older man added cryptically. "Maybe we should have proceeded differently, but there's no protocol for this. We just sort of stumbled into each other and after the initial shock, both sides did their best to wing it. We're still winging it."

"You did fine," Prentice assured him. "Nearly three hundred worlds drone-probed and only two show any signs of life. On the third we jump straight to an advanced, complete ecosystem complete with intelligent life. Humanoid life, no less. It's a bit overwhelming."

"We'll cope." Carnavon turned to engage Halstead. "How about it, Ted? Can you help Jack put together some kind of language program for Xica? Give us something we can all study while Jack's doing the pioneering work?"

Halstead pushed out his lower lip. "Maybe. From what I remember of preflight preparation, the lander's library is pretty extensive. If Jack can help me choose the grammatical algorithms I can probably hack out the rest. We're not talking about deciphering Mayan glyphs or anything as complex as that."

"I wonder if they've developed writing as well?" Prentice turned back to the ongoing convocation.

Carnavon grinned gently. "Let's not get greedy. We just found out that they have language."

"They have tools." Noosa had shifted over to Carnavon's other side. "Writing implements could be among them, even if it's nothing more complicated than a sharpened bone in the dirt." Even while he spoke he kept his eye glued to his recorder.

"You getting all this?" Carnavon asked him.

Noosa's reply was somewhat testy. "I know my job, Ced."

Carnavon advanced to Simna's side. The natives eyed his advancing bulk warily but held their ground. "How's it coming, Jack?"

Simna replied modestly, "I think I'm picking up a few words here and there, but it's too soon to be certain. Boutu just pointed to the ground and said *kes'wi'mi*. Now that could mean ground, earth, soil, brown, down, or Hell. Or it could be their name for the planet. Or he might have been asking me to kiss his foot, though I don't think so. Clarification will come only through repetition. The computers will help a lot." He smiled. "They're certainly willing to play the game, though I'm not sure they're as eager to learn from us." He looked back at the patient, smiling Boutu.

"When he pointed downward it struck me that they have neither toenails nor fingernails."

Carnavon's brows rose as he looked. Sure enough, smooth skin covered the natives' fingers and toes. "I guess all their keratin's gone to their hair. Simplifies hygiene, anyway."

Boutu had turned and was gesturing back into the forest. "*C'ulme*," he said insistently. "*C'ulme ch'wala.*"

"What's that?" Prentice asked.

Simna shrugged. "Your guess is as good as mine, Galvor. He may be referring to his home, or to what they were looking for when they ran into us, or the fact that he has to go visit his mother-in-law. I'm only working with a couple of words here. I don't even know if they have a permanent residence or if they're wandering nomads."

"The sophistication of their gear suggests a place of long-term occupation," said Carnavon. "It takes time to make clothing and baskets, time that's hard to find if you're moving around all the time. I'll bet they have a cave somewhere, or maybe a real settlement. Any people who can make baskets and clothing can build a hut."

"They have such beautiful eyes," Lejardin murmured. "Males and females. Look at how clean they are: clothing, skin, hair, it's all neat and brushed. Based on that, I'd have to say they're very advanced."

"Good point," agreed Simna. "Hard to stay clean if you're always on the move, too."

"Hey," O'Sandringham blurted, "they're leaving!"

Apparently Boutu's pronouncement referred to something of importance, as he and his three companions had pivoted to start back toward the trees. They would walk several steps, then turn and beckon, the gesture as unmistakable as their shy smiles.

"Interesting." Halstead looked up from his humming recorder. "They all seem to be lefties."

"Or maybe they always use their left hands when asking others to follow them," Simna pointed out.

"Oh." The big man was slightly crestfallen. "I hadn't thought of that."

"*C'ulme.*" The natives called back to the entranced explorers in unison. "*C'ulme eswaj!*"

"They want us to go with them," Carnavon declared. "Or *c'ulme* with them, whatever that might be."

"Dinner?" suggested Ramirez. "As guests, or as the entrée of honor?"

"Did you notice their teeth?" Simna asked him.

Ramirez blinked. "No . . . why?"

"I'm not sure they have individual teeth as we do. I couldn't very well stick my fingers down anybody's throat and ask them to say '*ah.*' The insides of their mouths appear to be lined with solid ridges of bone, angled like incisors in front and flattened for grinding elsewhere. Nothing like fangs or canines. That suggests they eat meat only occasionally, if at all."

"Then what were the spears and clubs for?"

Simna considered. "I could be wrong, or they might have some meat in their diet."

"Or maybe the stickers and bangers are for defense," Lastwell declaimed unexpectedly. That gave everyone a moment's pause.

The natives maintained their pace, pausing less frequently now to beckon back to their newfound friends.

"We'd better get some gear together if we're going with them," Carnavon announced. "They could be headed just over the first creek or halfway down the coast."

"We could break out the transporter," Stevens offered.

Prentice shook his head. "Take too long, and I'd be very surprised if something that size didn't frighten them away. They're sure not going to get into one on our say-so. Besides, we don't know if it can negotiate the woods."

"It'll bloody well knock over anything in its path," Stevens assured him.

Prentice was unpersuaded. "I'm not sure that's the best way to insinuate ourselves into their good graces. They may regard the forest with some respect."

Simna started forward, looking back over his shoulder. "We don't want to lose contact. I'll go with them now." He tapped his service belt. "Anyone who wants to follow can track my communicator signal. I'll try to ask a lot of questions about the flora and fauna. That should keep us on a slow pace."

Lastwell was somewhat less enthusiastic. "All the smiles and sweet talk are nice, but we don't know anything about these people. They could be arranging a nice, happy, grinning ambush."

Prentice started to object, thought better of it. "I agree that it would be wrong," he said slowly, "to go off half-cocked and overly optimistic. Have we got anything we could use as weapons? It probably wouldn't take much to overawe these people."

Stevens snapped his fingers. "I'll dig out a couple of hand cutter-welders. They're battery-packed, not too heavy, and they'll weld composite or metal. So long as you can get within four meters of your subject, on high setting they'll fry or melt it for you."

"That should do," Carnavon admitted dryly. "We should carry some minimal supplies, too: water purifier, some concentrates, first aid. Recorders."

The Xicans were nearly out of sight now. Not knowing what else to do, Simna waved and yelled excitedly. This set the natives to caucusing among themselves which, if nothing else, kept them in view a few moments longer.

"I'd better get going." He checked his communicator. Any of his companions could track him with their own devices, and stay in voice contact with him while doing so. He wondered how the Xicans would react the first time he answered a call and they heard the talking box.

His colleagues watched as he strode off through the trees. The natives waited for him. Those left behind saw them chat for a long moment. Then Simna waved and disappeared into the forest in the company of the others.

Prentice prodded his companions. "Let's get it together, people. Some of us may have a long walk ahead of us."

Ramirez intercepted him on the way back into the base. "Why can't we all go, Salvor? The natives aren't going to circle around and make off with the lander. Those spears of theirs can't break into the camp. Why can't we just put everything on standby and all go with Jack?"

"Bad procedure." Prentice was unwavering. "Doesn't allow for the unforeseen."

"Okaaay," agreed Ramirez slowly. "So how did you determine who gets to go and who has to stay?"

Prentice replied after a moment's thought. "Fair enough.

Ced goes because of his experience, but I'll sit this one out." He looked around at his sweaty companions. "Any other volunteers?"

"I'll hang around." Halstead was compliant, though it was clear he wanted to go.

"Tell you what," said Stevens reluctantly. "You all go. I can look after things here." He worked up a grin. "That is, if you think you can take care of yourselves without me."

"That's sweet of you, Kauri," said Millie Carnavon.

"Sweet nothing." Stevens was uncomfortable with praise. "It's my job."

Lastwell let out a snort. "Well, I'm going. Wouldn't miss this for an extra couple of zeroes on my credit account."

"I really ought to stay," Halstead insisted. "Get started on that translation program, so that when you all come back with full recorders we can put something useful together. I'll hit the library and start extracting. Then when you get back we'll dump everything into the hopper and see what kind of babble comes out."

"That's good of you, Ted," Prentice told him gratefully. "If they're as friendly as they seem, you'll get your chance to visit. Hopefully they don't live a hundred kilometers or so from here."

"They'd better not," grumbled Lejardin. "I'm not much on cross-country hikes."

"If you get tired, I'll carry you." Carnavon wore a decidedly unpaternal grin.

"Thanks." She smiled back knowingly. "I'll manage." She failed to see the look Millie Carnavon gave her husband, but he didn't.

V

Light packs riding high on sweat-soaked shoulders, they caught up with Simna and the four Xicans in less than an hour. Since the traveling scientist had prepared them for the arrival of his friends, the natives showed no surprise at their appearance. The group was welcomed onto the journey with few words and without ceremony.

The walk through the forest was even more fascinating and instructive than their previous solo journeys, now that they were traveling in the company of guides and interlocutors not only ready but eager to point out items of interest. Everyone kept their recorders on in hopes of matching up as many plants and animals as possible with their native nomenclature.

For their part the Xicans treated their visitors' curiosity as one component in some great game, squealing instead of laughing with delight whenever Simna or Carnavon or one of their companions struggled to pronounce a Xican name. Simna was better at it than anyone. He might not be a professional linguist, but he turned out to be an excellent mimic.

The Xicans displayed a keen if untrained intelligence. For example, they quickly picked up the generic word "tree" and used it alongside their own equivalent whenever possible. They darted lithely under fallen trunks and through thick brush as they sought out specimen after specimen for their newfound friends to admire.

"They're not keeping any kind of watch or lookout," Carnavon commented.

"Yes," agreed his wife pleasantly. "If there's anything really dangerous on this part of Xica, they're certainly not worried about running into it."

"Maybe they just know how to avoid the dangerous places. Or maybe the local carnivores aren't very fast, like the Bellies. Why don't you ask them about that, Jack?"

He looked back at the botanist. "Because I don't know enough to frame a question yet. You might give me a day or so."

"Sorry," she replied testily. "I was just asking."

Lastwell kept falling behind. Unencumbered by the need to classify or detail what he was recording, he rambled freely in their wake, drifting delightedly to whatever growth or small creature took his fancy. The recordings he was making would serve as an excellent supplement to their own work, Carnavon thought.

Noosa looked up from his communicator. "We've turned due west, toward the ocean. Unless they plan to hike along the coast, we're almost to wherever we're going."

"I hope so." Carnavon squinted at the sky. "Because there's no way we're going to be able to make it back to camp before nightfall."

"Maybe they're fisherfolk," Lejardin opined.

"If so, they've left their gear behind." Simna gestured toward Boutu's spear. "Wrong kind of point for fishing."

She glanced up from her recorder, her tone mildly sarcastic. "Anything you don't know?"

He smiled back at her. "It would take me a thousand years of study just to learn how to begin to ask the right questions, Favrile."

"Ask 'em if it's much farther." Lastwell had moved up to rejoin his companions.

"That's a simple enough request that I just might give it a try." Simna edged closer to Boutu, who did not shy away. A soft exchange of Xican words, and then Simna addressed his colleagues.

"I *think* he said that we're not going as far as the sea, but I can't be certain because I'm not sure of the word for ocean, among other things. Like their time-frame. But wherever it is we're going, we're not there yet."

Lejardin's tone grew even drier. "Now *there's* scientific precision at work for you."

"Check this out." Prentice had found a creature about the size of his foot that most nearly resembled a crawling cactus. The spines on its back were short and hooked. Dozens of long brown cilia sent it humping forward as it scoured the ground in search of new buds and other low-growing vegetation. He was trying to figure out how it fed without having to pick it up when his communicator buzzed for attention. Already familiar with the operation of Simna's unit, Boutu and the other Xicans didn't even look around.

"Prentice here. That you, Ted?"

"No," crackled the voice. "It's Cody. We've developed a slight problem back here, Salvor."

Prentice slowed and glanced around. His colleagues were ignoring him, intent on the Xicans and their exotic surroundings.

"Already? I didn't think we'd been gone that long. What's going on?"

"Don't get excited. We're not exactly in crisis." Noosa sounded only slightly hesitant. "You remember that dozen or so specimens we thought had escaped? Well, they're back."

Prentice wiped sweat from his cheeks and forehead. The

forest was like a sauna. "Back? What do you mean, they're back?"

"Just what I said. In their original cages and holding containers. As if they'd never left. Ted and I have been thinking about trying to devise a test to measure invisibility."

"That's a joke, right?" Prentice replied.

"Hell, Salvor, my first thought was that the whole business was a joke. You know Ted. I wouldn't have put it past him to have arranged the whole business. He swears up and down that's not the case. We quizzed Stevens about the reappearance and he acted properly insulted, so I'm pretty certain he's in the clear."

"I wouldn't suspect Stevens." Prentice held the com unit loosely, not knowing what to believe. "What do you think happened, Cody? Some kind of collective delusion?"

"Not likely. After meeting our remarkable and friendly locals, I thought for a minute that they might have had something to do with it, but even assuming they could slip inside undetected, why steal specimens only to return them later? Anyway, the three of us have been here working since you lot left and we haven't seen a sign of them."

"Metamorphosis," Prentice muttered to himself. "Reflex mutation."

"What's that, Salvor?"

"Nothing. I'm babbling. This situation allows for a little babbling, I think."

"I might buy metamorphosis of some kind." Noosa's voice hissed softly over the unit's speaker. "Except that when something metamorphoses it only does so one way. Butterflies can't go back into their cocoons, much less turn back into caterpillars."

"This is another world, an entirely new biosystem," Prentice reminded him. "Don't let's allow any superficial similarities to blind us to that fact."

"Yeah . . . right."

"Keep an eye on the returned specimens and let me know immediately if they disappear again."

Noosa replied with feeling. "No kidding. Ted's busy with his language program, so I guess it's up to Stevens and me. We'll take care of it. Meanwhile you keep a close watch on our jovial, smiling native friends."

"What are you suggesting, Cody?"

"You don't want them suddenly disappearing on you. They might reappear at an awkward time. Base out."

Prentice thoughtfully clipped his com unit back onto his duty belt. They'd been right from the start. The missing specimens *had* never vanished. They'd never left their cages. Which presented the question of what, exactly, had happened to them as opposed to those watching them. What peculiar transformation had they undergone? Or was it something else entirely, some alien phenomenon as yet unimagined? And a dozen of the specimens had been involved.

What about those who had managed to escape their cages and containers? Had they somehow likewise transformed themselves? But they had appeared normal and unchanged when they'd been recaptured. And more than half the collection had neither disappeared nor temporarily escaped.

He nearly tripped over a projecting root. Lejardin reached over to steady him but he irritably waved her off. Things were happening too quickly. He badly wanted to turn the key in the proverbial clock backward, slow things down.

The Xicans kept up their unvarying, fluid pace, forcing him to leave the curious cactus crawler behind. That creature represented a minimum of another week's work, another entire dissertation that would have to await more time. He was drowning in a flood of biological riches.

As the forest began to thin slightly, clumps of thin green grasslike fronds began to appear. The natives gave these a wide berth. When Simna managed to ask why, Silpa took off one of his sandals and drew the sole across the edge of one harmless-looking leaf. The groove it left in the tough leather was clearly visible.

"Haukik." The native spoke brusquely as he slipped his toes back into his footgear.

"That's for sure." A grim Ramirez reached for a frond with thumb and finger, thought better of it, and looked around guiltily to see if anyone had caught him.

Though abundant, the *Haukik* tended to grow off by itself, as though the other vegetation feared it equally, and the travelers were able to avoid it with relative ease. But it was a fresh reminder that not every living thing on Xica was harmless and inviting.

Prentice considered whether to inform the others of his conversation with Noosa. He decided to wait. Just now they had enough on their minds, which were wonderfully focused on their field work. Why complicate matters by presenting them with an inexplicable puzzle they couldn't solve until they returned to base anyway? Until then he'd ponder it himself. It was the kind of burden he willingly accepted.

As they pushed on, Boutu and his companions continued to reel off the names of numerous plants and animals. The humans plied their recorders avidly, making mental as well as verbal notes as rapidly as possible. Nothing could be overlooked, nothing forgotten. The opportunity might not be repeated as the Xicans might decide to leave at any time, without explanation.

Silpa paused to peel back the thick bark of one gray-green tree to reveal a broad hollow place beneath. Instead of growing directly on the wood, the bark grew like a shield, supported on innumerable tiny pillars of cellulose approximately a centimeter above the xylem.

Within this protected cavity lived a host of flattened

black creatures about the size and length of a man's thumb. Tiny swept-back spines grew from their flanks, giving them a fuzzy appearance, like flattened caterpillars. But when O'Sandringham tried to pick one up for a closer look, Jesh'ku hurried to intervene. Her exact words of warning were unintelligible, but her attitude and expression were not.

Plucking a newly fallen leaf from the ground, she touched it to the back of one of the black bark dwellers. The leaf instantly curled up and turned brown. The demonstration was as effective as it was brief.

Simna's tone was respectful. "So not every life form here is cute and benign."

"Some kind of organic acid." O'Sandringham examined the leaf gingerly, without picking it up. "Or toxin."

"Look, don't touch," Prentice reminded her.

She nodded. "I know, but it's easy to forget."

A cry reached them from Ramirez, who was striding along out in front of everyone, including the Xicans. Boutu jabbered excitedly and everyone increased their pace.

They'd been smelling the sea for several minutes. Now they emerged abruptly from the edge of the forest to find themselves standing on a low headland. Spread out before them was the body of water they'd prosaically named the Western Ocean. In appearance it was breathtakingly normal: white foam, the echo of waves crashing against the red rocks below, the wide sweep of blue. Only the raucous chorusing of seabirds was missing.

The eroded cliff on which they stood rose some ten meters from the water. A few low, rocky islands were visible halfway to the horizon, ringed by halos of pure white sand. To the north a sandy beach worked its way between piles of pitted dark volcanic rock, the basaltic material strikingly different in color and appearance from the surface on which they were standing. Ancient lava flow, Simna decided. The shoreline swung around in a smooth, plateaulike curve to the north.

All was in startling contrast to the blue water, the colors enhanced by the pristine, clear, but humid air.

A few puffy white cumulus clouds, their undersides lightly grayed as if soot-stained, hovered near the horizon, trying to organize some rain. Palm trees would have completed the picture, but there were no members of the *Palmae* family here. Only the strange, scraggy trees and bushes with their gray bark and purplish-green verdure, which had nothing soft or inviting about them.

Twenty minutes later they reached the village.

VI

It spread out across a low knoll, far enough back in the forest to make use of the trees for shade but high enough to catch those rare breezes that all too infrequently drifted in off the ocean. The simple round huts had peaked thatched roofs and walls of sticks cemented together with dried mud and clay. All entrances faced the sea, and there were small but functional windows. Woven fabric sufficed for window screens and doors. The only other visible structures were racks fashioned of wooden poles on which hung the curing shapes of outlandish, boneless water dwellers and plants.

Smoke rose from two cooking fires tended by older members of the tribe. Children scampered about in the manner of youngsters everywhere, though their play seemed more formalized when compared with that of human infants.

The appearance of the bizarre, tall visitors occasioned curiosity and surprise, but none of the astonishment or panic one might have expected. While Boutu and his friends were greeted by friends and relations, Prentice kept searching for indications of a chief or nominal leader. None materialized. If anything, Boutu seemed as much in charge as any of his fellows. The heat and humidity in the village was only slightly mitigated by its proximity to the ocean.

Young Xicans clustered together a respectful distance

from the strange visitors. With their tiny mouths, delicate shell-smooth ears, and wide round eyes they were even more attractive than their parents. Instead of having the long, flowing hair of the adults, the heads of the children appeared to have been shaved. For that matter, he realized, save for their flowing tresses neither male nor female Xicans had any hair under their arms or anywhere else on their smooth bodies, their long eyelashes excepted.

With Boutu taking the lead and the rest of the villagers escorting them, the humans allowed themselves to be led into the settlement. Though he would not have recognized it as an anthropological oddity, Prentice was immediately struck by its cleanliness. The village grounds were cleaner than the surrounding forest floor, and there was a thankful absence of noxious smells. There were many varieties of cultural sophistication besides the technological, he decided.

There was little difference in appearance between the older Xicans and the younger. Though it was enough to mark the gap, it was not near enough to estimate age. Facial lining was much finer than in humans, taking the form of reduced elasticity of the skin rather than deep furrows. Elder Xicans also moved with much greater deliberation than did their offspring.

Beautiful people, Prentice decided afresh. Kind and considerate to one another as well as to strangers. But where was the village chief or elder? He remarked on this absence to Simna.

"Maybe they don't have one," the other scientist replied. "The community is small enough to function as a cooperative democracy. In an extended clan situation like this, a group of respected individuals may make decisions for the whole. Nor is it a given that the weight of an individual's opinion is proportionate to his or her seniority. They may respect other things more, like intelligence or competence at certain tasks." He smiled flatly. "Or the chief may be off hunting. Until I get a better grip on the language we're shooting blind."

Cedric Carnavon was watching two Xican females turn something in a clay pot. "Government is a society's way of responding to outside pressures. These people don't look like they need one. Notice there aren't any readily recognizable totems or idols blatantly hanging about, either. These people are very basic in their response to their environment. They may not even have a religion."

"Not dissimilar to the early Greeks," O'Sandringham suggested.

"Early geeks I calls 'em," Lastwell said, then wandered off to examine the patterned fabric blocking the entrance to a nearby hut. Several natives accompanied him curiously, neither awed nor intimidated by his large presence.

"Look at this." Lejardin stood watching a group of children off to one side. The young Xicans sat in a cleared circle. In front of them several dozen small arthropods with metallic green backs were marching along in single file, each using specialized gripping organs to maintain contact with its relative immediately in front. The children would snap them apart like toys and then reconnect them to form different marching patterns, creating multiple columns and even multiple shapes. The single-minded arthropods were not the first example of communal living they had observed among the Xican fauna, but they were by far the most attractive and amusing.

As they wandered through the village they encountered further examples of the Xicans' highly developed tool-making abilities: sharpened stone axes and digging implements, fishing spears and hooks, obsidian knives, bone needles, and relatively sophisticated looms for weaving their fabrics. Behind the village was a well-tended and irrigated garden. The natives were far more advanced than their initial appearance would have suggested. In the presence of such sophistication, the absence of any sort of primitive jewelry or other objects of individual adornment was surprising.

Prentice watched as potters turned jugs and weavers worked at fashioning the clothing and rugs that covered the floors of the huts. Males and females seemed to share equally in such tasks and to boast equal skill. The only overtly sexual division of labor related to the care of the children, which tended to be more of a female enterprise. They later learned that the males compensated by doing most of the difficult fishing. While there was little difference in height, the still supple males were somewhat more muscular than the females. Perhaps most remarkable of all, there was no sign of any disease among the population.

There was no writing and no sign of the wheel. The patterns that decorated their earthenware and weavings were wholly abstract and as admirably proportioned as their manufacturers. Representational art of any kind was entirely absent.

He walked back to where Simna was seated with Boutu and Mahd'ji. Simna's recorder rested nearby, rendering their conversation into history. "How's it coming, Jack?"

The other man looked up. "Better than I might have hoped. Like I said, I'm no linguist, Salvor. But their idiom is simple, and easy enough to pronounce. They're teaching me by repetition. I'm starting to pick up some verbs, or verb equivalents. I'm sure they find my efforts highly amusing, but they're being very patient."

"I've got some questions I'd badly like to ask them."

"So do I," Simna told him, "but it's all going to have to wait until I can understand the answers."

Carnavon was strolling absently through the village when he spotted Ramirez fondling the female. It wasn't Mahd'ji, who was working with Simna, or Jesh'ku, the other one who'd accompanied them back from Base Camp. This female stood placid and unmoving as the human ran his hands across her lightly clad body. She seemed every bit as engrossed in the proceedings as did Ramirez, smiling enigmatically at the human with her cupidlike mouth.

"What the devil do you think you're doing, Stew?"

The younger man jerked around sharply. Another member of the expedition might have been embarrassed or at least nonplussed at being so discovered, but not Ramirez. He smiled impudently.

"Just a little field work, Ced. I guess the captain would call it feelwork." When Carnavon didn't respond, Ramirez continued in a more serious vein. "She doesn't mind. Why should she? We're not the same species. I surmised that their physical consistency would be similar to ours, but without actually touching one there was no way to be sure. I thought it was as good a time as any to clear up the ambiguity."

"It's not funny, Stew." Carnavon came nearer. His glowering appearance and stern tone caused the female to step away from Ramirez. The other man hastened to reassure her.

"It's all right," he said softly. "Ced's not going to hurt you." He turned to the other scientist. "Or me either. Right, Ced?"

"Don't be ridiculous." Carnavon forced himself to smile at the female, who relaxed and proffered a hesitant smile in return. "Isn't it a little soon to start exploiting the natives?"

"Look at her," Ramirez urged him. "By the way, her name's Chen'gi. Does she look exploited? Is she acting exploited? I'm not so sure I like you impugning my motives, Ced."

"I'll read your formal report on the consistency of Xican flesh later, Stew." Carnavon hesitated. "Maybe I am overreacting here. If so, I apologize."

"Hey, that's all right." Ramirez was in a magnanimous mood. "I know it must have looked funny, but you're the one who's letting the humanoid appearance of these people affect you, not me. And there will be a report, of course," he added formally.

"Right. Sorry." Carnavon glanced over his shoulder, back toward the busy part of the village. "I understand what you're saying, Stew. Just bear in mind as you carry on with your work that it might be harder to explain the scientific aspects to the Xicans. This particular female may not object to your field work, but if she's mated, her partner might. Their society may be rife with all kinds of taboos we have yet to encounter."

Ramirez nodded. "Like I said, my actions don't seem to be troubling Chen'gi. I don't think I'm endangering anyone here. But I'll be careful."

"See that you are." Troubled and uncertain how to best proceed, Carnavon elected to leave Ramirez to his avocation and rejoin the others.

The other scientist turned back to regard the young Xican female. At least, he presumed she was young. Her face and skin were completely unlined. As he resumed his endeavors, her full smile returned. Nonhuman she might be, but she was also considerably less standoffish than Lejardin or O'Sandringham.

He shut down that line of thinking fast. They were colleagues, as well trained and prepared as he was. Maybe even better. It wouldn't do to think of them in any other way. For one thing, it was much too early in the expedition. But it was difficult sometimes not to do so, especially when it came to Lejardin.

Something bright pink with blue stripes was skittering across a nearby tree trunk. He made pacifying motions to the female. "We'll get back to this later, okay?" Eyes like lapis dominated her endearingly baffled expression as he picked

up his humming recorder and hurried over to examine the
creature that was now munching on exfoliating tree bark.
She stared at him for a long moment, then moved off to re-
sume the work she'd been doing before he'd interrupted her.

It was Prentice who made contact with Base Camp and
informed those working there that they had successfully
reached the Pendju village and were going to spend some
time in its environs. Not knowing how far they had to go or
what to expect, they hadn't brought along a great deal in
the way of supplies, but there was enough to last for a few
days, at least.

When Simna, in his halting but increasingly fluent
Xican, managed to communicate their intentions, the
Pendju offered the strange visitors the use of two spacious,
adjoining, empty huts. Led by Mahd'ji, the natives rushed
to cleanse the structures of vermin and set woven rugs in
place on the hard-packed dirt floor. Large water jugs were
accepted but offers of food declined as Simna struggled to
explain that he and his companions had brought their own.

Lejardin, O'Sandringham, and the Carnavons moved into
one hut while Simna, Prentice, Ramirez, and Lastwell took
the other. To everyone's relief the crude buildings proved
cooler than they appeared. Set opposite the coast-facing
doorways, the arched windows allowed the occasional sea
breezes to blow straight through the structures, somewhat
mitigating the oppressive heat and humidity. The native design had not been arrived at by accident.

By the following morning they were moved in and feeling a good deal more comfortable about their situation. The
Pendju proved as willing and helpful as they'd been the day
before, though they no longer crowded curiously around
the visitors. They had daily chores of their own to attend to.

Prentice was working next to a fallen log when Millie
Carnavon appeared on the horizon, cresting the low bluff
that separated the village from the shore.

"Wondered where you'd got to." He looked up from his recorder. Its macro attachment was in place.

"I've been down on the beach." She exhibited a handful of shells, all beautiful, intricate of design, and startlingly transparent. "Be interesting to see if these are composed of the usual calcium minus tinting impurities or if they're simply pure silicon-based." She gestured back the way she'd come. "There are middens all around the high-water line, as well as signs of recent cooking. The males have several large, flat-topped rocks they fish from. I watched them, for quite a while. Spears and small nets." Pocketing the shells, she extracted what looked like a pearlized slipper from her pack.

"Isn't this one gorgeous? One of the females showed me how they scour the inside with scrapers and then polish the lining and exterior. They use them as utensils to hold their food but not as ornaments. Curious."

"Looks like they have plenty to eat." Prentice made an adjustment to his recorder.

Simna looked up curiously from where he and Lejardin were working nearby. "Looks like Millie's found some pretties. Can't be sure they're mollusks yet, though."

"What, no ready answers?" she chided him.

He gave her that penetrating stare. "I've told you before, Favrile; the questions interest me more than the answers. Answers don't require near as much brainpower to postulate. Just adequate memory." He tapped the sides of his head and grinned cavalierly. "Sometimes I'm afraid I'll run out of room before I die."

"Just concentrate on the language, Jack, so we can talk to these people. You should like that. You can spend most of your time formulating questions and leave all the answers to them."

His reply was in dead earnest. "Yes, that would be best." He sighed. "I'll think I have a name for something, and then Boutu or Jesh'ku or one of the others will call it something else. So I have to sort as well as learn. Strange to find a culture whose vocabulary causes more trouble than its grammar."

"You're doing fine, and you'll continue to do fine. I have confidence in you."

He looked up sharply. "Nice of you to say so."

She turned away. "Don't let your head get any more swelled than it already is."

With the village as a forward base they were able to fan out into the surrounding forest; exploring dense woods, creeks, shore, and beach without having to watch one another's backs. As Carnavon succinctly put it, "The natives may still be capable of treachery, but if they were going to try anything I think they'd have done so while we were sleeping. We can trust them and keep an eye on them at the same time." Prentice was against relaxing their guard and virtually splitting up, but seeing how the wind was blowing he bent with it.

They even had time to relax on the beach, though when O'Sandringham and Lejardin chose to do so it put a distinct crimp in the work ethic of their associates. It was a sign of how at ease they had become not only with their hosts the Pendju but with Xica itself. Its threats were implied rather than pending, its hostilities inwardly aimed. As visitors, they began to consider themselves outside the daily ebb and flow of the ecosystem. Not recognizing them, the herbivores did not see them as a threat, and the predators did not recognize them as prey. They were noticed but ignored.

The ocean was another matter. The Pendju knew nothing of swimming and were first frightened and then astonished when several of their visitors put on a demonstration. It took all of Simna's newly acquired linguistic powers to persuade them that the humans were neither amphibious nor suicidal. Thus assured, they observed their visitors' watery frolics with delight. There was scruba gear on board the *James Cook* for self-contained recycled underwater breathing, but it awaited another return visit to the ship to collect. Given their initial reaction to a simple swimming demonstration, Prentice couldn't help wondering how the Pendju would respond when scruba-equipped visitors disappeared underwater and didn't immediately come up for air.

Cedric Carnavon could barely restrain himself. Quick sketches of fish had produced only looks of consternation among the Pendju he'd shown them to, but rough drawings of octopi and squid caused them to babble excitedly. Dried tentacular bodies of great intricacy were thereupon drawn from village stores and proudly displayed to the visitors.

"Maybe there are no bony fishes or their analogs in the oceans of Xica," Carnavon deposed. "It seems that the seas here may be dominated by invertebrates. Interesting, as well as peculiar."

O'Sandringham challenged him immediately. "If that's true, then how do you explain the progress of vertebrate evolution on land?"

"We don't know if that's how life here has proceeded. We've seen and collected a lot of large arthropods with chitinous and silicate exoskeletons, and a number of other creatures that may or may not have true backbones."

"What about the Pendju themselves?" Lejardin wondered.

Carnavon refused to back down. "We don't know for a fact that they have bony skeletons like we do. Their humanoid appearance notwithstanding, their bodies might depend for internal support on some kind of complex internal tendon and ligament structure, or some kind of advanced cartilaginous arrangement."

"We can't very well ask to exhume a body for examination," Prentice pointed out. "Assuming they even practice burial. They may set their dead out for the forest creatures to consume, or dispose of them at sea."

"Would you like me to ask?" Simna inquired.

Prentice replied firmly. "No. It's much too soon to broach

such a potentially touchy subject. We've got plenty to keep us busy as it is. I don't want to do anything to compromise the relationship we've established with these people. Categorizing their internal structure can wait."

As the days passed they rotated between the village and Base Camp, giving everyone a chance to observe and study in the company of the Pendju. Prentice insisted that there always be a minimum of two of their number at Base Camp and that one of them always be Stevens or Lastwell. The two techs had no objection to the arrangement and were in fact delighted to be directed to avoid each other's company, of which they had enjoyed more than enough on the voyage out from Earth.

As for who would spend time at Base Camp, O'Sandringham always managed to volunteer whenever it was Stevens's turn to look after their refuge. The two of them exchanged insults with a frequency that fooled no one, and their colleagues were too diplomatic to allude overtly to the developing and deepening relationship.

Simna spent as much time working with Lejardin as he could reasonably manage, both drawn to and bemused by her. Her constant activity failed to mask his feeling that serious problems underlay her obvious dedication to her research. He sounded her out gently, with little success, trying to offer his assistance without appearing to intrude. It was a difficult balancing act to maintain, made worse by the fact that he had no idea how well or poorly he was managing it.

He wondered if she was aware of how they were all drawn to her; even Carnavon, somewhat to the wary dismay of his spouse. But there was so much work to be done, so many new discoveries to be marveled at and classified, that serious concern was unnecessary. For her part Lejardin tended to gravitate to Prentice, both as nominal leader of the expedition and for reasons she had no need to explain.

It was something Simna did not dwell on. He was quite used to being the outsider.

Added to his personal scientific agenda, his efforts to master the Xican language kept him more than occupied. Boutu proved a willing and even enthusiastic teacher, submerging Simna in a swirl of strange words and phrases. The Pendju drew as much pleasure from the strange biped's increasing mastery of their language as did Simna. Mispronunciation was cause not for disappointment but for laughter. The Pendju culture might not be advanced, but there was nothing primitive about their sense of humor.

A happy species, Simna decided. Content with their modest achievements, well adjusted socially, and in tune with their environment. He anticipated no difficulty on their part in adapting to the presence of a permanent human settlement in their vicinity. For such a settlement to serve the needs of greater science would surely be forthcoming as soon as the crew of the *James Cook* returned to Earth to report on its astounding encounter with the first nonhuman intelligence. As it had always been, the argument against intruding on a new and different culture would be overwhelmed by the desire to know, to learn, and to observe.

The two years the crew of the *James Cook* would spend on Xica would barely be sufficient to learn a modicum of its secrets. They needed more people, more specialists, more equipment, more supplies . . . more of everything.

It was toward the beginning of the second week spent among the villagers that the first blemish appeared on the gray-green skin of Paradise.

O'Sandringham returned from a collecting hike into the forest with one arm around Stevens for support. She was favoring her right leg and limping badly. The pain on her face was mirrored by the mate's expression of concern. As those of her colleagues who were in the village at the time gathered around, Stevens eased her down onto a rug Mahd'ji and Jesh'ku thoughtfully provided.

Her right calf was badly swollen. More concern was engendered by the red streak that ran from her calf up the back of her leg to disappear beneath the hem of her walking shorts. It was as distinct as if someone had sprayed the stripe on her with paint. The streak flushed angrily and was hot to the touch. The small hole in the meat of her calf was quite visible, a black puncture in the center of a slightly raised ridge of abscessing skin.

Halstead and Lastwell were back at Base Camp while Ramirez and the Carnavons were still out in the field, but Simna, Lejardin, and Prentice were available to help. Anxiety plain on their faces, a group of Pendju completed the circle of concern around the now prone form of O'Sandringham.

Lejardin took one look at her friend's leg and hurried back toward the hut they shared. Meanwhile Simna spoke softly to Mahd'ji. *"Bul'yan niu chosas, m'menmet."*

Stevens frowned up at him. "What?"

O'Sandringham's eyes were shut tight, her teeth clenched. "It hurts," she hissed softly. Her fingers gripped her injured leg hard.

"What the hell happened?" Prentice asked the mate.

Stevens looked like a man who'd just received a large dollop of bad news via long distance. "I'm not sure." His eyes never left O'Sandringham's face. "She was recording and making notes on some of those little tree climbers we found several days ago. About a dozen centimeters long, eight gripping legs, blue eyes, little furry heads and tails?"

Prentice nodded. He was familiar with the species.

"She's been working with them off and on for days. I've handled them myself for her: picked them off branches and bark, turned them over for examination, put 'em back on their tree. Never had any trouble.

"Bella-Lynn went to pick one herself and all of a sudden

this . . . appendage . . . just appeared in the middle of its back. Never saw anything like it on any of them before. It was like . . . I don't know . . . a little tube, or something. It *shot* something at her. Whatever it was went right into her calf. It was attached to the crawler by a strand of silk, or something like silk. Couldn't have been more than a second or two before the little bastard reeled it back in and the whole apparatus disappeared into the fur on its back."

"Natural needle." O'Sandringham grimaced. "It must've injected some kind of poison."

"That much is obvious." Prentice studied her swollen leg.

"We never noticed anything like it on any of the crawlers before," Stevens went on, "and we've handled dozens of them in the past week. I don't get it."

Simna had ceased his conversation with Mahd'ji and bent to examine the wound. "Different developmental stage of the same creature. More mature, less mature: it'll take a lot more study to determine which."

O'Sandringham's response was blunt and almost angry. "It didn't look any different to me from all the others we've examined."

Simna replied coolly. "Internal variations wouldn't be obvious. A different genus or subspecies, perhaps. Or a completely different species that mimics its harmless cousins."

Lejardin returned, clutching her medical kit. A quick scan and intrusive analysis of the injured, inflamed region yielded readings that she rapidly transferred into the kit's computer. It processed the information for a couple of minutes before supplying a prescription. More minutes passed as O'Sandringham lay stoic and silent on the rug, the sweat pouring off her face, while the kit's pharmacite synthesized an appropriate dosage. Only after Lejardin swabbed the area and delivered the injection did O'Sandringham begin to relax.

"What kind of poison?" Simna leaned close.

Lejardin shook her head. "This field kit's not sophisticated enough to carry out a full breakdown. We'll have to do that back at the lab. Some kind of anticoagulant hemotoxin. I made a best guess and blended it with a general painkiller." She was wrapping the other woman's leg in an antiseptically impregnated bandage. It would protect the wound and fight infection.

"Can you do anything else for her?" Prentice asked.

Lejardin wiped the ever-present sweat from her forehead and considered the results of her handiwork. "Not now. The antivenin has to have time to work. The best thing we can do for her is make her as comfortable as possible."

"What about getting her back to Base Camp?" Stevens looked thoroughly miserable.

"I don't think she should be jostled around until we get rid of that redness. I want to keep her circulation steady." Lejardin looked over a shoulder. "Let's move her into the hut, but keep her near the door where she can get as much fresh air as possible."

Together Stevens and Simna lifted O'Sandringham and carried her to the shelter. By the time they set her down on a clean rug inside, she was breathing easier. She eyed Lejardin thankfully.

"I don't know about the swelling, but the pain's a lot more bearable."

The other woman nodded. "Hopefully the antivenin will work as fast as the painkiller."

Half an hour later O'Sandringham's tumescent gastrocnemius had almost returned to normal, while the initial shooting pain had been replaced by a dull, distant ache. There was no sign of abscessing around the wound and the puncture had closed up. Only a little of the original inflammation remained.

The incident seemed to have upset the entire village. They clustered in small groups around the human's hut before shuffling off, conversing in anxious tones among themselves and neglecting their daily tasks. It was heartwarming to witness such a display of concern, but there was more to it than that, Prentice decided. There was something else. Simna spoke to several villagers without receiving enlightenment.

As soon as Lejardin could assure him that O'Sandringham was going to be all right, the expedition leader took Simna aside.

"What do you think of all this, Jack?"

Simna shrugged slightly. "Some kind of hemotoxin, like Favrile said." He glanced back at the hut. "Competent, isn't she?"

"We're all competent," said Prentice impatiently. "I'm not talking about Bella-Lynn's injury, necessarily." A number of Pendju females were smoking some kind of meaty cephalopods or mollusks on a nearby wooden rack. "I'm talking about the Pendju's reaction."

Simna blinked. "I thought it was nice of them to show an interest."

"They showed more than that." Prentice was persistent. "Doesn't it strike you as odd? I mean, I expected Boutu and Mahd'ji and maybe a couple of others we know reasonably well to come over to see what was going on, and maybe express some sympathy, but it seemed like the whole village checked in on us. Activity practically came to a standstill."

The other man shrugged slightly. "So they showed a little more than an interest. What are you getting at, Salvor?"

Prentice chewed his lower lip. "Probably nothing. I was just wondering if anyone else had noticed." He took a deep breath. "You know me, Jack. Mildly paranoid."

Simna put a comradely arm around the younger scientist's shoulder. "I know, Salvor. And far be it from me to try to change you. With you tormenting yourself all the time, it means the rest of us don't have to worry as much."

Prentice arranged a smile he didn't feel.

VII

As the days passed, Lastwell and Stevens worked out a regular, comfortable schedule for shuttling supplies back and forth between the ship, Base Camp, and the village. While the Pendju often accompanied such journeys, they made no move to assist or interfere. They seemed to find everything the humans did of interest, yet they rarely asked questions or tried to probe more deeply into the activities of their visitors. They continued to manifest unfailing hospitality and courteous indifference.

Meanwhile discoveries and confusion multiplied simultaneously, leading to increasing tension and argument among the humans. Simna and the Carnavons attributed much of it to the oppressive climate, did their best to soothe irritated feelings, and prescribed extended duty tours in the more comfortable air-conditioned surroundings of Base Camp. Not that they were any less affected by the heat and humidity: together with the two techs, they simply understood it better.

Moving a climate-controlled building or two to the village, as Ramirez suggested, was out of the question. Not only were the logistics daunting, given the rough terrain and dense patches of forest, but Prentice was already worried that their continued presence among the Pendju was affecting the natives' behavior and therefore compromising the team's studies of village society. So everyone kept to huts and rugs and dirt floors and tried to refresh themselves with the aid of systematic griping.

Despite the ongoing discomfort, no one requested to be assigned permanently to Base Camp. Everyone knew that the real discoveries were to be made out in the field.

After Simna had acquired a certain amount of fluency in the Xican tongue it didn't take long to learn that a good deal of the local fauna was nocturnal, including the larger predators whose absence had heretofore puzzled everyone. Not that they slept to avoid the heat of the day. It was hardly any cooler and no less humid after dark. Adverse climatic conditions persisted throughout the tropical Xican night.

The stealthy Silpa tracked down a moon-faced creature the size of a cow. On four stumpy legs it browsed the *Haukik* as if grazing on lettuce, somehow masticating the razor-edged growths without shredding its wide mouth or insides.

There was a creature Boutu called a *Chneidi*. While evincing no especial fear, the Pendju gave it a wide berth. It resembled a large, smooth-topped boulder atop which all manner of symbiotic growths flourished. No less than half the animal seemed to consist of mouth. In place of teeth it displayed a flexible, rubbery palate, and swallowed whole any unfortunate creature that ambled too near, demonstrating a determinedly democratic appetite.

Venturing at night to the edge of the desert, they collected a great variety of burrowing things, and gazed wistfully at a huge high-flying creature with vast membranous wings that were almost transparent. Like the ocean dwellers, the inhabitants of the forest and desert exhibited great bodily flexibility. Those that were not confirmed invertebrates boasted skeletal structures composed of ligaments and cartilage instead of bone. It was a view confirmed by the first use of the laboratory scanner at Base Camp. Absolute confirmation would have to await the start of systematized vivisection of their specimens.

Shoreline research continued to produce a preponderance of xi-cephalopods, xi-molluscs, and xi-crustaceans. Everyone was particularly delighted by the iridescent gold and red being that turned up one morning in a fishing net. Cylindrical in shape, slightly more than a meter in length, it lay gasping on the rocks where it had been laid, futilely flapping the dozen or so delicate diaphanous wings that normally propelled it through the sea. Within the water it would surely demonstrate the grace and bearing of a prima ballerina. Gripping palps surrounded the round mouth as it sucked uselessly at the air.

"Sarjesju," Boutu called it. They hauled it up the sandy bluff and back to the village to smoke, a mixture of beauty and grotesquerie. Simna took an uncommon interest in the curing process as the creature was gutted and hung up to dry, lacy wings spread wide like a crucified and bejeweled gargoyle.

One day Boutu guided them on an all-day march to a nearby river valley. As they descended a ridge, an unexpected flush of verdure closed in around them. The usual unyielding gray-slabbed trees gave way to softer plants and richer, deeper greenery. Spherical airy growths beside which a fern would have looked crass seemed to drift in the breeze that rose from the river, barely wedded to the soil by incredibly thin stems. Fairyland it might not be, but it was a welcome change from the endless forest of the red and maroon plateau.

As capture after capture followed close upon discovery, new cages and holding facilities optimistically provided by the scientific establishment had to be brought from the lander, unpacked, and installed in the increasingly crowded labs at Base Camp. Halstead and Noosa took charge of uncrating and setup, seeing to it that newly arrived specimens had food (hopefully appropriate), water (hopefully sufficient), and a halfway familiar environment in which to comport themselves. It was a credit to their efforts that once consigned to their care, hardly any of the collected died.

"I wonder how much of this we'll be able to get back alive," Prentice commented as he studied the squawking, gurgling inhabitants of Lab Cubicle 3.

"All of it." Noosa was enthusiastic. "Can't even imagine the stir this will cause back on Earth. Can't even imagine." He turned more somber. "We *have* to get it all back. It's our responsibility. There's no telling how long it will take to mount the second expedition out here." He stood a little taller. "If necessary we'll fill the two backup deepsleep capsules with the overflow."

Prentice nodded approvingly. "So long as Frank concurs." He turned to the stocky captain, who was squinting at the contents of a nearby cage.

Lastwell glanced back. "The coffins worked fine on the way out. No reason to assume any of 'em is likely to fail on the way back. Ain't that right, Blondie?"

"Don't call me that, Frank." Since she didn't look up from her work, O'Sandringham didn't see Lastwell grinning at her. She and Lejardin found themselves alternately appalled and amused by Lastwell.

"I can call you anything I want." He continued to tease her. "I'm the captain."

"On the *James Cook*," she shot back. "Not here."

Simna was worried about Prentice. The younger scientist was taking on too much responsibility, especially considering how well everything was going. He'd be of no use either to himself or the team if stress or overwork put him in the infirmary.

Just now he was cautioning Ramirez and Noosa, who

were about to leave the village on a nocturnal gathering expedition.

"Watch yourselves out there," he admonished the other men. "I've seen you two go charging through the woods. You don't want to stumble into something vicious. A carnivore that's shocked awake is likely to react violently."

"Not as violently as Stew would." Noosa adjusted the straps on his pack. "You ought to see *him* when he's been jolted out of a sound sleep."

Prentice grinned, feeling around the rim of the joke like a mouse searching for a rip in the lining of a foodpak.

Simna turned from the byplay to find himself eyeing Lejardin, who was standing outside one of their two huts stacking a half dozen recently collected arthropods held in compact observation and display cases. As no one seemed to be watching, he allowed himself the quiet pleasure of observing her comely, unconscious grace. Her black hair was tied back in a utilitarian ponytail and her body moved supplely beneath the beige work shorts and vest.

He didn't think his critical faculties were clouded by their isolation or a dearth of viewable alternatives. She would have attracted similar attention in New York or Greater London, Roma or Delhi. Not for the first time since resurrection from deepsleep, he found he had to force his eyes and mind elsewhere.

There was something living in a hollow in a tree a couple of hours' hike into the interior. Simna fully intended to climb that tree and seek out the owner of the reverberant, echoing cries that issued from within. He'd already asked Mahd'ji about it. She'd told him that it was most likely an *Ee'fhohn* and, as always, marveled at the human's interest in something so ordinary. Though his Xican vocabulary had increased considerably, it was not equal to her description of the animal. This naturally made him that much more curious to see it in person.

When he informed her of his intent to climb the tree she laughed and assured him it was impossible. That was a word Simna had heard frequently in his life and one he had as often refused to acknowledge. It would take much more than a mere tree to change that attitude.

Unable to restrain himself, he wandered over to join Lejardin. The specimens she was sorting were all new and unique.

"There's at least one major thesis and a year's worth of research in that single set of boxes," he commented. "It's kind of overwhelming."

"I know." Green eyes flashed. "Look at this one here." She tapped the topmost case. Something with eight legs and an unusual number of antennae was scuttling about as it explored the restrictions of its new home. Wavy yellow stripes fluttered down a body the hue of polished mahogany, terminating in blue compound eyes that wrapped around the entire front of the head. Its wing cases were translucent yellow.

"This thing has so much sensory equipment it must know where it is even when it's asleep." She grinned. "Mahd'ji found it under a log for me. It wasn't easy to extricate without breaking anything, either on it or me." She examined the creature thoughtfully. "I'm still trying to decide what to call it."

"Running out of names already?" he quipped.

"You know what I mean," she countered playfully. "It's neither insect nor arachnid. A lot of Xican life looks very earthlike, but when you probe just a little deeper the standard nomenclature never quite fits. That's as true of the buglike creatures here as it is of the more advanced forms. I have to decide if this is an almost-beetle or almost-spider."

"It's Xican," he replied, as if that constituted an adequate explanation. "Maybe we'll finally be able to utilize some real taxonomy instead of just applying randomly descriptive labels when we commence formal vivisection next week. With all the collecting and recording, no one's had time to classify by internal structures yet. Cody and Ted have run physiotomography on some of our specimens but that's not the same as getting inside and taking a look that's up close and personal. It's lab time."

"Overdue," she agreed readily. Her gaze accidentally locked on his. "I suppose you can run the tomographer too?"

He held the stare as long as he dared, then looked away. "As you know, I can do a little of everything. My real specialty is that I don't have one."

She continued to toy with him, only half innocent. "Imagine holding all that knowledge in one head. Doesn't it hurt after a while?"

"No, but there are times when I feel that I'm running out of space." He took a long breath. "Look, there's something making really weird cries in an emergent over by the river gorge. Mahd'ji says there's no way I'll be able to climb up to check it out, but I plan to surprise her."

"You won't surprise me."

He very gently rested one hand on her shoulder. "Would you like to come along? There's the usual fascinating stuff in the underbrush, and if Mahd'ji's right you'll be able to whistle, cheer, and add whatever sound effects you like as I plunge to my doom." He hesitated. "Also, I could use a hand with some of the gear."

She considered for the briefest of instants, then slid gently away from his fingers. "I'm not big enough to catch you if you fall, Jack. And right now I'm pretty overwhelmed with my own work."

"No problem. Just thought I'd ask. If you don't ask, Favrile, you never know." After an exchange of smiles, he left in search of Mahd'ji. Not because he needed the Pendju's help to find the tree again, but because he wanted someone else to talk to, and at that particular moment he'd just as soon it was a nonhuman.

Her shoulder tingling ever so slightly, she watched him as he strode across the cleared ground of the village. What was he about, Jack Simna? Most of her companions were relatively straightforward. She had no trouble dealing with Ramirez, or with Noosa or Halstead. Prentice she knew, and she'd struck up a real friendship with Bella-Lynn O'Sandringham. Simna fit into no easy category. He was an authentic enigma.

An awkward moment had come and gone, passing into history. It belonged now to memory and time. As a consequence of her extraordinary beauty, over which she had no more control than a molting macaw, she'd been forced to deal with such moments ever since she'd turned fourteen. It immensely complicated her professional life and made it that much harder for her to carry out any serious work. As a result, she'd had to evolve a regimen and protocols to deal with it. She doubted she'd have any trouble with Simna. Unusually, he admired her work as much as everything else.

If she continued to dwell on it she'd never get any work done. Resolutely, she turned back to the cases.

"Tou'alia."

"Kou'aliaj." Behind his wide yellow eyes Boutu looked puzzled.

"No. Not *Kou'aliaj. Tou'alia,*" Simna insisted. They were standing near one of the five traps that had been placed deep within the forest.

Presently it contained a blue-gray creature the size of a basketball. Round and covered in fine dense fur, it was exploring its confines with several of its sixteen small, black, prehensile limbs. These were scattered all over its spherical body, enabling it to move in any direction without having to turn. Not that it had anything to turn upon, having no discernible front or back. A small, flexible organ protruded from the nominal crown. Multiple eyes and antennae were scattered about the rotund surface as haphazardly as the grasping limbs. There were two or four rubbery mouths: the thick fur made it difficult to tell for certain.

"Kou'aliaj!" Boutu argued vociferously, showing an unusual amount of animation.

"It's not a *Kou'aliaj*," Simna argued. *"Tou'alia."*

"What's going on?" Prentice arrived, with Noosa and Halstead close behind.

Simna was mildly exasperated. "We've caught another *Tou'alia*. Boutu keeps insisting I'm misidentifying it. He persists in calling it a *Kou'aliaj*."

Prentice peered closely at the creature testing the boundaries of its cage. "Don't we already have two of these back at base? It looks like a *Tou'alia* to me." He glanced at his companions. "Cody?"

Noosa didn't hesitate. "No question about it. It doesn't look like anything else we've encountered, but it does look exactly like the pair we picked up a month ago."

"Spherical body, multiple small limbs and scattered oculars, dorsal sensory organ: it's a *Tou'alia* for sure." If anything, Halstead was even more positive than his colleagues.

Simna turned back to the attentive Boutu, pointing repeatedly at the cage as he did so. *"Tou'alia,"* he reiterated patiently.

His manner adamant, the Pendju gestured negatively with one of his four-digit hands. *"Kou'aliaj."*

Turning to his companions, Simna spread his hands helplessly.

"Different names for different stages of development," Noosa suggested. *"Tou'alia's* the juvenile, *Kou'aliaj* the adult. Or vice versa."

Prentice was shaking his head slowly. "I don't see any difference between this one and the pair we're holding back at camp. Same size, number of limbs, color, markings; as near as I can see, everything's identical. So why the different name?"

"Ask him about the discrepancy," Prentice suggested. "Straight up."

Simna nodded and turned back to the native. Boutu listened with his usual intensity, then took a step back from the three men, stamping the butt of his ever-present spear firmly into the ground in an unmistakable effort to drive home his response.

"Kou'aliaj. Vesec Kou'aliaj!"

"I don't get it." Simna was thoroughly exasperated. "This is starting to be a habit. In the past week he's given me different names for half a dozen creatures I've positively and repeatedly identified. It only involves motiles. No plants, objects, natural phenomena like clouds or waves: only animals."

"Maybe," Halstead posited thoughtfully, "the names change with the time of year? Could they have a seasonal nomenclature?"

"That's an idea," Simna conceded. "Not necessarily a valid one, but an idea." The scientist could be and frequently was unintentionally sarcastic. There was a tone, a quality to his voice he could do nothing about. It was as prominent a part of his makeup as a permanent limp.

"It doesn't make any sense," he went on. "We *know* it's a *Tou'alia*."

"Could its presence in the trap affect naming?" Noosa theorized aloud.

"One way to find out." Halstead stepped over a Crawling Bush toward the cage.

Noosa promptly nudged him aside. "Let me, Ted. I can get in easier than you and I've handled the pair back at base on several occasions." Flipping the latch on top of the trap and easing the door aside, he reached in with both hands.

With deliberate speed the *Tou'alia/Kou'aliaj* extruded one of its multiple mouths three times the length of its own body and fastened onto the scientist's forearm. Noosa let out a startled oath and tried to withdraw. The creature refused to relinquish its grip.

It took their combined strength to pry the rubbery lips away from their comrade's arm. As soon as the suction was broken the *Kou'aliaj* spun sideways on half its tiny limbs and burst out of the cage into the forest. Its former captors displayed a unanimous disinclination to pursue.

Noosa's forearm was covered with a welter of tiny red punctures where the *Kou'aliaj*'s fortuitously tiny teeth had penetrated. It looked as if he'd been attacked by a drunken acupuncturist. While Simna fumbled with his first-aid kit and set to work treating the wounds, Prentice and Halstead looked on anxiously. At least there was very little bleeding.

Boutu peered over Simna's shoulder, his voice barely audible. *"Kou'aliaj. Resek Tou'alia."*

"He's saying . . ." Prentice began.

"I know what he's saying." Simna interrupted his friend more harshly than he intended. "He's saying that was a completely different type of animal, just like he'd been trying to tell us all along." He ripped open a package of antiseptic skin patches. "The *Tou'alia* back at base may look identical, but they've never shown any tendency to bite, much less hang on and try to swallow somebody's arm."

"Mimicry," Halstead murmured. "Offensive instead of defensive."

"We don't know that," Simna argued. "More likely it's the *Tou'alia* who mimic these predatory *Kou'aliaj* for protection."

"We don't know that there are any anatomical differences," Prentice pointed out. "The only one we can be sure of at this point is behavioral."

"No shit." Halstead looked on as Simna bandaged

Noosa's arm. Lejardin would have done a better job, but she was back at the village.

Simna pulled out a small container and sprayed the wrapping. "We're missing something. I know we are. Or at least I am. Boutu's been giving me that feeling for more than a week. Maybe the language mutates, though that would be a remarkable sophisticated development for a primitive people. Damn, I wish I was more of a linguist!"

"Maybe you should talk to somebody else," Prentice suggested.

Simna shook his head brusquely. "Tried that. These name changes are consistent among the Pendju. If Mahd'ji was here, or Silpa, or any of the others, I guarantee they'd also have called that thing a *Kou'aliaj*."

Halstead knelt next to Noosa. "How you doing, Cody?"

The smaller man nodded reassuringly. Perspiration beaded up in his short beard. "I'll be okay. I've been bitten in the field before. Not *this* field, though."

"Any reactions? Eyes focusing all right, hearing okay?" Prentice was obviously concerned. "How's the pain?"

Noosa examined his left arm. "Bearable. More of a dull throbbing than anything else. The teeth weren't very big."

"I'm surprised it had any teeth at all." Simna straightened. "This isn't a language problem. We're overlooking something important. He made a point of smiling at Boutu, who had observed the goings-on with considerable solemnity. "That is, unless our happy confidants the Pendju are having some kind of elaborate joke at our expense." He looked around at his companions.

"This isn't the first time this has happened. Remember the 'harmless' bark-climber that harpooned Bella-Lynn?"

"That's right." Prentice considered. "Another mimic?"

"Maybe mimicry is widespread among Xican fauna," Halstead proposed. "If that's the case we're going to have to start treating every animal as potentially dangerous, no matter how comfortable or familiar we think we are with it. For every fifty harmless browsers there could be one dangerous predator that looks exactly the same." He glanced at their guide. "Somehow the Pendju can tell them apart. We're going to have to get Boutu and his friends to show us how to pick out the differences."

"I'd say the first order of business is to get him to point out any unsuspected dangers lurking among the little zoo we've assembled back at base." Prentice turned to Simna. "That's assuming we can get him to enter the buildings. Jack?"

"I think he will. It's clear that the Pendju have a well-developed sense of curiosity, and from what I've observed so far Boutu's foremost among them. Just because nothing we've collected has attacked us so far doesn't mean there aren't one or two specimens playing possum."

Halstead straightened and arched backward, stretching his spine. "It's definitely time to start opening some of these critters up to see what they're like inside. That's how we'll spot significant variations. Digestive systems can't utilize protective coloring."

"Speak for your own stomach." Simna grinned. The observation brought a smile from Noosa, which was its intended purpose.

Boutu stepped forward and murmured to Simna, who conversed with the native while the others waited impatiently.

"What was that all about?" Prentice finally inquired when the conversation ended.

Simna looked back at him. "Boutu's worried about Cody."

Noosa gazed approvingly at the native as Halstead helped his friend to his feet. "Nice of him to be concerned."

"I thought so." Simna stood on the smaller man's other side, ready to help if needed, but Noosa had no trouble standing by himself. "I told him that you'd be treated with our medicines and that you'd be fine. I'm not sure how much of that he accepts, but they've learned to appreciate what we can do."

Halstead offered his arm, but Noosa waved him off. His stride as they started back toward the village was deliberate if not exactly jaunty.

"It's going to be awkward," Halstead muttered, "if we have to treat every specimen as potentially dangerous. We won't always have a Pendju along to make positive identification."

"We're not exactly pressed for time," Prentice reminded him. "Better to be cautious." He glanced over at Noosa. "How's the arm, Cody?"

"Stings a little. Not worse, not better. Just different."

"A sign of healing." Prentice sounded hopeful as he led them across a small creek, picking his way carefully over the water-smoothed stones and pebbles.

"We can't be sure yet that mimicry is what's responsible for the confusion here." Simna was more than merely curious about what had transpired; he was upset. Ignorance always made him angry, as though it were a personal enemy. "Maybe once a month half the Xican fauna turns belligerent?"

"Now there's a cheery thought." Halstead studied the undergrowth through which they were hiking with more than usual intensity.

His obvious unease muted Simna's frustration. "Don't panic, Ted. Boutu'll warn us away from anything threatening."

"We're just going to have to . . ." Prentice began.

"Proceed with more caution than in the past." Simna had an unfortunate habit of finishing other people's sentences. The fact that he was usually right only made things worse.

"Well, I have my reminder." Noosa smiled wanly as he held up his injured, bandaged arm. Everyone smiled with him except Simna, whose frustration was not so easily alleviated.

VIII

They were almost to the village when Halstead paused to peer through a gap in the trees. "Seems like an awful lot of smoke from the cooking fires."

Noosa wiped sweat from his lightly freckled, pale forehead, taking care to use his uninjured arm. He knew that if he wanted to stay outside that afternoon he would have to repeat the ritual of applying sunscreen. He envied Simna, Ramirez, and Lejardin, who alone among the expedition members didn't need to bother with chemicals or shade.

"Sure does. I wonder . . ." He broke off as Boutu pushed past him. "Hey . . ."

The native shaded his large eyes with one hand and babbled something indistinct.

"What's he saying, Jack?" Prentice asked anxiously.

Simna made pacifying motions. "Just a second. He's speaking a lot faster than usual." The scientist hesitated, listening. "I can't get too much of it. He keeps repeating the proper noun '*Quwanga*' a lot."

Suddenly Boutu rushed forward, his limber, muscular legs carrying him over obstacles and around trees. His startled human companions stumbled after him, bashing unceremoniously through the brush and doing their best to avoid the occasional knife-edged clumps of bright green *Haukik*.

"What's a '*Quwanga*'?" Halstead was wheezing hard as

he struggled to balance his big backpack and keep up with the others. "Some kind of dangerous animal?"

"I don't know." Simna was having breathing problems of his own. "Whatever it is, it sure set him off." He raised his voice to a shout. "Boutu? *Sej necsa* Boutu!" Maintaining his flat-out sprint, the native was already out of earshot and widening the distance between them. He neither replied nor looked back.

Simna slowed. "Look, I can't keep this up and I'm not so sure it's a good idea to go charging after him anyway. If something bad's happening we might not want to go blundering right into the big middle of it."

"That's right." Prentice reduced his pace to a walk. A gasping Halstead didn't have to be told twice. Only Noosa continued to breathe easily.

"Maybe we'd better go on that assumption." Simna unclipped the modified cutter-welder from his belt, checked to make sure the battery was charged and the power on. Prentice eyed the makeshift weapon uneasily.

"You think that's necessary, Jack?"

"No, I don't. I just don't want to take any chances." He smiled slightly at the other man. "I'll try not to shoot myself in the foot."

"The hell with your foot." A grateful Halstead was sucking in long, deep breaths. "Just don't wave that thing in my direction."

Simna nodded as they resumed their forward progress.

By the time they reached the village it was all over. The Pendju milled about in a state of organized chaos, those who were unharmed assisting the injured, others trying to keep the flames that leaped from the thatched roofs of two of the huts from spreading to their neighbors. Overturned drying racks lay crumpled where they had been knocked down, food stores were scattered about, and drinking water and soup spilled from upset crocks and pots sank quickly into the thirsty ground.

As he stumbled open-mouthed into the village, Simna saw that the devastation was not as severe as it appeared at first glance. The drying racks had been knocked over but not destroyed. The same was true for most, though not all, of the laboriously fashioned crockery. The mud-impregnated walls of the two burning huts would resist the fire, and their roofs could be quickly replaced.

The Pendju themselves seemed to be handling it well. Females organized a pot-and-bucket brigade to supply water for dousing the fires. Others stamped out flaming embers that threatened to ignite nearby structures. Even more wide-eyed than usual, children clustered silently in small groups, keeping clear of the busy adults. Village elders watched over them while groups of armed males went from hut to hut. Others could be observed diligently patrolling the forest's edge. There was very little conversation and no moaning or crying.

The four humans split up to check the two huts that held their equipment. Neither had been damaged or disturbed. Prentice breathed a sigh of relief when he saw that none of their laboriously gathered specimens had escaped. Supplies could be replaced, but not weeks of effort spent traipsing and sweating through the bush.

Prentice looked up from checking the seal on one of their storage cases. "I'll tend to this. See if you can find out what happened here, Jack."

Simna nodded as he slipped out of his pack straps. He turned off the cutter and replaced it on his belt as he exited the hut. In the absence of any breeze the smoke lingered, burning his eyes.

"Jack? Over here!"

Squinting through the smoke, he spotted Millie Carnavon waving at him. The members of the other collecting party were gathered around her. Relieved greetings were exchanged.

"Everyone here okay?" he inquired anxiously.

"We're fine." Cedric Carnavon gazed past him. "We saw the smoke and hurried back as fast as we could. What happened?"

"Don't know yet. I tried to ask Boutu, but when he saw the smoke he took off like a shot and I haven't seen him since." He gestured to their right. "There's Mahd'ji." They followed him in a body as he hurried to intercept her. Considering the condition of her surroundings, she seemed remarkably calm.

So did her reply. "Quwanga attack."

"Quwanga?" The smoke made him blink. "What are Quwanga?" She proceeded to explain.

"What's she saying?" O'Sandringham asked edgily.

"She says the village was attacked by another tribe, which calls itself the Quwanga. Don't look so surprised. The Xican population has to extend beyond this one village. In fact, when you think about it, it's surprising none of the Pendju have mentioned another tribe or two before." He continued to question Mahd'ji and translate for his colleagues.

"She says they've suffered two losses: one dead, one taken prisoner."

"They take prisoners," Lejardin muttered to no one in particular. "What do they do with prisoners?"

"Give us a little room." Simna gestured for his friends to step back. "Don't crowd her."

"Never mind that now." Carnavon was looking around warily as he fingered the cutter he carried. "Ask her if she thinks these Quwanga will be back."

"No," said the female in response to Simna's query. "Our people chased them away." Her deep lavender eyes regarded the semicircle of visitors. "You seem upset, J'ac. Are you angry with Mahd'ji?"

Simna blinked in confusion. "Angry with you? Why would we be angry with you, Mahd'ji? We feel sorry for you and your people because of this bad thing that has happened."

Now it was the female Pendju's turn to look puzzled. "Is not a bad thing, J'ac. Is only Quwanga attack."

A lack of adequate grammatical knowledge, he told himself, had probably resulted in more broken treaties and new wars down through history than any actual disagreements.

"Jack?" Lejardin prompted him.

"Hang on. Their language is still full of surprises. I'm not sure I'm understanding what she's saying, beyond the fact that they've been attacked by another tribe. Also, she asked if we were angry with *her*." Ignoring the baffled comments of his companions, he pressed on with his questioning.

"Now listen, Mahd'ji. Who, exactly, are these Quwanga and why have they attacked your village?" He insisted she speak slowly, as if to a child. This time when she'd finished he felt reasonably certain he'd understood her correctly.

"She says that the Quwanga," he told his companions, "are their hereditary enemies, though I'm not entirely certain about the term I'm translating as 'hereditary.' It's imprecise, but it's also the only interpretation that makes any sense to me. She says that they fight on a regular basis, that the Pendju carry out periodic raids on the Quwanga just as the Quwanga do on the Pendju.

"I asked about the absence of wounded. She said that they heal very quickly. Usually all either side has to deal with are prisoners or their dead."

Millie Carnavon frowned. "I don't understand. There have to be wounded. It doesn't make any sense."

Simna's tone was grim. "It doesn't make any sense for

the Pendju to be fighting, either. This isn't a warlike society. They have few weapons, no war chief or war leader,
and the village is wide open. If they're raided on a regular
basis, why aren't there any defensive fortifications? Admittedly Boutu and Silpa aren't exactly graduate engineers, but
if they have the skills to make weavings and pottery surely
they could have figured out by now how to build a palisade
or moat." He turned back to Mahd'ji.

"When you attack your enemies, the Quwanga, who
leads you?"

"Whoever is strongest at that time," she replied innocently, and then compounded his confusion by saying
something that sounded like, "The Quwanga are not our enemies. They are the ones we fight with."

"I don't think I understand you, Mahd'ji. You fight the
Quwanga because they raid your village."

"Well, of course," she told him.

There, he thought. *That at least made some sense.*

"And because it is the right way to live," she added.

"That's crazy," Carnavon insisted when Simna had finished translating. "There's no reason for these tribes to
fight each other. There's no competitive pressure here. The
forest is full of small game and nutritious vegetation, the
sea is bursting with edible life, and despite the proximity of
the desert there are free-flowing streams that provide a
steady and reliable water supply. These Quwanga didn't
come to kidnap females for procreation, and neither tribe
apparently practices slavery. There's no complex exchange
system involving precious metals or gems or even shells.
So what do they fight about?"

"Maybe they have something like an old clan feud,"
O'Sandringham suggested.

"Or maybe it's just in the nature of intelligent life to
fight," Prentice commented sadly.

"It's too soon to be profound," Lejardin chided him. He looked back at her sharply.

"It's as valid a supposition as anything else. How would you explain it?"

"I can't," she said simply. "The Pendju have been so friendly and hospitable to us. The last thing I'd have expected was for them to be involved in periodic combat with others of their own kind."

"Hell," murmured Stevens, "we didn't even know for sure that there *were* others of their own kind." He eyed the surrounding forest nervously. "I wonder if these Quwanga will consider us enemies because we're guests of the Pendju."

Prentice blinked. "Jack, ask her if she expects the Quwanga to come back." Simna complied.

"Not come back," Mahd'ji cheerfully assured her human friend. "Must excuse me now. I have to help with the preparations."

"What preparations?" Simna put out a hand to restrain her. "To bury the one who was killed in the raid?"

"Bury? What is that?"

"When one of our kind dies, they are placed in the ground and covered with earth."

Mahd'ji considered this. "That seems wasteful."

"I see." He hesitated, ignoring the inquiring stares of his companions. "What do you do with your dead?"

"One who dies must remain with the village, with one's friends and relations. The body is cooked, and eaten." She smiled innocently at him, as though it were the most natural thing in the world. Which for her and her people it apparently was, he decided.

He considered her objectively—breathtakingly wide eyes the color of pale amethyst; flowing hair and tiny, cupidlike mouth; supple, unblemished skin—and tried to envision her chowing down on the well-done shin of a close friend.

Given the unexpected subtleties of Xican grammar and his own uncertainty, he sought further clarification. "Do you also consume," he asked hesitantly, "the bodies of the fallen Quwanga?"

"Quwanga or Pendju," she assured him briskly. "It is the same with all. None must go to waste. Naturally the Quwanga would do the same for us."

"Jack?" He felt fingers gripping his arm. It was Prentice. "What's she talking about now, Jack?"

"Recycling," he replied curtly, continuing his conversation with the native. "Are you sure about what you're telling me, Mahd'ji?"

She seemed puzzled by his confusion. "Is it not what I have said?"

"But you're not getting ready to do that right now?"

"No."

He was relieved. "Then what are these preparations you speak of for?"

"Why, since the Quwanga have raided us, it would be very bad courtesy if we did not respond promptly. We must make ready to attack the Quwanga village, if only to get back Gmou'le, who they took with them."

"What will happen if you don't get there in time?" Simna persisted. "Will the Quwanga kill and eat her?"

"Certainly not!" The notion obviously shocked Mahd'ji. "She is not dead."

"What if you don't succeed in rescuing her?"

Mahd'ji considered this. "Then the Quwanga will make her one of them and she will become part of their village. Just as I was once a Quwanga."

Simna felt as if he were sliding helplessly down an increasingly steep slope. "*You* were once a Quwanga?"

"Oh, yes! The Pendju raided my village and took me when I was but this high." She held her open palm out waist-high and parallel to the ground. "Since then I have been Pendju."

"But your parents, your relatives and childhood friends, must still be in the Quwanga village."

"Yes, but they are Quwanga and I am Pendju."

Simna had given up trying to steer the conversation. Now he fought simply to follow its utterly unexpected twists and turns. "If they were killed and their bodies captured in one of these periodic battles, would you . . . would you eat them?"

Mahd'ji didn't hesitate. "Nothing must be allowed to go to waste." She slipped lithely from beneath his restraining hand. "Please, friend J'ac. You must let me go. If I do not help with the preparations, I will not be allowed to go along on the raid."

Simna took a step forward but made no move to stop her. "You mean you're looking forward to this?"

"Of course. It is one of the most exciting parts of the right way to live." She turned and hurried off, a definite bounce in her step.

Prentice had to step into Simna's line of vision to get the other man's attention. "What was that all about?" He peered closer. "You look like you've just eaten something unpleasant."

Simna glanced back so sharply it startled Prentice. "Why would you say that?"

"Hey, take it easy, Jack. It was just an observation."

Cedric Carnavon looked thoughtful. "I caught some of it, but I'm not as fluent as Jack. A lot of it doesn't make sense."

"It doesn't make sense to me, either, Ced." Simna regarded his companions. "We're going to have to rethink this image we've constructed of the delicate, sensitive, peace-loving Pendju."

"How do you mean?" asked Lejardin. "They were the ones who were attacked."

Simna turned to her. "That's just the way it worked out this time. Apparently they raid the Quwanga on a regular, recurring basis. They're every bit as warlike as their assailants, and if Mahd'ji's anything to go by, they seem to enjoy it." He gestured in the direction the Pendju female had taken. "That's where she's off to now, to help the rest of the village make preparations to go after the raiders. She was in a hurry to leave us because she was afraid she'd miss out." He stared evenly at Lejardin.

"They also eat their dead."

O'Sandringham's jaw dropped. Lejardin assumed a look of disbelief. "No. Not the Pendju."

He nodded slowly. "Not only their own dead, but those of their enemies as well. According to Mahd'ji, they don't believe in letting anything go to waste, up to and including a freshly killed corpse. Furthermore, it seems that Mahd'ji herself was once a Quwanga. She's a Pendju captive, raised to be a citizen of this village."

Carnavon was sympathetic. "That explains some of the expressions you were running through, Jack. I was wondering what the hell you two were talking about."

Simna eyed his friend. "You know me, Ced. I wear my feelings on my face. I've always been a lousy poker player."

"Mahd'ji doesn't have any regrets about being a captive?" Millie Carnavon inquired.

"If she does, she didn't express them to me. She seems to be fully integrated into the Pendju tribe. I detected no indication of bitterness on her part."

"I wonder if they fight over possession of the dead," Stevens remarked. O'Sandringham gave him a look to which he responded defiantly. "Just because you've got the degrees doesn't mean you're the only ones who can speculate, Bee-el."

"Great, just great," Halstead was murmuring. "No alien Rousseaus here. In addition to being combative, our cheerful, pastoral Xicans also turn out to be cannibals."

"We're starting to encounter animals that aren't what they're supposed to be at first glance," Carnavon noted. "Why should the Pendju be any different?" His tone was cool, objective. "I think maybe we've overly romanticized this part of our discovery here. I'm not saying it was conscious, mind. But Xica isn't Paradise, so we shouldn't expect the Pendju or their cousins to be particularly innocent."

"Cannibals." Lejardin kicked gently at the dry earth. "Necrotism."

"There's no worship involved," Simna went on. "Mahd'ji as much as told me that she'd eat part of her own mother if the circumstances were appropriate."

She licked her lips as she gazed back at him. "You admit that your knowledge of the Xican language is still far from perfect, Jack. Are you sure you got all this right, that you didn't miss something in the translation? Thought Mahd'ji was saying one thing when she was actually saying something else?"

"I'm doing the best I can. I had far more followup questions than I did time to ask them. She was very anxious to be on her way. See, delicate little Mahd'ji wants to go kill some relatives, because that's the right thing to do." He let his gaze rove among his companions. "That's more or less what she said: that it was the right way to live."

"Retribution, revenge . . ." Halstead looked unhappy.

"I'm not sure that's a correct interpretation of the situation, Ted," Simna told him. "I got the impression it wasn't that straightforward. It's more subtle. I'm just not sure of the differences."

"It was all too easy." Prentice encompassed the entire

village with a sweep of his hand. "This was too simple, too idealized from the start."

"No kidding." Noosa made no attempt to restrain his cynicism. "Ted's right. We wanted to see a nonhuman intelligence living in an alien paradise, so we didn't dig too deep. Instead, they turn out to be as morally deficient as a comparably primitive human society. Maybe more so."

"I'm not so sure the analogy's that simple, Cody." When Simna was deep in thought, you could practically hear the wheels turning inside his skull. "Mahd'ji spoke of attacking the Quwanga, but she didn't speak of killing. There was no malice in her tone, not a hint of anger. Despite the village's losses she sounded almost content."

"Careful, Jack," Carnavon warned him. "Trying to learn an alien tongue is tough enough. Emotions, overtones, social subtleties . . . you might be interpreting everything backwards. There used to be places on old Earth where a smile was taken as a challenge."

"I know, Ced. Again, I'm doing the best I can. Bear in mind that when I give my opinions, that's all they are."

"So what do we do?"

They all turned to Stevens. "What do you mean, what do we do, Kauri?" Prentice asked him.

"Well, I mean, do we just sit here and wait to see how many of our new friends make it back home?" He caressed the cutter clipped to his workbelt.

Prentice was horrified. "We can't participate, Kauri. You know that."

"No, I don't know that. Don't tell me there are regulations about not interfering in native affairs, because no one ever expected to encounter any natives." He looked around at the others. "We could tag along with this raiding party and put an end to these Quwanga permanently. It'd sure simplify things around here."

"We can't, Kauri. We need to be everybody's friend. We're outsiders in the truest sense."

"It doesn't matter," Simna said. "We can't do anything."

"Sure we can." The mate was persistent. "A few carefully placed shots here and there ought to send these Quwanga running."

"Then what?" Lejardin asked him. "We sit down and join in the after-battle feast?"

Stevens never backed down, and he didn't now. "I don't know. What do you suppose Xican tastes like?" Thoroughly disgusted, she turned away from him.

"Kauri," Simna declared, "I got the distinct impression from Mahd'ji that even if we offered our help it would be refused."

"But you don't know that, Jack."

"No, I don't. It's just an impression. There's a lot I'm not sure about, a lot more now than yesterday. Overtones," he murmured. "I realize that I'm missing something critical . . . but I still know more than you."

"Granted," Stevens admitted.

"We could go along as observers," Carnavon suggested. "If they ask for our help, say in the heat of battle, we can make a decision at that time. If not, we stay out of the way and keep our recorders running." He looked at Prentice. "It will be a valuable document."

"I don't like this," Prentice muttered. "I don't like being involved in this sort of thing at all."

Carnavon put an arm around the other scientist's shoulders. "We can set our own precedents here, Salvor, without fear of criticism. The nearest complaining authorities are more than a few light-years away. It's up to us to write the first manual for contact as it develops. How the Xicans treat one another is not our concern. What is our concern is properly documenting every aspect of that behavior."

"Ced's right." Noosa turned to Stevens. "Kauri, we can't

take sides because we don't know which, if any tribe, is in the right. We don't know who started this. Maybe we should be siding with the Quwanga."

"I don't know the Quwanga," the mate replied. "The Pendju I know, and I rather like 'em. They've been real nice to us, real helpful."

"Maybe the Quwanga would have done the same." Prentice took a deep breath. "All right: we go along, but we don't take sides." He offered the mate a bone. "If somebody, Pendju or Quwanga, comes at one of us with a spear or axe, then that person can defend himself or herself. Otherwise I don't want to see anything going off during the attack except recorders."

"Everybody relax here for a minute." Simna jogged across the open area to confront Boutu. Human and Xican talked for a while before Simna rejoined his friends.

"It's as I thought. I offered our assistance in the forthcoming attack. . . ."

"Jack," Prentice began warningly, but the other scientist waved him down.

"Don't worry, Salvor. I offered our assistance. Even though Boutu's seen what our cutters can do, he declined." Simna eyed Stevens. "They don't want our help, Kauri. In fact, I got the distinct impression they'd resent any interference."

The mate shrugged. "If that's the way they want it. Did Boutu happen to say why?"

"He told me that with our help they could probably wipe out the Quwanga. They don't want to do that."

"Ah," murmured Millie Carnavon, "ethics. Morals."

"Not at all." Simna's tone was unchanged as he corrected her. "He said that if we kill all the Quwanga, then they'd have no one with whom to fight. The next nearest tribe they know of . . . yes, they do know of and have occasional contact with others . . . lies an inconvenient distance away, far to the south. They *like* fighting the Quwanga. They've apparently been doing it for some time and they feel comfortable with them."

"So they're against our helping them to slay their enemies even though it might save Pendju lives and prevent other Pendju from being taken captive." O'Sandringham ventured her conclusion carefully.

"That's exactly right," Simna told her. "Boutu all but pleaded with me to stay out of it."

"Now I'm really confused." No one took advantage of the opportunity to tell Noosa that he was always confused. At that moment none of them were feeling particularly jovial. Their precious Pendju had fallen from grace.

"Don't want us to share in the fun." Halstead was grim. "No, they're not what we thought they were."

"It goes deeper than that," Simna told him. "There's more to this than simply taking joy in battle. It's clearly a vital component of their culture."

"I still think it's crazy that they don't want our help," Stevens declared.

"Just don't let it affect your neutrality," Prentice warned him. "We're not a part of this. It's the way I want it, and it's the way they want it."

The mate nodded his understanding, but reluctantly.

O'Sandringham stared at Simna out of hard blue eyes. "Of course, we have only your word for any of this, Jack."

Simna's voice dropped. Oddly, it was more intimidating than if he'd raised it. Carnavon, who knew him better than any of the others, had once characterized it as a ferocious whisper.

"What's that supposed to mean, Bella-Lynn?"

His tone took her aback. "I mean . . . I was just wondering if you might have misinterpreted something badly."

"Are you saying that I'm making some of this up, that I'm maybe faking what I can't understand?"

"I'm not saying that at all. It's just that . . ."

Carnavon hastened to intervene. "Right, then; none of us is perfect and we've all managed to misinterpret the actual nature of Xican society. Observation and study will rectify that. So let's get on with it, shall we?"

"I'm doing the best I can." Simna was only partially mollified.

"Somebody needs to call Base Camp and let Frank and Stew know what's going on out here. I'll take care of that." Efficient as always, Millie Carnavon headed for the hut she shared with her husband and the other two women.

Halstead made an effort to lighten the atmosphere. "If Stew were here he'd be off whittling his own spear by now. We'd have to tie him to a tree to keep him from joining in."

"Get himself run through," Lejardin avowed readily.

"Then we're agreed." Prentice turned to Simna. "Jack, see what else you can find out. When is this war party or whatever they call it going to leave, how far back does Boutu insist we stay: that sort of thing."

"Right." Simna turned and headed toward a trio of conversing males.

O'Sandringham watched him go. "I don't know about the rest of you, but I'm going to concentrate on the language recordings Jack's putting together. The more of us who are fluent, the less confusion there'll be about what's really going on here." As an afterthought she added quickly, "Not that Jack isn't doing a really great job."

"Nice of you to approve," murmured Halstead. She looked at him sharply but found his expression unreadable.

It was both intriguing and depressing to watch the convivial, affectionate Pendju prepare for war. Most notable was the complete change of costume they adopted. Instead of the simple, light, one-piece garments they wore every day, they produced from the depths of woven chests elaborately fringed and decorated kilts and body vests. The utter absence of jewelry in everyday life was contrasted with the elaborate use of pierced shell necklaces and shell-, bead-, and seedpod-decorated battle regalia.

Shields, hoods, and light body armor fashioned from the tanned skins of various sea creatures completed the attire. It was as if the majority of their communal aesthetic was reserved for and directed solely toward preparation for elegant combat.

"It is important to make an impressive appearance during battle." Boutu took time from his personal preparations to explain things to Simna. "It is a way of boasting of one's skill in combat and also a sign of respect for one's opponent."

"But with all that ornamentation, all those shells and beads," Simna pointed out, "you can't possibly hope to sneak up on your adversaries."

"Sneak up?" Boutu looked confused. "What challenge is there in that? Better they should know we are coming."

"But you'd have a better chance of winning if you left off the noisemakers and bright clothing and employed surprise."

Boutu made a face. His response, despite certain linguistic uncertainties and allowing for possible semantic confusion, translated roughly as, "Winning isn't everything, friend J'ac."

The everyday spears and throwing sticks were replaced by a depressingly elaborate and even precocious assortment of javelins, halberds, pikes, axes, maces, and knives, in addition to the familiar bone- and volcanic glass-tipped arrows. Like the Pendju's battle attire, these were elaborately carved and decorated, sometimes with beads and feathers. The wooden handle of one axe was inlaid with a wonderfully iridescent green pearl shell. As usual, all of the decoration was abstract and nonrepresentational.

When at last final preparations had been concluded, the peaceful, pot-making and weave-dying Pendju had succeeded in transforming themselves into as bloodthirsty-looking a group of barbarian humanoids as could be imagined. They remained, however, unfailingly polite and courteous. A comparable group of primitive humans would have been working themselves up into a proper blood frenzy with yells and shouts, symbolic bonfires and war dances. In contrast, the Pendju continued to speak softly to one another, discussing the forthcoming retaliatory raid as genteelly as they might have a new fishing locale or garden site.

They could change their appearance, Prentice mused, but not their nature.

Furthermore, they continued to speak of the Quwanga, who had raided and burned, killed and taken captives, with something approaching open affection. It confused Simna, who had to try to explain it to his companions, to the point of irritation.

"Don't ask me to explain it to you," he told Carnavon, "when I don't understand it myself. All I can do is fall back on the self-evident: while they're very humanlike, they're not human." He hefted his pack higher on his shoulders.

"Boutu!" Compliant as ever, the native left his little cluster of warriors to join his human friends. "Boutu, what happens if you should defeat the Quwanga utterly this time?"

"That will not occur." The native was quite positive. "The Quwanga are as strong as we are. Both tribes are equal in strength."

"Well then, what happens if the Quwanga turn the tables on you and start to push you back?"

"Then we will retreat," replied Boutu, calmly stating the obvious.

"And if they follow you and pursue the fight?" wondered O'Sandringham. Simna eyed her in surprise: she'd made a lot of progress with her language lessons, using the recordings he'd been preparing.

"Then we could turn and trap them in the forest," Boutu informed her. "In the forest everyone is always equal, just as everyone is always different."

"Different?" Simna frowned. "How can you be equal and different at the same time?"

O'Sandringham didn't give Boutu a chance to reply. "Why don't you just make peace with the Quwanga? Wouldn't that be better than these regular, predictable bouts of killing?"

The Pendju pondered this notion before responding brightly. "Of course not. If there were peace between us and the Quwanga, then who would we fight? How would we improve ourselves?" With that he turned and went to rejoin his fellows, no doubt tired of inexplicable alien questions and concepts.

Simna sighed. "We've been down this road before. You know: the one with the familiar dead end?"

"Maybe it's a good thing they like to fight these Quwanga," Stevens declared. "I mean, I'm no scientist, but it strikes me that if they like to fight and they didn't have this other tribe to pick on, they might have chosen to fight with us. That would've complicated your work here no end."

"Don't be ridiculous." Lejardin was obviously irritated by the thought. "Why would they want to fight us?"

Stevens shrugged. "Why keep fighting with these Quwanga? You can't deny that they're looking forward to it."

"They just like to fight. Plenty of primitive human tribes liked to do the same," Cedric Carnavon pointed out. "We may not like that fact, but it looks like we're going to have to accept it."

"Maybe," added his wife, "we were expecting too much from the Pendju from the start. Or hoping for too much."

"Me, I'm ready to do some vivisecting." Halstead rubbed his hands together. "It's about time we started getting into some of these specimens. Take our minds off inexplicable native customs."

Prentice shifted his own pack on his back. Since the Pendju were firm in their insistence that they carry out the raid unaccompanied and unobserved, Prentice had decided that they would all return to Base Camp so as not to interfere in any way. Besides, as Halstead had correctly pointed out, there was plenty of work to catch up on back at camp.

"I couldn't agree more, Ted. I think we've all spent entirely too much time trying to puzzle out our native friends and not enough focused on our individual disciplines. We need a break. Compared to unfathomable Pendju-Quwanga ritual combat, it'll be a relief to get back to something as straight-up as internal biology."

But he was wrong.

IX

Ramirez was feeding the specimens housed at the back of Dome Three when he happened to look around and see Noosa staggering toward him.

"Cody?" Straightening from his crouch, he set the feed tray aside. "Cody, you all right?"

Noosa was clutching his left shoulder. His face was ashen. His lips worked but no sound came forth.

Ramirez started toward the other man. "Jesus, Cody, you look like hell."

Noosa took another step forward. "P . . . puh . . ." His eyes rolled back in his skull and he keeled forward as if he'd been axed. Ramirez reached him in time to keep him from slamming into the floor. He knelt on one knee, supporting his unconscious friend's upper body and looking around helplessly.

"Hey . . . hey, somebody! We need some help in here! Dome Two, it's Cody, we need help!"

The open intercom picked up his cries and distributed them throughout the camp. Computers were left open, chores set aside, conversations interrupted as one at a time the other members of the expedition came running.

They eased Noosa down and turned the short, compact body onto its back. The scientist's eyes remained shut and he was starting to shiver. His breathing came in uncertain, shallow gasps.

"Respiratory interdiction." Lejardin cracked the medical kit she'd brought. "Possible cardiac infarction." Yanking down Noosa's shirt, she slapped a couple of A-T contact patches onto the rosy skin of his shoulder, then fumbled for an ampule and injector. "What the hell happened to him?"

Ramirez hovered close by, looking miserable. "I don't *know*. I was doing the morning feeding when I turned and saw him. He tried to say something but he didn't get it out before he went down."

"What was he working on?" Simna was studying the unconscious man speculatively, his voice calm and controlled.

"Again, I don't know. He made some kind of 'puh' sound before he collapsed."

"Shit," O'Sandringham growled. "Poison? Maybe he was trying to tell you he'd been poisoned?" The unhappy Ramirez looked blank.

Prentice peered toward the far side of the dome, where numerous cages and containers held dozens of specimens considered to be harmless. Until now. He could detect no excitement, no unusual activity within. Which of them had unexpectedly struck Noosa? Or was his condition a consequence of circumstances as yet unimaginable?

Stevens arrived carrying a collapsible pallet under one arm and began to unfold it. Lejardin had jabbed the loaded injector against Noosa's upper chest and emptied the contents into his torso. By now the color of his shoulder had deepened from a light pink hue to a fiery red as his body's defenses went to war against the hostile intrusion.

Noosa's shivering grew worse. His heels pummeled the floor.

"Hold him steady." Lejardin's tone was grim. "Let's get him on the board." With Stevens and Simna taking the smaller man's legs and Halstead hefting him under the shoulders, they managed to shift him onto the carrying pallet. At that moment Lastwell arrived.

"Holy Christ," he blurted as he caught sight of the twitching, florid-faced Noosa. "What bit him?"

"We don't know," Prentice replied. "Stew gave the alarm, but Cody went down before he could tell him anything. We don't even know what he was working on."

The captain ambled over to peer down at the gravely ill scientist. "Doesn't look like natural causes to me." He glanced over at Lejardin. "What's your diagnosis, Blossom?"

She responded without looking up at him, her attention focused on her helpless patient. "I haven't a clue. I'm not a doctor, Frank. We think *maybe* he was trying to tell Stewart that he'd been poisoned, but we're not even sure of that. Something's sure as hell messing up his respiration and motor control."

"Is he going to die?" Lastwell inquired coolly.

"One hopes not." Simna's reply was as dryly reproving as a desert wind.

Prentice considered calling the Carnavons, decided it was not a priority. They were out combing and collecting in the desert-forest transition zone. Neither possessed any special medical knowledge, and it was already crowded around Noosa. They'd learn what had happened soon enough.

"We've double-checked all the specimens in here," he reminded his colleagues. "We've had no trouble with any of them. Cody must've stumbled into something else."

"Stumble's the word." Ramirez's feeling of helplessness made him bitter. "When I turned and saw him, he could hardly stand up."

The expedition leader nodded. "Maybe it would be a good idea to check the cages. See if anything's missing."

Ramirez blinked, upset at himself. "Damn, I should've done that already." Turning, he hurried to the far side of the dome and embarked on a furious inspection of the specimen containers.

"I'll give him a hand." Lastwell moved to join the scientist, but the first thing he checked wasn't one of the cages. Instead, he inclined his head and began running his hands experimentally along the seams of the double door that led outside the base.

Ramirez was down on hands and knees now, squinting beneath benches and tables. "All present and accounted for so far!" he called back to his companions.

Prentice thought to reply, decided it wasn't necessary. Surely Ramirez had told them everything he knew.

Satisfied with his inspection of the main entrance, Lastwell strode purposefully toward the single door that connected Domes Two and Three. "Internal integrity's intact. I'll try the entrances now."

"You think something may have slipped inside?" O'Sandringham queried him.

"I've no idea. But if it's a possibility, I sure as hell want to check it out. I don't like the idea of waking up in bed with anyone I haven't been introduced to previously. Or anything."

Noosa's trembling had eased. Halstead bent close to their resident medic. "How's he doing?"

She checked the field scanner she'd strapped to the prone scientist's chest. "Not real good. Readings are consistent with the reaction you'd expect to result from the absorption of a strong neurotoxin. He's been poisoned, all right. The molecular structure is complex and resisting breakdown. Until the active ingredient or ingredients are identified, I can't instruct the synthesizer on how to try to synthesize an antidote." Lips tight, she leaned over the body. "Heart rate has slowed and seems to be steadying."

"Goddamnit." Halstead was cradling Noosa's head in his hands, praying that the sheer physical contact might have some tiny benefit, wondering if Noosa could feel it or hear the conversation around him.

O'Sandringham exhaled slowly. "Maybe we ought to try to move him to the lander's dispensary."

Lejardin was doubtful. "I don't know. Moving him might do more harm than good. I'm doing all I can." She looked up at Prentice. "It's your call, Salvor."

"If you've no strong opinion either way, I think we should move him. Especially if there's a chance he's still going downhill. If nothing else, we can put him into deep-sleep to try to stabilize his condition." He bent and gripped one of the handles built into the side of the composite fiber pallet. "Let's get him up."

With Halstead at one end of the pallet and Simna hefting the other, they moved Noosa from the lab out into the heat of the Xican day. Ramirez remained behind, intent on his ferociously detailed inspection of cages and holding cylinders. Lastwell's seemingly casual attitude notwithstanding, he checked the doorway very carefully as he exited to make sure nothing, however tiny, followed them outside. Much to Simna's surprise, the captain was whistling the last movement from *Swan Lake*.

Cody Noosa; B.S., M.S., double Ph.D., Fellow of the International Academy of Advanced Biology, noted specialist in the classification and taxonomy of arthropods and crustacea, author of several books and numerous papers on same and recipient of the Haldane Prize for original research, died halfway back to the lander, just as they were about to step clear of the last ground cover and omnipresent *Haukik*. The scanner strapped to his chest announced his demise with a sorrowful, serene beeping. Lejardin painfully switched off the electronic lamentation as she inclined to read the screen one last time.

"His heart seized up," she informed her companions. "It just stopped."

"We could still put him in deepsleep," O'Sandringham insisted. "Maybe they could do something when we get home."

Lejardin eyed her friend sadly. "He'd have been dead too long before we could put him under." She eyed the still-distant bulk of the lander. "Even if we ran like hell from here and activated a sleep capsule in record time, he'd have lost all brain functions before we could get him under. There'd be nothing left to revive but a vegetable." She nodded at Halstead. "Might as well set him down. He's not going home."

The men complied. Simna was watching Lejardin carefully. There was not only a lot there; there was a great deal more than he'd suspected.

No one said anything for a long time. The shock of Noosa's death had stunned them into immobility. Not surprisingly, it was Lastwell who got them moving again.

He mopped at his forehead as he indicated the pallet and its motionless cargo. "Well, right now he's the only one here who's not sweating a bucket. This is about enough sun for one day. If we don't get back under shade pretty quick, chances are we'll be burying our first heatstroke victim alongside him."

Prentice nodded reluctantly. "Ted, Jack; let's get him back to camp."

There wasn't much interest in lunch, or conversation. They sat around the mess table picking lethargically at their food while largely ignoring the all-important tumblers of cold liquid. The energy and excitement of the previous days and weeks had sighed out of them like air from a balloon.

"First we find out our friendly, kindly Pendju are war lovers, and now this." O'Sandringham slumped back into her lightly built chair and moodily contemplated her feet.

"This is bad," Prentice mumbled. "Very bad."

"You can't prepare for what you don't expect." Cedric

Carnavon did his best to prod his colleagues. "Maybe we've grown a little lazy, a little sloppy. Since nothing's given us any trouble, we've come to expect none." He gazed around the table. "Maybe this seems a benign world, but don't forget that Old North America's a benign, civilized, urbanized continent and part of it's still inhabited by poisonous reptiles and insects."

Prentice looked up, his voice a little firmer now. "Benign but alien. From now on we treat everything we come in contact with, be it plant, animal, or unclassifiable, as potentially dangerous. That includes the natives."

Stevens objected. "You think, say, Mahd'ji's likely to suddenly stab one of us in the back?"

"No, I don't. But I plan on being prepared for the possibility." A few murmurs of agreement sounded from the assembled.

"There's no harm in caution." Carnavon was in complete agreement. "We've made remarkable progress here. Discoveries have come so thick and fast we haven't even been able to catalog them properly, much less embark on any kind of systematized study. A little conscious slowdown, a little more care, won't hurt."

"We've all fallen a little bit in love with this place," Simna pointed out. "We need to retrench and remember who as well as where we are. Xica isn't paradise."

"We can't afford another incident." Prentice looked past the table to the far side of the room where Noosa lay stiffening and cold.

"What now?" asked O'Sandringham.

"We bury him." Lastwell's tone was no-nonsense, his expression hard. "If you lot don't feel up to it, Kauri and I will handle the chore."

"No." Millie Carnavon smiled gently. "We should all participate. It will help to drive the lesson home. Poor

Cody. He just wanted to be better at his work than anyone else."

"It has gained him a dubious distinction," Simna declared.

"Oh, for God's sake!" Lejardin exploded. "Do you always have to try to be clever?"

An unperturbed Simna met her gaze without blinking. "We all suffer from our little personality-specific ailments, Favrile. I'm afraid that where I am concerned, cleverness is an endemic condition. I'm not boasting here, understand. There are many times when I wish it were otherwise." He looked toward the back of the room. "Cody would understand."

Lejardin started to say something else. Instead she turned away, furious at the situation far more than at Simna, and stalked out of the mess.

They buried Noosa in an empty packing crate that Stevens sealed against intrusion, assuring his companions that it was tough enough to resist the efforts of any burrowing scavengers. The silent gray-barked trees of the Xican forest stood sentinel over the chosen plot, which looked out over the tranquil ocean and its cavorting cephalopods. Prentice recited the words, simple but effective, and then they left him there, their number reduced by one.

Work was resumed, but with a noticeable lack of passion. What had formerly been unrelieved anticipation gave way to resignation, investigation became drudgery, and fervor over new discoveries was muted.

Only Lastwell exhibited no lingering effects, and to a lesser extent, Simna. The captain was all for returning straightaway to the Pendju village to see how the raid on the Quwanga had turned out. After suitable contemplation (and continuous badgering by Lastwell), it was conceded by the team members that despite their general depression, that was a situation that could not be ignored.

"I'll stay here," O'Sandringham volunteered. "I want to finish up the work I've been doing with that new fungi we discovered."

"I'll hang back too," Stevens added, a little too quickly. It didn't matter. Their unusual relationship was as acknowledged by everyone else as it was unspoken, just as O'Sandringham's fondness for spirits of the liquid kind went unremarked upon. To her credit, her intake increased only slightly following Noosa's death.

Slowest to emerge from the consequent gloom was Ramirez. He'd been closer to Noosa than any of them, and the death of his fellow scientist and explorer generated grief the normally ebullient researcher was unable to shake. His usual bravado was subsumed in a persistent melancholy. Although two could satisfactorily look after the camp, he volunteered to remain behind with Stevens and O'Sandringham.

The rest of them shouldered packs and began the familiar hike back through the woods. In addition to the usual field gear, supplies, and scientific apparatus, this time everyone carried one of Stevens's specially modified cutter-welders.

For the first time in a long while, the forest looked different. The usual exclamations of wonder and amazement were replaced by wary sidelong glances and hesitation. Sudden cries or whistles within the woods drew sharp, nervous stares, and any movement was cause for alarm. There was no panic: they were too disciplined and experienced for that. But the sense of wonder they had felt on earlier plunges into the wooded depths had been replaced by something else. No one commented on it directly, but they all felt it: a persistent uncertainty that nothing was what it seemed, an incertitude that threatened on occasion to spill over into dread. And underlying their newfound unease was, as always, the profound heat and humidity.

Nothing interrupted their march. They encountered a fair

amount of wildlife, including a new species of grazer as big as a human that shuffled through the brush on eight thick, padded feet and vacuumed up tubers and soft roots with a flat-tipped flexible proboscis. It had a blunt, comical face with mournful eyes and drooping ears.

It took an encounter that spectacular to finally rouse them from their grief. Humming recorders documented the lumbering, thick-bodied creature for posterity. When it caught sight of them it turned and bolted into the bushes, loping along at a breakneck three kilometers an hour. The exertions drew smiles from several members of the group; the first smiles in several days.

No one pursued it into the thicker brush for a closer look. The creature looked slow and clumsy, but . . . nothing was certain anymore. Not if it was Xican.

The Pendju were delighted to see them and had begun to worry at the continuing absence of their tall, hairy friends. Mahd'ji and Silpa were eloquent in their concern.

"We have lost one of our number." Simna explained the reason behind their long absence as he and his companions sloughed off their packs and sank exhausted to the waiting mats the villagers thoughtfully provided. "Cody Noosa."

The pupils expanded in Mahd'ji's wondrous lavender eyes. "Ah. The shorter male with the hedge of hair that framed his face." Simna nodded, a gesture the Pendju recognized. "He was nice. I am sorrowed."

"Yes, he was," Simna replied absently. "Something killed him. Something he was studying. We don't know what it was."

"Something we didn't think was dangerous," added Cedric Carnavon from nearby. He'd mastered enough of the Xican tongue to carry on a modest conversation.

Mahd'ji blinked at him. The Pendju often drew out the gesture, the speed with which their eyelids descended and rose constituting an entire vocabulary of its own.

"But anything can be dangerous if it is disturbed. That is the way of living things."

Carnavon reflected. "I suppose that's true to a certain extent. On our world we have many creatures that appear harmless, but which can be deadly if they're sufficiently provoked."

That explanation seemed to satisfy her. "I understand. There are big dangers and small dangers."

"Cody was probably killed by a small danger," the senior scientist told her.

"How do you know that?"

"Because a big danger would have been obvious to him." He smiled across at his wife, who had settled down under a tree to catch her breath.

"But all dangers are obvious." Mahd'ji was clearly bemused.

"Maybe to you, because you live with these particular ones," Simna told her, "but we're not familiar enough with them yet."

"That's enough about Cody." Prentice sat on his mat and sucked fruit juice from a cold cylinder. "She wasn't there and so she can't offer any possible explanations. Ask them about their raid on the Quwanga." He gestured languidly. "The village looks as peaceful and prosperous as ever, so whatever transpired couldn't have been too cataclysmic."

Simna put the question to their friend.

"Oh, yes!" Her response was brightened by the familiar childlike Xican enthusiasm. "There was a *big* fight. Though we made lots of noise as we approached their village I think we surprised them a little, like you said we should. We didn't mean to, but we did." As she spoke she gestured emphatically, her two opposable thumbs crossing repeatedly behind the pair of long middle fingers.

"Several Quwanga were slain."

"And the Pendju?" Simna inquired. "Did you have casualties?"

"Two wounded. They are recovering still. And two dead. Tumati, and Boutu."

Simna sat up straight on his mat, unsure he'd heard correctly. "Boutu? The Boutu who always went with us and who showed us around the forest? Your Boutu?" She responded affirmatively.

His companions had immediately picked up on his emotional shift. Simna often appeared preoccupied, but dazed was another matter.

"What is it, Jack?" Lejardin inquired anxiously. "What's wrong?"

His voice was slightly unsteady. "It's Boutu. Boutu's dead. He was killed in the raid on the Quwanga village."

Halstead didn't speak. Instead he wrenched off his wide-brimmed hat and threw it angrily at his pack. Prentice picked at a loose mat fiber between his legs and sighed heavily.

"Not Boutu." Millie Carnavon's face expressed the unexpected sense of loss they all felt. "He was so sweet. I always had the feeling that he not only wanted to help us, but that he actually cared about us."

"He was a good . . . person," her husband added.

Mahd'ji sensed their concern even if she couldn't understand their words. "He fought well. He brought credit and honor to the Pendju." She did not seem particularly distraught.

"So what happens now?" Carnavon's tone was uncharacteristically bitter. "The Quwanga attacked you, you've retaliated against the Quwanga. Is it their turn again? Should we expect an attack tomorrow, or the next day?"

She looked startled, as if the very notion was utterly alien. "Oh, no! Of course not. The fighting is over for the Season."

"What season?" a baffled Prentice inquired.

"Why, the Fighting Season, of course. They have made their raid, and we have made ours. Both sides have suffered loss. Now there is the time to rest and recover. You were not here to greet us upon our return, but we only just came home. We were helping the Quwanga to repair the damage we did to their village. Soon they will come here, to help us with ours."

Carnavon frowned. "So after you get through killing and maiming and burning, you all go out hunting and fishing together?"

"Some of your words are not right." It was her way of politely deferring to Carnavon's less than ideal pronunciation. "But I think I understand most of what you are saying. Yes, after the fighting is over we help each other."

"Then why fight in the first place?" Carnavon doubted she could sense his exasperation.

"We have talked about this before. Fighting is what gives life its flavor. It stimulates and invigorates."

"Unless you get killed." Simna raised his voice as he addressed his colleagues. "You all hear that?"

"You know we don't, Jack," said Lejardin. "We don't have your command of the idiom."

"Sorry. Mahd'ji says that now that they've done their best to beat one another's brains in, they're going to get together like old buddies and help repair each other's war damage." He shifted his backside on the rug. "See, nonhuman sociology isn't that hard. You slaughter your neighbors and when you've done an adequate job of it, you get together and party."

"Barbaric," she murmured.

"Not at all," he corrected her. "It's just an alien intelligence at work. That's what we keep forgetting here. We don't have to empathize with their ways; just accept them. Understanding can come later."

Lastwell had selected a shady spot beneath a *Ch'civ* tree and, after checking the ground for crawling things, had settled down for a long sip from his pack cooler.

"I don't see evidence of much intelligence at work here. Me, I wouldn't be lifting a second thumb to help these Quwanga. They killed Boutu, the best friend we had among the Pendju. How can Mahd'ji think of workin' with them? Wasn't he her mate, or something?"

"That's how I understood the relationship." Simna hesitated. "I could have been wrong."

"Well, even if he was her fucking occasional boyfriend," Lastwell continued in the same even tone of voice, "I wouldn't have left that Quwanga village until I'd gutted every last one of the sneaky four-fingered bastards."

Simna commented with his usual dryness. "That is hardly a scientific attitude, Frank."

"It's not how they work it here, Captain." Prentice adjusted his own rug. "Remember what we decided after Cody died? Assume that nothing here is quite what it seems? That goes for the Pendju and the Quwanga as much as for the rest of the fauna and flora."

"No shit." Lastwell punctuated his understanding with a sardonic smile.

"When we go to help the Quwanga," Mahd'ji informed them, "you could come with us. I am sure they could help you as much as we have."

Carnavon shifted until he was sitting on his knees. "But they killed your mate. They killed Boutu. How can you be friends with them, much less work alongside them?"

Her response was somber. "There are not that many Pendju or Quwanga. We must help each other. This is an important principle."

"I agree, I agree," Carnavon replied impatiently. "So why kill each other and make fewer of each tribe?"

"Because it stimulates and . . ."

"We know." A thoroughly vexed Simna interrupted her as readily as he would have one of his own colleagues. "I don't know if we're ready to meet the Quwanga, Mahd'ji. I don't know if I want to meet the people who killed Boutu."

"Why not?" She was genuinely perplexed. "I know they would greet you as we have and try to help you in your work. We have already spoken to them of you."

Lastwell caught enough of her declamation to sit away from the trunk of the tree and look around nervously. "The Quwanga know that we're here?"

"Certainly. We would not keep such fine news secret from them."

"Alien sociology. Expect the unexpected. Nothing's what it seems." Halstead nodded to no one in particular. "I think I'm starting to get the hang of it."

Simna rose and walked to stand close to Mahd'ji. She looked up at him expectantly. "Mahd'ji, don't you *miss* Boutu?"

"Of course," she replied softly. "I miss him very much."

"Maybe we can find her a new husband among her good pals the Quwanga," Lastwell snorted. Prentice shot him a warning look, and the captain raised his hands innocently. "Hey, I'm just trying to see things from their perspective. Isn't that what we're supposed to be doing? Why don't you ask her if she thinks that's a good idea, Salvor?"

Prentice considered, but quickly decided he'd rather not know the answer.

X

Over the next three days they discovered and rapidly catalogued forty-two new species of arthropod, half a dozen new, large, warm-blooded creatures, and as many more of *Octixica,* the new order Simna and Halstead had devised to include certain extremely odd creatures that seemed to fit into no recognizable class. Simply gathering and assembling their boundless cornucopia of specimens kept them too busy to dwell on developments within the village.

Simna was alone in one of their two assigned huts. Seated at a portable lab table, he was struggling to bottle a cross between a legless lizard and a millipede, when Mahd'ji gave him a serious start by sneaking up behind him and slipping both fluid, limber arms over his shoulders. Her body temperature was lower than his own and her skin was cool to the touch. An understandable adaptation to the Xican climate, but one that could be disconcerting when encountered in person.

It was not the difference in temperature that startled him, however, so much as the familiarity suggested by the gesture. Putting aside specimen and holding bottle, he whirled around in the chair so fast that she retreated. There was uncertainty in her expression and her voice.

"Did I hurt you, J'ac?" Fathomless orbs of magenta spilled their concern into his own.

"No. You didn't hurt me." He punctuated his denial with a native gesture to further reassure her. "I was concentrating on what I was doing and you just surprised me, that's all."

"I did not mean to."

"It's all right." His damnable sharp tone again, he cursed himself. With care he explained, "It's just that ever since our friend died we've all been a little jumpy, a little on edge."

"We sorrow for your lost companion."

"That's good of you, but you needn't concern yourselves. You have your own dead to mourn. Though I admit I haven't seen you doing much of that."

"We celebrate those who are no longer with us, friend J'ac. We do not mourn them."

"We're trying to understand that." He found himself drawn to the very human folds and ripples of her lightly clad form, still feeling the coolness of her arms against his bare neck. If you squinted a little so that the *sui generis* face blurred, and made yourself blot out the strange hands and feet . . . he was suddenly apprehensive.

Surface semblances, perceived equivalences. They were admittedly striking, and in some ways the differences could be viewed as exotic rather than alien. There was a striking symmetry about the Pendju that had been apparent from the first time they had been observed bathing in the stream near the village or at the beach.

With plastic sealant over the door and single window, the portable cooling equipment they'd hauled all the way from Base Camp kept the temperature in the hut tolerable. No Pendju could stand it for very long before they began to shiver. Still, Mahd'ji displayed no inclination to leave.

O'Sandringham and Stevens had struck up a relationship practically from the time she'd emerged from deepsleep. The Carnavons had each other, and he was convinced Pren-

tice and Lejardin enjoyed at the very least a deep understanding. Lastwell was busy being captain and Halstead de-
voted himself to his work. Simna . . . Simna's mind was too
encompassing to restrict itself to assignments and programs.

A halting, uncertain voice he barely recognized as his
own spoke into the silence of their stares. "What . . . what
did you want here, Mahd'ji?"

"There's going to be a feast. A feast and a celebration."

"A feast?" Something more than sweat slid away from
him. "That should be interesting. You came to tell me about
a feast."

"Yes. The Quwanga are coming."

He struggled to wrench his thoughts back to where they
belonged. "We've already told you, Mahd'ji, that my
friends and I don't want anything to do with the Quwanga.
We will leave the village while you have this feast and return later."

"No!" She was visibly upset. "You must stay. There is
something . . ." She cut herself off. "I am not supposed to
say."

Suddenly he was interested. "What aren't you supposed
to say, Mahd'ji?" he prodded her.

"No." Exhibiting the air of a child caught fumbling at the
lid of the cookie jar, she started backing toward the exit.
"You will find out at the feast. In three days. All of you
should be here."

"If it's that important," he said slowly, "all of us who can
and are willing to do so will try to participate." What was
she so reluctant to reveal? Was there some kind of treachery afoot here? Something in those guileless lavender eyes
he was missing. Did their Xican hosts want their visitors all
in one place at the same time so that both tribes could fall
upon them and slay them?

The fear and paranoia engendered by Noosa's death

tended to spread like a fever. He was being overly suspicious, reading consequences into her hesitation that were not supported by evidence. That didn't mean that he and his companions could not take precautions.

Since it was so important, it seemed that at least a few of them would have to put in an appearance at this intertribal gathering. There was much to lose and nothing to be gained by offending the Pendju.

"Does Silpa believe it is necessary for us to attend this meeting?"

"Oh, yes," she assured him, halting her retreat. "Everyone knows." She looked down. "I was not supposed to tell you today. It was to be a surprise."

"So it was supposed to be a secret?" Wariness surfaced afresh.

"Yes . . . and no. We know how you feel about the Quwanga. There is no reason for it, friend J'ac. We and the Quwanga are different tribes but the same people. There can be fighting without anger."

"That's kind of a difficult concept for my friends and me to accept. Especially since the Quwanga killed Boutu."

She faltered before replying. "Boutu's goneness makes me sad, but not angry. It was a part of life." She brightened. "I am glad you like Silpa. I like him also, and we will probably mate."

Unbidden, the image of the supple, lithe Mahd'ji and the harder, more muscular male Silpa mating coalesced in Simna's mind. He envisioned them writhing, entwining in the throes of a cooler alien passion, an almost human conjugation.

What the hell is this? he thought angrily. While it was true that all scientists were voyeurs by trade, such visions ought only to stir the mind, not the blood. He was being pummeled by his own rebellious thoughts.

The internal torment must have been more than a little

visible. Mahd'ji took a step toward him. "Are you all right, friend J'ac? I did not mean for my news to upset you."

He turned away from her and concentrated on the worm-shape he'd been trying to stuff into a collection bottle. "Yes, I'm fine," he said curtly. "I'll be at your feast. I can't assure you that anyone else will attend, but I promise that we'll discuss the matter among us. Regardless of what is finally decided, you should know that several of our number must stay at our Base Camp."

"They have time to get here," she said encouragingly.

He shook his head, not turning to face her. "We have a lot of work to do, Mahd'ji. Our own priorities. Your feast doesn't change that." A sudden thought made him turn again. "What if the Quwanga decided to raid *our* village?"

"Oh, no." She was genuinely shocked. "The Quwanga would never do that."

"Why not?" He was watching her carefully. "Our village contains a great many valuable items that the Quwanga would probably like to possess."

"But that would be stealing," she protested. "We never steal from each other."

No, he thought. You only raid and kill, and then make up and have a big feast.

A sudden impulse made him rise and walk over to put a hand on her shoulder. Wide, innocent eyes gazed steadily back into his. Seeking enlightenment within those viola-ceous depths, he found only his own reflection.

"Thank you for the invitation, Mahd'ji. I will try to convince the others to attend."

"You are a good friend, J'ac." Displaying a flexibility not even a double-jointed human could have matched, her left arm reached up and around to grab his wrist. A deli-cate, four-fingered hand pressed his own fingers into the cool flesh of her shoulder and neck. Inclining her head to her left, she leaned it against the two hands, closed her eyes . . . and purred.

Then she straightened and flowed as much as walked out the door, the electrostatically charged plastic curtain parting to pass her.

Fingers tingling, he watched her depart. Notably unscientific thoughts rattled around loose in his brain, fragments of a hitherto solid but now rapidly crumbling structure.

What's happening here? What's happening here? He resumed his seat, his mind far from his work, drifting out to sea like a lone swimmer caught in a sudden rip tide. *Have to get ahold of myself.*

Why fight it? Consider it, as you do nearly everything else, as an object of scientific curiosity. Would there not be a wealth of information to be gleaned from such an encounter? It was not necessary that he lose himself. He could remain objective, observant, and analytical throughout. Of course he could. Hadn't Ramirez, that day he'd caught him with the female?

What if Silpa objected? But why should he? Hadn't Mahd'ji just told him that they were not yet mated? What would Boutu have thought, or did that matter now? Did much of anything matter except what he was thinking?

Stop this, he told himself. Put it out of your mind. It's not something you can justify. While hormones might be capable of remarkable feats of rationalization, your mind is still in charge. Under siege perhaps, but still in charge. Act like it. Besides, he told himself with a smile, if anything *were* to happen and the results became known, Prentice would be all over him for interfering with the workings of native society.

They had discovered a bush that produced the most peculiarly attenuated, finger-length yellow berries. The seed structure was remarkable. He diagramed it in his mind and the activity put that deviating vessel back on course. His hands fumbled for the equipment on the workbench. To his immense surprise he saw that they were shaking.

This is absurd, he decided firmly. He had a worm to bottle. Willing steadiness into his fingers, he resumed his work. He also found solace in what had become their overriding criterion for the study of Xican life.

No matter how benign the circumstances, assume always that nothing was as it appeared to be.

Besides, Mahd'ji had already promised one surprise for the forthcoming feast. He would content himself with that.

Ramirez had no idea where O'Sandringham and Stevens had taken off to, but he was confident it had little to do with camp maintenance or basic research. That suited him fine. He'd been waiting for a time when he had the lab complex to himself.

He climbed efficiently into the ecosuit, gathering the thin but incredibly tough material around him. It would keep an individual safe and protected in any environment short of empty space. The small backpack maintained a steady insuit temperature while the dense white polyfiber weave was impervious to penetration by any known life form on Earth, Tycho V, Burke, and presumably Xica.

Adjusting the integral faceplate, he ran a check of the suit's biosystems and fine-tuned the pressure-sensitive regulator so that it would supply a little extra oxygen. When he finished he was as fully protected as he'd been the day they'd first set foot on the Xican surface. It was not that external environment that drew him, however, or inspired such extensive preparation.

He made his way through the compound, careful as always to make sure each doorway was sealed behind him before opening the one ahead. He was gratified to find no sign of O'Sandringham or Stevens.

The double door to Dome Three was properly closed.

Entering, he examined the shelved and stacked containers, the miniature habitats he and his colleagues had thrown together to house their burgeoning collection of live specimens. Slightly off to his right, near the back of the room, was the examination bench where Cody had been working while Ramirez had been feeding the herbivores. The same bench he had staggered away from before he'd lapsed into his pre-death coma.

Checking a last time to make certain he was alone in the room, he advanced on the bench and began to activate and position equipment. It did not take any time at all to duplicate the setup Cody had been working with. Then he rose and moved to one of the many occupied cages.

It contained three basketball-sized, black-splotched, gray-furred animals. Their four legs were all but concealed by the dense fur, which covered their spherical forms completely save for a pair of pupilless red eyes that could extend outward on flexible stalks. These flanked the curious, probing snout with which the creature siphoned its diet of small arthropods. In appearance and activity the Puffball was utterly harmless.

"Puh." It was the last sound Cody Noosa had made in this life. "Poison," his friends had assumed he'd been trying to say. Much later Ramirez had gone back and checked his friend's work records. Noosa hadn't filled in his work sheet for the day on which he died, but he'd been doing a lot of work with the Puffballs. Enough to raise suspicions, enough to provoke what-ifs. Not enough to enable anyone to draw any kind of conclusions. Those awaited further proof.

Which Ramirez intended to produce.

Noosa might well have been trying to say "poison," as O'Sandringham and a few of the others had surmised. Or he might have been trying to say something else. Like "Puffball." It was as good a place as any to start.

The equipment Cody had left in place told Ramirez as lucidly as any instruction sheet what sort of work his friend had been engaged in at the time of his death. Ramirez's intention was to try to duplicate his friend's activity on that day as closely as possible, only with considerably more in the way of defense at hand than poor Noosa had possessed.

With deliberate care he unsealed the Puffball habitat and reached in with both gloved hands. The individual he removed squeaked softly but could not resist with its soft snout or small, unclawed feet. Cuddling the creature gently to soothe it, Ramirez resealed the cage as the rubbery proboscis probed curiously at his suit. Soft and flexible, the organ looked about as dangerous as a rolled tissue.

Ramirez placed the specimen in the holding pan on the dissecting table. He was just as experienced in the use of the gleaming, sterilized equipment as Noosa had been. The Puffball offered no resistance as he strapped it in place, continuing its amiable examination of its immediate surroundings with both eyes and snout.

A single injection ought to put it under, Ramirez mused. Then he would get to work. With the aid of computer-generated guidelines, he drew a dose of a lethal soporific and loaded the injector. It would kill quickly and painlessly. The Puffball would slip quietly into a permanent sleep, never knowing it had been affected. The autoscalpel hummed nearby, ready to probe and invade, to expose and reveal.

Stroking the thick gray fur, Ramirez pressed the tip of the injector against the creature's approximate anterior region. He felt no emotion whatsoever. According to all accounts and observations, there were plenty of Puffballs. One would not be missed. In the course of his professional career he'd performed hundreds of operations like this on as many different creatures, and while he was more alert than usual, he really expected nothing untoward to result.

The Puffball gave no indication anything was happening to it. Ramirez thumbed the trigger. Under his stroking left hand the specimen abruptly went rigid.

Then it went crazy.

Or maybe it was Ramirez who went crazy. That's what it felt like.

The Puffball's fur rippled wildly as each soft, flexible hair swelled and stiffened into a needle-sharp spine. Both bright red eyes ballooned to ten times their normal size. The flexible snout retracted into the rotund body, as did the four legs. Even as a startled Ramirez was dropping the injector and withdrawing his hands, the Puffball detonated.

Perhaps two seconds had passed.

It only gave the appearance of exploding. What actually happened was that no less than a quarter of the now modified hairs were blown off the epidermis, propelled by air pressure compressed within the spherical body. Several stuck in the ceiling, then relaxed and drifted down to the floor. Others punctured plastic vials or bounced off cages and habitats.

The ecosuit turned most of them. A few penetrated partially, only to lose their rigidity and hang limp from the fabric. One struck the seam where glove met wrist. He felt the point scrape his skin and penetrate. It was no more than a pinprick.

The flesh just back of the little finger on his left hand went numb.

Gaping through the suit's faceplate, he stumbled backward. There was no pain. He could envision his hand, then his arm, turning fiery red like Noosa's shoulder. The numbness spread with incredible rapidity up to his elbow and down to the tips of his fingers. As neuromuscular control was lost, his left arm slumped at his side.

Ripping with his right hand at the emergency release on his neck he tore off the hood and flung it aside. A glance revealed that the Puffball had snapped its restraints and vanished from the workbench. He looked around wildly, wondering how quickly it could rearm and if it would be inclined to pursue its would-be vivisector.

Careful to keep his distance, he located it beneath the bench, huddled up against the wall and respirating hard. Its fur had relaxed again and in that dense mat the missing hairs were not noticeable. He wondered how many times it could fire.

Fascinating defense mechanism, he mused drunkenly. But the hairs hadn't merely stiffened; they'd changed. So had the bulbous red eyes. He was sure of it. This portended even more than it revealed.

He bumped up against a shelf, sending vials and containers crashing to the ground. Fashioned of unbreakable polymers, they didn't shatter, but the seals on several cracked and their contents leaked out onto the smooth, sterile floor. His good hand fumbled for a first-aid kit. That much he knew how to use, if he could only find one of the damn things. His vision was blurring and the numbness had advanced as high as his shoulder. He knew what would happen if it reached his lungs or heart. Knew because that's what had happened to Cody Noosa.

Oddly, what bothered him was not the very real possibility of dying, but the fact that there was no one present to observe his passing.

His fingers wrapped around the familiar kit. With difficulty he popped the seal and fumbled at the contents. Blinking tears from his watering eyes, he struggled to read the labels on the self-contained injectors. He found that he was starting to shiver, just as Noosa had done.

No time to read any more. No time to see if one ampule contradicted another. Tearing the wrapper from one of the compact tubes with his teeth, he jabbed the business end against the side of his neck. Pressure surged through him.

He repeated the action with a second tube, jamming it against his left cheek. He considered emptying a third, but by that time he was shaking so badly he couldn't hold the tube.

Nor could he make it to the chair by the door. As he lay shivering and shaking on the floor, his head lolled to the right. Something moved at the edge of his vision.

It was the Puffball, its eyes shrunken back to normal, its four little legs motivating the corpulent fuzzy body in his direction.

Whimpering, he tried to roll onto his belly so he could try and crawl, but all he could do was lie there and shake. The Puffball drew close, its manner curious. The flexible snout investigated his suited shoulder, then his exposed neck, drawing back from the sweat that had broken out on his face.

It squeaked softly, pivoted, and ambled off. Ramirez would have screamed except that his vocal cords seemed to be paralyzed.

"Maybe we should look in on Stewart." O'Sandringham pulled away from Stevens.

"Why? Stew likes his solitude. So do I." He tried to drag her back.

She resisted. "We're really supposed to check in with one another periodically. It's been quite a while."

"Don't worry about Stew." Stevens's fingers marched.

She squirmed. "I'd feel better, Kauri." They were lying in one of the hammocks that had been set up outside the main entrance to the camp. Off in the distance Faery Lights, as they called the tiny flying creatures, swarmed in the heat of day above the reflective mass of the lander.

He sighed and rolled smoothly out of the hammock. "Anything to make you feel better, darlin'." Naked, he extracted his com unit from the duty belt encircling his pants and flicked it to live.

"Ramirez, it's check-in time." There was no response. "Stew, you there?" The tiny speaker's thin electronic hiss mocked his efforts.

Alert but not yet worried, the mate smiled reassuringly at O'Sandringham, who was now sitting up in the hammock, her legs dangling over the side. "C'mon, Stew, old boy," he murmured into the com's pickup. "If you're asleep, wake up. If you're not, talk to me." There was still no reply.

Thoroughly irritated, he shut down the com. "Probably left it by his bed, or he's in the can and doesn't want to be disturbed."

O'Sandringham shook her head. "That wouldn't bother Stewart. He'd be happy to talk to you while defecating. Something's not right." She slid out of the hammock and picked up her jumpsuit.

Stevens looked resigned. "All right, we'll go check on the stupid mucker. I suppose his unit could be malfunctioning. Checking on it'll give me a chance to pretend I'm doing *something* useful around here."

She sealed her suit and reached over to tousle his hair. "Kauri, you know I'd pine away if you weren't around to keep me posted."

He had to grin. "Three bad puns in one line. Keeping my company's improved the hell out of your disposition, Bee-el."

A quick check revealed that Ramirez wasn't in his private cubicle. Nor was he in the mess, engaged in his favorite pastime of raiding the food stores.

"Don't tell me he's working." O'Sandringham evinced mock disbelief. "Out in the field you can't slow him down, but he's not big on laboratory methodology."

"I think you underestimate him there, Bee-el." Stevens led the way down a connecting corridor. "Stew's just a hyperactive type, that's all. From what I've seen, you have to sit still to do proper lab work, and he's not a sitter. He just has a lot of energy."

"Yeah, right." O'Sandringham absently flipped the seal on the barrier to the next chamber.

Stevens let out a moan even before the door had finished opening. "Oh, man." Rushing forward, he practically slid on his knees up to the prone figure. His fingers felt briefly of the other man's body. Then he was tearing at the ecosuit.

"Give me a hand, Bee-el!"

"What do you think I'm trying to do?" She was already working at the leg seals. "What happened to him?"

"I don't know. Except for the doffed hood, his suit looks intact. He's still alive."

"How alive?" she asked tersely. "Look, he's trying to say something!"

The mate bent forward and positioned his ear a couple of centimeters above Ramirez's lips. They moved, but nothing audible issued forth. Stevens rose.

"He can't talk. He's trying to, but he can't make sounds."

"Paralysis." O'Sandringham leaned back as she yanked on the pair of integral boots. The cracked ecosuit began to slide off Ramirez's slim form. "Just like Noosa."

Stevens moved to help, and together they freed the body from its fabric container. As the mate folded the ecosuit and carefully placed it to one side, O'Sandringham recovered the two empty injectors and held them up to the light.

"Both empty." She glanced back down at Ramirez with new respect. "He had enough sense to do this much, anyway." She looked nervously around the dome. Everything looked normal. Just as it had when Noosa died.

"He can tell us what happened," Stevens was saying.

"If he lives. Let's try to get him off the floor."

"Hang on. There's a foldup near the other door."

The mate rushed to set up the cot. Together they managed to wrestle Ramirez onto it. O'Sandringham vanished back the way they'd come, to reappear in a couple of minutes with a pillow and a light blanket.

Ramirez was still shivering, but there was none of the convulsive trembling that had afflicted Noosa immediately prior to his passing. Stevens chose to take it as a hopeful sign. It was the only one.

"I don't know what else to do for him." Her frustration was evident. "I'm not trained for this. Favrile should be here."

"What did he manage to get into himself before he went down?" An anguished Stevens studied the face of their semi-comatose colleague.

"Eco-morphine, antibiotics, antihistamines, white cell booster, quartered adrenaline: a real grab-bag. I'm sure he didn't have time to diagnose himself." She put a hand on Ramirez's arm. "I don't know that we could've done any better if we'd been here. You need to buzz Favrile and the others, tell them what's happened."

He nodded and rose. "And Simna."

"Jack? Why him?"

"Because he seems to know something about everything." He paused with his com out and activated. "I know you don't much like that aspect of him."

"I didn't say that. He just gets on my nerves sometimes. Always watching everything and everybody."

"Funny. I thought that's what a good scientist out in the field was supposed to do."

"You're supposed to study what's in the field, not your companions."

"No? If he'd been here studying Stew, maybe he wouldn't be lying on his back paralyzed and half dead." He thumbed the autovoice pickup. "I hope to hell they're not all out working."

XI

The village had been decorated with vegetable-dyed hangings and streamers stripped from various cooperative plants. Some of the scarce white and yellow native flowers brightened windows, while fruits and berries framed individual entrances.

East of the compound a space some twenty meters square had been cleared of rocks and debris, its surface packed hard by the ceremonial pounding of bare adolescent feet. Bowls and trays piled high with the harvest of forest and garden, shore and sea, were assembled on the village side of the clearing. A substantial bonfire was prepared in the center, ready for subsequent lighting.

All this, Prentice thought, to greet those who had murdered their friends and kin. Next time it would no doubt be the turn of the Quwanga to put on the feast, after the attacking Pendju had slain a suitable number of their relatives. He saw Mahd'ji and Silpa working at the preparations as hard as anyone else. Mahd'ji, whose mate had been slain by the Quwanga.

Someday all this would make sense, he knew. Someday when specialists had time enough to study the Xicans at length and more fully interpret their culture. Someday. But just then, at that moment, Prentice did not understand.

The children and prepubescents had painted their faces with red and green dye, while their older siblings put on special clothing. Everything possible was being done to honor their adversaries. Under the circumstances the least he and his companions could do, Prentice mused, was remain suitably neutral.

Noon became evening as the sun settled into a turquoise sea, bidding the land farewell with a last gust of ocean-cooled air. Prentice welcomed the capricious breeze, hoping it would linger. As usual, it did not, and before long he was once more reduced to dependence on the inadequate evaporative efforts of his thermosensitive shorts and vest.

Though they had no dresswear, he and his companions had donned clean jumpsuits or shorts out of respect for their Pendju hosts. As always, Lejardin managed to look unconsciously spectacular amidst the utterly ordinary. He doubted the Pendju or the Quwanga would appreciate her efforts, but her male colleagues certainly did.

As it began to grow dark, the entire population lined up on the village side of the clearing; adults and seniors in front, adolescents and children in back striving to peer through the surging mass of their parents. Silpa stepped forward and with great dignity touched a flaming torch to the carefully constructed pile of dried wood and leaves. It ignited instantly, lighting up both the assembly and the silent forest.

The heaping bowls and trays of food were brought forward and placed on the far side of the blaze. When the last villager had returned to the line, definite movement could be discerned among distant trees. Prentice and his colleagues tensed.

They might as well have relaxed. The arrival of the Quwanga was very much an anticlimax, given the elaborate buildup executed by their eager hosts. In shape, coloration, and size they were identical to the Pendju. None sported fangs or bloodthirsty leers. Save for some minor differences in design and pattern, their attire might as well have been lifted directly from Jesh'ku's loom.

If they mixed freely, Prentice found himself thinking, it would be next to impossible to tell Pendju from Quwanga.

There were no children among them, he noted. Perhaps the journey from the Quwanga village entailed dangers the adults did not wish to expose their offspring to, or maybe in spite of everything he had been told the Quwanga feared possible reprisals on the part of their hereditary enemy.

There were no very young children or infants present among the assembled Pendju either. They would be in the nursery, attended to by designated elders. The nursery was the one part of the village the Pendju had not allowed their human visitors to see. In that they had been very insistent. With so much else to see and study, Prentice and his companions were hardly about to force the issue.

As Boutu . . . poor, lamented Boutu . . . had once explained in response to their queries, infants were not presented to the rest of the community until they reached a certain stage of development, until they had learned how to make themselves presentable in society. Prentice fully intended to have a look at the nursery, but it would have to be under the right circumstances. He wasn't about to risk the excellent relationship they had established with the Pendju by violating what seemed to be their one formal taboo. The nursery could wait its turn.

He doubted it would turn out to be anything special. Elders caring for young until they were old enough to appear in public. Several primitive human tribes had once tended to their offspring in very similar fashion.

At the moment he was much more concerned with and involved in the interaction between the Pendju and the Quwanga. His recorder, like those of his colleagues, hummed away, noting every detail of the formal proceedings.

The Quwanga emerged from the forest by twos, with no segregation by gender. They alternated turning to left and right, forming a line opposite the Pendju on the wooded side of the crackling bonfire. When all had finally assembled, their nominal leader, an impressive-looking male wearing an elaborate headdress fashioned of polished *c'soufa* shell that trailed down the back of his long hair, stepped forward.

He was met by Troumo, who had the equivalent status of a respected elder. The Pendju and presumably also the Quwanga did not have formal chiefs. Decisions within the tribe were made by a vote of the majority, with certain respected individuals carrying additional weight but with no one possessing anything like a veto power.

As he watched the two elders converse, Prentice was struck by their solemn aspect and imposing appearance. The Xicans seemed not to age gradually, but to jump directly from adolescence to young adulthood, thence to middle age, and lastly to seniorhood. There were no seam-visaged middle-aged, no youthful-looking elders. Transitions between the generations were much more abrupt than in humans. Someone had once told him Balinese women aged in similar fashion. He'd thought it a joke, never having been to Bali. Only later had he learned the reality of what was a striking human phenomenon.

Both elders were smiling now; those same petite, shy smiles that had proven so charming to the explorers. They exchanged an odd sort of handshake, or rather, armshake. The gesture reminded Prentice of snakes mating. The two males walked three times slowly around each other, then turned toward their respective, respectful peoples and waved. This was the signal for both sides to break out in enthusiastic cheers.

As near as Prentice could tell, there was no difference in language, no variations in dialect, between the tribes.

Members of both groups rushed to embrace one another. At the appropriate time they would try their best to massacre those they were presently hugging. But not this night.

Cheeks rubbed against cheeks and there was much casual, affectionate touching. It was all one big, happy family, and as baffling as ever.

Hands began to clap and primitive musical instruments were brought forth. Like the Pendju, the Quwanga made use of wood flutes, drums, and your basic primitive percussion: sticks, shells, and stones knocked together. There were no stringed instruments. Individuals were laughing and chanting as a grand communal dance blossomed around the flames.

Then a pair of Pendju were pulling him forward, the dancing blaze reflected in their capacious eyes, laughingly urging him to join in, to participate. He protested weakly: brazen public displays were not his forte.

Off to one side he saw the Carnavons displaying surprising vigor as they demonstrated several styles of human dance to the delight of the natives. A grinning Theodore Halstead lumbered about surrounded by slimmer Xicans while Lejardin's hair flew as Simna whirled her around the bonfire. The night had become a colorful, chaotic mass of swirling shapes, of flying hair and huge, multihued eyes, of tinkling-voiced aliens, throbbing music, and deep-throated human laughter.

His natural reticence fell away and he allowed himself to be drawn into the spirit of the celebration. Still running, his recorder bounced against his belt. The account it would make from now on would be exhilarating but difficult to study.

Someone pushed him toward the fire and he stumbled as he rollicked past. A pair of Quwanga . . . Pendju? . . . became his satellites, spinning and darting around him.

Maybe this was the more civilized way of conducting warfare, he told himself. Better a Jewish wake than a Greek tragedy.

For a while nowhere to be seen, the Carnavons reappeared soon thereafter, hauling with them a portion of the expedition's modest liquor supply. At their urging everyone, even the teetotaling Simna, was induced to have a sip. Or two. Prentice accepted his in the midst of a wild spin with Lejardin. As was often the case he couldn't tell whether she was laughing with him or at him. Her fingers slipped from his as she darted away to pirouette with Simna The two of them exchanged whispers before parting to link up with new Xican partners.

It was a shame the others couldn't be present, he reflected. O'Sandringham, Stevens, and Ramirez were stuck looking after Base Camp. He could already envision their complaints when they saw the recordings. They would not accept that had all been conducted in the spirit of serious scientific inquiry.

Another pair of bright-eyed Xicans spun him around, and for once he managed to forget about colleagues both present and absent.

Having quietly preceded the Carnavons both in thought and presence to the hut that contained their food supplies, Lastwell had appropriated for himself and subsequently consumed a disproportionate quantity of alcoholic spirits, with the result that his own were raised considerably.

He was standing, or rather swaying, off to one side in the company of an agreeable tree, observing the proceedings, when a blue-green-haired and unusually tall Quwanga maiden prodded him from behind the supportive growth. He couldn't tell if she was giggling at him or if his brain was fizzing, but he gave congenial chase with a sort of brontosaurian grace.

Her easy avoidance of his grasp made him only more determined to catch up with her. They bounced from tree to bush to tree, drifting away from the celebration and further back into the woods.

"That's enough tag-you're-it for me, miss two-thumbs. You've damn well tired me out." Wheezing deeply, he halted and took a healthy swig from the nearly empty plastic specimen bottle slung at his hip. He wiped his lips with the back of his hand. "This ain't my style." Tottering on his axis, he turned to gaze back through the trees toward the now distant fire and celebration.

She edged out from behind a shave-barked *kingu'a*. *"Ch'molta? Shi'mou taiy?"*

"Yeah, right." Lastwell's knowledge of the language had lagged behind that of his more academically inclined companions.

He felt a cool hand on his arm and jerked around sharply. "What are you up to, owl-eyes? I don't know what you're sayin', see?"

"Bsi asuch'ad." Her hands rose to the fabric ties at her shoulders, the fingers moving imperceptibly. As he stared, the loose garment fell to the ground. In the dim light of Xica's single large moon her skin had a lustrous sheen, as if her flesh had been pearlized. Fine china, it reminded him of.

She advanced slowly and deliberately toward him, her gaze deep and impenetrable, the tiny mouth parted, flat nostrils not moving at all. Unable to decide whether to run, call out, or crack another bad joke, he just stood and gawked. Delicate alien fingers encountered his chest and inched upward.

"Buddha almighty on a crutch," he muttered. "Is this part of the goddamn ceremony?" He belched softly.

"Milach." In a gesture that transcended species, she gently placed both fingers against his lips to still them.

Franklin Lastwell, though designated captain, had a healthy interest in education and exploration. Much more a creature of emotion and action than his learned companions, he was far more likely than any of them to react straightforwardly to a new situation than to step back and assess. The liquor he had consumed suppressed his analytical inclinations further still.

Months of inactivity spent in deepsleep coupled with long hours of unexciting, largely repetitive work coupled with too many idle days spent suffering in the Xican heat led him perhaps inevitably not to forthrightly reject the thought of coupling. There was very little Lastwell feared. Though not a particularly imaginative man, he was resourceful.

If he squinted hard at the tall humanoid within his grasp (and there the alcohol supplied aid unbidden), the expansive eyes shrank, the nose bulged, the mouth widened. The vision of long, flowing, straight hair required no mental adjustment, and the ears were not readily visible no matter what their shape. The result was a passably human face, one some might even consider attractive.

As for the rest, well, it was almost too human. He'd overheard the scientists speak often of something called convergent evolution. Smug smart-asses, the lot of 'em. Why shouldn't the Xicans be humanoid? Wasn't it a damn successful shape? And why should he be intimidated by a dumb native? The Pendju might fight among themselves, but they were anything but intimidating to a competent human.

Once more he felt those four-digited hands moving across his body, divesting him of his rumpled shirt and shorts. He didn't help, but neither did he resist. While she worked he finished the last of his bottle, pouting at the resultant cylindrical void. It matched the one growing in his mind as she drew him down with her.

"This is what you want, isn't it?"

Was that Xican she was speaking? He laughed softly to himself. Apparently he'd picked up more words than he'd realized. Bravo for me, he mused gaseously. Or maybe it *was* English. Before he'd been killed, wily Boutu had mastered several complete phrases, and Mahd'ji was taking occasional lessons from that know-it-all Simna. The female's accent was breathy but not unpleasant.

Supple hands maneuvered as she eased on top of him. Her movements were as lissome as those of a dancer, her skin soft as suede. A social experiment, that prissy Prentice

would call it. Lastwell chuckled, well pleased with himself.
They wanted research? He'd show them some research, by
God he would! Let them quantify *this*.

She was moving against him, and he was inside her, and
it all felt astonishingly normal. No, better than normal. Distant alien music and integrated laughter filled his head with
a sensual hum. Reaching up, he put his hands on breasts incontrovertibly mammalian. The nipples hardened immediately. He sniggered at the stars.

"Why are you laughing?" she asked wonderingly. "Your
laughter is so strange."

"You people have a giggle now and then, too."

"Yes, though we sound different from you. But we practice, and we are getting better."

Now that was an odd thing to say, wasn't it? Getting better—at laughter? What the hell did that mean? He made no
effort to hang onto the thought. Too many other sensations
were competing for his attention and demanding of his time.

"Your skin is so perfect," he mumbled contentedly.

"Does it displease you?"

"Not hardly. It's just hard to grip."

The tiny mouth formed an "O" of amusement in the
moonlight. "You seem to be doing quite well."

"I'm a persistent kind of guy." If that poffy Prentice was
here now, he thought, the expedition leader's eyes would
be as wide as a Xican's. Lejardin would either be disgusted
or blush to the tips of her pretty toes, the Carnavons would
find the circumstances alternately outrageous and amusing,
and Simna . . . he didn't know how Simna would react. The
generalist was impossible to figure.

Screw 'em all. This beat hell out of prancing around the
campfire with a lot of bulgy-eyed, rubber-limbed tribesfolk.

"Do you like it when I do this?" she asked inquisitively.

"Oh, yeah, baby. That's just . . . fine."

"I am not an infant." Her tone turned serious. "I am fully mature."

"Hey, you don't have to persuade me. I'm already convinced." He relaxed, letting her do most of the work. "You know, you folks look pretty good with your clothes off, and I ain't just saying that because I've been away from home a long time."

"Then you find my physical appearance pleasing?" There was an earnestness, an intensity to the seemingly casual inquiry that penetrated the fog that had enveloped his brain.

"Are you kidding? It's just that . . ." He didn't finish the thought.

"That what?" Her movements slowed.

"No, no. Don't stop doing that, luv." Motion resumed and his smile returned. "It's nothin', nothing really at all." He fondled her chest. "I was just thinking that maybe these could be a little bigger, is all. And your hips could be a tad wider. Not that there's anything wrong with either of 'em, you understand. It's just that ol' Cap'n Lastwell's tastes run to the more ample than those of the average chap, if you follow my meaning."

"You mean, like this?" She responded without hesitation.

Her breasts seemed to enlarge beneath his fingers and her hips to spread and flatten. His smile did not vanish, but it was joined by a querulousness in his eyes and an uncertainty within his mind that had not been there previously.

This was odd, he thought. More than odd. It wasn't right. Having asked, he had received. His fingers shifted, experimentally now. No, the permutation was definitely not a consequence of stuporous perception.

"How . . . how did you do that?" His stomach was suddenly churning, no doubt from all the excitement and drink. Something was wrong, very wrong. But it didn't *feel* wrong. It felt wonderful. And pretty soon now, he knew, it was going to feel even better.

"It was what you wanted." Her eyes glowed and her voice reassured him. Or maybe it was the other way around, he mused languidly. "I enjoy giving you what you want."

"You're sure doing that, sweet thing." He started to push against her, feeling the pressure begin to intensify and rise.

"I can tell that I am pleasing you. Would you like anything else to be different about me?"

"Well, now that you mention it . . ." Something in the back of his mind was trying to get the attention of the rest of it. Something bright and insistent, like a high-intensity light. A warning light. But it was far off and ignorable.

"I was just wondering what you look like all the time."

"Like this," she told him.

"No. You just changed. Not a lot, but you changed."

"You wanted me to change."

"But you can't do that just because somebody asks you to. It doesn't make sense. It ain't right."

"I want to please you. We try always to please our teachers." Her voice quickened. "I want to please you."

"You are, you are." He clenched his teeth, and the skin on his face tightened. Soon now, he thought. He planned to make it last longer, but he was only human. Of course, his partner wasn't. He suppressed the laugh. That could come later.

"Would you," she said uncertainly, breathing hard and riding fast, "really like to see me as I am?"

"We all like to see ourselves as we really are," he assured her. "You're seein' me as I really am."

"I know. I'm not sure . . ."

"Go on." He let out a mad laugh he could no longer repress. "Is this the real you? Show me the real you, baby. Come on, show it to me, show it to me. *Now!*"

She complied.

XII

Breathing hard, Lejardin stopped dead in her gyrations to stare into the forest. The scream came again. It was hard to hear above all the singing and chanting, the laughter and the music. Off to her left the Carnavons were demonstrating some surprisingly contemporary undulations. Prentice had shed his inhibitions along with his reluctance and was hopping madly about in the company of several delighted natives.

With its usual disquieting silence, a calm figure materialized at her side. "I heard it, too." Simna was eyeing the shadowed trees. "It sounded like Frank."

The scream did not come again. He took her hand and pulled her forward. "The majority of the big animals here are nocturnal. If Frank stumbled into something like a nest of Drill Worms or one of the larger predators he's liable to need help, and fast."

"What can we do if he has?" She hurried to keep pace with him. "Yell and wave?"

He lifted the hem of his long, armless shirt to reveal the cutter clipped to his belt. Her brows lifted.

"You brought a weapon to the celebration?"

"I only take it off to sleep, and then it's always within arm's reach. I admire everything we've found on Xica, and I trust none of it."

"What about us?" she inquired sarcastically as they pushed into the trees. In the near darkness she couldn't see his reaction.

"I trust everyone. Most of the time."

"Truly?"

"I told you before we made landfall here, Favrile. I always tell the truth. It gets me in more trouble than anything else I do." He turned away from her and raised his voice. "Frank? Frank, are you out there?"

"Are you all right, Captain Lastwell?" She found herself searching the brush as they slowed. "It's me, Frank. Favrile."

"Over this way." Simna turned to his right, beckoning for her to follow.

Groaning came from the undergrowth. She thought it a creepy mixture of fear and self-pity. Simna activated a light and played it over the brush. As not one but two forms were fixed in the bright beam, he reached with his free hand for the cutter. The light dipped briefly, and when he repositioned it only the nude form of Lastwell could be seen, sitting up against a tree with his thick arms crossed tightly over his chest. A quick search of the surrounding undergrowth revealed only trees and bushes, vines and clumps of the ever-present *Haukik*.

An empty plastic specimen bottle lay on the ground nearby. Simna picked it up and caught the odor without having to bring it close. "Having your own private party, Frank?"

Silent and distant, Lastwell didn't respond. Occasionally he'd mutter something unintelligible and shake his head violently, like a dog with a foxtail up its ear.

Ignoring his nakedness, Lejardin bent close to him and spoke encouragingly. "Captain Lastwell? Frank? Can you talk? Can you tell us what's wrong?"

"Here's his clothes." As he nudged the pile with his foot,

the scientist took another whiff of the bottle. He didn't drink, didn't smoke any stimulants, didn't take any chemical boosters. If not for his way with words, he would have been relentlessly boring. If he had any unusual vices he kept them carefully under wraps. At one moment full of laughter and camaraderie, the next would see him closed as a tomb.

Lastwell, on the other hand, hid nothing.

"Where is she?" He blinked repeatedly, as if his eyes were having difficulty focusing.

"She?" Still crouched over, Lejardin looked helplessly at Simna.

The other scientist flashed his light into the trees. Behind them, the sounds of high celebration drowned any nocturnal animal peepings.

"There's no one here, Frank." He moved to place a comforting hand on the other man's shoulder. "What happened here? Are you all right?" Lastwell muttered something unintelligible.

"D.T.'s?" Lejardin nodded at the empty specimen bottle.

Lastwell spoke up unexpectedly. "Wish that were all it were. Plain old D.T.'s. Wish that's all I saw. Wish that's all that I . . ." With unexpected suddenness he rose, threw his arms around Simna, and began to bawl relentlessly. Not knowing what else to do, Simna allowed himself to remain in the captain's grasp.

Gradually the sobbing died down, at which point Lastwell became angry. Ignoring them both, he dropped his head and began searching the undergrowth.

"My clothes, goddamnit. Where're m' stinkin' clothes?"

"Over there, Frank." Lejardin was careful to stay out of his way.

He nodded appreciatively and started toward them. Three steps saw him staggering. A fourth and he collapsed, landing hard on his right side. With a moan he rolled onto his belly and began crawling in the general direction of his shirt.

"Just stay put, Frank. I'll get them for you." Moving to gather up the captain's clothing, Simna noticed a peculiar odor and hesitated. When a touch of shirt and pants revealed nothing abnormal he gingerly picked up the rumpled attire. He'd hardly finished collecting everything when Lastwell unceremoniously snatched them out of his hands. Simna backed off, saying nothing. Muttering constantly to himself while using a tree trunk for support, Lastwell proceeded with some difficulty to dress himself.

"Got to be around here someplace," he was mumbling. "She-thing, Xica-she, got to be around. Will find her. Will find the bitch-thing."

"Frank, you're not making any sense." Lejardin stepped in front of him. "Tell us what happened."

"Nothing. Nothin' happened. Lemme alone." Fumbling with his waist fastener, he staggered and stumbled off in the direction of the celebration.

Lejardin and Simna watched him go. "Maybe he'll tell Stevens. They talk a lot when none of the rest of us are around," Simna murmured.

She frowned at him. "If it's when we're not around, how do you know they talk?"

"I'm a good listener. I'm around when people don't think I'm around."

"Too bad you weren't around just now." She indicated the small clearing where they'd found Lastwell.

"That's a real dangerous talent to have, sonny-boy. It could get you killed."

At first Simna thought the warning might have come from Stevens, but the figure that emerged from the depths of the forest was too tall to be the mate. Too tall, and too broad to be Cedric Carnavon. Slightly bowed, the venerable frame was thickly muscled. Long gray hair that had receded well back from the high forehead spilled in thick curls past the broad shoulders, while a tangled gray beard obscured the outer realms of the face.

He wore an intricately decorated Xican poncho of Quwanga design and wider than usual sandals to accommodate the extra toe. Breathtakingly detailed carvings decorated his wooden staff from top to bottom. It had been burnished to a high luster. A thick woven headband kept his long hair out of his eyes. Picked out by the flashlight, piercing blue eyes seemed to penetrate Simna's very soul. He took a reflexive step backward, then held his ground.

"By gods, you're afraid of me." The figure chuckled heartily. Nothing senile or feeble about that laugh, Simna thought. It expressed unimaginable joy, sheer delight in being alive. Its progenitor terminated it with unexpected sharpness, exposing as he did so the thin edge of insanity. He gestured past them, after Lastwell.

"I saw what he did."

"And what did he do?" Lejardin pressed the newcomer.

His eyes twinkled as he regarded her. "By my mind and places, missy, aren't you some piece of work? Why don't you ask him?" He chuckled again.

"We did," explained Simna coolly, "but he wouldn't tell us."

"Then why should I? I don't mind other people's business. I gave that up when I came here. Other people's businesses were always in a mess, and they were always coming to me to fix it for them. So I got good and sick of it and came here, to this place of peace." He made a sweeping gesture with an arm strong enough to floor both of them.

"Then you lot arrived." He lowered his voice. "I suppose I was naive to think it would go otherwise. Xica's too prominent in the catalog to be ignored for long. But I thought, I'd hoped, to have twenty or thirty years here to myself. Then I'd be worm-food and it wouldn't matter." He straightened.

"Well, you're here now. And getting along well with the locals, too. Except for him." He indicated the path Lastwell had taken.

"We're scientists," Simna told him.

"Not that one." The creature continued to stare in the direction the captain had taken. "I know his type. I've dealt with hundreds of 'em. See, I've been watching you, watching you all." He chortled softly. "Oh, yes, executing my own observations, I should say."

"We haven't seen you before now." Simna was utterly fascinated. What and who was this . . . person?

"Didn't want to be seen, boy."

"I'm no boy." Quiet challenge was implicit in Simna's reply.

"You are to me, sonny. So's that unhappy fella you found here. You're all kids to me." He leered openly as he studied Lejardin. "Except maybe you, missy. You're sure no girl."

She contemplated the impossible arrival calmly. Having dealt with those kinds of comments all her life, Simna knew, she was unlikely to be rattled by something that came stumbling and prattling out of a Xican forest.

"You've got five toes and five fingers," Simna pointed out matter-of-factly. "Also a beard. None of the Xican males have beards."

The figure leaned on its remarkable staff. "Go on." The voice was very deep. "You're a scientist, all right. Can't slip anything past you."

"You're not Xican," Lejardin declared firmly, "but you *can't* be human."

"Missy, I wish most fervently I could agree with you. Unfortunately, that is what I am." The outlandish figure hesitated, as if a large chunk of memory had suddenly gone missing. A blink seemed to signify its return. "I wonder what your bibulous friend would think of me. Probably be convinced that I'm Xican."

"Obviously you're not," avowed Lejardin.

He grinned at her. "Oh, so how it's obvious, is it? Learned a lot since you've been here, have you?" She bristled at his tone but didn't reply. "I'm human, all right. Believe me, if I could change that I would. Would've done so a long time ago." Eyes flashed in the glow from Simna's light, perhaps hinting of madness, perhaps of something else.

"If you're human," she responded, "you must have a name."

"Must I?" He shook his head sadly. "You're so positive, so sure of yourselves. Myself, I've done with names. Swore that when I came here. Done with names and mankind both. But since my existence is obviously a strain on you, I will be gracious and not stress you further. You may call me Conc. Old Conc, if you will, since I currently endure on the fallow side of the antediluvian." He chortled wildly to himself. "Not that I'm looking forward to dying, although now that you've shown up my previous indifference to the matter may change."

There was something concealed in this old man, Simna decided. A repressed power that didn't match up with the pose of cackling, half-mad geezer. Whoever he was and however he'd come to be on Xica, he bore close watching.

"That's quite a piece of carving." Lejardin indicated the old man's staff.

He nodded as he glanced at the intricately sculpted wood. "Thanks. Something I always wanted to master, but never had the time to practice. Here I have all the time I want."

"I thought one of the Xicans might have done it," Simna told him.

Instead of being offended, Old Conc cackled delightedly. "A Xican? Carved this? You ain't been payin' attention, boy."

Simna stiffened. "I don't see why that would be an unreasonable assumption. Their attire is elaborately decorated, and their mastery of pottery suggests the ability to work wood as well."

" 'Their mastery.' " The old man snorted derisively. "Boy, when I found 'em these folks were dumber than dirt. Hidin' in the bushes, running from the smallest predators, living off what they could grub from the soil and snatch from the trees. How do you think they developed their skills?"

"Beginning with primitive tribal association," Simna began, "they would naturally proceed on to . . ."

"Naturally my ass!" Old Conc gleefully interrupted the younger man. "They were loam toilers and nothing more until I got here. *I* organized 'em into tribes, showed them how to raise simple crops, fish the sea, and build basic shelters. They're quick learners, I'll give 'em that. Then I instructed them in the arts of weaving and pottery making, of weapons manufacture and hunting, of advanced hut design and food preparation." He shook his head, grinning all the while beneath the light of Simna's torch.

"These folks haven't evolved, boy. I evolved them. One day this'll become Xican civilization, but right now it's the civilization of Old Conc." He paused. "I see the doubt in your faces, right alongside the confusion. Don't tell me you haven't wondered about the similarities to primitive human societies, the comprehensible designs in the clothing and pottery, the shape and style of shelter construction. You may not be all that conscientious, but you're too observant to miss all that. There's too many clues." He chuckled. "I'm the missing part that binds the puzzle together."

Lejardin responded carefully. "If that's true, then all our toil here among the Pendju and the Quwanga is worthless. If there was no native society until you started working with them, then we've been spending weeks studying a bastard society. It's nothing more than your interpretation of what a primitive society should be. Everything from their social relationships to their manner of dress is a lie."

"You got it, girl."

"I don't believe you," Simna said abruptly.

"Hell, sonny, you don't have to take my word for it. Ask any Xican where they got the design for their poncho, or their spear, or their fishing net, and they'll tell you. They'll point you right straight back to me."

"Why didn't they tell us about you when we first made contact?" Lejardin asked.

"No reason to mention me," Old Conc told her. "Besides, they've come to think of all this"—he nodded in the direction of the ongoing celebration—"as their own. That's the way I want it to be. They've taken legitimate pride in their accomplishments, in raising themselves out of the muck. That's the way I want it. I don't want any credit from them. I'm trying to teach them to think for themselves, to be independent. I ain't going to be around forever."

"So we've wasted months probing what we thought was an alien civilization, only to find out it's nothing more than your hobby," Simna growled.

"Cheer up, sonny. You could've wasted years. Carried it all back to Earth and made prize fools of yourselves. You ought to be thankin' me for clueing you in on the way things really are. As you've probably learned by now, not everythin' here is quite what it seems." He winked. "Civilization's not the only thing I've given them."

Lejardin frowned. "There's more?"

"Oh, a bit, missy, a bit."

"For instance?"

Again that toothy grin beneath wide, staring eyes. "Why don't you ask your captain? I reckon he could tell you."

Simna glanced over his shoulder. "Frank doesn't seem to be in a talkative mood right now. So we still can't be sure whether you're telling us the truth or not."

Abruptly the old man straightened. It was a remarkable transformation. He seemed to grow broader and taller, not to mention thirty years younger. Even his voice deepened, the rattling cackle temporarily fled.

"When you take away a man's word, sonny-boy, there's not much left." His new tone was brusque to the point of being brutal. Simna blinked and took a wary step backwards. "My word is my rock." Then the old man seemed to shudder slightly and his voice cracked as he ogled Lejardin.

"You're a pretty little dollop of *schlagober,* missy. I'll bet you've heard that before."

Lejardin looked uncertain. "I'm not familiar with that particular terminology, but if I'm interpreting you correctly, I think you'd need a calculator to keep track of the times."

"You seem to have handled it well, as opposed to being well handled." He chuckled to himself.

"Lay off, whoever you are." Simna regained his confidence and the ground he'd given up.

The old man's expression changed to what could only be called a gentle glower. "Why? Missy here seems capable of taking care of herself." He moved nearer and Simna became acutely aware of those massive, if aged, arms. This self-proclaimed Old Conc was at least half crazy. What was the other half?

As quickly as it had gone, the old man's good humor returned. "I'd rather lay on, but I ain't one to rush things. I have my own amusements to keep me occupied. Not averse to sharing 'em, either, with them that might be interested. Your captain appears to have discovered that on his own. Interesting to see that humans haven't changed any. Not that I thought it would be anywise else."

Despite the difficulties inherent in acknowledging a painful reality, Lejardin had by now accepted the fact that the wild old man standing before them was indeed human, if a not particularly flattering representative of the species.

"How the hell did you get here?" she asked him point-blank. Behind them the music and chanting was beginning to fade as the celebration finally began to wind down. By this time the Carnavons and especially Prentice might be starting to wonder at her extended absence.

"Why, I were born here, missy." A gnarled finger reached out to chuck her playfully under the chin. She didn't flinch or retreat, maintaining her even stare. With a sigh he let his hand drop, gesturing with his staff. "We might as well join what's left of the party. I hate missing all the music. Lot of that originated with me too, you know. They didn't know anything about tempo or the crafting of musical instruments until I got 'em going on it. They're finally starting to devise some rhythms of their own, and it's fascinating to see what they come up with."

Having no choice, they accompanied him toward the village.

"What about this ritual intertribal combat, the raiding and kidnapping followed by celebratory potlatches?" Curiosity was rapidly overcoming Simna's wariness. "How much of that is native to the Xicans?"

"About as much as everything else," Old Conc told him, "which is to say, none of it. I got 'em started at fighting, too. They needed something besides me to give them a periodic mental push. So as soon as they'd developed enough to make weapons, I set them to this formalized fighting. It's good for them."

"It is what we do," Lejardin whispered, remembering the words of Boutu.

"Stimulation," the old man went on, "to keep the mental juices flowing."

"Then the only reason they fight and kill one another is because you told them it was good for them?" she asked.

"Naturally. Or unnaturally, as you prefer. Quite a jump for dirt-grubbers, I'd say." He halted. "Look, when I first arrived here and discovered they were intelligent, I was going to leave them alone. But the longer I watched the more I felt sorry for the ugly beggars, don't you know? Their enthusiasm and gratefulness for everything I taught them was heartrending.

"Now they've advanced to the point where if I were to die, they could take care of themselves, and even continue to make progress on their own. I've ignited the process of development here. They won't slip back into the muck."

Lejardin remained disapproving. "So because you felt sorry for them you've taught them war."

"Why not? It was one of the most useful things I had to teach them. It's civilized conflict, though. They only fight to a certain point and then they stop and reaffirm their Xicanhood. Beats hell out of the way we used to do it."

"It will never work," Simna declaimed confidently. "Sooner or later one group will try to dominate the other."

"Don't bet on it. Remember, they're not human. They accept what I tell them as gospel, without variation. They'll spread the benefits among those Xicans I haven't had time to help. Lift them out of the mud and teach them civilization. So that they'll have others to do ritual battle with. That's how I've set it up. That's how it'll continue. Conflict will stimulate them long after I'm gone."

"Not feeling well?" Simna inquired tactlessly.

The old man chuckled. "I feel fine, sonny. Immortality doesn't beckon quite yet. I sought out this world hoping to live out my last decades peacefully. Playing daddy-god to a race of berry-pickers wasn't quite what I had in mind, but to such uses we do all come. I didn't expect to find intelligent life here any more than you did. As soon as I made my little discovery, I knew others of my kind would be along eventually. I just didn't expect visitors so soon. I was hoping my Xicans would have at least another hundred years to develop on their own.

"By then all trace and memory of me would be gone, except maybe as some kind of transmogrified Ur-figure indistinguishable from the natives. Then the Xican civilization would be regarded as native, and accorded the respect they don't quite yet deserve. Instead you've gone and plonked yourselves down right in the middle of my timetable."

"If you wanted to keep your influence here a secret," Lejardin wondered aloud, "why did you choose to show yourself to us? We'd probably never have found you."

The faintly glazed look returned to Old Conc's face. "I ain't entirely sure. I think . . . I think maybe the sight of another human face, the sound of another human voice after all these years, was just too much for me to ignore." He looked away. "I'm not as strong and determined as I once was. Time and age mutes even the deepest anger. It's hard not to give in to certain temptations." He sounded confused. "At times I ain't sure why I do anything anymore."

"You still haven't told us how you came to be here," Lejardin reminded him. They had resumed their walk and were at the edge of the clearing now. Ted Halstead's unmistakable bulk was whirling among the natives, more relaxed than Lejardin had seen him at any time since revival from deepsleep.

At that moment Millie Carnavon caught sight of the three of them standing on the fringe. She waved and then came to an abrupt halt, her expression transforming almost comically as she sighted in on the old man standing between them. She immediately brought her husband to a stop, the two of them staring in disbelief.

"What difference does it make how I got here?" Old Conc tapped Simna on the shoulder with the tip of his staff. "I *am* here. Maybe some day I'll tell you the history of my travels, and maybe some day I won't."

As the Carnavons hurried over, a somber, anxious Prentice appeared from out of the darkness. He looked askance at the grinning oldster before directing his attention to his colleagues.

"I just heard from Bella-Lynn. There's been another accident at Base Camp." As he spoke he gestured nervously with his communicator. "It seems that Stewart decided to do a little research on his own."

"He would." Lejardin looked resigned. "What happened?"

"From what Bella-Lynn and Kauri could make out, Stew put on an ecosuit and tried to vivisect one of the Puffballs."

"Ah." Old Conc made it sound as if that explained everything.

Prentice's gaze narrowed as he fixed the old man with a penetrating stare. "Who are you?"

"Never mind that now," said Simna. "What about Stew?"

"He's alive. Apparently he managed to get enough universal antitoxin in him to counteract the effects of the Puffball's poison. Bella-Lynn and Kauri have been following up as best they can."

Millie Carnavon was murmuring to herself. "The Puffballs manufacture poison?"

Prentice glanced back at her. "Bella-Lynn said there were Puffball hairs all over the place, and that Stewart told them they transformed into needlelike spines."

Old Conc was nodding sagely. "That's the Puffballs, all right. I'll use your name for 'em and make it easier on you."

"What's he talking about?" Cedric Carnavon couldn't take his eyes off the old man. "Who *is* he? And what does he know about this?"

"Everything and nothing, apparently." Simna had reverted to his usual prosaic self. "He calls himself Old Conc. Favrile and I haven't decided if he's half mad or half sane. He won't tell us how he got here, but he seems human enough. Too human." He sighed. "According to him, there was no such thing as Xican society until he arrived here and fashioned one for them. If that's true, then we've been breaking our necks to record and study pure artifice."

"That's bullshit." Carnavon's reaction was understandably blunt.

"I don't think so," countered Lejardin. "What he's told us so far makes sense. He claims to be responsible for everything the Xicans are."

"That's right." The old man was smiling broadly, like an aged, muscular elf. "Hell, I even gave 'em their shape."

A sympathetic Millie Carnavon broke the shocked silence that ensued. "You are crazy."

"Am I?" Blue eyes locked on hers with unexpected intensity. "Don't tell me you didn't remark right from your first encounter on how humanlike the 'Xicans' are."

"Their faces are very different," she argued, "as is their apportionment of body hair. They have only four digits on each hand and foot, and two of them are opposable thumbs."

"Sure are." Old Conc was quick to concede the obvious. "I thought that would be more useful than five fingers and one thumb. As for human-type ears, never did much care for them myself, or big noses. Both get in your way. So I had them develop smaller ones. Oversize eyes for better vision, smaller mouths so they wouldn't make as much noise. I wanted them to appear both attractive and inoffensive to the human visitors I knew would be arrivin' here sooner or later. Call it defensive aesthetics. They're getting real good at the innocent, soulful look. With more time to practice, they'll get even better.

"I could've had them shape fangs and horns and pointed tails. Wouldn't that have been something to see when you first stepped off your ship?"

"This is crazy," Prentice was mumbling.

"No, sonny. This is Xica. You've been here long enough to wonder why you haven't seen any Pendju or Quwanga infants." When no one disputed this he continued. "That's because they're raised in a special private place both in the villages and off in the forest until they've learned their shape well enough to join the rest of society. Besides being appallingly grotesque, their natural form is unsuited to civilized life. Nobody cuddles babies here." He looked thoughtful. "Usually takes the kids about four years to get the humanoid body pattern down pat. That's why the youngsters and adolescents here look just like miniature versions of the adults."

"The young of many species are like that," Simna argued weakly.

"Are you trying to tell us that the Xicans are shape-changers?" Cedric Carnavon stared at the old man. By now Halstead had joined them. He stood behind Prentice, listening intently, the sweat pouring down his face.

Old Conc didn't hesitate. "Not just the Pendju and Quwanga. Every soft-skinned, mobile life form on Xica."

"There's no such thing as shape-changers," Prentice replied carefully. "It's a physical impossibility."

Lejardin was murmuring to herself. "Nothing here is what it seems."

"Impossible, is it?" The old man was not chuckling now. His manner was somber and disturbed. "Certain cephalo-pods on Earth possess pliant chromophores, epidermal cells that allow them to radically adjust their skin color and surface pattern. Except for internal organs and cartilaginous pseudo-skeletons, the solid parts of all the fauna on Xica I've been able to study are comprised of thixotropophores. In other words, physiologically they're quasi-thixotropic."

"What?" In such circumstances Lejardin turned instinctively to Simna, as did the others.

He replied carefully. "Thixotropy is a property possessed by certain solids that when subjected to physical stress become liquid or gelatinous. When the stress is removed they solidify again."

"Not bad, sonny-boy." The old man nodded appreciatively. "Excepting the hard-shelled arthropods, most Xican animals have the ability to alter from one shape to another. It's an instinctive, evolved metamorphosis. Carnivores can sprout longer legs, or bigger teeth, or sharper claws. Herbivores respond by adopting a defensive shape radically different from their usual inoffensive browsing forms."

Carnavon started. "The Puffball?"

Conc nodded. "Threaten it and it swells up, changes shape. The body hairs become poison-filled spines that the animal is capable of firing at a predator. I suspect gas pressure builds up in special sacs under the skin. Other apparently equally harmless critters have evolved comparable defense mechanisms, some of 'em so exotic you wouldn't believe."

Prentice was not satisfied. "That doesn't explain the Pendju and the Quwanga."

"No, it don't. See, they were so pitiful they never even evolved a decent defensive shape. Being intelligent, they can control the process to a certain extent, but because they didn't have a clue what to do, that ability didn't help them at all until I came along. I supplied them with a humanoid model. At first they had to try to copy me. Then I made modifications, gave them their distinctiveness, showed them how to customize differences among individuals. You don't want to know what they really looked like."

That prompted Simna to peer past the gathering, into the native assemblage. "Anybody seen Frank?" All responses were in the negative.

"He'll be all right," the old man assured them. "He got a glimpse of something he wasn't meant to see. Under trying circumstances, too." He laughed uproariously.

"So every soft-skinned creature on Xica has two shapes," Simna concluded.

"That's it. Makes for tricky taxonomy, sonny."

Lejardin framed her question carefully. "If I asked a Pendju to show me its natural form, would it do so?"

"Hard to say. I'm telling you, missy, you don't want to bother. They're much prettier to look at as they are now. They think so, too. I think you'd have a tough time getting a positive reply to that one. But far be it from me to try to stop you. The older they get, the easier it is for them to maintain these shapes. They're very proud of their accomplishments."

"Your accomplishments," Simna insisted glumly.

"Not me, sonny. Don't give the teacher all the credit. They're apt pupils."

"We've only your word for this." Prentice was diplomatic, but firm.

The old man shrugged. "Don't take my word for it. Ask the Xicans."

"What if you've ordered them to lie to us?"

He shook his head sadly. "I'm just a teacher here, not a god. They appreciate what I've done for them, but they have minds of their own. Again I say, ask your captain." He chuckled. "If you can find him."

More than their months of work among the Pendju had been rendered instantly invalid, Prentice knew. The presence on Xica of this remarkable and eccentric old man meant that the crew of the *James Cook* were not the first from Earth to set foot on the planet. It seemed that honor, too, was to be denied them. Their triumphs and achievements were shriveling before their eyes. The glory of discovery rightfully belonged to this half-mad old man.

Who would and could make the effort to travel, apparently alone, to a place as distant and unexplored as Xica? Whatever else he was, this Old Conc character was no scientist. So why, then, had he come, and how had he managed it? In secret, no less.

The tribes continued to celebrate, but by now several of the Pendju and Quwanga had paused to turn in their direction. Prentice continued with his questioning despite a growing unease, trying to keep himself between the old man and the cavorting natives to prevent any signals from passing between them. Given his age and precarious mental state, there was no telling what the oldster might do next.

If he had taught them how to fight and they had willingly complied, could he not also instruct them to fall upon the visitors? There was no doubt in Prentice's mind that despite the friendships they had cultivated with the likes of Mahd'ji and Silpa, the natives would respond to any command Conc chose to give them. For the first time in a long while, he was glad of the solid presence of the cutter-welder that was fastened to his belt.

Not that the old man was hostile. Gruff, certainly, and less than pleased by their presence, but confused and uncertain about how to proceed more than angry.

At the moment he was rubbing his chin and sounding thoughtful. "Who am I and where am I from, you ask? Well, I'm from Kinshasha and Broome. I'm from Port Moresby and Vanuatu. I'm from New Caledonia and New Delhi, from Dushanbe and Kuang-chou, from Kiev and Cairo." Unexpectedly, an extraordinary sadness filled his face.

"I'm from all of those places and from none of them. Most especially, I'm from Tananarive. Yes, Tananarive. I'm from there because that's where she was from. I *have* to be from there. Don't you see?"

Extraordinary, Prentice mused. In seconds Old Conc had gone from being alternately crazy and intimidating to a wretched shell of a human being. Pity welled up in him. A glance showed that his companions were similarly affected.

Lejardin asked the question as gently as she was able. "Who was 'she'?"

"She was Melanie, Melanie she was," he whispered. Framed by that thick, unkempt beard and yellowed teeth, his smile was a wondrous thing to behold. It was as if the sun had burst through a permanent cover of black clouds hard on the heels of forty days and forty nights of pure misery.

"Melanie, my Melanie, was from Tananarive. She was the color of fine café au lait, and as sweet. Hair black as onyx wire, eyes of eveningtide. Tall, too. Tall as you." His eyes flicked past Cedric Carnavon. "But she didn't look down on me." For just an instant his voice deepened and darkened. "No one looked down on me.

"She was kindness personified, and thoughtful, and understanding of others. She had the face of an angel and the body of a succubus. She was so naturally kind and sweet she could stand even me, unlike all who had preceded her. So many others. For the first time in my life someone liked me for myself, for who and not what I was. I had never thought to see that moment, to experience that feeling. So alien was it to me I didn't even recognize it at first. When I did, I experienced what I can only call nothing less than a personal epiphany.

"I would have accepted that feeling from a broken, leprous beggar. Instead it flowed like a river of honey from someone as desirable as her, from Melanie. There was no pretense in her, no desire as in other truly beautiful women to hang a brace of scalps from her belt or to carve notches in a gun. No mental black book in which to record conquests.

"She just . . ."—he hesitated—"she just . . . *liked* me. You have to understand that I was not liked, no. Admired, yes. Looked up to, in certain circles. There were even those who worshiped me. But liked?" He shook his woolly head. "No one *liked* me. I didn't let on, of course, that I knew they didn't like me. I had evolved means for dealing efficiently with fawning sycophants before I was twenty.

"That was not my Melanie. She liked me, for me. And I liked her. But I was still so very full of myself in those days. Not surprising when you consider how I was treated. They didn't put me on a pedestal, you see. They put me on a pedestal on a pedestal. I could do no wrong. No matter where I was sent or what I did, it always seemed to be the right thing.

"Because I was good at what I did, and didn't have the sense not to be proud of it. I wouldn't say that I enjoyed my work, but someone had to do it, and I was better at it than anyone else. None of which mattered to Melanie. Nothing troubled her. She still liked me. Enough to see through what I had to do."

"What happened?" Lejardin inquired gently. The sounds of Xican revelry, the swelling night chorus of the forest, all seemed to fade around them.

"I made a mistake," he told them quietly. "That's what happens when you're full of yourself. Against my better judgment, just that one time, I took her with me on an assignment. I was so loathe to be away from her, you see, even for a moment, much less weeks. Also, I wanted her to see how I worked and what I did. And she did.

"Even then, even after that," he continued earnestly, "she still liked me. It had been my one lingering fear that when she discovered who I was and what I did, it would change the way she saw me. With that concern banished, I was so grateful and pleased that I actually relaxed. Relaxing with her had become my greatest joy in life.

"Those I had dealt with had been broken. That was my job, you see. But they were not dead, their organization not entirely eradicated. They saw that I was relaxed, and so they rose up in one final defiant gesture and struck at me. Blindly and thoughtlessly, as is the nature of such people. Knowing they couldn't do anything to me, not because I was immortal or invulnerable but simply because I was damned hard to kill, they struck at the one thing in the world that meant anything to me." He had to pause long there, to deal with the remembrance.

"They killed her," he said finally, his voice utterly devoid of emotion. "They killed my Melanie and left her as twisted and broken as a *grahpius* can break a vine-climbing *mou'son*. Melanie was only human. She didn't have a second, defensive shape to fall back on, like a Xican. It didn't matter to them. They didn't even have anything against her. All that mattered to them was that she mattered to me.

"They all died eventually, of course. I saw to that, even though my mandate didn't extend that far once my assignment had been completed. Those who knew me knew better than to try to stop me.

"I sought each of them out, one by one. Two I came across in Milan, having lunch at an outdoor café. I was so careful that none of the other diners saw them die. Another I tracked to Rangoon. He'd become a monk and shaved his head, adopting the ways of the Buddha. As he folded his hands before me, I strangled him with his saffron robe. Another led me into the taiga, far to the northwest of Novosibirsk. He was mining for diamonds, hopeful of replenishing the small fortune he'd spent avoiding me. I watched while he froze to death.

"There were others. It may seem like a lot to some, but

they were few to me. When I had done with them, I found that I was done with life. Too strong to kill myself, too stubborn to die, I sat and tried my best not to think.

"Those who thought or considered themselves my friends did their best to revive me. They did so out of admiration or need for my services or a sense of duty. Not because a one of them liked me.

"I became a voracious reader, because concentrating on the words of others kept me from remembering my own. In the course of my reading I came across the catalog of planets that had been designated for future exploration. It was not extensive. Intrigued, I pursued detail, and came eventually to the description of this world. There were others I considered, but having to settle on one and only one, I chose Xica." A thin smile crept back onto his face. "A fortuitous gamble.

"I made the necessary arrangements, I slept gratefully, and eventually I found myself here, set down among gray-green plants, duplicitous fauna, and a plaintive but innocently willing intelligence."

"How?" mumbled Halstead. "You can't just rent a deep-space ship the way you would a private vehicle. There aren't that many, and they're all controlled by the government or the dominant multinationals."

Old Conc fixed him with that piercing stare. "You'd be surprised what can be done, sonny, if you know a few of the right people and have access to adequate resources. Since the latter no longer meant anything to me, I was able to turn them entirely to one purpose, and in fact was glad to be rid of them.

"What you say cannot be done was done. What you claim is impossible, I did. Most remarkably, it was done quietly, without attracting aggravating attention."

"Not even the wealthiest individual could afford a private journey like this." Millie Carnavon was insistent. "Only a great corporation could mount the resources."

"But I was like unto a great corporation," Conc told her. "Besides, I was only going one way. That cut the cost more than you can imagine. Unimaginably expensive it still was, but it became doable."

"What if you'd come all this way," Simna asked, "only to find a barren planet, incapable of supporting life?"

"Then I would have died," the old man told him quietly, "but I would have died trying. And I would still have been done with Earth and with humankind, which took my Melanie from me. Done with people and their spiteful, mean-spirited, vapid arguments, done with tribalism and factionalism and all the petty excuses humans have always used for not acting human. I wanted to die someplace *pure*.

"I found that here. Then I encountered the Xicans, and rediscovered something I never expected to have again: a reason for thinking. Since I no longer had need of it myself, I've tried to give them the hope I relinquished, like passing a baton in a relay race. They've taken it and run with it pretty well, don't you think?"

"It's not natural." Prentice was touched, but not overcome. "You've stepped in and interrupted the natural flow of evolution. Who knows what kind of unique civilization these people would have developed if they'd been left alone?"

"What, with humans studying them? You would've been just the first. I know exactly what would have happened if I'd left them in the state in which I found them. They would have never become anything more than the equivalent of intelligent laboratory rats, with others like you sitting around watching to see how they'd develop. I chose to give them the stimulus, the boost they needed to leap beyond that.

"I'd hoped they'd have a hundred years in which to make the society and shape I've given them their own, but if it's only to be the time it takes you to return to Earth and another expedition to get back out here, so be it. I feel confident my Xicans will survive your attention."

"You wouldn't . . . you won't try to stop us leaving, then?" Carnavon did his best to hide his concern.

"Why should I? Don't you listen, man?" Conc tapped the side of his head. "I've given up fearing or worrying about what humans may do. Continue with your studies. Falsify your records, if you choose. If you so desire, it should be easy for you to eliminate me and my presence here. Say that the Pendju and the Quwanga represent the highest stage of unsullied native development. I don't care. I'm not interested in you and your perceived little glories. My kind and gentle Xicans will survive your presence, and any that follow. That's my only concern."

" 'Kind and gentle,' " Lejardin repeated, "and you've taught them war."

"So they can continue to make progress after I'm gone, not to mention have the basis for understanding humans and their motivations. Each seasonal battle teaches them something, about their surroundings and about themselves. They'll share what they've learned with other tribes. Humanoid shape and civilization will spread across Xica. It will be their salvation from an eternity that would otherwise be spent under glass.

"Perhaps I've gone about this in the wrong fashion, but I did what I thought best. My only regret is that I won't be around to see how it all comes out."

"You look pretty healthy to me," Lejardin observed.

"Why thank you, sweet missy. I could almost, almost fall in love with you, if only you weren't human. Too much baggage, you see. So in my last days I'll keep the company of my Xican friends, if you don't mind." His expression twisted. "Strange to see again human faces, hear again the human voice. I didn't think it would draw me so powerfully. You surprise me. I surprise myself."

Prentice chose to take a calculated risk. "Since you say you won't oppose us, will you help us?"

"Help you?" Old Conc stared at him. "Have you heard nothing I've said? Not a word, not a phrase? Or has it so quickly filtered out the back end?"

"We could learn so much from you." Prentice was undaunted. "About the flora and fauna here, for instance. Aren't you interested in increasing the store of knowledge, if not for yourself or for us, then for generations to come?"

"I'm not interested in generations to come," the old man replied stonily.

"What if we were to make duplicate records of all our work here?" Carnavon suggested. "We could leave behind our spare reading devices. Some day the Xicans could make use of them. We could supply information about Earth and human society as well. Leave behind a whole library. Maybe they're not sophisticated enough to make use of electronic readers now, but someday they will be."

"They don't need that kind of help."

"You've helped them. Don't prejudge us so harshly. Help us, and you can judge us at the same time. Then you can make your decision. You're not the only good person around, Conc."

"Good person? I never said I was a good person. I said that my intentions were good. There's a vast difference there, my young friend."

Behind them, the Xican wailing rose to a crescendo. The celebration must be winding down, Simna thought. How much of that music was original with the Xicans, how much inspired by a casual lesson of Old Conc's? Xenology had become a sideshow. The local culture was all Conc culture. It was a bitter disappointment.

"Did you give them their language, too?" Halstead asked.

"No. That much they had. But I showed them how to build upon the basics, how to expand meaning and conceptualization. Otherwise I'd simply have taught them ours. Their grammar was simple."

"Yes, it is," agreed Simna.

"I haven't changed what they were," Conc went on. "Gentle and understanding. That is pure Xican. That is what has to be protected.

"There are some impressive predators on this world, most of them nocturnal. They used to pick off individuals at their leisure. That doesn't happen anymore. To me that's worth any amount of interference with 'natural development.'"

Prentice stole a glance at the slackening celebration. "We need to check in on Stewart and see what we can do for him. Then we need to revise our plans. We still have a whole world to explore and study. Maybe the natives aren't what we thought, but they're still the first nonhuman intelligence humankind has encountered. They're still worthy of our time and attention."

Carnavon gestured expansively. "There are still reputations to be made." He glanced at Old Conc. "You don't object to that, do you?"

"I told you, I could care less. Besides, you have weapons." He indicated Carnavon's cutter-welder. "I haven't seen real *weapons* (he made it sound like a bad four-letter word) since I left Earth."

"You didn't bring any with you?" Lejardin was openly surprised.

"I preferred to allocate the room in my lander for worthwhile supplies. I journeyed here expecting to die, not hoping to. If all I wanted was a quick death I could have accomplished that outside the orbit of Neptune."

"Favrile, Bella-Lynn, and Kauri are doing the best they can, but Stewart really needs your skills." Prentice eyed Lejardin expectantly.

She acquiesced tiredly. "I'll get back there as fast as I can. But I'm not going alone." She tried hard not to look in the old man's direction.

"You won't have to. I think most, if not all, of us could use some time back at camp. We have to completely re-think our plans and redesign our programs anyway. And somebody has to go and look for Lastwell and tell him what's going on." He turned back to Old Conc. "Whatever your motivation for coming here, you're still human. You're welcome to come with us."

"I might tag along for a while. You intrigue me against my will. The sound of voices, I suppose." He trailed them as they started back toward the village.

"How did you get them to start fighting each other?" Carnavon inquired curiously.

"They trust me," Old Conc explained. "They've seen what a difference I've made in their existence. They've no reason to dispute anything I tell them." A sly smile crept across his face.

"You know, there's only one of me and many of you. If you did away with me, the Xicans would probably enshrine me as some minor deity and forget all about my corporeal presence among them. You could return to Earth with your studies unchanged, with your fantastical native culture in-tact and unblemished by human interference."

Carnavon shook his head. "It wouldn't work. There are too many similarities with primitive human societies. Ex-tensive study would reveal them, and the truth would come out. So we might as well be truthful now."

"Besides," said his wife, "you haven't done anything to us. Why would we think of hurting you? You've obviously been hurt a lot already."

"I don't want your sympathy. I don't want anything human."

"That's too bad." She smiled maternally.

"It's just as well. You couldn't kill me anyway. Not the lot of you working together, not with whatever weapons you may have brought."

"Because the Xicans would protect you?" Carnavon said.

"No. Because of who I am." He straightened anew and that hard shine returned to his gaze and his posture. "Don't even think about it, people. Like everything else on Xica, I'm rather more than what I appear to be. Don't judge me by my current appearance."

"Nobody wants to kill anybody," Millie Carnavon assured him. "We just want to carry out our work and depart peacefully. You've complicated our intentions, but you haven't diverted them."

"Too bad. As I said, I won't hinder you and I won't help you. Maybe we can stay out of each other's way."

"If you do feel the need to hear a human voice, or engage in a simple conversation," she went on, "we're always available. We're not as dogmatic as you seem to think."

"Ah, dogs!" Old Conc looked wistful. "Now there's a species I miss. Give me a good dog over a human any day. Loyal, trustworthy, true, there when you need it."

"Robotics," Cedric Carnavon murmured. "It's not very rewarding to coexist only with robotics."

"A dog is warm, a machine ain't," Conc objected. "It's the same with most humans."

"I think," said Millie Carnavon, "that you have a problem with perception more than anything else. If you'll give us a chance, if you'll give yourself a chance, you might find yourself surprised." She and her husband continued onward as the old man halted, following them with his eyes.

No, woman. There's nothing wrong with my perception. Only with yours. He resumed his stride, intending if nothing else to join in what remained of the joyous celebration.

XIII

Eventually the celebration died down. The Quwanga performed their farewells and melted back into the bush, while their hosts the Pendju set about carefully dousing all remaining fire and retiring to their huts.

Choosing not to wait for dawn, the visiting scientists gathered their equipment and set off by flashlight for Base Camp. Their thoughts were in turmoil and no one had any idea how they were going to restructure their programs, but Prentice was adamant about continuing with the work. The strange figure who called himself Old Conc had spoiled and infected only a portion of their research. There was still a great deal to be learned.

Conc considered accompanying them but decided against it. They'd already lost one of their number, another awaited them badly injured, and the sanity of a third was at risk. All of which was none of his concern.

But he did inform his escorts the Quwanga that he would be remaining with the Pendju for a while. The Quwanga did their best to hide their disappointment, while the Pendju were openly delighted. Wherever Old Conc was, good things invariably happened. Nevertheless, the Quwanga would not have thought of objecting to the decision. One might as well dispute God, for all that the Old Conc had taken numerous pains to repeatedly point out that he was

199

only an individual, living being like themselves, no greater or lesser. Only more educated.

The Pendju assigned two of their best to see to his needs, which were minor. Though his useless lander still contained some sealed foodstuffs brought from Earth, he'd long since adapted to a diet of local edibles. The native seafood, in particular, was nutritious and tasty.

He'd learned which fruits and nuts were edible and which were likely to contain potentially harmful parasites. He was not above dining on the local arthropods when other food was scarce, spading them from the soil or digging them out from beneath the bark of the peculiar trees. He had adapted completely.

He hadn't recovered from the sounds of human voices. They rang still in his ears, echoes of a past he fully believed he'd consigned to time and space. Certainly he'd never expected to hear one again.

Had he heard a human voice? Or was he imagining again? He'd done enough of that over the past several years to begin to worry about it. In fact, he worried about it all that day and well on into the evening.

It was dark when he found himself on the bluff overlooking the sea. Below lay a rocky point that thrust out into the ocean, and he climbed lithely to its very tip, where ancient cooled lava agitated the gentle surf.

Turning to his right, he found that he could look far up the coast along the endless beach that fronted the black, moonlit sea. A warm, gentle breeze caressed his bare skin, the salt it deposited a small sacrifice in return for the welcome cooling.

Along with the salt the breeze carried with it out of the night the haunting cry of some unseen sea-dweller. Behind him the forest murmured as some of its more daring nocturnal inhabitants began their nightly ritual of flitting from tree to tree or bush to bush. After dark the land was at once quieter and more crowded, the paradox explained by the determination of those who might be prey to avoid those who would feast upon them. In the forests of the Xican night, silence meant life.

They'd asked him about himself but he hadn't told them. Or had he? He shook his head, unable to remember. If he hadn't, then had they guessed? How could there be anything for them to guess? They were only scientists. High-beam searchlights, all their brilliance focused on a small area of particular concern, no breadth of vision at all.

Certainly they felt that he was harmless and posed no real threat to them. In that they were half right, just as he was only half mad. Or half sane. In any event he was by now at least half harmless, he told himself. He'd worked very hard to get that way.

Below the point the moon ladled strips of gold into the water. As far as he could see there wasn't a sign of human interference; no artifacts, no debris, no plastic excrement. Save for a few Xican coelenterates that had been stranded on the beach by high tide, the sands were as unblemished as the mind of an embryo, washed pure by an unpolluted sea.

Though hot and steamy, Xica was a beautiful world. He was sorry he hadn't been able to spend more time in isolated contemplation of its natural wonders, but the demanding natives required his attention. Raising them up was his form of penance for all those on Earth he had laid low. Having no personal submersible or diving gear meant the mysteries of the ocean depths would remain forever closed to him. Not that it mattered. There was enough on land to occupy his attention for several lifetimes.

At least the one allotted to him was substantial. He was in remarkable health for a man of fifty (no, that wasn't right). He was long past fifty, wasn't he? Like so many other bits of knowledge, the fact of his age continually escaped him, washing in and out of consciousness like the unfortunate coelenterates on the beach. He was far older than fifty.

How old, then? Seventy, ninety, a hundred and ten? Was he Lazarethan, or simply lazing? Did he forget because he wanted to, or simply because it no longer mattered? He chuckled aloud, and the peculiarly shaped crustaceans clinging to the rocks below spared a glance for the sudden noise.

That was what he'd wanted all along. To be ignored. He'd sought out a venue for that mode, only to find himself implored by the most pitiable aliens one could imagine. He'd lifted them up out of pity, but they implored him still, and he was too gracious, or guilty, to ignore them.

He sensed the presence long before it sat down next to him, recognizing it by smell. The Princess did not speak. She knew Conc that well. Her hair was dark and her eyes expansive. The flattened double nostrils and small mouth did Xican tricks with atmosphere. She was Quwanga, and had remained behind with him. As he'd known she would.

He could have encouraged her to greater modification. The nose could have become a prominent ridge, the ears substantive and convoluted. She could have sculpted from her being five fingers instead of four, and a corresponding number of toes.

But that would have made her stand out too prominently from the rest of her kind, would have put undue pressure on her, and that he was unwilling to do to satisfy a mere dream. She was enough as she was.

I molded you, he thought. I took the clay that was Xica and the innocent, distressed intelligence of your self and shaped you into something better. To do more would be unfair, though I know you would comply and gladly. Push the nostrils out so, add ears thusly, shorten and twist and bring forward the hair. Better to do so in imagination only. Better to be fair. It was right that he should bear the pain.

"Melanie." He dropped it upon the waters, and the waves cast it back. Melanie, who did not deserve to die but who had made the fatal mistake of liking him. Of loving him.

A sinuous, flexible arm slid across his shoulders, behind his neck. It was cool against his fevered skin, and the voice affectionate as always. It was the voice of a species, grateful.

"Always," the Quwanga Princess breathed, in her simple language.

Time passed. The moon precessed. Constellations rotated. "So often you sit and stare at the ocean," she whispered to him. "What is it you expect to see, Old Conc?"

He swallowed. "The horizon. The place where the sea meets the sky. The sun and the moon."

"But it is always the same, no matter the time of day or night. The horizon is nothing but a line that divides the air from the water. You taught us that."

"I know." He rested a gnarled palm on her knees. "But I think that if I keep looking I'll find something I've lost, and I don't know where else to look."

She peered into the moonstruck night. When she spoke again, petulance had crept into her voice, a small irritant with legs.

"There is nothing out there. Why do you so often have to speak in riddles, Old Conc? It makes it hard for me to understand you."

"It's not your fault, *Tchi'al'line*. It's not anybody's fault." He turned his face to hers, studying the impossibly wide, questioning eyes. "I don't understand me, so you shouldn't fault that failure in yourself."

The arm contracted gently. Even in the natural gruesomeness into which they were born, the Xicans were close.

"Please help me to understand, Old Conc."

He turned away from her. "Stop saying that. I wish all of you would stop saying that. I keep hearing your whimpering in my sleep."

She tried another tack. "Why can't you relax and enjoy

the life that remains to you? You have already done so much. We want you to relax." She gestured at the shifting sea with her free arm. "There is clean air, good water, plenty to eat since you showed us how to farm and take food from the sea. It is because of you that we are now able to enjoy these things. Why can you not enjoy them as well?"

"That's not my destiny, *Tchi'al'line*. I'm fated to listen to your complaints, and to respond."

"Then show me something, Old Conc. Show me something new. Please."

A great exhalation escaped him. "There isn't much I haven't shown you, *Tchi'al'line*. Why don't you show me something? Maybe it'll stop me from thinking."

"I have nothing to show, Old Conc. Only that which you have shown us is worthwhile."

"Not true. Not true at all. You always had much inside you."

"Why should you want to stop from thinking?" Her vast eyes contemplated him sorrowfully, in their plaintive glow both reflecting and challenging the moon.

"Because on my home world I spent too much time thinking, and only learned too late how to feel."

"The world where your friends have come from."

"They're not my friends," he said sharply, causing her to recoil. Instantly regretting his tone, he slipped his own arm reassuringly around her back. "They're not my enemies, either. They're just an intrusion. Humans."

"Like you."

"No. Not like me. I surrendered my humanity when I left my world."

"Then what is it you give to us, if not your humanity?"

His gaze narrowed. The Xicans were maturing at an impressive pace. Hopefully it would be fast enough.

"Knowledge. A future. A defense."

"You mean the way we defend ourselves against the Pendju when they attack our village?"

"No. It's not the Pendju you have to fear. It's what I once was."

With that he drew her smooth form, half alien and half remembered, tightly into his arms.

XIV

"You're not going to tell us who you are, are you?" Prentice sat next to the old man, the two of them ensconced side by side on the bluff not far from the village. They were gazing out to sea where strange cephalopodian creatures were leaping clear of the water. Their feelers fluttered as if they were feeling of the empty air, and the internal propulsive system by which they drove themselves would remain a mystery until one could be captured. They had eyes faceted like golden topaz and sleek bodies streaked with iridescence.

The old man called them Blowzers, a descriptive if unscientific appellation.

"That's not what the Pendju call them," he added cheerfully, "but it's adequately descriptive. The native name would mean less to you. Why are you so interested in my background? I thought you came all this way hopin' to learn about an alien world. I may be a bit strange, but I ain't alien. More's the pity."

O'Sandringham stood nearby, her recorder focused on the cavorting cephalopods. Clad only in duty shorts and vest, the sweat rolled off the pale, fair skin of her legs and arms. She replied as she lowered the instrument from her eyes, aware that the old man was staring at her.

"You're like those airborne Blowzers, Conc. An interesting specimen whose origins understandably intrigue us. We hardly expected to find anyone had preceded us here. If you're telling the truth, you must've been a person of some importance back on Earth. Otherwise you'd never have been able to muster the resources to reach Xica, not even on a one-way ticket."

"How about if you leave me alone?" As always, his sharpness of manner struck them forcibly whenever it manifested itself. At such moments his voice took on a quality that could not be ignored. "Why don't you just concentrate on the Blowzers?" He turned back to face the sea.

"I regret the omission on my lander of a boat. The Xicans, of course, haven't the foggiest notion of how to build one. Nor have I attempted to show them, yet. It's not a priority in their education. Hopefully I'll begin demonstrating the process some time next year, I think mastery of the sea is vital to the dissemination of local culture because of the natural barriers posed by the deserts. With luck I hope to get them to the point of understanding steam technology before I die. They have a voracious appetite for new things that can be appalling at times." He nodded northward.

"I've hiked quite a distance up the coast. There are funnel-shaped bays that have thirty-foot tides. Very impressive, but no place for coracles or dugout canoes. Fortunately they've proven to be skillful weavers. Sail-making should come easy to them."

"If not, you could induce them to grow finer, longer fingers," O'Sandringham commented sarcastically.

"It's not as simple as that," he told her. "It took years before the adults could lock into these humanoid shapes without having to concentrate on them all the time. If I were now to vary the formula it would cause more confusion and harm than possible good. These shapes have become automatic to them. I don't want or intend to tamper with that. Instituting even small changes risks causing them to snap back to their natural form. I don't want to chance that. *You* don't want to chance that." He changed the subject. "How's your Puffball-punctured colleague?"

"Feverish. Sometimes coherent, sometimes not." Prentice kicked a pebble over the edge, watched it slide down the sandy slope. "Stevens is keeping watch on him, back at Base Camp. We managed to extract a sample of the toxin. A couple of our people are working with it right now, trying to synthesize an antivenin. It's a complex neurologic agent and the proteins are proving difficult to replicate."

"Will he live?"

"We hope so. There doesn't seem to be any permanent damage."

"He's missing a lot." Wiping perspiration from her forehead, O'Sandringham gestured to where an especially large cephalopod leaped five meters clear of the tepid surface and fell back with a thunderous splash.

The sun hammered mercilessly at the naked beach, but up on the bluff they had the benefit of shade trees and the cooling breeze. Conc glanced over a shoulder, turned suddenly.

"Be quiet, and look there," he advised them.

Snuffling through the woods behind them was a creature the size of a small, obese antelope. A wide, flattened proboscis extended from its face to the ground. Slitted yellow eyes intently scanned the soil as it advanced methodically on wide, splayed feet that appeared better suited to treading lightly on lily pads.

Conc's voice was soft. "A Groomer. I told you if you paid attention you'd see something. They usually keep to the denser woods."

"Don't tell me it's a burrower." Lejardin was working her recorder, captivated by the creature's antics. "Not with those feet."

The old man chuckled. "There are suckers under each foot. Watch."

As they looked on in silence, the Groomer came to the base of a tall tree they'd named a Fracturebark. Head back, it surveyed the vertical, dark gray trunk. With great deliberation it circled the base several times, testing both the trunk and the soil around the roots with its remarkable snout.

That organ led Simna to suspect it was some kind of arthropod siphoner, like an anteater or echidna. Just as he thought he had it classified, it stood up on its hind end and wrapped its front legs around the sides of the tree. Using the unseen but obviously efficient suction cups Conc had alluded to, it began to climb, its four legs and broad flat feet almost encompassing the trunk's circumference. The sucker-equipped feet gave it an unbreakable grip.

About halfway to the crown it halted. Oblivious to their presence, it began to change. O'Sandringham held her breath.

"Another thixomorph." An elated Lejardin stood very close to Simna, her attention concentrated on the eyepiece of her instrument and the singular creature she was recording for posterity. Acutely aware of her proximity, Simna edged sideways, putting a little more space between them, the better to maintain his scientific detachment. His action went unnoticed and unremarked upon.

While the Groomer's lower body remained stable, muscles seemed to blossom in its shoulders, as if its mass was flowing forward beneath the skin. The flexible proboscis stiffened and straightened, except at the tip where a corkscrewlike spiral formed. With a rotating motion of its head, the Groomer proceeded to screw the end of the organ right through the outer bark and into the tree. The result was a hole some three centimeters in diameter.

As the Groomer withdrew its organic drill, a couple of diminutive, brightly winged creatures burst from the freshly cored cavity. Quickly the agile climber reformed its original broad snout while its body ballooned with inhaled air. The pliable organ whipped around to suck in the slower of the two flying things as its companion escaped.

Placing the broad tip of its snout over the opening it had drilled, the creature proceeded to vacuum out the unseen contents of the hole, its body expanding and contracting beyond the bounds of simple respiration.

"Now that's an interestin' critter." Old Conc regarded the rapt scientists. "Carries a tool chest in its nose and a bellows in its gut. Kind of puts the venerable elephant to shame." He resumed his contemplation of the languid ocean.

"Except for the arthropods, everything that moves through the Xican forests is like that. There's the shape you see and the shape you don't, unless you're lucky like we've been this morning. It's not all that different from human society. People have their public faces and their private ones. If folks' faces matched what they were thinking, relationships would be a lot more honest. Of course, there would also be a lot fewer of 'em." He jerked himself back to his company. "You should see a *Vrilil*."

Lejardin looked up from her recorder. "What's a *Vrilil*?"

"The most deceptive predator I've seen on this planet. Not much bigger than a man and it goes on all fours, like the Groomer. Has the look of a fat, clumsy teddy bear and spends most of its time huddled up in a shallow burrow. You can get right up close to it and it doesn't move. Just lies there looking like a giant furry pillow. But try to step over it and the burrow suddenly sprouts teeth.

"My fourth month here I saw it take a Quwanga. The poor creature was shuffling along, pointing out different plants and their fruits, and then there was this quick, high scream and he just sort of disappeared from the midsection down. I ran like hell. Looked back just long enough to see the rest of the *Vrilil* emerge from its burrow to engulf the unfortunate native's torso. It had bitten him in half, faster than the eye could follow."

Lejardin made a face while, as usual, Simna's expression didn't change.

"I'd like to get one of those," O'Sandringham avowed.

"How would you mount it?" Old Conc smiled at her. "In its predation state or waiting mode?"

She grinned back. "Whatever was scientifically most applicable."

"Predictable response. You disappoint me. I had you pegged as less of an intellectual than the rest of this bunch. I was hoping to be surprised." He glanced at Lejardin, a twinkle in his eye beneath the heavy, gray brow. "I bet you could surprise me, missy."

Lejardin replied without missing a beat. "No, somehow I don't think I could. Of course, if you'd tell us more about yourself, I might be able to give you a better answer."

"You sure you still want to know about me?" His expression narrowed. "I might be like a *Vrilil,* you know. All cute and cuddly on the surface, all teeth and destruction inside. You might not like what you find."

She started to reply, but there was something in his face, something in his expression behind the wild hair and fluttering beard, that gave her pause and stifled the ready quip she'd intended to deliver. She placed the recorder against her right eye and resumed her scrutiny of the Groomer.

Simna observed the byplay with interest. Lejardin might look fragile, but he'd never before seen her back down from a verbal confrontation. It was noteworthy. The old man was indeed like a Xican life form, though, Simna thought, probably something very different from a *Vrilil.*

Drawing him out was going to take time and expertise. Not only was he reluctant to explain himself, his lucidity varied unpredictably. One moment he was as clear and straightforward as anyone in the crew, while the next could find him staring off into the distance muttering incomprehensibly to himself.

Simna was an extraordinarily patient man. He would query Conc when the time seemed propitious, and he would not give up until they had some answers.

As if reading his mind, the old man turned and threw him a look not unlike the one that had disconcerted Lejardin. But Simna didn't back down, didn't turn away. He was able to resist the effects of that glare because he concentrated on analyzing it. Was it a conscious effort on Old Conc's part, or a byproduct of his madness?

Movement near his feet distracted the scientist. A glimpse of brilliant pink and indigo made him instantly vigilant. On Earth, bright contrasting colors signified danger, or at the very least proffered the promise of unpleasant possibilities to roaming predators.

It had a dozen legs, six to a side, each as neatly jointed as a human's. The shiny body rose to a hump near the posterior, ending in a short tail covered with fine bristles. The three eyes that dominated the anterior end gleamed like faceted tourmaline.

Simna made no move to pick it up. After what had happened to Noosa and now Ramirez, anything furry or bristly was off limits to physical contact. The skimpy tail might be as harmless as it looked, or it might pack another thixotropically metamorphosable toxic surprise.

As he kept a prudent eye on its progress, the creature slithered underneath a fallen log and did not reemerge. Another unclassifiable discovery, he mused, neither mammal nor reptile nor arthropod but combining aspects of all three. And that only described its normal, dominant form. If it was threatened, who knew what it might change into? Biology on Xica consisted of the observable and the imaginable.

Yet while fantastic, these life forms were not without precedent. Precambrian Earth had featured a profusion of phantasmagoric forms the majority of which had died out, leaving no direct progeny. Perhaps some had been thixotropic. It was now known that instead of advancing in a steady, predictable arc, evolution bounced around all over the place, influenced by chance and a host of random, capricious factors. Life on Xica had simply taken a different but no less valid path than it had on Earth.

Detailed study of Xican cell structure, with its remarkable flexibility, would lead to a standardized taxonomic structure capable of encompassing even shape-shifting. After all, it wasn't as if the forest dwellers had access to dozens of different forms. Each could manage only a single change. Only the intelligent natives were able to exceed that restriction, and then only with time, concentration, and great effort.

A sudden thought made him turn to consider Old Conc, who continued to tease and toy with Lejardin. If a Xican could learn to hold a humanoid shape, why not one wholly human? Was it any more preposterous to assume that Old Conc was merely a clever Xican than a lone one-way traveler from far distant Earth?

No, he decided. It was one thing to imitate form, another to imitate substance. Conc was too quick mentally, too versatile in his responses, to be even a trained Xican. More than what he seemed he might very well be, but he was incontrovertibly (inconctrovertibly?) human all the way through. To assume otherwise was to countenance unsupported possibilities.

And just to make sure, he voiced the absurdity. "Hey Conc, you're not by any chance a genius-level Xican, are you?"

The old man turned sharply, then grinned. "That's right,

sonny. Tomorrow I'll be something else, and then into your tent I'll creep."

Simna was satisfied. It was the kind of reply only a human could make, one afflicted with chronic cynicism.

That didn't mean their occasional guide and companion could be trusted. They had no way of knowing how much of what he told them was truth and how much something entirely else. In that he was not unlike his adored Xicans.

Take nothing for granted here, he reminded himself. Not even testimonials of temporary insanity. Not on a world where giant teddy-bear mounds became motile fangs and claws, fumbling tree-climbers turned their nostrils into drills, and cute fuzzy Puffballs slung poison-filled quills at curious investigators.

He wanted badly to document the pink and indigo crawler that had vanished beneath the log. Halstead carried the best macrorecorder, but though he'd accompanied them as far as the bluff, the big scientist was now nowhere to be seen. Ted tended to become preoccupied. Probably he was back in the forest, recording something under a rock.

Shrugging, Simna ambled over to examine the log, as interested in the fallen timber as in the creature that had taken refuge beneath. If he found anything of especial interest he would point it out to O'Sandringham, whose specialty it was. He forgot about Halstead.

Off by himself, the big man had indeed found movement to occupy his attention. Having espied something very unspiderlike that was responsible for the spinning of a unique, complex web, he focused his recorder on the transparent, pigmentless, winged blob and silently tried to urge it into action. It had the wingspan of a sparrow.

The web itself consisted of a series of concentric cubes. As he looked on, a large flying arthropod became entangled in the outermost cube. It broke free, only to tumble deeper into the boxy maze. Disturbed, the cubes collapsed onto themselves, until the unlucky flier was completely and hopelessly entangled.

All but invisible against the sky, the crystalline spinner fluttered down from its branch to inspect the collapsed web. As an entranced Halstead watched, the wings flattened and thinned. Their now sharp edges plunged into the thicket of web, slicing and cutting until they reached the struggling prey trapped in the center.

Nothing as arachnoid as fangs manifested themselves. Instead, the bladed wings attacked, slicing the helpless prey into a dozen manageable chunks. Lifting one tiny gobbet in its clipperlike forefeet, the web-spinner reformed its wings and soared back to its branch. Dumping the meat into a dark hole, it returned to gather another.

Halstead knew that he ought to climb up and have a look in that hole, but as he watched the web-spinner ascend with its second chunk of oozing protein he decided against it. Metamorphosing organic blades might mangle flesh as readily as chitin. He was alone, and if anything happened to him there'd be no thoughtful Lejardin or Simna handy to patch him up.

A tap on his arm made him whirl so sharply that he nearly dropped the precious recorder. With great relief he saw it was only a Pendju. A female, gazing back at him out of those wide, imploring eyes. They were a striking shade of pale yellow.

"Why do you watch the Weaver?" She offered no apology for having nearly startled him out of his boots.

He exercised his inadequate but improving Xican. "To learn about it, as we have been trying to learn about everything that lives in the forest."

"I could tell you about it. There are many different kinds of Weavers." When he didn't respond she added, "My name is Diha'na."

"You surprised me, Diha'na. My people do not like it

when someone sneaks up behind us unannounced." He struggled to convey the concept of "sneaking."

Her head dropped. He'd forgotten how sensitive they were. "It's all right," he hastened to assure her. "I forgive." Her eyes came back up and the shy smile returned to her unblemished face. It seemed only natural for him to smile in return. "The more we learn about life on your world, the more of it we will be able to share with others of our kind when we return home. For instance, there's nothing on our world like that." He gestured at the busy Weaver.

"Because it can change its shape?"

"Because of that, among other things."

"You are surprised by our ability to change, aren't you?"

"We certainly are. On our world there are creatures that can change their color, but except for a very few, not their shape. I'd like to see what you'd make of a frilled lizard. Anyway, it's not the same thing." He carefully placed the recorder in a notch in the tree and left it running on auto as he found a seat nearby.

"Tell me about changing, Diha'na. Does it hurt when you alter your body?"

"Hurt?" She looked at him sideways.

"You know, is there pain? Physical pain?"

"Sometimes. When you are young it is hard to learn the adult shape, and you must work all the time to maintain it. As you grow older it becomes much easier. Eventually you stop thinking about it. Your body . . . learns. You keep the shape even as you sleep."

"Do you ever change from the shape Old Conc taught your people back to your natural form?"

She seemed uncertain how to reply. "Hardly ever. This shape is much more pleasing to us. Is it not pleasing to you?"

"Well, yes. I suppose so. Your cells must memorize the

new configuration. I wonder how thought affects the change, or if it's entirely a physical operation."

"I do not understand."

He smiled encouragingly. "It's all right. We don't understand, either. At what age did Old Conc start to instruct you in your present shape?"

"Old Conc? He did not instruct me. My mother did."

"Oh." Then Conc had been telling the truth when he'd told them that the natives preferred the humanoid shape to their own. "What about your insides? Those don't change at all?"

"Oh no. How could you change your heart, or your stomach? Why would you want to, if they were working well?"

"Good point. I had an uncle who had to get an artificial heart." He tapped his chest, wondering if she would relate to the gesture, or the area. "He'd have been real happy if he'd been able to change his insides."

"An artificial heart." She mulled the notion. "What an odd idea. You mean, like a spear or a pot?"

He nodded, grinning at her technological naivete. "Something like that. A machine."

"Like that?" She gestured with a four-fingered hand at his active recorder. "Like the devices you use to study us?"

"That's right." He tapped the device. "This makes a picture of everything it sees. Right now it's watching the Weaver."

"Would you like to make pictures of me, too?"

He smiled. "Maybe."

"And then you will study that?"

"That's right."

She ran one hand absently through her long hair. "Do you enjoy studying us?"

"It's not a question of enjoying. It's to increase our knowledge. Humans want to know everything about Xica. About its plants and animals, its weather and geology. Its people."

"I know that. I want to know if you enjoy studying me. Just me."

"You mean you, personally?" She responded with a gesture Old Conc had taught the Pendju. "Sure. I like studying all of you."

"I am pleased," she replied. "I want your people to like me. I want you to like me." A lithe, four-fingered hand reached out to touch his forearm and he felt the coolness of her, the contact rejuvenating in the humid confines of the forest. It was almost like talking with a child, he reflected, except that Diha'na was a fully mature representative of her species.

The hand began to stroke his arm. After a moment's hesitation, he pulled back. "That's enough. The feeling is that our captain, Frank Lastwell, already went through something like this, and he hasn't been the same since. I have no intention of suffering a similar experience."

The fingers withdrew and the alien, humanoid face fell into a recognizable pout. "F'rank was with Koil'yi. Koil'yi doesn't know what not to do." She looked back up at him. "While you have been studying us, I have been studying you."

"That's very admirable of you." He didn't know what else to say. At the same time he found himself wondering if he should wind up his observations of the Weaver and rejoin his companions. There was no one else in view or earshot. Not that he worried about becoming lost. *Not physically, anyway,* a part of him whispered.

The fingers returned to his arm. "I learned well what Old Conc tells us, and I have studied you all closely. Particularly B'ella and K'auri. I want to do what is right. I want to learn, and while learning, to make you happy."

"I am happy." Though taken aback, he didn't want to offend her further. The situation was getting out of hand.

When had she studied O'Sandringham and Stevens, and why especially them?

Nothing was going to happen to him. He wasn't Lastwell, and he hadn't been drinking. The heavy, tepid atmosphere, the rich organic fragrance of the forest, the muted sounds of mutable creatures rustling unseen in the undergrowth, and the light sandpapery feel of the tree bark where it brushed against his bare skin, all combined to weaken his resistance. But not break it.

"I'm not going to go through what Frank went through," he warned her. "He mumbles about it constantly. He saw something that I don't think I want to see."

"You won't." She moved closer. "He wanted to see us as we were, not as we are, and Koil'yi made the mistake of showing him. She should not have complied, but she wanted to please. There are better ways to please." The four-fingered hand moved against him. He inhaled sharply.

"I have studied hard and I am very able," she whispered. "I can become anything you want. Anything. The Elders warn against experimentation but I have done it. Alone, deep in the forest. It is hard, and it does hurt, but I would do it for you, if you asked. Please let me please you. You who have seen so much could show me new shapes, teach me new things."

"Christ." Halstead found himself staring at her. "I . . . I wouldn't want you to hurt yourself."

"You won't, you won't." When a Xican was close, it was impossible to focus on anything except those astonishing eyes. There was nothing hypnotic about them: they were simply deep, and beautiful. Seeking to verify that he was still in control, he deliberately looked away. Nothing pulled him back. Nothing, except his own desire. His own secrets.

Her voice was a pleading whisper. "I can be, T'ed, anything you want. I want to be. Teach me," she whined.

XV

"Where's Ted?" O'Sandringham wondered aloud. Prentice blinked at her.

"Where'd you disappear to?"

"Down to the beach." She hefted a collecting bag. "There's some fascinating mollusks in a big tidepool. At least, I think they're mollusks. They have valves, and hard shells, but of course in this place all taxonomic bets are off." Reaching into the sack, she extracted a cross between a scallop and a spearpoint and tapped it against a rock.

"These don't change shape. Not every life form on this ball of dirt is different from what it seems."

"Pretty hard to liquefy and restructure your cells underwater." Simna looked past her. "I thought Ted was with you."

O'Sandringham shook her head as she returned the specimen to her bag. "Haven't seen the big goof all morning."

"There he is." Prentice relaxed as the subject of their discussion emerged from the line of trees. His recorder dangled loosely from his big right hand.

Simna called out to him. "Hey, Ted! Find anything interesting? Like a bug that turns into a helicopter?"

For a moment Halstead appeared not to hear his friend. Then he looked over and grinned sheepishly. "No. Nothing much. Just stuff."

"Well, c'mon," O'Sandringham urged him, "don't keep it all to yourself. What kind of 'stuff'?"

Halstead strode past her and took a seat on the edge of the bluff, concentrating on the gentle wavelets below. Laying the recorder across his lap, he began fiddling with its latches and slides.

"Nothing special. The usual native life."

"There's no such thing as 'usual' native life on Xica." Simna strolled over to sit down next to the big scientist. Lejardin watched with interest. Not Halstead, but Simna. She could tell from the latter's attitude that something was amiss. She just couldn't tell what. She continued to mess aimlessly with her own instruments while keeping an eye on the two men. Meanwhile O'Sandringham was displaying the results of her beach walk to an interested Prentice.

"What did you find, Ted?" Simna kept his tone even and conversational.

Halstead didn't look up. "I told you, Jack. Nothing special." He continued to clean the recorder.

Simna gestured at the instrument. "Got it all in memory?"

"I'm not sure. Won't know for certain until I play it back. I'll let you have a look tonight." Now he did look up at his companion. "I promise."

Simna nodded as he rose. "Good enough. I'll look forward to it." He turned to gaze speculatively into the woods. "You never know what you're going to run into in this place. Even if you did, it could always turn out to be something else before you have time to figure out what you're up against."

"You know something, Jack? Sometimes your wordplay gets a little tiring."

Simna smiled apologetically. "Hey, I'm sorry. Just trying to make small talk."

Halstead looked quickly back down at the recorder. "I didn't mean that."

"Yes, you did. It's all right. I'm used to it. It's the way I've been since I was old enough to talk. I just have to watch myself. I tend to ramble too much. Just like you tend to be pretty closemouthed."

This time Halstead's grin was genuine. "What, me? I'll show you what I found today when we sit down for the daily postmortem tonight."

"I know you will. If there's anything I can do to help, just ask."

Halstead replied a little too quickly, a little too sharply. "Help? Help with what?"

"Your presentation." Simna indicated the recorder. "If you're having any trouble, I know that model inside and out."

"So do I, and I'm not. But thanks just the same. Anybody ever tell you that there's such a thing as being too smart? That it can make you, even without you being aware of it, appear real overbearing at times?"

"Oh sure. People tell me that all the time." The older scientist smiled.

"You ought to be a teacher."

Simna shook his head. "No could do, Ted. They'd want me to specialize, and I'd be bored senseless within a year. See you." He turned and wandered over to see what Prentice and O'Sandringham were up to.

Halstead resumed working on the recorder, to all outward intents and purposes wholly absorbed in the task of cleaning the device and checking its seals. His concentration was wonderful to behold, a quality for which he was noted among his colleagues. So no one noticed that he was actually doing very little. His fingers, like his thoughts, were straying.

Back to the deep forest, into which he dared not turn and look.

Though he did his best to hide his condition, over the following days it became more and more obvious to his friends that the big scientist was seriously preoccupied with something.

"What do you think's going on with Ted?" Lejardin put the question to Simna one morning as the two of them were examining an extraordinary new fungi. It crawled halfway up the northern flank of a large tree, sending out questing filaments and lacy flying buttresses in all directions. The complex brown-and-white structure stood out sharply against the dull gray bark of the host growth. According to the Pendju who had led them to the mycotal phenomenon, it would eventually engulf and kill the entire tree, whereupon the entire integrated structure would topple to the ground, resulting in the death of host and parasite alike.

But by that time the fungi would have fruited several times over, sending its feathery spores drifting through the forest. Major-league mycelium, Simna called it. Working smoothly side by side they cut and bagged samples, maintaining the distance they had established by unspoken mutual consent. The constant proximity was considerably harder on Simna, who nonetheless concealed it well.

"I haven't a clue," he replied in response to her query, "though I've tried my damnedest to find out."

"I know. I've watched you."

"How about you, Favrile? Any ideas?" Carefully he tweezed a fragment of fruiting cup from its stem and deposited it in a waiting plastic vial. A touch sealed the container, which he proceeded to mark.

"No, and don't try to tell me you haven't speculated on the reasons for his current behavior. I know you better than that."

Simna looked away, into the woods. A few edgy peeps

and squeaks reached them, small rusty hinges flapping in the wind. They were far from the coast, and perspiration flowed freely. Simna tolerated the heat better than anyone, but that didn't mean he was immune to its effects.

"Maybe he's shape-changing. You haven't noticed if his nose is shrinking, have you? Or his ears becoming shell-like?" To his surprise Lejardin didn't smile.

"That's not funny, Jack."

"Hey, lighten up! It's too soon to turn serious on me. We've still got more than a year to go here and I can handle just about anything this planet dishes out except unrelieved pensiveness."

"I can't help it. Haven't you noticed that he takes off by himself as soon as he's able? Every time, every day."

A reflective Simna set his collecting gear aside. "No. No, actually I hadn't noticed that. Really? Every day?"

She nodded. "I've been watching him. He watches you, and Cedric, and Salvor, but he pretty much ignores me. When he's sure none of you are paying any attention to him, he slips away."

"His work doesn't seem to be suffering. He comes in with as much new stuff as anyone else."

"I know. He tries to beg off Base Camp duty every time, too."

Simna shrugged. "You can hardly blame him for that. With all the finds waiting to be made out here, I'd rather be out in the field gathering glory myself than back at camp tending to mundane chores."

"He balks even at the little that's asked of him. We're doing all we can for Stewart, and Kauri and Frank take care of most of the maintenance."

Simna nodded thoughtfully. "Speaking of our illustrious captain, how's he doing? I haven't seen him in a while."

"He keeps to himself a lot, spends a great deal of time mumbling. But the work gets done."

"I guess that's what matters."

She looked away, eyeing the remarkable fungi with sudden indifference. "I've known Ted longer than you have. It's not like him to be that assertive, to argue before complying. Something's bothering him."

Simna spread his hands wide. "I don't know what to tell you, Favrile. If he's up to something, he's keeping it well hidden."

She leaned forward, her manner earnest. "Talk to him, Jack."

"I have been talking to him. Just like I talk to everyone else."

"I don't mean ordinary, everyday conversation. *Talk* to him. Try to find out what's on his mind."

"If it's that important to you, why don't you try to draw him out?"

She shook her head impatiently. "He wouldn't be honest enough with me. Besides which, I don't know the right questions to ask, how to push the appropriate buttons. I don't have your talent for getting to people."

He grinned wryly. "Thanks . . . I think. All right. If it's bothering you that much, I'll see what I can do."

"It's not just me. Bella-Lynn's commented on it, too. And Millie."

"Ah. Female perception."

"I don't think so. I think everyone's noticed. Including you. You just don't like to discuss things unless you're absolutely, positively sure you have all the answers first."

"I'll talk to him," the older scientist reiterated.

"Good. You're not fooling me, Jack. I know Ted's attitude's been bothering you, too. You don't miss anything."

"Like the color of your eyes?"

"You know what I mean," she replied without missing a beat.

As he rose he slipped the carefully marked and filled

vials into the carrying case. "You know, you could be making too much out of this. Maybe he's just immersed in his work. Maybe he's found something that requires a great deal of concentration to classify and analyze, and when he's finished he's going to surprise us with the results."

"We're not supposed to engage in private studies. This is an open expedition. We're supposed to share all findings with each other, no matter how speculative."

"I'm not disagreeing with you. It's just that Ted's such an easygoing guy that in the heat of discovery he may have momentarily forgotten some of the rules. I still think he's planning to surprise us." He slid the carrying case into his backpack. "People are full of surprises."

"That's right," she admitted readily. "Even you."

He had no clever reply for that.

Though the forest was more fecund and the desert more alien, the beach was Simna's favorite place. There more than anywhere else he felt almost at home, while the waves regularly washed up fresh discoveries of their own. Sometimes he felt he should have had his blood tested, certain that its composition would vary little from that of seawater.

There was something uniquely soothing about the sound of the waves, the feel of even alien sand beneath his feet, the play of sunlight on water and surf. The ocean was a warm, wet, salty cocoon he knew he could slip into at any time and feel rejuvenated. The original survey probe's identification of oceans on Xica was what had first excited interest on Earth. They were probably also what had convinced Old Conc to gamble his one-way, one-shot flight on this particular extrasolar system.

The sand was very fine-grained and tinted green in places due to the presence of residual volcanic olivine. His polarizing glasses muted the glare as he probed with shovel and siphon in search of tiny shore-dwellers. Not everything

of interest on Xica was immediately visible to the overwhelmed explorer.

That's when he detected movement out of the corner of
one eye. It was further down the beach, but not so far that
by squinting he couldn't make out Halstead's lumbering
silhouette. Nor was the younger scientist alone. Though he
had excellent distance vision, Simna was unable to identify
his colleague's companion. At first he thought it might be
Lejardin, but soon changed his mind.

Reaching up, he adjusted the knurled knob on the side of
his glasses. As magnification increased, the two distant figures leaped toward him. It was Halstead, all right, clad in
light shorts and multipocketed work vest. Like an extension
of his own arm, the ever-present recorder hung from his fist.

The other figure was not Lejardin nor, for that matter,
any member of the crew of the *James Cook*. It was a Xican,
female, and from the distinctive designs on her poncho, a
Pendju. She held Halstead's free hand in her own smaller
grasp.

Flipping the lenses back to normal, Simna surveyed his
surroundings. Save for the two figures ambling down the
beach he was quite alone.

Slipping his recorder strap around his neck, he returned
siphon and shovel to their brackets in the backpack, which
he then snugged behind a wave-polished boulder just above
the high-tide line. No one would bother it. Unless explicitly
granted permission beforehand, no native would touch any
of the visitors' gear. Old Conc might have educated them in
the arts of primitive war, but both tribes observed strict pro-
hibitions against theft.

He's afraid we'll corrupt his precious aliens, Simna
thought. What he doesn't realize is that he's corrupted them
already. No matter how fond they are of the physiques and
culture he's given them.

Hugging the edge of the bluff, he started down the beach.

The large, exposed granite boulders that dotted the southern portion of the berm provided him with ample cover as he tracked the anomalous pair. He expected them to stop anytime. There was no reason for Halstead to hike very far down the shore. Dozens of new discoveries were to be found within every meter.

But they kept going, piquing the senior scientist's curiosity still further. Was she guiding him? Was there a secret place where Halstead was carrying out the special research Lejardin and the others suspected him of? Simna didn't for a moment anticipate a replay of the captain's unhappy confrontation. Halstead was far too intelligent to risk anything so chancy. If such thoughts had entered his mind, there was the everyday example of the mumbling Lastwell to remind him of where such misguided bravado could lead.

Unique arthropods and other creatures deserving of investigation peeked out at him from holes and burrows in the bluff. It took an effort to ignore them and concentrate on his patient pursuit. They would be there for him to examine or collect on the way back.

Whenever the opportunity to take a longer look at the couple presented itself, Simna tried to identify Halstead's Xican companion, but try as he might he couldn't place her. The Xicans did not possess a great many distinguishing external characteristics. Not in their present, learned humanoid form, anyway. Old Conc might have done it, but Simna wasn't that proficient.

Tired and thirsty, with his canteen back in his pack, he was just about to give up on the tracking when the objects of his interest suddenly halted. With his glasses turned to full magnification he stared as the Pendju turned to face Halstead and put both flexible arms around his waist. Simna froze.

Far from rejecting the embrace, Halstead responded in kind. Bending over to accommodate the Xican's slighter stature, he kissed it. That in itself was astonishing. What was more remarkable still was that it appeared to kiss him back.

When confronted by the inexplicable, Simna was invariably able to assume a wholly objective and analytical position. Apparently Old Conc wasn't the only one capable of volunteering complex instruction to the Xicans. Was this what Lastwell had experienced? The captain had proved less than voluble about the matter.

Halstead seemed to be tolerating the experience rather better. He appeared not only at ease but familiar with the methodology.

The kiss lingered. Simna was at once enthralled and repulsed. What, for example, would a Xican tongue feel like? Would it be as humanoid as the rest of the acquired configuration, or entirely different under such incongruous circumstances? Would a Xican mouth and lips be warm or cold to the touch? What sensations could result from a thixotropical tease?

As he stared, the two of them lay down side by side, not bothering to see if they were alone. Doubtless experience assured them they were, he thought. There was no reason for anyone to be this far down the beach. In spite of his scientific detachment he felt a certain twinge of guilt. There was no reason for it, he knew. His continuing observations were entirely consistent with the best guidelines for biological research.

He fingered his recorder. Though not as large or elaborate as the one Halstead always carried with him, it was still a very sophisticated instrument. Certainly it was adequate to the moment. He fumbled with the strap, and then his fingers fell away. There were some things it was better to record with one's eyes and mind.

Would Halstead be embarrassed if his secret were to be revealed? Judging from the familiarity with which they progressed, this was obviously not the first such tryst or rendezvous. Human and Pendju knew one another well. Simna wondered how long it had been going on. It certainly explained Halstead's fondness for solo forays into the woods and elsewhere. The information he brought back from such solitary expeditions was always valuable, the specimens easily the equal of those acquired by his colleagues.

He simply wasn't being forthcoming about his preeminent discovery, Simna reflected.

The actual details were not particularly revelatory. Certainly he saw nothing of sufficient magnitude to explain what had happened to the unfortunate Lastwell.

And then the Pendju began to change.

Even with the glasses it was difficult to be precise about details at that distance. *Design-a-female,* Simna found himself thinking. Indulge in physical as well as mental compliance with your fondest dreams. No wonder Old Conc was so protective of his primitive charges. Such thoughts were impossible to avoid as he watched human and Xican making love.

Halstead didn't change, of course, and the Pendju could only catalyze her outer form, but that was enough. Organs could not transmute, but they could stretch and twist to accommodate a different external alignment. Muscles could elongate or contract. Not that Halstead was embarked on any ride so radical. If this was akin to the experience Lastwell had endured, he mused, that must have been very different from what he was presently witnessing.

How else could the natives mutate, he wondered? If provoked, did they possess a defensive mode, like a Puffball? Could they also inflate and explode, driving poison into their adversary? Nothing of the sort had happened to Lastwell. He suffered from a malady more subtle.

Because of their ability to exercise conscious, intelligent control over their thixotropic talents, of all Xican life forms only the humanoid natives had the ability to teach their bodies new tricks. Or be taught, he decided as he watched Halstead. Could they realize hostile as well as compliant shapes? With this possibility in mind, the seasonal war-play between the Pendju and the Quwanga took on a far more sinister aspect.

How did the tractable Pendju female see such encounters? Were her maneuvers defensive, or did she have an entirely different purpose in mind: one that might escape the attention even of Old Conc? Though he found himself wishing he was closer, he didn't want to risk exposing himself. Nor was his desire founded entirely on scientific objectivity. He was male enough to admit to a less than laudable interest in the nuances of the skirmish.

When, after sustainable activity had subsided, they rolled apart, the Pendju seemed to flow more than figuratively into Halstead's arms. The tall scientist held the native close. Both gave every indication of having secured what they wanted from the experience.

Was the encounter purely physical, he wondered, or was there more to it than he could see, something on a deeper level? An emotional as well as a physical satisfaction? He continued to watch as they whispered softly to one another. A part of Simna was quietly pleased: Halstead had plainly found the language recordings his colleague had compiled of considerable value.

His thoughts churning, Simna chose to leave them to themselves. As he made his way back up the beach he wondered if he should share his observations with any of the others. He knew that not everyone would react to the information objectively. Not to mention the effect a general dissemination would have on Halstead. Ted was certainly as sensitive as anyone on the team and perhaps more than most.

Better to delay, and to consider, he decided. There was always time for disclosure. Better first to learn all that he could if for no other reason than to see if he was missing something vital. Something at once more important and less visible.

He confronted Halstead later that same night, drawing the younger man aside. Except for the two of them, the laboratory hut was unoccupied. The voices of Lejardin, Prentice, and O'Sandringham drifted across from the other hut, the one they used for sleeping.

"Say, Ted, can I talk to you for a moment?"

Halstead looked up from the recorder viewer. "Sure, Jack. What's up?"

"Not in here. Come outside. It's a nice night."

"They're all nice nights, if you don't mind being hot and sweaty." Halstead grinned companionably as he rose from his workbench.

The sounds of preadolescent natives and chattering adults accompanied them as they strolled to the periphery of the village. Numerous Pendju had warned them about wandering too far into the forest after dark, since that was when the large nocturnal predators were about. As neither man was carrying his cutter-welder they were scrupulous about halting well short of the first underbrush. Overhead, Xica's single large moon, three-quarters the size of Earth's, bathed the uncompromisingly upright trees in its pale light.

"Over here." Simna led his friend further to the west, following the line of huts, until they were a good distance from the one occupied by their colleagues. By now Halstead was eyeing him with open curiosity, wondering what was going on.

When he was sure they were alone and out of earshot, Simna turned to confront his colleague. Though the subject was delicate, his approach was not.

"I was on the beach this afternoon, Ted. I saw you, and your Pendju."

Halstead absorbed this silently before responding in an ~en, tremorless tone. There was no evasion in his reply.

Evasive types were not chosen to go on deepspace missions. Directness and straightforwardness was valued, and awarded appropriately.

So instead of mumbling something along the lines of "I don't know what you're talking about," Halstead said, "All right, you saw us. What are you going to do, Jack?"

Simna stared into the forest, wishing he could see the owners of the strange sounds that continued to issue forth. "For the moment, nothing."

Halstead nodded stoically. "I appreciate that, Jack. I really do."

"I don't see that any real purpose would be served." Simna nodded in the direction of their huts. "The others would badger you incessantly for details; some out of sincere scientific interest, others for reasons wholly personal. I have the feeling you'd rather not deal with that just now."

"Right. What about you?" Halstead was scrutinizing the more experienced researcher intently. "You're not personally curious?"

"Of course I am. I just feel that you'll elucidate all this in your own good time, when you feel ready. Rushing you won't help matters." Unable to restrain himself, he added, "Would I not be correct in assuming that you find the experience enjoyable?"

Halstead broke into a wide grin. "You ought to try it, Jack. There's something about the Pendju that goes beyond their ability to shift shape. I think it has to do with their innocence, and with a desperate need to learn. Like a kid desperately trying to please his parents. It's a trait that humanity's lost."

"You haven't second-guessed yourself? You're not wondering what you're doing?"

The grin remained strong. "What I find myself wondering is how a male Pendju would accommodate O'Sandringham or Lejardin. Haven't you?"

"Not really, but now that you've gone and mentioned it I

suppose speculation's inevitable. Be careful, Ted. You're treading uncharted waters. I'd hate to see you drown, even with a smile on your face." He hesitated. "You're pursuing this purely as a matter of scientific interest, right? You're not doing anything stupid like developing an emotional attachment to this creature, are you?"

Halstead's smile vanished. Simna had touched a sore spot. "You're not serious, are you?"

"Yes. On rare occasions I am. I've been straight with you so far, Ted. In return I ask only the same."

Turning away, the other man plucked a leaf from a nearby bush, staring at it as he rolled it between his fingers. "I'm not sure, Jack. I'm really not."

The older scientist took it upon himself to be reassuring. "It'll never work, Ted. Has she taken you home to meet her parents?"

Halstead jerked around, relaxed when he saw the smile on his friend's face. "You really do have a hard time being serious, don't you? I don't think they do that here. Don't lose any sleep over this, Jack. I know what I'm doing."

"Yeah, but do you know what you're doing it with?"

"Everything's under control. I'm maintaining a proper distance. No one's going to get hurt, least of all me."

"I'm pleased that you can be so positive about it." Simna knelt to examine the base of a small bush. The roots were glowing slightly due to the presence of symbiotic phosphorescent bacteria. "What happens next year, when it's time for us to leave? We know that the Xicans are capable, if not of love in the human sense, of forming strong emotional attachments. What becomes of the innocent subject of your ongoing experimentation when it's time for us to depart?"

"It's not like it is with us, Jack. *They're* not like us. Remember Mahd'ji's reaction when Boutu was killed by the Quwanga? She sorrowed, but there was no weeping and wailing. I think Diha'na will react the same when I leave."

"Diha'na. So that's her name." Both men were quiet for a long moment, listening to the contented prattle of the Pendju and the background murmurs of the forest. "I saw her change when you were . . . exchanging information. Did she volunteer options, or did you provide instructions?"

"A little of both." Halstead kicked at the ground. "I proffered what I thought were some aesthetic variations. Some she made on her own. She enjoyed the physical variety. I have the feeling that if this Conc person wasn't around to constantly ride herd on them, the Xicans would experiment more with their shape-changing talents. Stretch their ability, so to speak. Whether that'd be good for them or not I can't say, but they'd certainly have more freedom."

"That's not always a good thing," Simna declared. "Did she ever revert to her natural form? The one that apparently gave Lastwell such a fright?"

Halstead shook his head. "No, never. Neither of us suggested it. She did say that she knew what had happened to Frank and that she knew it would be rough on me if she did the same. So she avoided even the suggestion."

"Would she do it if you asked her?"

The other man looked up. In the pallid moonlight his expression was hard to read. "I think so. But I'm not going to ask her. Because it would stress her, and because I'm not sure I'm any mentally tougher than Lastwell."

"Just make sure you stay mentally strong enough to retain your objectivity. Keep in mind who and what you are and where you're from, as well as what we're here for."

"Hey, no problem."

Simna turned pensive. "I don't suppose there's any harm in you continuing these assignations. You seem to have things under control, and it's highly unlikely you're at risk of contracting any kind of disease."

"Christ, Jack!" Halstead muttered.

"These things have to be said, Ted. If you're not going to

think about them, then I'm going to have to do it for you. We've already lost Cody, and Stewart's having a rough go. Something happens to you, and I know Salvor. He'll cancel the whole expedition on the spot. We'll be back in deep-sleep inside of a week." He stared hard up at the other man, utilizing a look and tone of voice he usually kept carefully in check.

"I, for one, don't want to be ordered off this planet prematurely. There's too much to learn here. Xica's the most important stop in the history of humankind's travels. I plan on learning all there is to learn about it in the time that's been allotted to us, and I don't plan on you or anyone else fucking it up. You understand me?"

Halstead stiffened. "When did somebody die and make you king?"

"I'm just telling you how I feel, Ted. It's not a threat."

"Sounded like a threat to me."

"If I wanted to make trouble for you I'd go parade this in front of everyone right now."

Halstead finally looked away, his voice dropping. "I'll handle it, Jack. No one's pulling out, and nothing's going to happen to me. I'm not Lastwell. I know how to watch for danger signs."

Simna nodded slowly. "Then we understand each other. I'll keep your 'research' a secret. I'll even help you: I'll deflect any questions from the others as to your whereabouts. Hell, I won't even track you anymore. You and your experimental subject can have your privacy. As long as you're discreet you shouldn't have any trouble with Salvor. Just, when you're pursuing your investigations, keep a sharper eye peeled, okay?"

"I didn't know anyone was spying on us," Halstead told him.

"Nice try, Ted, but it won't wash. In watching you, I was doing *my* job. At least as well as you were doing yours."

Halstead took a step into the woods. "If you meant what you said about respecting my privacy, I could use a little right now, Jack."

Simna almost asked the other scientist if he was planning on seeking out a sympathetic ear in the form of his alien paramour, but he kept the thought to himself.

"All right, Ted," he said gently. "I wanted you to know where I stood on this, and I wanted to know the same about you. Just watch yourself, all right? I don't care how warm and understanding and empathetic your Pendju popsy seems to be, she's still a thixotropic alien humanoid, the operative word in this instance being 'alien.' They're only as human as they are because they've had years of instruction at it from this crazy old geezer Conc. We don't know that their learning is immutable, or, for that matter, what else he may have taught them. Remember, he wants them to be able to defend themselves against too much human intrusion. Take care that she doesn't suddenly decide to defend herself against you."

"I'm not worried about anything Old Conc may have told them, or her. He's half loony. He'd have to be, to do what he's done."

"Sure he is. It's the other half of him that concerns me, the half we don't know much about yet. For instance, why won't he tell us who he is?"

"Maybe," said Halstead slyly, "he wants his privacy."

"Go ahead and joke about it. If you persist in pursuing this line of study, it's your neck that'll be on the line. Not to mention other things." He paused. "I wonder if this old man's breezy lunacy is all part of an act, to keep us off our guard. Or from asking the right questions."

"You're too suspicious, Jack. I kind of feel sorry for you."

"Because I'm not into what you're into? Don't count me out on that, either."

"No?" Halstead turned a challenging face to the other

man. "You ought to try it, Jack. Don't tell me you're not lonely out here. O'Sandringham and Stevens have each other. So do Prentice and Lejardin. For as long as we're here I have Diha'na. I'm sure any one of the unattached females would be delighted to accept personal instruction from the great human teacher Jack Simna. What about Mahd'ji? Why don't you ask her?"

Now it was Simna's turn to look away. "I couldn't be that forward, Ted. Especially not with Mahd'ji. I'm not sure I'm ready for the whole conception."

"You're thinking in human terms, Jack."

Simna whirled. "This isn't what we're here for, Ted!"

"No? If this isn't xenobiological research, I don't know what is."

The senior scientist was silent for a long moment. "It's research you choose to pursue; not me." He nodded in the direction of the huts. "I think we've been gone long enough. Someone's liable to miss us." He started back. After a moment's hesitation, Halstead fell in alongside.

"Thanks, Jack. Thanks for understanding." He didn't offer a hand. There was no need to.

"Yeah, sure. We'd better understand each other, because this world is going to take all the understanding we can muster, and then some. Just watch yourself, Ted. You're a good guy, and you're smart. But I've been around a lot more than you, both on Earth and off it, and I know how easy it is to forget you're not working in a lab or class back home. I just don't want you to get into something you can't get out of."

"Who, me?" Halstead's expression twisted into a self-deprecatory smirk. "I'm just your typical disinterested observer. Keep to the sidelines and do my work."

"Yeah, right. Try to remember that."

They parted as they reentered the camp, Simna resisting the urge to trail his companion.

XVI

Prentice was anxious to catch up on his work. Having done his turn at Base, tending to necessary maintenance and helping to look after the still feverish Ramirez, he was anxious to see what breakthroughs had been made in his absence. Meanwhile he'd left Base in the capable hands of Lejardin and O'Sandringham.

The babble of energetic Xicans had been growing louder all morning. Now he turned from his bench to walk to the open doorway.

"Seems to be a lot of activity."

Cedric Carnavon scratched at the back of his head as he sauntered over to stand next to the expedition leader. "Sure does. It's unusual to see all the females and so many of the children out and about this time of day. I wonder what's up?"

"I was hoping someone would come enlighten us."

"They won't."

Both men whirled. "You shouldn't sneak up on people like that," Carnavon told him.

Old Conc edged around to the front of the hut. "It's my manner. Don't mean to, nothing personal. You afraid of me?"

"Hardly," replied Carnavon.

"Glad to hear it."

Prentice was paying as little attention as possible to the old man. "What's all the excitement about?" He indicated the village center, frenetic with Xicans.

"Mean to say you don't know what's going on?" Conc stroked his luxuriant if unruly beard.

"I presume," Carnavon prompty him dryly, "you do."

The old man cackled. "Not much to know. It's their time of the month."

Prentice frowned. "You mean, all this commotion has something to do with reproduction?"

"Just the opposite. It's time for the Pendju to raid the Quwanga village. They trade off, you know."

"Have we been here that long?" Carnavon looked around for his wife, who was busy mounting arthropods. At least they could be handled with some impunity, their hard exoskeletons being incapable of permutation.

"Then there's going to be another fight." Prentice looked unhappy.

"Pretty hard to mount a raid without fightin'."

"According to what you've told them."

The old man's voice fell an octave. "Let's not get back onto that, sonny. This is their society now, and they're happy with it. It's nothing to you, so don't think of interfering."

"Did I say anything about interfering? How could I interfere with your interference?"

"Tch. Touchy. Just see that you don't."

Carnavon was not intimidated. "What if we did decide to say something to the villagers, or suggest a modification of their behavior? What could you do about it?"

Old Conc straightened and a gleam came into his eye. At such moments he seemed to become another person entirely.

"Don't cross me, Carnavon. You'd cause me no more trouble than would these kids you call colleagues. I've put my soul into raising these people . . . and they are people, make no mistake about that . . . up to where they are. I won't tolerate any interference in their affairs from you or anyone else."

"Take it easy," Carnavon told him. "I didn't say I was going to do anything. Frankly, there's no reason to, unless someone had a thought about preventing them from slaughtering one another. But I guess you wouldn't find that constructive, would you?"

"Slaughter?" The old man chuckled. "They don't slaughter each other. They're very judicious when it comes to numbers. Have you forgotten already? There'll be no more than one or two killed or severely wounded; nothing either village can't absorb. Then they'll call a mutual halt to the combat, and it'll be time to celebrate. Lookin' forward to it, myself. Personally, I think the Quwanga do a better job of mountin' the postmortem festivities than do the Pendju."

Prentice was not placated. "I'm surprised you don't join in the killing. Your active participation wouldn't make any difference one way or the other, since for the Xicans intertribal warfare isn't natural behavior."

"It is now," the old man chortled. "Until I showed 'em how, they didn't have enough sense to fight. Didn't have nothin' to sustain stimulation of their development."

"Since the timing is so formalized, will the Quwanga be waiting for the attack?" Carnavon asked curiously.

"Only within a certain window. They'll know a raid is coming, but only within pretty vague parameters. That still gives the Pendju the advantage of surprise." He gazed fondly toward the village. "What I'm really waiting for is some Xican Caesar or Hannibal to wake up and realize that they don't *have* to wait for a particular season. That they can attack their opponent at any time. I'm waiting, in other words, for initiative. That'll mark a great leap forward for these people."

"It'll also allow them to wipe out their adversaries," Carnavon argued.

"Not hardly. Their triumph would consist of having achieved total surprise. The killing would still stop at the same ritual number. Then the other tribe would get the idea, and the notion of taking the initiative would spread. Not only to ceremonial combat, but to other areas of development as well. I could slip either side the notion, but my whole intention here is to get them to think for themselves."

"So they can kill each other more efficiently," Prentice grumbled.

"Do I detect the pungent, stale aroma of acrimony? Of cynicism? Remember, there's no hate involved here. We're not talking about a couple of primitive human tribes. They do battle in the spirit of uplifting competition. As for the actual deaths, the Xicans have a much more prosaic view of personal loss than we do, bless 'em."

"Yes, you've greatly ennobled them," Prentice acknowledged.

"Look," Old Conc responded earnestly, "I didn't come all this way with the intention of educating a brace of innocent intelligent aliens. I wanted freedom from thought, among other things. Then I stumbled onto these people and I just couldn't leave them to their own nonexistent resources. Not while knowing that other human beings would eventually arrive here. I didn't seek this responsibility; circumstance thrust it upon me."

"Oh, yes," Prentice avowed. "You're noble, too."

Old Conc shook his head resignedly. "I found teratoids grubbing in the dirt, and to replace that I've given them form and substance. Before I started working with them they weren't even functional. Now they're building a culture and maybe a civilization. I make no apology for any of it." His tone turned steely. "I've never apologized for anything I've ever done and I'm not about to start now." Carnavon eyed him sharply, but the old man did not elaborate.

"We ought to accompany the next raiding party," the senior scientist declared. "Right from the initial preparations. It beats sitting here and waiting for them to return so we can question them about it." He regarded Old Conc. "How about it? Think they'll let us go along this time?"

"Don't see why not."

"There's plenty to study around here, Ced. You know that." Prentice was uncomfortable with the proposal.

"I'll get a team together." Carnavon was plainly taken with the idea. "Speak to Jack about communications." He turned back to the old man. "How long before the Pendju set out?"

Old Conc considered. "Judging from the current level of activity, I'd say that they're planning to move within a day or two. Better get yourselves together or you'll be left behind. Or you could ask Troumo straight up. But even he might not know precisely. They like to wait until the auguries are right: weather, physical condition, that sort of thing." Unexpectedly, he asked, "It's March, isn't it?"

"I don't know." The request took Prentice by surprise. "There's leaving Earth orbit, leaving the system, returning to the system and reentering Earth orbit. For us that's pretty much it on a journey like this, as far as keeping track of time goes."

"I think it must be March." The old man looked wistful. "I've tried to keep a sort of calendar."

"Then you haven't abandoned your humanity as completely as you'd like us to believe," Carnavon asserted.

Penetrating blue eyes met those of the scientist. "A man has to keep some kind of order in his life. Otherwise sanity tends to slip away like a cat on owl shit. Me, I'm livin' proof of that." He cackled delightedly as he turned and hobbled off toward the village center.

Prentice tracked his shifting, loping stride. "We're never going to figure him out. He may not be able to tell us about himself because he may have forgotten, or intentionally wiped it from his memory."

Carnavon nodded. "If he fled Earth to put something behind him, he may have succeeded." He rubbed his chin thoughtfully. "Or maybe for reasons we haven't yet divined he'd prefer for us to think that he's crazier than he actually is."

"If it's an act, it's a good one." Prentice grunted scornfully.

"No matter." Carnavon put a comradely arm around the younger scientist's shoulders. "We've got a native sneak attack to document."

"I wonder how much real value all of this is going to have when we get back to Earth. Maybe all the time we're spending on the Pendju and the Quwanga could be put to better use elsewhere."

"We've got time enough. Everything they do can't be Conc-inspired. He doesn't choreograph their daily behavior. He just makes suggestions. They're intelligent, and they're nonhuman. To me that makes *everything* they do of value, even how they interpret the old man's instructions. I say we record everything and leave it to the specialists to determine what's enlightening and what's not."

Prentice nodded slowly. "You're right, Ced. We're here to observe and record, not draw conclusions."

"I knew you'd see it that way." Carnavon removed his arm. "So what are we sitting here wasting atmosphere for? Let's get on with it."

This time Troumo, Silpa, and the rest of the war party had no objection to the humans accompanying them on the raid. On the contrary and much to Prentice's dismay, they were eager for any suggestions the humans might care to make. As always, their desire for knowledge was boundless. Prentice was convinced that Conc had prepared them for the request.

The rest of the village followed the war party at a discrete distance. They would remain behind until the fighting concluded, only then advancing to join in the ensuing revelry.

It was distressing to Prentice to see the best of the Pendju decked out in weapons and shields, war paint and other primitive combat regalia: the mature, healthy males in front, the females and adolescent males behind, with the elderly shepherding the children in the rear. It seemed such a waste of energy. The Pendju, of course, would have soundly disagreed.

He wondered what would happen if a Quwanga succeeded in slipping up behind the war party to dispatch a child. Would that count as one of the requisite dead? Or was infanticide against the rules Old Conc had set down for them, and would a warrior who so fell from grace be disciplined, exiled, or executed? He thought to ask Mahd'ji, but she was busy, and the old man seemed to have melted into the forest.

Conc had assured them that they could carry out their work in the heart of the battle in perfect safety. What if one of the team decided to get involved? Prentice wondered. Would that then make them a legitimate target? Surely not even Carnavon would be that foolish. Fortunately Ramirez was well out of it, back at camp. If Stewart were with them, concerns would have instantly multiplied.

The Quwanga community was situated several days' march to the south, also close to the coast. This made it a simple matter for one village to find another. Nor, when they finally came upon the collection of huts and drying racks, was it any better defended than the Pendju hamlet. No moat, no palisade; nothing. Doubtless Old Conc was waiting for Xican initiative to assert itself in the realm of defensive fortification as well.

The raiders managed to avoid a group of females out collecting edible roots and berries. Although the Quwanga knew that an attack must be in the offing, the gatherers did not look particularly vigilant.

With cries, whoops, and whistles, the Pendju swept down upon their neighbors. Though surprised, the Quwanga responded swiftly. Practice, Prentice thought bitterly. He stayed well back in the trees as the battle developed. Maybe Old Conc was right when he insisted neither Pendju nor Quwanga would deliberately try to injure a human, but that didn't mean you couldn't succumb through accident. Not given all the spears and arrows flying through the sultry mid-morning air.

Several Quwanga tried to execute an unnoticed flanking maneuver, hoping to get behind the main line of invaders. They were spotted and cut off by a group of warriors under Silpa's command. Prentice watched as a single Quwanga, his spear and shield gone and armed only with a knife, went down bravely beneath the combined assault of three Pendju. As the native was lanced his contour seemed to shiver and flow. Then he stiffened, holding the long-practiced humanoid configuration even in death.

Prentice was perspiring profusely as he recorded the painstakingly decorous carnage. With cries of triumph, the trio of attackers ceremonially impaled their downed adversary several times as he struggled to crawl to the imagined safety of a nearby hut. The butchery was carried out with an impassiveness hitherto unobserved among the Pendju. Or maybe the chill was in his mind and the natives were simply acting in what they would regard as a matter-of-fact fashion. They were not human, he kept reminding himself.

Tonight the three executioners would frolic and feast in the company of the slain Quwanga's relatives. And they would be welcome. Senseless, he thought. All so senseless. There had to be more civilized ways to foster development.

A hand on his shoulder caused him to jerk sharply, but no native spear thrust at his forehead. It was only Simna, who had a way of appearing silently at one's back. Berated for so startling his colleagues on more than one occasion, he continued to insist that the effect was quite unintentional. As he raised his arm to point to their right, his expression was grimmer than Prentice could remember.

Three Quwanga had a female Pendju pinned up against a tree. She was bleeding profusely from a chest wound, parrying as best she could with her short spear the robust thrusts of her tenacious assailants. It was clear that she was weakening. One jab after another slipped through her guard.

Another Quwanga arrived to join his companions in pressing the attack. But the conflict itself wasn't what had drawn Simna's attention.

A large male form came bounding out of the trees, waving a whole intact branch over his head while howling madly at the top of his lungs. Taken by surprise, the four Quwanga turned to meet this unexpected threat.

Describing a sweeping arc as it descended, the massive branch shattered two of the modest Quwanga spears at a single blow. Thus partially unarmed, the attacking quartet, even more wide-eyed than usual, beat a hasty retreat toward their village.

Murmuring something neither Prentice nor Simna could catch, given the distance between them and the surrounding chaos of the rapidly abating battle, the almost-victim confronted her savior. Breathing hard, the tall male let the branch fall from his fingers as he reached out to embrace and comfort the injured female. Instead of sagging into his arms, she raised her own weapon and placed the point against his chest.

The male appeared to plead, whereupon after conspicuous deliberation she set her spear aside and somewhat reluctantly let him put an arm around her. Hurriedly the male considered their immediate surroundings, as if to see if anyone was watching. Then he led her away, into the safety of an uncontested portion of the forest.

Throughout this lowly but extraordinary drama Simna and Prentice had not spoken. It wasn't necessary. As always, Simna wore his emotions on his face, and Prentice had no difficulty interpreting them.

"You *knew*."

The expedition leader voiced the accusation with confidence. "You knew something like this was going to happen."

"No." The other scientist was clearly uneasy. "Why would I have known about anything like this?"

"You knew something was going on with Ted. I've seen you watching him, Jack. I'm not as blind as everyone thinks. There was confirmation in your expression, just now."

"Damn my face, anyway." An unhappy Simna gazed into the woods that had swallowed up Halstead and his Xican paramour. "What the hell was he thinking of?"

"He interfered." Prentice took a deep breath. "Implicitly and with forethought. He could have killed a native."

"I know that, Salvor." The other man's recorder hung loose from its neck strap, humming softly as it documented the ground. His own plans completely forgotten, Simna made no move to turn it off.

The skirmish was definitely winding down around them. War whoops and battle cries were being replaced by cheers and shouts of joyful recognition as strife gave way to fraternization. No longer was Prentice looking forward to the post-combat celebration. A new and utterly unexpected problem had been handed him to deal with.

Simna was elucidating quietly. "That Pendju female on whose behalf he intervened? Let's just say that Ted's interest in her goes deeper than ethnology."

Prentice frowned. "Lastwell went through that, and he still hasn't recovered."

"Frank was dealt a sight he couldn't cope with." Simna squinted into the trees. "Apparently Ted's had no such problem. Her name, by the way, is Diha'na."

"You know her name?"

Simna's lips tightened. "When I called him on it, Ted admitted to the relationship . . . if we can call it that. We may have to invent some new descriptions."

"This is insane, impossible." Prentice turned away from the fighting to gaze into the forest. "I can't have a member of the team involved with . . . with an alien."

"You're half right. It's crazy, but impossible it's not."

"How long?" Prentice inquired quietly.

"Weeks." Simna was uneasy. "I promised Ted I wouldn't tell anyone, that I'd let him bring it up in his own time. Actually, once the novelty wore off I thought he'd tire of the situation and call a halt to it. It hasn't affected his work any."

"No, not that I've noticed," Prentice had to admit. "What I've been able to review of his field notes is exemplary. The equal of anyone else's." He glanced over at his colleague. "But this is wrong, Jack. Not only isn't this good science, it's conflicting with science."

Simna found himself defending Halstead without quite knowing why. "It's certainly that, but nothing like what this Old Conc's been up to."

Prentice's gaze narrowed. "Are you defending Halstead's behavior?"

"No. No, I'm not."

"There could be consequences we can't imagine. Diseases, native mistrust. Anger could now be directed at us.

On the basis of this the Quwanga could come to regard us as an enemy worthy of 'ritual' killing, no matter what the old man thinks."

Simna considered philosophically. "All I can say is that so far no harm seems to have been done." With a straight face he added, "He's certainly gathering a great deal of distinctive and valuable research. It's not like he's neglected his work or responsibilities in favor of lolling about with a Xican harem. It's just him and this one individual."

"You're rationalizing for him, Jack."

"What can I say? Ted's my friend."

"He's my friend, too. That's why he has to be confronted with the truth and brought back to reality. As soon as I can get him aside . . ."

"No." Simna interrupted insistently. "He trusts me on this. Let me talk to him first."

"You saying he doesn't trust me?" Prentice wavered. "Perhaps this should be handled by a third party. O'Sandringham, maybe, or Lejardin. Or even the Carnavons."

"Just let me try." Simna glanced back over his shoulder. "I wonder if he knows that we saw him."

"I don't think so. If he did, I think he would've reacted."

"Let's do this," Simna proposed. "Let's keep it quiet a while longer. Now that I've filled you in, there's no need for any more speculation or conjecture on your part. You can keep an eye on him too. Let's let the two villages enjoy their celebration and a good time be had by all. We'll deal with this when we get back to the Pendju village and everything has calmed down some."

Prentice deliberated. "All right, Jack," he replied finally. "I'm going to defer to you on this one. I trust your analysis."

Simna smiled gratefully. "You need time to consider all the possible ramifications, Salvor. I know I did, when I first found out what was going on. I don't think native culture's been adversely impacted yet." He waxed philosophical.

"We have to decide how to handle things like this as we go along. There's no handbook for Alien Affairs because we never expected to find any aliens. Everything's improvisation. Ted isn't violating any procedures because there aren't any applicable procedures to violate. Hell, maybe he's even doing some good. Maybe he's counteracting some of Old Conc's strictures."

"That's not what concerns me the most, Jack. I'm worried about what he may be doing to himself. You saw the look on his face."

"Yeah, I saw it. He definitely needs a serious talking-to."

Prentice nodded slowly. "Then we're agreed. You talk to him, Jack, and I'll hold off. But I am going to talk to him myself, later."

"That's fair enough. I'm as concerned about his mental health as you are." He gestured in the direction of the Quwanga community. "Look, the fighting's about stopped."

"One dead Quwanga, one dead Pendju," Prentice muttered. "Time to kiss and make up." Indeed, the former combatants could be observed chatting amiably with each other as they filed into the village. Their shapes seemed to be shifting subtly as they walked. Did fighting put a strain on their ability to sustain their prescribed humanoid form? Or maybe it was only the sweat in his own eyes, the expedition leader decided.

Off to one side he espied Old Conc discoursing on matters unknown to a cluster of attentive Pendju and Quwanga. No doubt admiring his handiwork, Prentice mused sardonically.

They could abandon Xica tomorrow, he knew. Pack up and depart knowing their careers and reputations were assured. Upon their return they would become instantly famous and, unlike many hard-working academics, maybe even rich. They would not have enough time to accede to all the requests for dissertations and interviews.

Then why, as he trailed Jack Simna toward the Quwanga village, did he feel so uneasy?

XVII

The festivities differed only in minor but interesting detail from those that had been put on by the Pendju. The same enthusiasm and sincere affection was on display, the same camaraderie in the face of traditional rivalry and death. When they arrived, the Pendju elders and children were greeted with open kinship and presented with the best food and drink their adversaries could provide.

Once again the humans participated in the dancing and feasting, but this time with obviously less enthusiasm than before. Even Old Conc took note. Simna could tell from the way the old man watched them. But he said nothing, merely grimaced and cavorted wildly as ever.

Prentice waited several days after their return to the Pendju village before deciding to share his thoughts. They had resumed everyday routine and all were present for the morning meal except O'Sandringham and Stevens, who were back at Base Camp looking after their supplies and the improving but still weak Ramirez, and Lastwell, who as had been his habit since his unfortunate encounter had taken to rising before sunup to go walk about in the woods.

They sat at the long folding bench in the larger of their two huts. Outside, the Pendju went about their daily business: patching clothing, drying and storing foodstuffs, educating children, repairing weapons and fashioning pottery, maintaining their learned shapes. With no winter to worry about there was no reason to slave morning to night storing several months' supply worth of food. It seemed a salutary and contented life.

However essentially artificial, Prentice brooded.

"We have to move," he informed them, abruptly and without introduction.

"Move?" Lejardin forked something from her plate and swallowed delicately. "What do you mean, move?"

"You want to switch operations to the Quwanga village for a while?" Millie Carnavon asked.

"No. I mean we have to *move*. Everything. Our operations here"—he gestured at the interior of the hut—"Base Camp, everything. We need to reload the lander, boost back to low orbit, and find another site. A couple of hundred kilometers would be sufficient, but if it was up to me, I'd set down somewhere halfway around the globe. There are at least a dozen outstanding possibilities."

Cedric Carnavon chose his reply carefully. "There might not," he said slowly, "be any intelligent Xicans where we set down."

"That's possible." Prentice was unswayed. "If so, we can do a brief survey of the immediate vicinity and keep moving until we encounter them again. The important thing," he went on with uncharacteristic forcefulness, "is that they'll be uncorrupted Xicans, existing in their natural state . . . whatever that is. Any recordings we make of them, any studies we carry out, will not have to be stained with an asterisk named Conc!"

"We observe what exists," professed Millie Carnavon. "Affected by outside influence or not, the Pendju and the Quwanga *are* the local intelligence. And they can communicate. If we're lucky enough to stumble across any in their 'natural state,' we may not be able to parley with them at all."

"I refuse to accept that." Prentice gazed unblinkingly around the table. "They communicated among themselves before this antique intruder arrived here. If there are differences in dialect or even the language itself among any undisturbed natives we encounter, I feel confident we can master it. Jack?"

Attention shifted to Simna, who nodded reluctantly. "Salvor's correct. With the files I've assembled we should be able to talk to any natural-state natives anywhere on the planet, assuming they share common linguistic roots with the Pendju and Quwanga."

"Assuming they have anything to say." Millie Carnavon was not convinced.

"Salvor, what if intelligent life is restricted to this part of Xica? I don't mean the immediate coastline, but this general region."

"Then we can always return." He changed his approach, pleading for understanding. "Look, I'm getting really worried. I'm starting to wonder if despite our accumulated experience we're not getting in over our heads here. We handled Tycho V and Burke without any trouble, but this world, where everything has a twin something else and where the natives can make of themselves what they wish . . . I'm just afraid it may be too much for us.

"Then there's this Old Conc character. Is he more or less than what he seems? We already know he has his own agenda, one that puts the natives paramount. So far he's been tolerant of our presence here, but what if his attitude changes? He knows infinitely more about Xica than we do. What if under the weight of his own intentions or his fickle madness or whatever, his tolerance abruptly gives way to open hostility?"

"You afraid of one old man?" Simna challenged him.

Prentice shot him a look. "You know better than that,

Jack. I'm just saying that we should be cautious. Science should always be cautious."

"I always understood that the cautious scientists ended up in comfortable retirement and the bold ones in history books," Cedric Carnavon declared.

Prentice rarely lost his temper. "Damnit, Ced, this planet has enough deceptions to cope with without having to deal with a human one as well! What do we really know about this character? Nothing! What do we *really* know about what he's told his local Xicans? Nothing." He took a deep breath.

"I'm just saying that maybe we ought to try another spot. We're not doing too well here as it is. Noosa's gone, Ramirez is better but still shaky, and Captain Lastwell . . . he's been damaged. I don't know how severely, but I have the feeling that a change of scenery would do him a world of good. I've already spoken to him about this matter." Simna looked at the senior researcher evenly. "And he concurs."

"He would," Lejardin deposed. "He's terrified of this place. But should we be guided by the desires of an obviously disturbed paranoid?"

Prentice responded without hesitation. "He's still the captain of the *James Cook*. My conversations with him have convinced me that technically, he's sound. That's all we need be concerned about. He can rant his personal opinions day in and day out, so long as he can handle the ship." He scowled down the table at her.

"In reply to your question, no; I don't think we should be ruled by his desires, or anyone else's. Mine included. I think we should be guided by reason and common sense. With one team member dead, another seriously injured, and others who have demonstrated impaired judgment"—now it was Halstead's turn to look up in surprise—"and surrounded by an uncertain, unpredictable cultural situation over which we have no control, I think circumstances dictate our removal to a safer, if possibly less interesting, work site.

"If nothing else, everything we'll be studying will be the truth." He gestured toward the doorway and the bustling village beyond. "This place . . . this is at best a half-lie. Frankly, I'm fed up with it. I feel that we're being manipulated, if not by the Xicans then by this crazy old man. Haven't any of you experienced similar feelings?" He tried hard to avoid Halstead's gaze, though he was well aware that the bigger man's eyes were locked on him.

It was hushed around the table. Lejardin looked over at Simna. "Jack, what's your opinion?"

Simna leaned his elbows on the table and steepled his fingers in front of him. "I admit I wish we knew more about the old man, not to mention his actual state of mind. Sometimes I'm sure he's crazy, and then I get this inescapable feeling, like an itch I can't scratch, that the whole business is an act and that he's just putting us on.

"One thing we can't argue about. Willingly or not, these two tribes have become his plaything, individual Pendju and Quwanga his toys. It's his experiment and his study project, not ours. That's not to say the information we've gathered here is useless. Howevermuch influenced by outside forces, this society demonstrates native adaptability and talent to a considerable degree. In fact, it might help us to raise up any Xicans we encounter in their natural condition."

Prentice gaped at him. "I thought the whole idea of moving was to allow us to study the Xicans as they are and not to interfere with their native culture."

Simna shrugged absently. "According to Old Conc, Xicans in their natural state have no culture. Can we deny them those benefits because we want to study them?" The two men confronted one another across the table. Eventually it was a stern-faced Prentice who looked away.

"This only confirms my fears. We're becoming entirely too involved here. We're losing our distance, just as this crazy old man has. As scientists we can't afford that."

"What about our status as humanitarians?" Simna murmured.

Prentice slammed an open palm down hard on the table. "We weren't sent here as humanitarians! I say we move."

"I don't see that it's worth coming to blows over," sighed Millie Carnavon. "There'll be plenty to study at the next site. If we're lucky, even more."

Her husband nodded. "I agree. We can always come back here, perhaps with a constructively different perspective. It'll be useful to be able to compare unaffected natives with those that have been instructed by the old man."

"What about the rest of you? What do you think? Favrile?" Prentice eyed her expectantly.

"I guess I'll go with the majority decision. What about Bella-Lynn and Stewart?"

"They'll have to accept a *fait accompli*. Jack?"

Simna's answer was delayed, but agreeable. "I'm not one to rock the ship."

"Good." Prentice turned to his left. "Ted?"

Halstead looked away and said nothing.

Simna had stepped outside. Now he returned with Lastwell. Currently there was no sign of the detachment that had afflicted the captain off and on ever since his unfortunate encounter. He eyed them all openly, nodding to himself.

"Ready to spade fresh ground, eh? Suits me." His voice dropped to a garbled slur. "Damn sick of this place. Fucking heat and natives never let go of you. Get their slimy tendrils into your guts."

Prentice ignored the commentary. "Captain, what are our prospects for executing a prompt move?"

"Depends on what you mean by 'prompt,' Salvor. The lander's not a crude tool. You don't just jump aboard and push *start* and whizz, off you go. That said, I can state that fuel's no problem. There's enough on board to allow two or three takeoffs and landings, depending on how far afield we decide to range. More than that and we'll have to make a rendezvous with the *Cook*. Mechanically, everything's solid." He paused. "You want a minimal time frame?"

"That's what I'm asking for," Prentice told him.

"Couple of days. That's if we can get all your junk loaded by then."

"We'll hold up our end." Prentice turned back to his colleagues. "It's decided. We leave as soon as we can pack everything up and the captain and mate can get the lander ready."

"It's not decided," interposed a disputatious voice. Everyone turned to Halstead. He had his head down, not looking at them, but his eyes were open. "I think somebody should stay here. The future of these people is too important to leave in the hands of this Conc person. I know they want to learn from us and not just from him."

Prentice was taken aback. "Is that so? And how do you know that, Ted?"

Halstead raised his head. "Because that's what I've been told."

"You don't say? By your own personal Xican contact, maybe? I've no doubt she wants to learn from you."

The big man glanced sideways at Simna.

"Sorry, Ted. I kept it quiet as long as I could."

About to offer a retort, Halstead instead slumped visibly and just nodded. "I know. Thanks for the consideration, Jack."

Cedric Carnavon's countenance was severe. "What's going on here? Salvor? Jack?"

Simna waited for Halstead to speak. When the younger man remained silent, the generalist reluctantly explained. "Ted's established a relationship with one of the Pendju. A closer relationship than the rest of us have enjoyed."

"Oh," murmured Millie Carnavon. Lastwell grunted something unintelligible.

"I think it's vital that we retain contact with and influence over these two tribes," Halstead declared firmly.

"And you nominate yourself for primary contact," said Cedric Carnavon.

"Why not?" Halstead replied crisply. "I'm as qualified as anyone."

"That being an entirely rational and scientific decision on your part." Prentice was unable to bridle his scorn.

Halstead twitched perceptibly. For an instant Simna was afraid the other man was going to rise from his seat and physically assault the expedition leader. He primed himself to step between the two, but Halstead kept control of his emotions and intervention proved unnecessary. No doubt Halstead realized that such a reaction on his part would give Prentice all the excuse he needed to have his colleague sedated and moved bodily onto the lander.

"All I'm saying," Halstead continued fretfully, "is that it would be better if some continuity were maintained in our study of the Pendju, the Quwanga, and this part of Xica."

Prentice readily agreed. "No doubt. But not at the expense of undermanning the rest of the expedition. If we were at full strength I *might* consider your suggestion, but we're down two, at least until Ramirez fully recovers. Frankly, Ted, I don't think you're being sufficiently objective. We all make the move."

Meeting their gazes as candidly as he could, Halstead rose slowly from the table. "You all can do what you want.

Take all the supplies if you feel you'll need them. These people crave my help. I'm staying here."

Prentice gawked at him. "You're what?"

"What do you mean, you're staying here?" Cedric Carnavon spoke with quiet authority. "You can't stay here, Ted. You're part of a scientific *team*. Salvor is nominally in charge. We can debate minutiae and adjustments, but when it comes down to what we do next, it's his call. If he says it's time to try another site, we go to another site."

"Authority's a long ways from here, Ced." The big man turned back to Prentice. "What are you going to do, Salvor? Fire me?" Pushing away from his chair, he strode toward the doorway. "I think it's wrong to leave here when we're just starting to learn what these people are about. But I can't force you to stay with me, and I obviously can't convince you. Leave me a small transmitter. If your new site isn't too far, we can stay in touch. If not, you can use it to locate me when you come back."

Prentice rose. "Ted, you're not being rational. Come back here, Halstead!" But the other man was already out the door.

Lejardin looked first at Prentice, then turned to Simna. "This must be some relationship, Jack."

He smiled thinly. "Ted's infatuated, Favrile. Salvor's right: he's not acting sensibly."

"Oh, man." Lastwell rolled his eyes. "The fool's gone troppo."

Lejardin frowned. "Gone what?"

"Old expression from back home. Gone tropic, gone native, gone wild." He looked around the table. "If we leave him here now we may never find him again. He'll shut off the damn transmitter and go hide in the bush with his alien floozy."

"Surely not," argued Millie Carnavon. "After a few

months here by himself, surely he'll be glad of our company again."

"Don't count on it," Lastwell told her. "Look at this Old Conc."

"He came here seeking solitude."

"Maybe, maybe." There was a dangerous glint in the captain's eye. "Or maybe he's changed since he's been here. Maybe this place has changed him. He's told us how badly he wants to help these aliens. We're here a little while, and now Halstead swears essentially the same thing." He looked around the table. "Who's next?"

"What are you getting at, Frank?" Simna's curiosity was piqued.

"Probably nothing. But I can tell you this. I *don't* feel any overriding compulsion to help these happy humanoids. I just want to get the fuck away from here as fast as possible." He fastened Prentice with his gaze. "Want Kauri and I to initiate preparations for departure?"

Though a bit overwhelmed by the captain's sudden manic energy, Prentice didn't hesitate. "That's the decision."

"Good! I'm on my way." Rising from his chair, Lastwell stormed out of the hut.

Millie Carnavon pursed her lips. "He was very emphatic."

"Listen, I don't mean to sound cold in this." Prentice was very earnest. "I know these natives need our help. I can feel their desperation myself. It's like a palpable thing. But I don't think our situation here is healthy anymore. I feel, I know, that we need to get away. I don't want anyone else trading objectivity for altruism. We need breathing space, time to reflect on what we've seen here. So does Ted. He just doesn't realize it."

"I don't think we're going to be able to convince him."

Cedric Carnavon looked to his right. "I don't think even Jack will be able to persuade him."

"It doesn't matter," Prentice asserted. "When the time comes for us to lift off, Ted's coming with us. Whether he's ready to or not."

Carnavon's eyebrows rose. "You have something stronger than verbal persuasion in mind, Salvor?"

The expedition leader nodded. "Unless his impaired ability to reason has slid all the way over into paranoia, I think we should be able to get a sedative into him."

"Well, don't expect me to carry him," declared Lejardin.

"We'll take turns," Prentice informed her. "All we have to do is get him aboard the lander. Once we're away from here, he can yell and complain all he wants. I think that after a day or two free of local 'influence' he'll calm down and start to think. I know Ted. Once he does that, he'll be okay. He's just not thinking straight right now."

"He believes he's found something," Millie Carnavon pointed out.

Her husband frowned at her. "Don't romanticize this, Millie."

"I didn't say that was what he'd found, Ced. I just said that he's found *something*."

"The heat doesn't help." Lejardin's fingers fluttered in the air. "It makes your mind go muzzy."

Simna had to grin. "Is that an old expression from your home?"

She tried not to smile, and failed. "No. It's an original Lejardin expression."

Prentice remained all business. "Favrile, can I rely on you to fabricate a suitable pacifier for our contentious colleague?"

She nodded. "I don't like the idea, but I suppose it's better than letting Lastwell handle it. Certainly Ted can use the sleep."

"You'll need help when the time comes, in case there's trouble." Prentice peered around the table. "Jack? Ced?"

Both men looked resigned. "We don't want him to hurt himself," Carnavon murmured. "We'll be available." Simna subsequently gave his acquiescence.

"All you have to do is get one good dose in him." Prentice was very confident. "I don't want to lose any more people. Myself, I'm looking forward to seeing how the flora and fauna on the eastern continental mass differs from what we've collected here, if it does at all."

"Having a whole new ecosystem to decode should snap Ted out of this mood he's fallen into." Millie Carnavon made an effort to sound optimistic.

"If there are natives at the next site, we'll be more careful how we interact with them, natural state or not," Prentice added. "We've grown too close to the Pendju and the Quwanga, lost our scientific detachment. Their existence surprised us and we didn't handle it well. That won't happen again."

"Maybe," hazarded Lejardin hopefully, "we can find a cooler site."

"Now you're talking," agreed Cedric Carnavon. "I could handle that. There's mountains on this world. Maybe we can find a nice, luxuriant plateau. The fauna and flora higher up would have to differ significantly from what we've encountered here in the lowlands."

"I wonder if thixotropes are thermosensitive," Simna murmured. "If it's too cool, maybe the fauna can't shape-shift."

"Something else to check out." Prentice tried to muster some enthusiasm. "See? There's plenty to look forward to once we're away from this place. And when we've satisfied ourselves elsewhere, we can always return and conclude our research here."

"I know Bella-Lynn," Lejardin told him. "She'll be ready to go."

"I don't see Stewart objecting," Prentice added. "Not after what he's gone through here. And Kauri doesn't have a vote one way or the other.

"We'll start breaking down our facilities here first thing in the morning. I'll communicate our decision to Bella-Lynn and Stewart so they can get started there." The expedition leader seemed rejuvenated. Even the heat in the hut seemed to recede. "Now that we're agreed on what we're going to do, we don't need to rush. We'll move rapidly, but with care. I don't want to overlook anything."

Millie Carnavon spoke as they all rose and prepared to return to work. "Just one thing. What about the Pendju? We haven't considered them."

Prentice's expression twisted. "What about the Pendju?"

"We haven't talked about how they're going to react to our proposed departure. Our presence here has made a difference to them, perhaps to the point of altering their behavior. Particularly the behavior of certain individuals. Ted was right about one thing: they really do want to learn from us, want us to stay and teach them."

"They've still got the old man to supply instructions," Prentice reminded her. "I don't think they'll miss us. Anyhow, we can't worry about that. We need to concentrate on getting the expedition back on track."

"I know," she admitted. "But I am curious to see what their reaction is going to be."

"It'll give us something to record and study on our way out." Prentice deliberated. "Which brings to mind something else we should consider.

"I don't care how much money this Old Conc has, or had, or what his motivation was for coming here. Maybe there was a conspiracy on the part of his business partners to get rid of him. Or maybe greedy relatives are responsible. As we've already discussed, his whole story may be the product of a deranged imagination. Maybe he fabricated it to help preserve what's left of his sanity. We know for a fact that at the very least he's seriously addled."

"What are you saying, Salvor?" Cedric Carnavon wanted to know.

Prentice became dead serious. "I think we'd be seriously derelict in our responsibility if we didn't take him with us, all the way back to Earth. Look how a short stay here has affected Ted. This old man's been here a lot longer. Once free of the influence of this place, I'm betting he'll soon revert to normal."

Carnavon was uncertain. "I happen to agree with you, Salvor, but I'm not sure this falls within the province of our expedition charter."

"He'll thank us for it. If he doesn't change or otherwise improve, if he fusses or mopes over our altruism, we can always return him to his beloved natives." His gaze shifted to Lejardin. "When you're mixing your brew, make two doses."

"What if he resists?" Millie wondered.

"We won't give him the chance, any more than we will Ted. Besides, he's just a tired old man. I don't anticipate any difficulty." Prentice was quite sure of himself. "We'll feed him real food for a while, let him listen to music and watch some new entertainment recordings. He'll snap out of his stupor, same as Ted will. His sanity may even return without the need for medical attention."

Cedric Carnavon was convinced. "All right. As you say, if he becomes difficult we can always bring him back." He eyed his colleagues. "I know that if I were marooned in this place and had gone half off my head I'd want someone to offer me a helping hand, even if I didn't have sense enough to accept it at first."

"The Pendju may not like us taking their teacher away," Millie Carnavon pointed out.

Prentice had a ready reply. "We'll make sure they're not looking when we offer our help. We'll invite Old Conc to have a look at Base Camp, or the lander, or something. If the Pendju inquire, we can tell them Conc's gone to stay with the Quwanga a while. By the time they can check on the story we'll be out of here. Not that I think we'll have any trouble with him, or with the natives.

"Besides, I think they deserve a chance to mature from this point on based on their own abilities and without external distractions."

"Can we handle Old Conc and Ted at the same time?" Lejardin looked uncertain. "We only have the one truck. Everything else has to be moved by hand."

"If we have to, we can leave some of the gear and come back for it later," Prentice declared. "Getting Ted and the old man aboard are more important. Once on the ship we can isolate each of them in separate rooms until they calm down and come to their senses. I wouldn't be surprised if Old Conc straightens out before Ted. Underneath all his gabbing and mental drifting I have the feeling there lies an eminently sensible individual."

"Who do we grab first?" she wanted to know. "If Ted sees us sedate the old man he may get suspicious and bolt."

"Good point," agreed Simna. "I say we go after Ted. If we get the old man too, that's fine, but Ted's one of us. He's our real responsibility."

Carnavon nodded approvingly. "And if the old man witnesses anything we can explain that Ted's gone over the edge and is in need of some serious medicating. I don't know how perceptive he is, but even in his half-mad state he ought to understand that."

Prentice was fatigued, but pleased. "Everyone get a good night's sleep. Tomorrow's going to be a busy but rewarding day."

XVIII

"Hey, Ted! What do you have on tap for this morning?"

Halstead looked over and down at Simna. The senior scientist had materialized behind him in his usual infuriatingly silent manner.

"Nothing special," the younger man replied guardedly. "I thought that since O'Sandringham's still back at base I might take some samples of those seed-shooting flowers she discovered. Very carefully, of course." He grinned. "Maybe run some internal pressure measurements on the blossoms."

Simna squinted at the sky. "Nice day for it."

"It's always a nice day on Xica, Jack."

"*I* like it. The climate gives some of the others fits, though. Imagine spending a morning taking measurements of the muzzle velocity of a flower."

"I wonder." The picture of casualness, Carnavon joined them. "If you weren't careful and you caught one of those fruiting seeds in the chest, would it kill you or would you just bloom?" The three men shared a mutual chuckle.

"I'm not particularly busy this morning," Simna informed the younger man. "Sure you don't need any help?"

"No, thanks. I'm fine on my own." Halstead hesitated, then wondered why. "One of the Pendju will be assisting me."

Simna nodded understandingly. "Going off to the southeast? There's a sort of glade back that way that's full of those shooters."

The younger scientist blinked. "I don't remember a spot like that. I thought I'd been over that ground."

"So much of it looks alike," Simna replied, "that sometimes it's tough to tell one place from another. At least the plants here don't have a second suit of clothes to change into. Of course, we don't know what effect seasonal variations might have on the local flora."

Halstead considered. "That's assuming that this region experiences climatic fluctuations when . . . hey!" He spun sharply. Carnavon was already stepping back from him, the compact injector clutched in his right hand.

Halstead twisted and strained to see the back of his right leg. A small red spot was visible just below the hem of his shorts. Face flushed, he straightened slowly.

"What's the idea, Ced? What's going on?" His attention shifted back to Simna, who explained apologetically.

"I'm sorry, Ted. It's for your own good. Really. We're leaving this place together, or we're not leaving at all. Since you've been exhibiting a certain amount of reluctance here lately to comply with majority decisions . . ."

"I told you." The younger man seemed on the verge of tears. "I told you I wasn't . . ." He raised his voice suddenly. "Dih!" He tried to call the Pendju's name a second time as he turned, a tall pole wobbling unsteadily on its axis.

Simna caught him under his arms as he fell, supporting the much larger man easily. With Carnavon's help he lowered the scientist's bulk to the ground. Halstead was mumbling steadily, but so softly he could not be understood.

Carnavon slipped his arms under the other man's legs, well up above the knees, while Simna took the rest of the weight under the arms.

"Ready? On three. One, two . . ."

Together they carried the semiconscious form back to the nearest human-occupied hut. Suspending their daily chores, several Pendju paused to look, their wide eyes full of curiosity and concern.

Carnavon spoke to one who took the time to inquire if anything was wrong with Halstead-friend. "No problem. You know how soundly we can sleep. Ted here's just taking a nap." The native blithely accepted this explanation and went on about his business.

They entered the hut and set Halstead down on a waiting medical pallet. Carnavon moved to the doorway and peered cautiously outside.

"No sign of his female. I think we've pulled it off."

Lejardin ran a quick check of Halstead's vital functions, pronouncing him healthy and sound. In the rear of the building Millie Carnavon was carefully repacking delicate instrumentation.

"The poor dear." Bunching up a native weaving, she slipped it beneath Halstead's head.

"Hopefully when he wakes up on the lander his mind will clear fast," her husband murmured. "All of it. He may weep and wail for a while, but he'll get over it as soon as he realizes how silly it makes him look."

"I hope so." Lejardin considered the scientist's motionless form thoughtfully. "Would you say his problem was that he was attached, infatuated, or really in love?"

"I'd say he was emotionally overwrought and seriously confused," Carnavon responded.

Simna wiped sweat from his brow. "So much for the easy part." He eyed Carnavon meaningfully.

The senior scientist nodded and reloaded the injector, addressing Lejardin as he carefully checked the power setting.

"You sure you measured this accurately? He's an old man and I wouldn't want to overdose him."

"Are you kidding?" she retorted. "Living here for years among the Xicans has probably made him as tough as some of those vines whose internal structure you've been struggling to analyze."

He nodded and gestured to Simna. The two men slipped out of the hut.

"I hope they don't have any trouble." Millie Carnavon gazed after her departing husband.

"They'll be all right," Lejardin assured her. "Jack knows what he's doing." She smiled. "Jack Simna could talk a Xican out of his alternate shape."

The older scientist glanced in surprise at her colleague. "You like him, don't you? I thought you found him too dry."

Lejardin shrugged. "I don't know, Millie. Jack puzzles me. He knows so much, but there is an awful lot of disparity between us. I just can't figure him. Personally, he's an enigma, and I'm not used to dealing with enigmas. Sometimes I think I've got him figured, and then . . ." She sighed and turned back to the business of packing. "This Old Conc character isn't the only one wandering around with secrets bottled up inside."

"Maybe on board they can puzzle each other out," Millie Carnavon suggested. "Can you give me a hand with this luminoscope?" Together the two women gently wrestled the sensitive device into its shipping container.

The two scientists found Old Conc relaxing at one of his favored spots, atop the highest point of the bluff that overlooked the sea. The wind blew his long gray hair and beard backward, giving him the aspect of a biblical prophet working on his tan. Carnavon was relieved. They hadn't had to go bashing through the woods to find him, and in this isolated spot they could get on with it untroubled by passing, querulous Pendju.

"Hello, gentlemen." The old man spoke without turning.

Not that he had eyes in back of his head, but he *was* highly sensitive to movement around him. Simna readied himself. Conc wasn't *that* old . . . however old he actually was.

Not for the first time since Prentice had put forth his philanthropic proposal, Simna found himself wondering if they were doing the right thing. Surely, he told himself, the old man would be better off returned to Earth. He'd embarked on this solitary fling and it had unquestionably damaged his mind. Once his sanity had been restored by rest, decent food, and medical treatment, he'd likely seek out his saviors to fall at their feet in gratitude.

A noble perspective, the scientist mused as he approached, but a difficult one to instigate. Who had Old Conc been, and what had he done? They would have plenty of time to find out once and for all when they were safely back aboard the lander.

"Come out here for the view, have you?" Old Conc inquired spritely.

Simna glanced back the way they'd come. The gaps between the trees remained deserted. No suspicious Pendju had trailed them. The three men were alone.

"Don't you ever get bored here?" Carnavon was prosaic as always.

"Bored? From gazing out across an unspoiled sea, an uncontaminated beach, through unpolluted air? Why would I grow tired of that, Cedric?"

Simna sat down next to Old Conc while Carnavon lingered behind. "Even paradise can get boring. And once it's boring, it's no longer paradise."

"Why, Mister Jack Simna, you're a philosopher." The old man guffawed; a deep, quaintly skewed sound. "And here I thought you were like all the others, your mind and attention forever glued to the eyepiece of magnifier or telephoto. Don't tell me you actually take time to think about what you see?"

"I've done my share of analysis," Simna told him.

"I'm not talking about 'analysis,' sonny-boy. But then, if you don't know what I'm talking about, there's no use talking about it, is there?" With a sweeping gesture he simultaneously encompassed and blessed the unparalleled panorama before them. "Isn't this worth preserving for the Xicans? They want to preserve it, too. They just aren't sure how to go about it."

"So you tell them, just like you've told them everything else."

"Yes," the old man murmured. "I teach them. They're hungry for knowledge, sonny. They crave it the way an addict craves chocolate, or theta-endorphin. They are without question the *neediest* folk I've ever come across. Shoot, they even needed a decent *shape*." He turned so suddenly that Simna started in spite of himself. "Why don't you teach them, Jack Simna? You've a lot to share and no one to share it with. They hold you in highest regard. I tell you, the sense of satisfaction you get can't be compared to any other feeling you've ever experienced. One of your group has discovered that already."

Simna replied without hesitation. "Halstead. You know about that, then." His expression clouded. "Did you put the female Pendju up to that?"

Old Conc laughed uproariously and Carnavon took a discrete step back. "Me? Put a Pendju up to asking for help? Name-of-a-God, sonny, I don't have to propose anything like that to the Xicans. They're fully capable of manifesting their cravings without the intervention of a wrinkled old intermediary like myself. No, sonny-boy, your friend found something he needed all by his lonesome. I had nothing to do with it."

"If you're so anxious for the Pendju to receive instruction, I'd think you'd want to see as many expeditions come here as rapidly as possible, to disseminate even more knowledge, to feed the Xican craving even faster."

The old man wagged a finger at him. "Ah, but it has to be the right kind of knowledge. Not everyone is suited to teach, not everything suitable to learn. Now a few of your lot, like your young associate Halstead, and you yourself, seem fit for the job. I haven't decided about the others."

Taken aback by such profound conceit, Simna could only sputter, "*You* haven't decided."

Old Conc smiled through his beard. "That's right."

Simna leaned forward. "Tell me something, old man. What's the secret of the Xicans' lure? What compels you, and now Ted, to give up everything to help them? Is it the promise of malleable sex? Of something telepathic the rest of us can't or haven't felt yet? Or is it the opportunity to be treated like an absolute ruler or king?"

The old man lowered his voice conspiratorially. "Well now, sonny-boy, it ain't the sex, because I had plenty of that before I ever set foot on this world. And if it's tele-pathic it's breakin' all the rules and laws of biology, not to mention physics. Not that I'm sayin' it ain't a possibility, mind. As for the chance to be an absolute ruler, well, I had all I wanted of that, too.

"No, it's a good deal more basic than any of that, sonny. It's need, pure and simple. Need immutable, in a form so elemental we've forgotten it on Earth. If there are some kind of telepathic undertones, I haven't caught on to 'em yet, but it doesn't matter. The need's genuine enough all by itself. The potential of these people is beyond imagining. All they *need*, all they ask for, all they want, is a chance to meet outsiders on equal terms.

"And you ask me if I'm bored. Wake up, sonny-boy, and smell the quantum roses."

Simna shook his head. Out of the corner of an eye he could see Carnavon edging closer to the old man's back.

"So it's curiosity that keeps you going here? The desire to see what's going to happen next, the surprises posed by a developing culture?"

Old Conc was shaking his head sadly. "Once I used to be like you, sonny. Wanted to know everything, see everything, do everything. I came about as close to achieving that as any one human could, and you know what? It didn't make me a better person. More knowledgeable, more experienced, yes, but better?" He shook his head anew.

"Eventually I decided that all I wanted was peace. Peace and silence."

"The Pendju talk plenty," opined Carnavon, not wanting to appear the silent shadow.

"They approach politely, and when solitude is requested, they honor it. Two characteristics sadly missing from human society." He returned his gaze to the sea.

"Are you saying that we're bothering you now?" Simna asked him.

"A sense of humor, too. You have potential, Jack Simna."

"No, it's plain that we're bothering you."

For an instant the old man hesitated. Then he sat a little straighter and turned to look directly around at Carnavon, who was very close now. Much to his surprise, under that unexpectedly withering stare Carnavon stiffened and retreated several steps.

Simna descried the byplay. Though his physical skills exceeded those of most of the expedition members, he chose to keep them largely under wraps. Now he had to consider how much force he might have to employ. He wasn't going to hurt the old man in order to save him, even if it meant disappointing Prentice.

Carnavon lunged quickly and then stepped back. Perhaps Conc could have avoided the strike, perhaps not. In any event he made no effort to dodge the descending injector.

Stiffening momentarily, he addressed them without taking his eyes from the blue waters.

"How long before it takes effect?"

A hesitant Simna glanced briefly at Carnavon before deciding simply to reply. "It's pretty fast. There's no pain."

"Am I supposed to be grateful for that?" The woolly head turned to regard the scientist. "Why?"

"We're convinced this is for your own good. You're obviously unstable and a danger to yourself. We think a change, the company of good people, the familiar surroundings of modern civilization, would do you good. We can always bring you back."

The old man smiled gently. "But I don't want to leave." So far he was showing no effects from the sedative. He should be wilting, Simna thought worriedly.

"You can always come back here." Carnavon echoed his colleague's sentiment.

A soft chuckle emerged from the deeply lined throat. "Are you going to study me, too?"

"No," Simna told him. "We just want to help. To do what we think is best for you."

"Really?"

"That's all we have in mind."

"Sure you're not feeling guilty about something?" He was blinking rapidly now.

"Why should we feel guilty about anything?" Simna watched the old man closely.

"Because everyone carries a pocketful of culpability around with them. None of us is guiltless. To claim otherwise is to admit to a bald-faced lie. Take it from me. I'm an expert on guilt." He inhaled softly. "Do-gooders. Worse than assassins." With that, his eyes closed and his head fell forward.

Simna hastily grabbed the old man's wrist and felt for a pulse. "Hell, I hope we didn't kill him."

"Favrile was very meticulous about the dosage." Carnavon was leaning forward to examine the unconscious oldster.

Simna's fingers rose to the wrinkled throat, probing beneath the beard. Only then did he sit back and heave a sigh of relief.

"He's okay. He just went under differently from Ted."

Carnavon flexed his fingers. "He'll be a lot easier to carry, that's for sure." He bent forward again. "Here, let's get him up."

"He's not that big. Let's trade off. We can move faster that way and one of us can always be acting as lookout." With Carnavon's help, Simna hoisted Old Conc into a shoulder carry. "Keep a watch for meandering locals. Since they were curious about Ted's condition, they're liable to be positively engrossed in Conc's."

Keeping to the trees as much as possible, they hurried swiftly back to the village. Most of the Pendju were out gathering foodstuffs, working their gardens, or collecting the special clay they used for making pottery. The two men and their burden arrived at the hut unseen.

Looking harmless and very old, the man was laid in the open truckbed alongside Halstead. Millie Carnavon found a light, porous sheet to place over them both, pulling it up high enough to cover the old man's face. The thin material would conceal him without impairing his slow, steady breathing. To any casual observer the truck would appear to be piled high with sealed containers, bound gear, and a single large, irregularly shaped lump.

"Let's keep moving." Carnavon was peering out the single window. "We don't want to linger here until he's missed."

"We don't know that anyone checks in with him on a regular basis," Lejardin pointed out. "We shouldn't have any trouble." She swung her bulging backpack up onto her shoulders and took a final look around the hut.

"I'll miss this place. But I guess it's time to move on."

"A fresh start at a new site." Prentice adjusted his own, slightly larger pack. "Everyone ready?"

They headed out across the by now well-marked and widened trail that had been cleared between the village and Base Camp, the heavily loaded little truck humming silently through the forest. There was one tense moment when a few passing Pendju, who had been out gathering edible roots, waved but did not stop to chat. The energetic trio were the only villagers the expedition members encountered on the long drive back, and they did not look closely enough to remark on the presence of the strange shapes that shifted loosely within the vehicle.

Lastwell and Stevens were waiting to greet them. Prentice was pleased to note that several of the domes had already been broken down. They formed a gleaming monolith in the clearing, awaiting transport back to the lander. For her part, the heavily perspiring O'Sandringham had made good progress at repacking their research materials and other equipment. Her own personal effects were ready to go.

Three buildings with their connecting tubular passageways remained to be dismantled, along with the gear inside. With all of them working together that shouldn't take more than a couple of days, Prentice decided. Their planned departure was on schedule.

"Any trouble with the Moon-eyes?" Lastwell came over to examine the contents of the truck.

Carnavon shook his head. "Ted wasn't happy about it, but we got to him before he realized what was going on. The old man didn't even resist."

"He just sat there after we dosed him." Simna flung

sweat into the brush. "Said a few words and went to sleep. He was less trouble than Ted."

"Let's put them in with Ramirez," Lastwell suggested. "The dome housing the infirmary'll be the last one we take down. They can keep him company for a while."

"How is Stewart?" Prentice slipped off his pack.

"Up and about pretty good," O'Sandringham told them, "but he still hasn't got all his strength back. It's been a humbling experience for him."

Lastwell looked better than he had in some time. "As soon as we've got everything back on board, I'll flash-activate the auxiliaries. Then we can sleep in real beds. Or at least in real bunks."

"That'd be a change. And strange." Lejardin looked back at the forest from which they'd emerged, then out across the intruding finger of the great Xican desert. The sleek bulk of the lander gleamed metallically against the russet sands, its nose pointing into the wilderness.

"Despite all the hardships, I've come to like this place. It's so different from what I'm used to. You can get a fresh perspective on existence here, put aside a lot of your every-day concerns."

"And have them replaced by new ones," Prentice avowed. "Like the old man was told, we can always return."

"Any idea where we're going to try next?" O'Sandringham asked him briskly.

"If I remember the final charts correctly, there's a wide, shallow bay of unusual dimensions on the west coast of the other continental mass. There could be some intriguing shallow-water life forms there, and it would be a logical place for native Xicans, however primitive, to establish a homesite or two." Prentice was showing more enthusiasm than he had in many days. "We'll get on the rest of this stuff tomorrow and be out of here in a couple of days."

"You don't think we should say farewell to the Pendju?" wondered Millie Carnavon. "Let them know that we intend to return?"

"I don't think that's a good idea," her husband said. "We don't want them hanging about, querying us about Old Conc's extended absence. They're clever folk. One might spot him and tell the rest, and then there could be trouble. I don't think that would be the case, but I see no point in chancing it."

"I concur," said Prentice. "In fact, I think it would be a good idea to mount a watch on the camp tonight and not rely solely on the automatics. Just as a precaution. They can't get into or do anything to the lander."

The senior scientist nodded agreeably. "I'll take the late watch. Give me a chance to look for interesting nocturnals."

"I'll take the two hours before or after you, Ced," Simna volunteered.

They parceled out the watches between them. Tomorrow they would pack up the rest of the equipment, and then the domes. With the aid of the truck, it wouldn't take long to transport everything back to the lander. As for their two heavy sleepers, the sedative Lejardin had concocted should keep them comatose until at least tomorrow night. If either man gave signs of causing trouble, she could work her pharmaceutical magic a second time.

Leaning on his improvised cane, Ramirez wandered out to greet them. He was sufficiently recovered to express his frustration to anyone who would listen at his inability to get around faster. The paralysis seemed to be lingering longest in his legs.

Steadying himself, he shook the cane. "I'll toss this tomorrow. Day after at most. When we move to the ship I'll eave it here, a present for some lucky Pendju."

"Think of it," Prentice teased him. "There'll be a whole new ecosystem for you to get up close and personal with."

"Very funny, hah-hah." Ramirez spared a perfunctory glance for the two somnolent bodies in the bed of the truck, then raised his eyes to the forest. "I'll be glad to be away from here. My memories of this place aren't as idyllic as some of yours."

"Who said anything about them being idyllic?" Prentice came back. "It was business. We've learned a great deal here, but now the time has come to move on." He was almost content with their progress.

There was little movement within the camp that night. Everyone was tired, fatigued either from participating in the hasty breakdown of facilities or the bumpy drive from the Pendju village. Anticipation over their imminent departure gave way to the demands engendered by physical exhaustion.

Prentice took the first watch, to be followed in turn by Lejardin, Simna, and, early in the dark morning, a weary but attentive Cedric Carnavon. A few night-dwellers shuffled about in the underbrush, and once something clumsy and slow ingested an entire clump of *Haukik* right under Carnavon's delighted eyes, but of the natives there was no sign.

Within the compound everyone slept soundly. All was peaceful and devoid of movement when the old man's eyes snapped open.

He blinked. Whence the comforting night sky with its sly arthropodial buzzing and drifting thixotropic shapes? Where were the familiar alien constellations so lovingly memorized? The unfamiliar, nearly forgotten odor of artificially cooled air tickled his nostrils. The dryness suggested that a dehumidifier was also hard at work.

Air is not clay, he mused, *to be so indifferently tailored and molded.*

Raising his head, the first thing he saw was the unconscious figure that had been laid alongside him. In the dim light he recognized the tall young scientist named Halstead. In a dash of delicious irony, the pillow that cradled his head was of Xican manufacture.

A quick survey of his surroundings revealed living space largely filled now with sealed crates and packing tubes. Looking like a retired robot in the dim light, a sterilizing cabinet stood off to one side, carrying handles affixed to both sides.

As he sat up the feathery sheet fell away from him, bunching in folds at his waist. Memories flooded back: of a conversation on the bluff, a fleeting sting, promises unlikely to be kept. He'd been aware of the tautness in the two men but had been curious to see what they intended to do. Neither could imagine the resistance his body had built up during a lifetime of strain and exertion to medication of every type.

Other memories spilled into consciousness, remembrances he had done his best to forget. A great sadness welled up in him. He'd spent years trying to put all that behind him. But mankind, bursting with its usual insulting good intentions, had followed him even to this place, even to impossibly isolated Xica.

From the start he'd done his best to be civil with them, though cultivated manners had never constituted a significant part of his makeup. He'd fled such constraints and embarrassments, not only for his health but for mankind's as well. Now these interlopers were doing their damnedest to bring it all back. To bring back the *him* he'd heretofore so successfully abandoned.

There was still hope, still time. With great difficulty he repressed the instincts that were welling up in him with all the force of a tsunamic wave. Silently he turned and slid off the pallet. He didn't want to be quiet. What he wanted to do was scream, to howl and bray as he'd done exuberantly so long ago. Life among the Xicans had enabled him to subdue such emotions. As he edged toward the doorway he knew his control was shaky.

Though he knew nothing of the camp's internal layout, he'd studied it from outside. The setup was not complex. The portal before him would lead to a tubular tunnel, which would lead to another domed structure, which would offer a way out. The cooled air chilled him as he opened the door.

Someone was standing there.

"Christ, you startled me!" Ramirez blurted. "I was coming in to check on Ted. Hey, you shouldn't be up yet."

Eyes of blue fire gazed unblinkingly back at him.

"I'm going to have to tell Favrile. She's not going to be happy at being awakened this late." Ramirez took a step forward. "Right now I need for you to get back on your cot."

"You're in my way." The old man's voice was deeper than the researcher remembered it. He hesitated warily.

"You look different in this light. The others think I'm inventing things, but I could swear I've seen you somewhere before. Not in person but . . ." His eyes grew wide. Not as wide as those of the Pendju, but very wide indeed.

"Madre de Dios," he muttered. "Majestatus."

"Aye." Suddenly Old Conc didn't look so old, or bent.

"Concarry Clive Majestatus," an astonished Ramirez continued. "I'll be damned."

"Probably," whispered the old man huskily. "As for myself, I already was, a long time ago. So you recognize me."

"Yeah. Yeah, I do. From the histories. I know who you are."

Conc shook his head slowly, sadly. "No, you don't. You don't know me at all. No one does, no one ever did. I am all you ever wanted to be, or could be, or ever feared becoming. I am your savior and your nemesis, your god and your devil. I was, unfortunately, only a man. Now I am healed. But, woe is to say, not completely. You put me to sleep and now I have awakened. Something better than you or I depends on me. Therefore I will not let you put me to sleep again."

With a movement so swift not even Simna could have avoided it, he struck out with his left hand in a distinctive, peculiar fashion. It caught the startled Ramirez on the side of his neck before he could even begin to jerk away. He blinked, shuddered once, and collapsed to the floor.

Bending over, the old man picked up the cane and raised it slowly over his head. Trembling, it hovered there for a long moment before Conc lowered it slowly.

"No," he whispered as much to unseen demons as to himself. "No. You won't have me again. I won't let these put me to sleep and I won't let you wake me up. Do you hear? I choose to remain median. I fight for the average me!" With that he rushed in absolute and eerie silence down the corridor, leaving the scientist crumpled behind him.

XIX

It was O'Sandringham and Stevens who found Ramirez as they completed a perfunctory check of the camp near the end of their joint watch.

"What the blazes happened to him?" Stevens's bafflement was plain on his face as he bent to look at the unmoving scientist.

Kneeling beside the body, O'Sandringham spoke without looking up. "Go check on Ted. Then get everyone else up. And watch yourself." Nodding, Stevens whirled and rushed to comply.

O'Sandringham shoved a hand beneath Ramirez's head and raised it as much as she was able. "Stewart! Stewart, tell me what happened."

Stevens was shouting to her from the far side of the dome. "Halstead's fine! I'll go wake the others."

"Right." The head in her hands shifted slightly. "Stewart?"

His eyelids twitched as he turned to face her. That's when she saw the half-dry stream of blood that had been flowing from his nose and the coagulated pool that formed a dark, horrid halo beneath him. Her insides jumped, but she continued to support him. Lejardin was needed here. The quantity of blood hinted at more serious damage within.

Abruptly he reached up and grabbed the hem of her duty blouse. "I know who he is," the injured scientist mumbled weakly.

"What?" She leaned closer, trying to comfort him. "Take it easy, Stew." She glanced anxiously back down the corridor. *Where were the others, damnit?* "Just hang on a minute, Stewart."

"No, you don't understand. *I know who he is.*"

Her lips flexed. "Who *who* is?"

"Him. The old man. Concarry Clive Majestatus."

It was her turn to blink. "Who? That name means nothing to me."

"Majestatus." The grip on her shirt slackened. "Watch out for him. Watch out for . . ." He settled back, a dead weight against her, his eyes staring at the featureless ceiling.

"Just take it easy, Stew." Cradling his bloody head, she repeated those words like a mantra, but it did no good. By the time a sleepy Lejardin arrived with medical kit in hand and Millie Carnavon close behind, Ramirez was gone.

O'Sandringham stepped back and let Lejardin go to work. The other woman's skilled fingers fluttered only briefly over the motionless figure before she sat back, staring blankly. "Internal hemorrhaging," she elucidated emotionlessly. "He bled to death. What could have *happened*?"

"Here." Bending, Millie Carnavon brushed aside dark hair and pointed to the dead man's neck. It was impossible to miss the deep, ugly bruise above the carotid artery.

"The Puffballs," O'Sandringham suggested. "Or something else in the lab. Stewart never could leave well enough alone."

An out-of-breath Stevens burst back into the dome. "The old man's definitely gone. So's the cane Stewart was using."

"This doesn't look like it was made by a cane." Lejardin was fingering the bruise.

"Of course it was," O'Sandringham growled. "What else?"

"Then he is dangerous."' Millie Carnavon looked up from her contemplation. "Who was on watch last?"

"We were. Bella-Lynn and I." Stevens rubbed at his eyes. "We didn't see or hear a thing."

"What the bloody hell is going on?" Lastwell appeared at the mate's side, took one look at Ramirez's body, and snapped out a terse obscenity. "That's it. We're getting out of here today. You can sort out unsecured gear once we're all back on board the lander. I ain't staying here another night."

"What about Old Conc?" Millie Carnavon asked.

"What about the old shit? If we're lucky, a *Vrilil* will get him."

"We can't leave him now," she insisted as Prentice and Simna arrived. "We have to . . ."

"We have to what?" Lastwell was openly furious. "Bring him to justice? Query his motives? Forget it, Millie. Come sundown, we're out of here."

"He said that he knew his name." O'Sandringham looked up at her colleagues. "He said that he knew who the old man was." Everyone was looking at her. "Majestatus."

"Maje . . ." Lastwell choked on the pronunciation. "Concarry Majestatus?" She nodded. Whereupon he turned to slam a booted foot into the corridor wall, denting it severely. "Goddamnit! A thousand times over son-of-a-bitch!"

"Hard to believe." A phlegmatic Simna was unaffected by the violent display. By now they were all used to the captain's violent mood swings.

Lejardin's gaze flicked from one man to the other. "Who is this guy? I never heard of a Concarry Majestic."

"Majestatus," Simna corrected her. "He was a little before your time. Old Conc. Concarry Clive Majestatus. Field-Marshal Majestatus. Think back to your history texts, Favrile."

Her brow furrowed, then relaxed. "Oh," she murmured. Her eyes widened slightly. *"Oh."*

"Not especially eloquent," Simna deposed, "but to the point."

"Well, I don't recognize it," a frustrated O'Sandringham insisted.

"As I said, before your time. Before mine too, actually, though less so than yours." The scientist meditated briefly as he leafed through the encyclopedia that was his mind. "Was it thirty years ago? Probably more. I was just a kid, but it seems I can remember reading about it."

"About what?" O'Sandringham prompted her colleague.

"His abdication. The greatest military mind of the Posttribal era, they called him. Head of the Global Commonwealth Police Active Response team. I remember reading about how he personally took charge of the suppression of the Kanaka Anarchics rebellion in New Caledonia in '83, and made peace among the Martian colonists in '86. Those are just a couple of the high points. His brilliance was universally acknowledged, though as I recall there was considerable controversy over his methods."

Cedric Carnavon had arrived later than the others. But his memory was as sharp as Simna's. "Military historians ranked him with Caesar and Alexander, though he never really had a chance to demonstrate his *abilities* on that kind of scale. So he made the best of the more limited opportunities contemporary society offered. He was a soldier's soldier."

Simna nodded. "Then one day he just disappeared."

"The sneaky bastard." Lastwell was looking around nervously as if he expected the old man to leap out at him

from a dark corner. "And we wondered how he had the resources and connections to pull off a voyage like this."

"Certainly he was well connected in the global financial
community," Simna commented, "and with the space program as well. Not many individuals could have orches-
trated an inconspicuous one-way ticket on a deepsleep ship,
but he had the wherewithal. Clearly he used it."

"But why this?" O'Sandringham indicated the inanimate
body before them. "Why kill Stewart?"

"Maybe because your friend recognized him," Lastwell
snarled softly. "Maybe because of something else that was
said. Maybe because the old bastard is just out of control.
We'll never know. I do know that we'd better watch ourselves from now on, and not just because of this." He indicated the corpse on the bloody floor.

"What are you saying, Frank?" Carnavon asked him.

"That he may not want us going back and telling the
world that he's out here."

Simna disagreed. "I think you're buying trouble. He
could have knocked us off one at a time before we ever ran
into him, or had it done quietly while we slept in the village. No, something specific happened to set him off."

Millie Carnavon was never reluctant to speculate. "Could
the sedative you gave him have had unanticipated side effects? Maybe it helped to jog old memories, old reflexes."

"He must've surprised Stewart." Stevens was unruffled.
"There are seven of us, and he's still just one old man."

"Yeah." Lastwell continued to scan his surroundings uneasily. "The most dangerous old man alive. We've got to
get away from here, and we've got to get away *now*."

"Not until the rest of our equipment is ready to move."
Prentice was unyielding. "We don't have spares enough to
allow us to abandon all this. Wherever we make landfall
next, we're going to need it. He's gone, and I don't thi

he'll bother us anymore. All he probably wanted was to get away from us."

"Forget your life for a moment," growled Lastwell. "You willing to bet somebody else's on that?"

Prentice hesitated. "We'll do this as fast as we can. Captain, you and Kauri continue to break down the camp infrastructure. The rest of us will help as time allows.

"You don't have to tell me twice." Now Stevens was beginning to share his superior's sense of foreboding.

The expedition leader offered a sop to Lastwell's anxiety. "Anything bulky and nonessential we'll leave. For now." He looked around the shrunken circle. "Everything important goes on board as quickly as we can move it."

"That's more like it." Lastwell was mollified. "We'll be out of here before sundown tomorrow." With Stevens in tow, he whirled and hurried from the dome.

"Meanwhile, I guess I'm still on watch." O'Sandringham rose. "Millie, maybe you could join me? I don't like the idea of trekking a night perimeter alone."

"I'd be happy to. Ced?"

Her husband nodded approval. "I'll handle our responsibilities here. Just make sure you two look out for one another."

Lejardin was querying Simna. "You think he'll give us any more trouble?"

"Who knows how a man like that thinks when he's sane, let alone when he's obviously been unbalanced?" Simna's lips tightened. "We should have left him alone."

"We should maybe have done a lot of things differently," Prentice confessed, "but we could only do the best we could. Like we're going to do now."

They dispersed throughout the camp, furiously cramming gear into gaping packing containers and crates. Everyone was too busy to talk about what had happened to amirez, or what theoretically might happen to them if they didn't get away fast. Care and precision were overlooked in the rush to complete the work as quickly as possible.

Stevens took time from the arduous task of infrastructure breakdown to set up several powerful portable lights. They bathed the edge of the forest in splendid glare, stunning those nocturnal creatures unfortunate enough to stumble into the powerful beams.

Two of their number gone now and a third reclining in enforced slumber. There would be, could be, no more losses.

As soon as the truck was loaded, Stevens drove it recklessly across gravel and sand, dumping the contents onto the lander's belly hoist. The moment the vehicle's integral skids could be shoved into the hold, he returned for another load. With everyone working frenetically, the Base Camp vanished in huge chunks into the waiting ship.

They worked on through the rest of the early morning hours and into the torpid light of morning, alternating watches and catching up on missed sleep a few hours at a time. On several occasions the alarm was raised and work halted when curious Pendju were spotted watching from the forest fringe. The natives would stand and stare at the shrinking camp and the antics of the humans, only to eventually turn and melt silently back into the woods.

Halstead had emerged from his induced stupor enough to moan and complain about his condition. They shifted him to a medical pallet and secured him with straps, ignoring his increasingly intelligible protests.

By mid-afternoon the heat and constant activity had laid low even the most energetic among them. They rested in the secure, unnaturally cool confines of the lander.

"Why don't we just leave now?" Stevens was staring out the vessel's front port.

"We sill have too much irreplaceable material to load." Prentice nodded in the direction of the campsite. "Just a few more trips and we'll be on our way. I'm not any happier about the delay than you."

"Then what are we sitting here for?" Stevens's energy was prodigious. "Let's go get the rest of it."

"There's too much for the two of us," Prentice contended, "and everyone else is exhausted. You can't expect people to work round the clock in this heat."

As he continued to gaze out the port, the mate chafed at the delay. "It'll be dark soon."

"A couple of trips," Prentice said soothingly. "Under the lights. Then we can lift off." The expedition leader tried to free the other man's thoughts from the anxieties that were tormenting him. "How's the programming look for touchdown at the new site?"

"Don't worry. Frank goes off a little wild sometimes, but he could plot an arcing descent from orbit in his sleep."

Prentice nodded absently as he squinted in the direction of the forest. It was too far to tell if any natives were lingering in the vicinity of the camp, and he didn't feel like hunting for a set of lenses. In any case, in the event of an emergency the most valuable equipment was already on board.

By the time everyone was roused from the essential afternoon nap to bolt down a hastily prepared meal, the sun was already setting. Head- and spotlights blazing across the rolling red sand, they rode the axleless truck back to the campsite and resumed work.

It wasn't until just before nine that the captain, upon delivering another load to the ship, made a discovery that he shared in his usual tactful fashion, which consisted of bellowing it at anyone within earshot.

"Well, the dumb bastard's gone and snuck off."

"What?" O'Sandringham was collapsing extensible nanocarbon footings while Stevens tied them in bundles prior to stuffing them into their waiting storage cylinders.

Lastwell shoved back his cap and sunshield as he ambled over. "Your brilliant buddy Halstead. I checked the on-board infirmary. He isn't there, nor anywhere else on the lander as far as I could determine."

Lejardin abandoned her work to join the discussion. "How could he get up? He still had a lot of sedative in him, and he was cinched in place."

Lastwell's face contorted into a sneer. "Love doth do strange things to men, my dear." Espying Prentice, he yelled in the expedition leader's direction. "Hey, Salvor! Your alien-struck canary's flown."

When apprised of the situation, Prentice turned re-signedly toward the looming forest. "I suppose someone's going to have to go and look for him."

"Why assume he went that way?" asked Millie Car-navon. "What if under the sedative's influence he's wan-dered off into the dessert?"

"Because he's in bleedin' love, that's why. Or com-pletely out of it. Same thing, really." Lastwell gestured to-ward the gray-green woods. "I'd bet my retirement fund he's stumbling around in there, trying to find his way back to the village and his pliant Xican doxy."

"I'll have to go after him." As Simna took a step toward the truck, Lastwell blocked his path. The captain's expres-sion was bleak.

"You don't have to do anything of the sort." He looked sharply at Prentice. "How about it, Salvor? We don't know how long he's been gone. He could be anywhere by now."

"We can't just abandon him here," Prentice insisted.

"Maybe not, but if I'm right we have a pretty good idea where he's headed. First we finish loading and prepping the lander. *Then* we go after him. We'll organize into teams of three. That'll leave one of us here at all times, to keep an eye on things and greet him in case he comes to his senses and returns. This way once he's back in harness we can lift off straightaway, without giving him a chance at second thoughts or causing trouble."

Simna peered toward the forest, shadows against the moonlight, and wondered what eyes might even now be watching and listening. What alien thoughts might be coursing through alien minds? As for the musings of Old Conc, what proportion of them were still human and which alien? Did he now bear them malice, or was he content simply to be away? If the former, did he have anything to threaten them with besides his bare hands?

What sort of "supplies" remained on his own craft, the lander that had brought him safely down to Xica's all-embracing surface?

Behind him Lastwell finished his speech.

"That's decided, then. First we conclude operations here, and only then do we go after the lovesick little puppy." He put a shoulder to a large crate and winced as he began to shove. "Somebody give me a hand with this bitch."

They worked on into the late hours, the ragged little circle of artificial illumination holding back a night become suddenly hostile. It was as if they were drifting in space, as though there was no remarkable, fecund alien world lying just beyond the reach of their lights.

If he stepped outside the glow, Simna found himself wondering, would he step off the edge of reality? Would he find himself falling through a void speckled only with distant, uncaring stars and nebulae? Drifting toward the darkness, he was relieved to find only familiar sand and gravel underfoot. His thoughts, he knew, trod on less stable ground.

It was late when the last load was ready to be delivered to the lander. Exhausted, they prepared to climb aboard the heavily laden truck for the final run back to the ship. Just as Stevens was about to head it out onto the sand, a figure appeared at the edge of the forest: a ghostly gray wraith.

The steady voice of Old Conc drifted across to them. "You can't go out to your vessel now."

"Who the hell says we can't?" The normally low-key Prentice's uncharacteristic vehemence startled his colleagues.

"There's an *Arnagui* out there," the old man shouted.

"An *Arnagui*?" O'Sandringham drew a blank. "What the hell's an *Arnagui*?"

Lastwell had his lenses on and was staring hard at the strip of desert that separated the campsite from the lander. "The moon's up and it's plenty bright. I don't see a damn thing out there. He's trying to delay us for some reason."

"You killed Ramirez," Prentice yelled back accusingly.

"I didn't mean to." There was no quaver in the old man's reply. His voice was strong and steady, as it might have been in the old days. Steel undertones. It was a voice that had *commanded*.

In the present circumstances and surroundings, however, it carried little weight.

"I don't know what you've got on your mind," Prentice responded, "but we're going to finish loading our ship and then we're coming after our friend. You wouldn't by any chance happen to know where he is, would you?"

"Where who is?" If the old man was feigning ignorance, Simna decided, he was doing an exceptional job of it. "I told you: I didn't mean to kill the other one. He was in my way and I . . . I forgot. Or rather I remembered. Remembered what I had come here to get away from. For an instant I was what I had once been. I'm sorry for that. My first sorry in a long, long time. You must listen to me. There *is* an *Arnagui* out there."

"If so, it won't be there long." Lastwell grinned nastily as he drew his cutter and set it on maximum intensity.

"Why should we listen to anything you say?" Prentice

stood on the back of the truck bed as he hailed the woods. "You're a self-confessed liar and murderer."

"What if he's telling the truth?" An uneasy Lejardin tugged at the expedition leader's jumpsuit.

"Shut up, Favrile." He pushed her hand away. "We've made over a dozen trips from here to the lander. All of a sudden we can't go because there's an *'Arnagui'* out there?" He leaned out to peer toward the front of the vehicle. "Frank, you see anything yet?"

"Sand," Lastwell told him. "Rocks. Moonlight." He glanced over a shoulder at Lejardin. "Why don't you go ask the old man for details? I'm sure he'll treat you with the same courtesy he accorded your friend Ramirez."

"Maybe it *was* an accident. Maybe he really only meant to shove Stewart out of the way, or something." Coming to a decision, she climbed down off the truck.

Prentice gaped down at her. "Favrile, get back up here."

"Go ahead and take the load back to the lander. I'll talk to him. I don't think he perceives me as a threat."

Lastwell laughed sardonically. "I'm sure he doesn't. An opportunity, maybe, but not a threat."

Clutching a portable light, Simna hopped off the vehicle and started deliberately toward the forest. "I'm not sure I believe you when you say Stewart's death was an accident, old man, but I'm willing to be convinced."

"Jack, for Christ's sake, come back here!" Prentice yelled.

"Don't be a fool, Jack." Cedric Carnavon added his own admonition to that of Prentice.

The scientist looked back at his friends and colleagues. "I can handle this. Go on ahead."

"If he's who he claims to be, no one can handle him," Carnavon shouted back. "Stewart couldn't."

"I'm not Stewart." As Simna strode purposefully toward the still trees, a tentative Lejardin moved to follow.

"Leave 'em." An impatient Lastwell muttered a curse under his breath. "We'll come back for them when we've finished loading."

"But . . ." Stevens started to protest.

"Go *on*." When the mate hesitated, Lastwell jabbed at the accelerator plate. The heavily burdened vehicle lurched forward.

"Hey!" Prentice hollered. "I didn't say it was time to go."

Lastwell bellowed back at him. "We'll argue about it later!"

The expedition leader scrambled onto the flange that ran around the side of the vehicle, clinging to the rocking machine by grasping the binding straps that held its cargo in place. He continued to yell as he worked his way forward. Sand began to hiss beneath the fat, independently mounted wheels.

"You can't leave them here with that fanatic!"

As Stevens drove, Lastwell shouted back over his shoulder. "Your man said he could handle things. Let's see if he knows what he's talking about or if he's just all air."

"But Favrile . . . !" Prentice's words were lost in the granular wail of flying sand.

Lejardin watched silently as the truck jounced toward the lander, its lights arcing silently across the red surface, the soft hum of its engine growing fainter with distance. She could see the Carnavons sitting in the rear seat, heads together, no doubt discussing how they would proceed once they reached the ship.

Putting her hands to her mouth, she yelled as loud as she could, though she doubted that her words could be heard. "Salvor, stop treating me like a child! I can take care of myself!" Thus unburdened, she turned to stare as Simna approached the edge of the forest.

When Old Conc advanced to meet him, she felt herself

tense. But the old man, or general, or whatever he was, strode right past the scientist. Conc's attention was focused instead on the retreating truck.

"There's an *Arnagui* out there, you idiots!" he roared in a voice to which strong men had once bowed. "Don't you hear me?" In point of fact they no longer could.

Simna stepped in front of him. "Don't get so excited, Concarry."

"Don't call me that," the old man muttered irritably. "I'm Old Conc. Just Old Conc." He reached out to shove the scientist aside. Displaying surprising speed and strength, Simna countered the arm thrust.

Conc blinked and turned. Looking the much younger man up and down, he seemed to see him for the first time. "Well, well. Could there be more to you than comely phrases, sonny?"

"Perhaps not unlike yourself, sir." Simna felt eerily calm. "What's an *Arnagui*?"

The old man's attention remained focused on the distant, brightly lit vehicle. "A nocturnal predator. Fortunately it's restricted to the desert. It's particularly active on bright, moonlit nights. Like this." He was silent for a long moment before adding, "They usually don't come in this close, but with all the constant noise and activity, and now the lights . . ."

Simna turned and squinted. There was very little moon. "I still don't see anything out there."

Old Conc sighed tolerantly. "Have you forgotten where you are? Have you forgotten the *Vrilil*, which can assume the aspect of an old rug half-buried in the ground?"

"They'll be okay," Simna told him. "They have weapons. Calm down."

"I am calm." Conc was very sure. "But they won't be okay."

Simna returned his gaze to the desert. The heavily laden

truck was almost to the lander. "So this *Arnagui* is a thixotropic predator. What does it look like in its nonthreatening guise?"

Wizened blue eyes scanned the shadowed, treeless terrain. "Sand."

A vast hissing sound made Simna whirl. On the skimpy slope below him, a startled Lejardin stumbled and fell on her backside. She immediately began skittering uphill, pushing herself away from the edge of the desert with hands and feet.

Distant screams and curses came from the truck as the ground opened up beneath it. Simna's skin prickled as he heard its engine whine. Wheels spun wildly, unable to find purchase.

"Close," Old Conc murmured softly. "They almost made it."

"How big *is* this thing?" Simna mumbled. The old man did not reply.

Above the squeal of crumpling metal and plastic, Simna thought he could hear Lastwell bellowing. A few strobes of coherent light came from someone's cutter, luminous streaks making lines on the blackboard of night.

All too soon, it was quiet again.

XX

Conc softly explained to a stunned Simna. "It lives just under the surface. In its dormant, camouflaged state it looks just like an expanse of sand. A very large expanse of sand."

The younger man didn't reply; just continued to stare in the direction of the lander. Of the little truck, its cargo, and its human passengers there was no sign. They had vanished as utterly as if they had never been.

"For such a big brute there ain't much to it," the old man continued. "Just a lot of contiguous bumps and ripples. And mouth. Actually I'm kind of surprised one of the stouter ones ain't tried to eat your lander by now. 'Course, the really big ones tend to stay further out, in the deep desert."

Feeling for the ground behind him, Simna sat down slowly, unable to take his eyes off the place where the *Arnagui* had appeared.

They couldn't be gone, he told himself. Not all of them, not everyone. The perpetually argumentative but supremely professional Lastwell and the more subdued Stevens, the quietly efficient Salvor Prentice, the lovely but confused Bella-Lynn, the jovial, tireless Carnavons. Colleagues and friends. Gone. Snatched away by Xica, just like Cody Noosa and Ramirez.

Nothing was what it seemed. What a maxim for a world. Not the natives, not any of the soft-bodied fauna. Not Old

300

Conc or his motives and intentions. Not the sky or the sea or the sand.

Am I what I seem? he wondered. Are these hands whose shaking I fight to still real, are these feet half dug into the soil? Are my thoughts authentic or merely a cover for some madness that took hold weeks ago, without my realizing it?

A firm hand was gripping his shoulder so hard it hurt, the worn, powerful fingers digging deliberately into the flesh. "Snap out of it, sonny-boy. There's real reality here. You just have to look a little harder." He released his grip and extended his fingers. "I've always considered a helping hand up a good litmus test for reality. Humans. Always in such a hurry."

Simna was too stunned to cry. As he accepted the assist, he stared straight into the old man's eyes. "And what about you, Conc, or whatever your name is? Are you a thixotropic mirage or are you really human?"

The oldster grinned. "God, I hope not."

The scientist turned back to the hushed desert. As usual there was no wind, no breeze, and the sweat poured in rivulets down his face. "We've got to go look for survivors. If not now, then as soon as the sun's up. If this creature is nocturnal it won't be around at daybreak."

Old Conc spoke gently. "Neither will any survivors, sonny. The *Arnagui* doesn't leave scraps. I've watched one eat before. Made supper out of a whole troop of *Pinitah*. They ingest *everything*." He considered the night. "If some of your supplies or gear was knocked loose you might find a little of it lying around. Eventually it'll regurgitate anything it finds indigestible. I'm afraid your companions don't fall into that category."

"Favrile," he murmured. She had stopped scuttling backward and, like him, was too dazed to do much more than continue staring out across the inanimate sands. Old Conc trailed him as he walked down to her.

"What was it?" She managed to look frightened and competent all at once, ready for what might come and yet fearful of it. "What happened out there, Jack?"

"It got them," he told her gently. "The creature Old Conc was trying to warn us about. The *Arnagui*. They're gone, Favrile. All of them. Everyone's gone."

With his help she rose to her feet. "Bella-Lynn. Millie." Like Simna, she found that reciting their names seemed to enshrine their passing, to render it inarguable if not acceptable.

"I tried to warn them," Conc swore. "But of course they wouldn't listen to me."

"Why should they?" Simna told him. "You'd just killed Stew Ramirez."

"I told you, that was unintentional. If I could, I'd take it back." His voice fell to a barely intelligible mutter. "I'd take a great many things back." He took a deep breath.

"This wasn't equable of me. I should have had the Pendju try to distract you. I should have tried."

"Why didn't you?" Lejardin was utterly spent.

"I'd have preferred that you never came here, but once you'd indicated a determination to settle in and study, I thought you might be of some use in helping to satisfy the Xicans' insatiable craving for more nurturing, for more succor. I determined to evaluate you to see if you were worthy."

"Not that it matters," Simna declared. "Nothing matters now. But were we?"

The old man eyed him somberly. "Some of you. At first I didn't want to help them either. I wanted only to be left alone. But need is a powerful thing. The Xicans are very needful. More so than one can imagine."

Lejardin rose shakily, brushing coarse sand from the backs of her legs. "There are survivors out there. I know here are!"

"Go on," Conc told her. "I did my best to stop you, and you ignored me. I won't try again." Tilting back his head, he judged the innocent, starry sky. "The *Arnagui*'s still out there. Its eating habits are very democratic."

Several strides into her journey she slowed and turned. "Jack, even when you're not sure what you're talking about you always have an opinion." She gestured in the direction of the lander's silhouette. "Can we get back to the *James Cook*?"

He had to turn away from the hope in her eyes. "I know what you're thinking, Favrile. Plenty of the lander's functions are automated, but I doubt they extend to lifting off, achieving orbital insertion, and consummating dockage on behalf of an inexperienced and unqualified would-be pilot. I could *possibly* get us off the ground. Rendezvousing with the ship would be more than problematical. And I couldn't land it. Frank and Kauri were assigned to this expedition for more than their ability to participate in snappy conversation."

"Then that's that. We're marooned here. There might as well not be a lander." She looked up again. "Manuals? On-board instruction?"

Simna wasn't one to encourage false hopes. "I can work with what's available. I *will* work with what's available. But if I'm able to accomplish anything, it's not going to happen overnight. You don't become one of the few individuals qualified to supervise the operation of a deepsleep ship in a few months, or even a few years."

She looked at him imploringly. "But you'll try. You have to try."

He shrugged helplessly. "What else is there to do?"

"How long?"

"I couldn't even hazard a guess until I've had time to dig into the on-board programming. A year, two or three. Maybe more, maybe never. Sure I'll try. The best I can

His gaze rose to meet hers. "One thing I am sure of. Xica's going to be our home for a long, long time."

"So there's just the two of us," she murmured.

"Not quite, missy," Conc reminded her.

She tried to compose a smile. They were going to be dependent on this mercurial old man for some time. "I didn't mean to exclude you."

"I wasn't referring to me. Have you forgotten your need-struck companion?"

Simna was slightly cheered. "Ted! Yes, I'd forgotten about him."

"He strikes me as a happy man. If I were you I wouldn't expect any help from him for a while, though. He's convinced you betrayed him."

"He betrayed us." Lejardin found herself peering into the moonlit woods. "He was ready to betray the expedition."

"Was he?" Conc suggested. "Maybe he only deceived himself. Regardless, he's much more content at the moment than either of you. He's with someone who makes him happy."

"She's not human," Lejardin declared tightly.

"That's right." The old man nodded agreement. "Personally, I consider that a point in her favor."

Simna fought to collect himself. "What do you expect us to do now?"

"Do?" Conc frowned at him. "I expect you to do whatever you want, Jack Simna. You are now short on resources and long on freedom." He gestured toward the forest. "You have supplies stored on your lander, which you can access whenever you please . . . so long as it's during the daylight hours. As I recall, they were intended to last the lot of you about two years. They should do just three of you a good deal longer. You've been here long enough to have learned how to live in the forest without being devoured or poi-
oned . . . I hope.

"Why not continue your studies? If you don't succeed in leaving, you'll have left something behind for those of your brethren who will come after. They'll find the lander, if not you. Your huts remain at your disposal, and your Pendju friends are eager to be of assistance.

"Work with me. Learn about Xica as you help the Pendju and Quwanga and the other tribes to raise themselves up, to flourish and mature so that they'll be able to meet the next humans who come this way on a more equal footing. This is a far more hospitable world than Tycho V or Burke. Life here can be good, if you meet it halfway. In any event, it beats the hell out of sittin' around waiting to die." He paused to catch his breath.

"Please pardon my polemic, but this is a matter I feel somewhat strongly about."

Simna cocked his head sideways. "Did the Pendju put you up to this?"

For the first time in a long while, the old man cackled appreciatively. "Now there's an amusin' notion. Why don't you devote some time to findin' out? Then you can tell me." Despite the laughter, Simna couldn't tell if Conc was being serious or not.

"We can share our supplies with you," Lejardin offered.

"Thanks, missy, but I don't need anything off your vessel. I don't need anything that stinks of Earth."

"Well, we won't starve," Simna declared confidently.

"No, you won't starve, sonny." Conc tapped the side of his head. "How you handle it up here is what matters. Me, I think you'll manage. Your wayward friend Halstead seems to have adapted pretty good already."

"I don't want to adapt." Fresh concerns were already pushing aside his images of the recent catastrophe.

The old man shrugged. "You chose to come here. N body forced you. You didn't choose to stay, but Xi made that choice for you. I suggest you make the best of it." Turning, he started back toward the forest.

"Wait a minute!" Simna took a step after him.

Old Conc looked back. "What for? You don't really want to talk to me. But I'll be around in case you're struck by the need for conversation. So will the Pendju. If you need their help, all you have to do is ask for it. They'll cherish the opportunity."

Moments later he was gone, swallowed up by the forest, as much a part of it as the flaky-barked trees and knife-sharp *Haukik* and the wondrous creatures that could don and efface physical templates at will. Simna found himself wondering how many masks that singular old man possessed.

Lejardin had returned to stand alongside him. She made no move to take his hand, and he resisted the urge to put his arm around her. Physical contact was unnecessary. Their condition automatically drew them close.

"What now, Jack?"

"I don't know. What about you?"

She turned her gaze to the waiting forest. "The history of science is full of failed expeditions. Not everyone comes back on schedule. Not everyone comes back."

In the morning they found the extruded ruins of the truck and those of its fixtures that the *Arnagui* had deemed unpalatable. Tremendous pressure had wrenched and twisted it like a toy. Of their former colleagues and comrades there was no sign.

Simna struggled to pull a small container packed with medical supplies from beneath a larger one. Though the sun was up and the day bright, he found he was continually searching the ruddy sands for hints of movement. He tried keep his own to a minimum.

With Lejardin's help he finally succeeded in extracting

the container intact. They sat down to rest in the shade of the crumpled vehicle.

Thoughtfully he considered the decussation of desert and forest. "You know, this really is a beautiful place. If you have to be stuck somewhere . . ."

She put a hand on his shoulder and smiled encouragingly. "You'll figure out how to operate the lander, Jack. I know you will."

He shrugged. "I wish I had as much confidence in my abilities as you seem to. That's always been a failing of mine. I've always compensated for a perceived lack of knowledge by trying to appear even more knowledgeable. I know it can get tiresome."

She squeezed his shoulder. "I'll let you know when you're boring me." She looked toward the forest. "Think we'll be able to survive here?"

"*He's* done it for decades, and we're supposed to be trained to survive an emergency. We'll manage. Maybe we'll get lucky and another expedition will arrive ahead of schedule."

She mustered a grin. "By the time they get here we'll certainly have mastered our subject."

He turned pensive. "We're going to have to watch ourselves, or we'll end up like Ted."

"I wonder," she mused, "if that would be such a bad thing? Call it adaptation, call it a survival trait. Old Conc's survived because he's blended in. He helps the natives and they help him."

"You know, I was a teacher once. Enjoyed it. I suppose I can teach again." He rose and wiped grit from his shorts and legs. "Let's get off this sand."

Together they began to shift the supplies they'd recovered from the wreck site into the shade of the trees. Later they would ask the Pendju for help in moving heavier equipment from the lander back to the village. With time and effort they could make the two huts that had been provided to them more than suitable. From now on the village would be their Base Camp. Without Stevens's expert help they'd never be able to reassemble the portable domes.

They would be comfortable. They would survive. And they would use the time forced upon them to learn and to teach.

A group of Pendju were waiting just within the woods. Simna greeted them as he laid down his burden.

"We are here to help you," one proclaimed. "We were told you could use some help."

"We *want* to help," entreated another.

"Like you helped T'ed?" Lejardin kept her distance.

A large, attractive male stepped forth. "If that is what you wish." Lejardin did not reply, but eyed the congenial alien speculatively.

As Simna set about instructing the arrivals on how to go about recovering their scattered equipment, Old Conc emerged from the underbrush.

"You see why they need to be educated," the old man told him. "You can imagine how they'd be received, and treated, by human society. All my life I was looking for something. I found it, lost it, and was convinced I'd never find it again. But I have, here on Xica. Anything you've ever wished for, anything you've ever really wanted, you can find here, if only you're willing to look."

"I've never had any trouble finding what I wanted," Lejardin countered.

"Haven't you? I'm not sure I believe that, missy. Maybe you don't even know what you want. First you have to recognize what you don't have."

"I could resent that," she shot back.

"Go ahead and resent it. People have more than resented me my whole life. It no longer bothers me."

"There's plenty missing here. This isn't Paradise," Simna reminded him.

"Have I ever claimed that it was? There's disease here, and death in quantity. Xica's a world for those who'll take the time to look carefully, not for anyone who claims innocence as an excuse on a regular basis. Give it a chance, though, and you'll find yourself rewarded."

Lejardin stepped past them. "Where are you going?" Simna asked her.

"To talk with the Pendju. Old Conc had his special questions for them. I'm sure you have yours. I have mine. I'm going to try to get some answers."

He nodded understandingly. "If you need any help, I'm here."

She smiled back at him. "I know, Jack. But as I always tried to tell poor Salvor, I can take care of myself." Gathering a group of attentive Pendju around her, she settled down on a convenient hummock of soft purple *Nasturtium* leaves and in her distinctive, hesitant accent, began to talk.

"There," Conc observed thoughtfully, "is a unique woman."

"If she were otherwise she wouldn't have been included on the expedition," Simna reminded him. "I'm just not sure she realizes it herself. Someday she will."

"And what of you, Jack Simna?" The old man was scrutinizing him intently.

Grateful to be under shade, he turned and watched as the busy Pendju gathered what was salvageable of the supplies that had been on the devastated truck.

"I guess in addition to everything else, I'm going to have to try to learn how to orbit a lander." He shook his head. "I never was much for astronautics." He looked sharply at his companion. "I don't suppose . . . ?"

"Sorry. Besides being pared down to the bare minimum, everything on what's left of my craft was fully automated.

In my life I have mastered many things, but deepsleep flight is not one of them. Once it had achieved landfall, my lander was not even designed to lift off again. The vines and creepers have long since invaded its innards. It belongs to the forest now. To Xica. Just like I do. Just like you will."

"Maybe. If so, it'll be an interesting new sensation. I've never belonged to anything except myself."

A twinkle came into the old man's eye. "Don't underestimate Xica. She can provide for needs you don't know you have, in ways you can't begin to imagine. The Pendju and the Quwanga like to help as much as they like to learn. In return, you will help them."

Simna watched the energetic Xicans for a long time before replying. "You know, Conc, sometimes I get so tired of *thinking*."

"Ah." A rare breeze ruffled the old man's beard and hair. "Common ground. I think you and I will get along fine." He nodded toward Lejardin, who was surrounded by responsive natives. "She'll find what she's looking for. Your friend Halstead has. You? You're going to be a little tougher to satisfy. But then, so was I, sonny, so was I."

"You talk of teaching them. What are you trying to teach them, most of all?"

"Ambition," Conc replied at once. "It ain't an easy concept to get across, and I'll be glad of your help, Jack Simna." He put an arm across the younger man's shoulders, and this time Simna didn't shrug it off.

From the depths of the forest, Troumo watched the two humans talking and knew it was a good thing. It was important that they get along. He knew there had been disagreements between them, but Old Conc had insisted that was a normal state of affairs for humans. Besides, disagreement was normal and sometimes even useful, so long as you didn't kill each other too much.

Though he sorrowed for those the *Arnagui* had taken, he was glad to see that some of the humans were going to be staying. Three more in addition to Old Conc! It meant that the Pendju would be able to learn at a much faster rate. He was very grateful because the hunger in him to learn was so strong that it sometimes hurt.

So excited was he that for a moment his left leg fluxed slightly. Automatically he visualized the way it should be, and the rippling stopped. Stability of shape was among the most important things Old Conc had taught them.

He watched as his fellow villagers carried armloads of strange stable objects to the feet of the humans. Someday he was sure that Old Conc and the others would teach him and the rest of the Pendju and the Quwanga how to make use of such devices. In return he and his people would try to share what they knew with the humans. Already they had learned more than they thought there was to know.

He wondered if the great vessel contained any more of the wonderful wheeled machines that could travel rapidly over the ground. He had admired that above all the other devices the new humans had brought with them.

So much so that he was contemplating the novel idea of trying to become one himself.